BURIED ROAD

Also by Katie Tallo

Poison Lilies
Dark August

BURIED ROAD

A Novel

KATIE TALLO

HARPER

NEW YORK · LONDON · TORONTO · SYDNEY

HARPER

BURIED ROAD. Copyright © 2024 by Katie Tallo. All rights reserved. Printed in the United States of America. No part of this book may be used or reproduced in any manner whatsoever without written permission except in the case of brief quotations embodied in critical articles and reviews. For information, address HarperCollins Publishers, 195 Broadway, New York, NY 10007.

HarperCollins books may be purchased for educational, business, or sales promotional use. For information, please email the Special Markets Department at SPsales@harpercollins.com.

FIRST EDITION

Designed by Jamie Lynne Kerner

Library of Congress Cataloging-in-Publication Data has been applied for.

ISBN 978-0-06-336071-6 (pbk.)

24 25 26 27 28 LBC 6 5 4 3 2

For my lovely mum

I SQUINT THROUGH THE BRANCHES, SEARCHING FOR ONE OF THE torn strips of her T-shirt that we used to mark our path. I can't see the sky. The dark woods close above me. The air is thick with dew. I gulp in heaping mouthfuls trying to steady my stuttering heart. If I'm lost, I might not ever find my way out. We were warned it would be rough trying to get through this twisted old forest. Warned there was some kind of dead zone right in the middle. But we didn't care. Death has been chasing us for a while now. It doesn't scare us anymore. We pulled on rubber boots and came anyway.

I felt pretty brave as we hopped the gate. But now fear claws at my throat because I didn't think I'd have to do this all alone. Without Gus. We were supposed to be in this together to the end. Mother and daughter. Gus is my mom. Her real name is Augusta. Augusta Monet. I haven't called her Mama since that awful day three years ago. And even though she wasn't the one who disappeared that August morning, she sort of did. I remember it like it was yesterday.

The sun felt warm on my skin that summer day. The
water was cool and skimmed with seaweed. Kids bobbed
in the waves and built sand forts on the foamy shore.
A family ate hamburgers at a picnic table and some
teenagers played volleyball over a sagging net. A dad

chased a red beach umbrella that tumbled and flapped
in the breeze like a warning flag. Everyone was where
they were meant to be that morning.

All except Howard.

He got a text as we were laying our towels in a row
on the sand. He said it was a lead—for the article he
was writing. Someone he had to go meet. He said he'd
take the camper van into the county. He'd only be gone
a couple of hours tops, he promised.

"Did you want me to get you anything on the way
back?" he asked.

"Ice cream." I smiled.

"Chocolate mint," he said, nodding. He knew my
favorite. Howard knew everything about me. Like a dad
does, even though he wasn't my real dad.

My real dad was an ex-convict. Gus doesn't think
it's right to hide the truth from kids. Especially from
her own kid. She never once pretended there was a
Santa or an Easter Bunny. So when I was old enough to
understand, Gus took me to see him. I was around five.
He wouldn't even look at me. We were strangers to each
other. All he said to me was that he hoped I didn't have
too much of his bad blood in me. I could tell he didn't
want me. Howard wanted me from the day I was born.
He told me so.

Howard headed up the beach. Gus didn't say
goodbye. When he got to the edge, he turned and
waved. Gus was staring across the bay toward the
horizon where Lake Ontario meets the sky. I waved to
Howard for both of us. He smiled then walked away.
He crossed the parking lot and headed down the road
leading away from Outlet Beach. I watched as he

rounded the corner to our campsite. Site 88. I watched until he was gone.

That was the last time I saw him.

A branch snaps behind me and I spin around to find a chipmunk scurrying across the black forest floor. I move faster. It gets stickier and stickier. My boots squish through muck. There's a break in the trees up ahead that I hope is the road. I lurch forward, splashing through puddles as I start to run for the clearing. Suddenly there's water everywhere. It pools around the trees and the rotten stink of it makes my eyes water. It's not a clearing. It's the dead zone. I'm nowhere near the road or the car or help. I've gone the wrong way.

"I like your swimsuit," I told the girl in the yellow bikini with orange polka dots. "It's very summery." It felt nice to have an instant friend to play with on the beach that day. Together, we collected shells and played Marco Polo in the water and did handstands on the sand. The sun crawled across the sky toward the dunes at West Lake on the far side of the bay. Gus wanted to wait on the beach until Howard came back. But the sun started to set, and everyone packed up and headed back to their campsites. Even the girl in the summery bikini left with her family. Gus was being stubborn. She was mad that Howard was gone so much this trip. She was trying to make a point. I didn't see it but when Gus was in a mood, I knew it was better just to go along with it.

It was weird having the beach all to ourselves. We were like two castaways. Like the world had ended and someone forgot to tell us. And in a way, it had. We just didn't know it yet.

I was doing cartwheels across the beach when I found a blue-and-green string bracelet in the sand. Someone's lost treasure that was now mine. I put it on my wrist and haven't taken it off since.

Right after it happened, all I would dream about was that last camping trip. In some of my dreams, Howard kept his promise. He heads across the sand with a cone in each hand, the chocolate mint ice cream dripping down his knuckles.

I'd also dream about real things—like the sweet taste of the apple cider from Waupoos. Like the snap and crackle of the campfire. Like the sting of marram grass on my ankles as I climbed the dunes. Sometimes I'd dream about running on the beach with my kite or skipping along the boardwalk over the marsh at Cedar Sands Trail. Howard would be naming all the plants we saw along the way. Spike rush. Jack-in-the-pulpit. Sweet flag. Gus would be holding his hand. I would look back at the two of them just in time to see Howard lift her hand to kiss it. At the last second, he would kiss his own hand. It was one of his silly jokes. And even though she kept a lot of herself inside, Gus would burst out laughing. He knew how to get her to crack.

I'd wake up from those dreams with a full heart. And for a few seconds, I'd forget. But then I'd remember he was gone and my heart would empty and hurt all over again. I'd twirl the woven strings of my bracelet, trying to go back to how I felt when I found it in the sand.

Before everything changed.

It's been almost three years. I was just a kid back then. I'll be a teenager in a few weeks. Practically a grown-up. It's up to me now. I can't believe it was only eleven days ago when Gus read that stupid obituary. That's what brought us back to the county. And now that we've come all this way, I can't give up and I can't be lost. Not after all we've been through. I have to do this for Gus and Howard. Even if it means heading straight into a dead zone.

I keep moving. Suddenly I hear voices up ahead. I pull the knife from my back pocket and move into the low brush, inching closer. I spot them a few feet in front of me. I freeze. I can see their faces. If they look this way, they'll see me too. I hold my breath and grip the knife. I steady myself. Ready to fight. Or even kill if I have to. I've changed in eleven days.

I am still Bly Monet. Augusta Monet's daughter. Howard's daughter.

But I can also feel some of that bad blood pumping through my veins.

I grip the knife and move slowly toward them.

PART ONE

1

THE OBITUARY

GUS IS NOSE-DEEP IN HER SECTION OF THE NEWSPAPER WHEN SHE gasps like she's been shot. I don't look up. She's being dramatic as usual. Chewing words under her breath. Huffing. She's sitting right across from me in the breakfast nook, but I keep my eyeballs glued to my section. I try to focus on the daily word scramble. It's my morning routine. Dress. Breakfast. Coffee and word scramble. Floss. Brush teeth. Comb hair. Pack lunch. Go to school. In that order. I have to solve the scramble before I can do anything else, but she's messing up my concentration. She lets out another big sigh and tosses the paper on the table.

"They finally did it," she says through clenched teeth. "Those fucking fucks."

I give up. I look at her even though I don't want to.

Her cheeks are hot pink. She picks up the paper again.

It comes alive in her trembling hand like the words printed on it are electrified.

I abandon the scramble and slide around to her side of the nook to see what's what.

I lean in close, my shoulder touching hers. I scan the newspaper.

She's reading the obituaries.

I spot his name and the electricity goes through me too.

> BAYLIS, Howard George. Missing and presumed dead, at
> the age of 34. A kind and loving son, Howard is survived by
> his parents, Vivi and Kirk Baylis. A friend and colleague to
> many in the National Capital Region, Howard was a talented
> freelance journalist. All are welcome to attend the celebra-
> tion of life at the Stone Chapel in Glenwood Cemetery. Sun-
> day, June 26 at 4 PM., 47 Ferguson Street, Picton, Ontario.

All the air leaves the room. This is bad. Life is about to go
sideways and there's nothing I can do to stop it. I down my coffee, slide around the bench, and slip out of the nook. I can't feel
the kitchen floor as I walk to the sink. My throat is dry, my chest
tight. I look back at Gus.

We have the same green eyes and red hair. Strangers go out
of their way to point at our red hair like we don't know it's on our
heads. Like they're surprising us with the news. People say I'm a
mini version of Gus.

Only what they can't see is how different we are.

I like neat rows. I like making homemade soup from leftovers
and organizing my T-shirts from lights to darks in my closet. Gus
doesn't do rows or color coding or cooking meals from scratch.
She barely does dishes. She only does laundry when she's got
nothing left to wear. I like to be early and I hate when people get
angry. Gus is always late and she likes a fight.

I know why she is how she is. Life's been really, really mean to
her. She lost a lot of people along the way. Both her parents. Then
her last living relative, her great-grandmother. Some friends. Even
Levi, her dog, got old and died. I think all that loss has messed
with her insides. She never cries. She barely eats and if she does,

she never eats vegetables. And even though she just turned thirty-five, I don't think she's ever really grown up. She didn't have anyone to show her how. Her dad died before she was born, and her mom was killed when she was just a kid. She mostly raised herself.

Then Howard came along. He was sort of geeky and a bit silly, but he was always kind and sweet even if he could be embarrassing sometimes. He was a journalist for a local paper when she met him. He wasn't really her type. At least not at first. He was awkward and skinny and way too romantic for Gus. But he liked her a lot. They grew close and he helped her when she was pregnant with me. He took care of her when she didn't take care of herself. He showed her a new way of being in the world. A lighter way.

And then out of the blue, he wasn't there anymore. The loss was huge for both of us, but she couldn't handle losing someone else so she acted like he'd be back any second. Like he was out running errands and he'd come home any day now. No one could tell her different. She searched for Howard for months. It was like she could see this faraway flicker that no one else could see. It gave her tunnel vision. All she cared about was keeping that flicker alive because it meant Howard was still alive and out there somewhere.

Eventually, we had to come home without him. Mostly because the entire town of Picton was pretty much done with her. But even when we got back to Ottawa, Gus still lived in that tunnel. I think she was afraid to come out. Afraid that if she walked around in the light of the real world, she'd lose sight of the flicker.

I turn my back to Gus and place my mug in the sink. I look out the back window at Howard's flower garden. I've kept the weeds from taking over. The pink toad lilies have bloomed early. The lilac tree has grown much taller than it was on the day we planted it together when I was six. I've been pruning it like Howard showed me.

I wash my mug, dry it, and place it in the cupboard next to Howard's. His mug has his name painted on it. I made it for him on his thirtieth birthday. I tap the side of his mug with my middle knuckle, like I do every morning—the same five-part rhythmic knock that reminds me of him because it was his favorite way of knocking on doors when he entered a room or tapping on a table when he got one of his bright ideas.

Rat-tat-tatat-tat.

I open the fridge, grab the lunch I made the night before, and shove it into my backpack. My morning routine is all wrong now. I can't bring myself to floss or brush my teeth or comb my hair and I'm already dressed so I hoist my backpack over one shoulder and leave the house.

Howard's house.

His parents own it now. At least that's what their lawyers told Gus. When we left Picton, Kirk and Vivi Baylis said we could stay in the house until we got ourselves set up somewhere else. They said it like we were guests who didn't belong here anymore now that Howard wasn't here. They said it like they thought he was never coming back. Gus ignored them. She never looked for another place for us to live and they never pushed.

Until maybe now.

I shiver even though the June morning is warm. I roll my bike out of the shed.

That obituary means only one thing. Howard's parents have really given up. They think he's dead. Why keep a house he's not coming back to? But I don't want to live anywhere else. This is my home and it's the only place where Howard is. He's everywhere. He's in the pencil marks on the doorframe where he measured my height every year. His initials are even carved into the wood armrest of the back porch swing. I know Howard isn't my flesh and blood, but he was my dad for almost ten whole years—thirteen if you count the ones he's missed.

We can't leave. We just can't.

My backpack feels loaded with bricks. I don't bother poking my head in the back door to say *have a nice day* or *see you later*. There's no point. And I don't want to see that look on Gus's face. The one she gets when she's about to do the one thing the universe is screaming at her not to do.

I put on my helmet and head down Ossington. I pedal faster and faster, trying to put as much sidewalk between me and my worries as I can. At school I can't concentrate. I fail a pop quiz on algebra. I can't eat my lunch. I get scolded by my French teacher, Madam Spicer-Pilon, for daydreaming. I only *wish* this was a dream. But it's not. My mind won't stop going around and around—spinning and rolling over and over and over—wondering how bad it will be when I get home. And what kind of bad it will be. That's what haunts me all through French class.

Quel genre de mal?

Will it be the kind where Gus is sitting frozen in time, right where I left her in the breakfast nook? Or will it be the kind where she's standing in the dining room with her head tipped to one side, staring at the evidence that's covered the walls for the last two years? Those newspaper clippings, photographs, police reports, interview transcripts, and maps have become our wallpaper. It's not like we use it for anything else.

I hate that room. Every time I walk past the dining room, it reminds me that not a single piece of evidence has ever been found to explain where Howard went.

The end-of-day school bell startles me and I almost fall out of my chair.

Madam Spicer-Pilon shakes her head and purses her lips. She thinks I've been sleeping.

I pedal home. Slowly. Weaving back and forth down the road. Killing time.

When the house comes into view, I spot Gus at the far end of the driveway.

That's when I know.

It's another kind of bad.

The kind she does best.

Gus is not letting this go. She's not retreating or hiding or crying or calling or begging. She's going to fight. This is the kind of bad that makes my neck break out in hives because it's the kind I can't predict or understand or reason with or sometimes even detect at first. But I know her too well. She looks like a normal everyday mother loading suitcases into the trunk of Howard's old Honda, like we're going on a road trip to Disneyland. Like everything's hunky-dory.

"Hey, Boo," Gus says when she sees me.

Boo is the nickname Gus gave me when I was little because I couldn't pronounce my own name. I kept trying but it always came out sounding like Boo instead of Bly so it stuck.

"Gus," I say flatly.

"Just about ready to hit the road," she says, keeping her voice light as if the trip's been planned for weeks.

I know exactly where we're going. Back to Prince Edward County for Howard's funeral. What they're calling a celebration of life. Back to the place where he was last seen and where his parents still live in a big house next to their winery in Cherry Valley just outside the town of Picton. Back to where we used to camp every August until that summer three years ago. The summer when he went missing and our search began. But after nearly a year in Picton, Gus said we needed to go home to Ottawa so she could get her head straight. She would keep investigating from a distance, and I'd go back to school. It was time for us to get back to our normal life and our normal routine. I do love routines, but there was nothing normal about being back at the house without Howard. Gus began taping her evidence to the dining room walls. Sometimes she'd add a new piece of research—an article or a document. Sometimes she'd take everything down and tape it up a different way. Hoping the new way would spark something. She'd stare at it for days before drawing a line or circling a picture with her red marker. But after two years, her head wasn't any straighter than when we'd left Picton.

She tried normal. She made tuna casserole every Friday night because it was all she knew how to cook. We went to the movies on Tuesday nights, and on Sundays we'd go walking in the Dominion Arboretum. All the trees were marked with these tiny metal plaques etched with the Latin names of the trees. We'd each choose a name, then spend the rest of our walk calling each other things like *Fagus grandifolia* and *Gymnocladus dioicus*. We'd almost pee ourselves laughing. But even on good days, I'd still go to bed with a hollow feeling in my chest, knowing nothing could ever really be normal without Howard.

Gus places my olive-green suitcase next to hers in the trunk. I know she hasn't packed the right clothes or arranged them in the right order, but I bite my tongue.

"I did my best, Boo," says Gus.

She knows exactly what I'm thinking.

"So, we're going back?" I ask, already knowing the answer.

Gus slams the trunk shut.

"Fucking right we are, kiddo," she says.

2

THE PURPLE CORDS

I REMEMBER WHEN WE FINALLY WALKED BACK TO OUR CAMPSITE and left the deserted beach that day. Gus made us grilled cheese sandwiches in a frying pan over the campfire. There were bits of ash in the cheese. Some of our cooking stuff, our cooler, and our water jug were still sitting on the picnic table. Left behind when Howard drove off in the camper van with most of our dishes and clothes inside. We had nothing to change into except for a couple of his T-shirts that were drying on the clothesline. We put those on over our swimsuits. It was still warm even though the sun had just set. Gus sent Howard a text but got no reply. There were no voice messages from him, either. It wasn't like Howard, and I could tell she was getting more and more worried.

I wanted her to say that she was mad as heck at Howard. That he probably ran into someone he knew and went for a beer or stopped by his parents' place and lost track of time. I wanted her to say it was just like him to get caught up chatting with someone. Or that he was forgetful or that he had blinders on when he was working. He loved doing research. He loved chasing leads. He was excited about his latest story. That's why he was late. I wanted her to say all those things or at least one of them. But mostly I wanted her to say she wasn't worried.

Instead, she said she was going to take a shower.

Gus walked over to one of the stalls at the comfort station across from our site, her beach towel around her waist. I settled into the hammock and tried to read until it got too dark to see the words. Gus sat by the fire after her shower and let the heat coming off it dry her long red hair. I fell asleep as the wind rustled the sugar maples, listening for the sound of the wheels of the camper crunching on the gravel road.

The sun woke me the next morning as it poked through the trees, already too bright. A beach blanket covered me. Gus was sitting in the same camping chair she'd been sitting in last night next to a smoky firepit, sipping coffee from a tin mug. I don't think she slept. I felt bad that I did.

"Want a cup?" she asked when she heard me yawn.

I looked around for the camper. All that was there were grooves in the dirt where it used to be parked. Two tracks snaked across the sandy site where the camper had driven away, fading at the gravel road.

We sipped black coffee. The smell of bacon from other campsites made my stomach growl. Gus didn't say much. Later that morning, we got a lift into town from the man who checks the water quality at the park pumps. We'd seen him around all week. He had friendly eyes and he didn't talk much. He dropped us on Picton's Main Street in front of a used clothing store called City Revival. We were still wearing flip-flops and swimsuits with Howard's T-shirts overtop. We looked like tourists who'd gotten lost on their way to the beach.

Inside City Revival, we picked out some clothes *to tide us over until he gets back*, Gus said. I was happy they were used. I don't like new things. Newness makes my skin itch. I picked out a pair of purple cords that were too big for my almost ten-year-old body, but the second I saw them, I had to have them. I loved them more than I'd loved any piece of clothing I'd ever owned. *Circa 1970* was what the woman at the counter told me, nodding in approval. She offered me a belt to hold them up. Gus picked out a pair of jeans. She was tucking Howard's T-shirt into the waist when she spotted a jean jacket. It reminded her of one she used to wear when she was young, so she bought it.

We walked down the street and got pancakes at Gus's Family Restaurant. We ate there at least once every summer. We sat in our usual booth. I remember the first time Howard saw the sign out front, he stopped the car and pointed.

"Gus, look, it's your place," he'd said with a laugh.

Tears ran down his cheeks he was laughing so hard. The car behind us started honking. Gus didn't get why he found it so funny, but Howard's funny bone was easily tickled. From then on, anytime it rained, he would say, *How about we head on over to Gus's, Gus?* Then we'd drive into town for pancakes and bacon. Most campers didn't, but I loved rainy mornings.

But this morning everything was different. The sky was as blue as a robin's egg and the sun was so bright it hurt my eyes. And Howard wasn't laughing. He wasn't with us. We ate without talking. When we walked out of the restaurant, Gus finally called his parents. I'd been wondering why she hadn't done it last night, but I didn't ask. Gus did things her way, in her own time. I think maybe she was afraid that he might be there and she didn't know why or what she'd done wrong.

But he wasn't there.

His father, Kirk, drove into town right away to pick us up. He took us to their place in Cherry Valley about a ten-minute drive from Picton. Howard's mother, Vivi, busied herself getting rooms ready for us. She fussed over me, made peach cobbler, let me play around on her piano, and when night came, she started knitting and humming to herself. She reminded me of a hummingbird hovering and twitching.

We were all in it together at first, united by worry and hope and love. They insisted that we stay with them until he was found, like it was only a matter of time. After a while, time was all we had. Days went by. Then weeks. When the school year started, I was enrolled at Marysburgh Public down the road. Gus spent her days driving around the county. Kirk and Vivi helped when they could, but the winery kept them busy. After months of searching and asking questions and handing out flyers and posting missing person signs and coming up with theories and tracking leads and arguing about what to do next, everyone was exhausted and sad and angry and lost. Vivi cried at the drop of a hat, which made me cry. She didn't like that Gus never shed a tear. But Gus didn't have time for tears. She didn't want them blurring her vision. Vivi thought she was coldhearted.

Summer turned to fall, then winter, then spring. And as warmer weather came, a chill set in. There was no more peach cobbler. Vivi and Gus barely spoke except through Kirk or me. Pretty soon, we all stopped talking. In that silence, a space opened up. At first, blame filled it. Then an ice-cold emptiness seeped in. Kirk tried to warm things up with lame jokes or predictions about the unseasonably hot weather. But in the end, he sided with his wife. It was time for us to go. We'd been living at the winery for almost a year. They'd been patient and generous, but they couldn't do it anymore. They said they had a business to run.

I knew the real reason they wanted us to go. We weren't theirs and we all knew it. I was sort of their grandchild, but not really. Gus was sort of Howard's wife, but she wasn't. They never got married. We weren't blood. We weren't family. We were just a reminder of what they'd lost. Their only son. Their real flesh and blood. So we left. The emptiness followed us home and we've been living with it ever since.

But now, as we head west on the 401, the afternoon sun streaks the clouds red and orange. We pass that familiar FLYING J sign just after Napanee, and suddenly I get the feeling we've left the emptiness behind. Something new has taken its place. I stare out the front window of the Honda and I begin to see what it is.

It is Gus's flicker.

3

THE PINK RIBBON

THE FUNERAL IS IN TWO DAYS.

It's late Friday afternoon when we get to our second-floor room at the Picton Bayside Hotel on Bridge Street. It's not even July yet, but the lady at the front desk says it's high season when Gus raises an eyebrow at the price of the room.

"Count yourself a couple lucky ducks. You scooped up a last-minute cancellation," she tells us.

We leave our door open to let in the breeze. While Gus settles in, I step out onto the balcony that runs along the back of the hotel. It overlooks a marina. I lean on the rail and watch as a man hoses down the side of a large boat. Some kids are playing tag on the grass near the dock. They're all squealing—especially a little girl in a pink dress. A teenager fills a wheelbarrow with weeds and deadheads from a garden. An older lady sits hunched on a wood bench tossing bits of bread to a couple of ducks bobbing between the boats. *Lucky ducks.* I stare at the sunlight sparkling on the water like jewels. My vision begins to ripple, making everything look like it's underwater.

I rub my eyes and when I look back at the marina, I see something flipping on the breeze. It's bright pink. It floats on the air then tumbles to the dock, before lifting and twirling like it's putting on a show just for me. I think it's a ribbon, but I need to find out.

Gus comes up beside me. She asks if I want to take a walk to the Agrarian Market to get snacks. I tell her to go without me. Then I race down the balcony to the stairwell. At the bottom, I scan the lawn then head for the dock. *Where did the ribbon go?* I race to the very end, checking between the boats, looking up and down, then back across to the parking lot and garden.

It's disappeared.

I can feel tears starting to well up and I don't know why.

But before they can spill, I spot it. The ribbon is caught in the branch of a rosebush at the edge of the garden. I run over and grab it. A thorn from the rosebush pricks my finger and a pearl of blood stains the ribbon. I try to wipe it off but the blood smears.

Another flash of pink catches my eye. I look across the parking lot just as a bicycle disappears behind the building. Before I can stop myself, I start running for it. I round the corner of the hotel. There it is. A pink bike with a banana seat with pink ribbons tied to each handlebar like pom-poms. It has to be a sign. I race after it.

The boy riding the bike is pedaling up the hill toward Main Street. He's a big kid with straw-yellow hair. He's struggling on the steep hill and the bike is weaving dangerously close to passing cars. The bike's too small for him. I follow as fast as I can. When he reaches the top, he doesn't head toward town. Instead, he goes northeast to the outskirts. I'm at least a full block behind him. He zigzags down the sidewalk for about a half mile as the road becomes a highway and the houses spread out and the sidewalk changes to a dirt shoulder. He's still teetering close to traffic. I don't want him to get hit. Someone sticks their head out the passenger window of a truck and yells *get off the road, you fucking moron* before tossing a soda can at him. It just misses his head. I jog after him. He turns onto a side road. I can't see him anymore through the trees. My legs are burning.

When I get to the side road, I spot the boy leaning his bike against a fence that surrounds a small church painted all white. He unlatches a metal gate and slips through. As he walks toward the church, I come along the fence. A sign on the gate says THE OLD CHAPEL 1809. He hasn't seen me. The boy has a limp and one of his shoulders is lower than the other. Now that I'm closer, I think he might be a grown-up. But he seems like a kid. Half skipping, half walking. Half boy, half man. He opens the chapel door and goes inside, leaving it open a crack.

I look around. The road is a dead end. Deserted. I slip through the gate. As I walk toward the chapel, I hear music. A beautiful, sad song. Someone's playing "Amazing Grace" on an organ. I step inside. It's all shadows. Once my eyes adjust, I can make out pews on the main floor and two balconies overhead. There's an old woodstove in the corner. Dust swirls inside a shaft of sunlight that streams in from an open window. The shaft angles toward the front corner of the chapel where it lights up the boy like a spotlight. He's sitting at an organ. He's the one making the beautiful music. His feet pump the pedals and his fingers dance across the keys. He's tipped to one side, just like how he walks. He's swaying to the rhythm. I inch closer. I can smell something earthy and musty. I think it's him.

I clear my throat. He keeps playing. I don't want to startle him. I try again.

"Hello?" I call out.

His fingers freeze and the music stops. He lifts his chin and sniffs the air like a dog.

Then he slowly turns and looks at me.

I smile and give him a little wave.

"I like your music," I tell him.

He looks like he's about to say something but just as he opens his mouth, a shadow blocks the sunlight on his face. I turn to look. A figure is silhouetted in the open window.

"That you in there, Dod?" shouts the silhouette.

The voice bounces off the chapel ceiling, making it sound crazy loud. The boy leaps off the bench, sending it clattering to the floor. He stumbles toward me. I lurch into the pews to get out of his way. He's out the door before I can stop him.

"Who else is in there? It's after-hours," barks the silhouette.

"I didn't know. I'm leaving," I say.

I hurry outside. I can't see the boy anywhere.

The silhouette belongs to an old man who hobbles around the side of the building, a rake in one hand. He's almost as thin as the rake and not nearly as scary looking as his voice sounded.

"Hello," I say. "Um, I'm sorry. I didn't mean to trespass. I saw the boy go in and—"

He leans on his rake and twirls his long white beard between his fingers.

"I've told him once, I'll tell him a thousand times, he's gonna get in right shit if those ladies from the historical society catch him with his grubbies on their precious antique organ," says the man.

"You'd think they'd want him to play when he can play like that," I say.

"You ain't from these parts, are ya?" he says.

"I'm here for a funeral," I tell him.

He crosses himself.

"I'm the groundskeeper here. Digby Vader. Site's closed to visitors for the day," he says. "But you're welcome back tomorrow."

I glance at the gate. The bike is still leaning on the fence.

"You called him Dod?" I ask.

He squints.

"Most folks 'round here call him Dud. 'Cause he's different. He was born a tad dim and he walks kinda funny on account of an accident a few years back," he says.

"Oh" is all I can think to say.

"Folks don't like different. But you got a point. Dod Perley's got the gift of music in him. Taught himself. Can't even read notes. Just picks up tunes by ear."

"He's very good," I say.

"Not much good ever came from the Perleys making more Perleys, I can tell ya that." Digby chuckles.

It's a mean thing to say.

I feel sorry for Dod Perley and I don't even know him.

"All righty then," he says as he grabs up his rake. He's done talking.

"Nice bike." He nods, thinking it's mine.

He turns and heads for the small graveyard next to the chapel.

I ride the bike back to the hotel. I'm sure it belongs to the girl in the pink dress and not to Dod Perley. It's too small and pink for him. Maybe he borrowed it and forgot to return it.

I'm right about the bike, but wrong about him borrowing it. It does belong to the girl. But her family thinks it was stolen and they think I was the one who stole it. They're staying in a first-floor room right below ours. The whole family is searching for the bike when I ride up. Two parents, two boys, and the girl in pink who's sobbing. Before I can explain what happened, they grab the bike. They make such a fuss that a policeman who's inside having dinner in the restaurant comes out to see what's going on. The manager of the hotel and some other customers gather around me in the parking lot. People look down from the balcony. I'm scared and flustered and red-faced and the girl's dad won't let go of my elbow.

That's when Gus comes around the corner of the building.

She has a grocery bag in each hand. Her face goes white. She drops the bags and chocolate-covered almonds roll across the pavement.

"Get your hands off her," Gus barks.

She glares at the dad. He lets me go and shrinks behind his wife. The pink girl wraps herself around her mum's leg like a baby monkey. The woman points at Gus.

"That's her," she spits. "That's the mother."

Then she points her long finger at me.

"As if it isn't obvious," she says, staring at my red hair like it's evidence of a crime.

Her boys snicker. Gus goes nose to nose with the woman. The policeman steps between them, facing Gus.

"It seems your daughter stole this girl's bike," he says.

Gus pulls me over to her.

"You okay, Boo?" she asks, ignoring the policeman. "Did they hurt you?"

The girl's mum makes a show of rolling her eyes.

"*We* are the victims here," she puffs.

The pink girl wails on cue.

"My daughter doesn't steal," Gus tells the policeman.

I feel a rush of love for Gus in that moment. She knows me and even if she doesn't always make sure I eat my vegetables or brush my teeth like most mothers do, she'll always fight for me.

"We caught her red-handed," says the girl's mum. "Or should I say red-*headed*."

She cackles. I now see that she's a witch.

Gus ignores her and focuses on the young policeman, who looks uncomfortable and hot in his stiff uniform.

"What's your name, Officer?" asks Gus.

He doesn't know who he's dealing with.

"Constable Journey. Able Journey. Picton OPP detachment," he says.

"Are you accusing my kid of a crime, Constable?" she asks.

"I'm just looking into an incident is all, ma'am," he says, looking down at his notepad.

"Wow, pretty slow day," Gus says.

"I was having a bite in the restaurant . . . and there was s-such a r-ruckus outside," he stutters.

He flips through his notepad and clears his throat. He shifts his attention to me.

"How old are you, miss?" he asks.

"Almost thirteen," I tell him.

Gus steps in front of me.

"You can't be serious?" she says.

"Did you leave your daughter unattended, miss, ma'am?" he tries.

"So now I'm the criminal," says Gus.

"What did you say your name was?" he asks.

"I didn't say," says Gus.

The witch folds her arms and gives the people around her a *what'd I tell you* look.

The pink girl ramps up her fake crying. I want to kick her bony shin so she has something to really cry about.

"Name?" repeats the constable, trying to take control back.

"Augusta Monet," says Gus. "M-O-N-E-T."

The constable hesitates like he's forgotten what to do next.

"Oh," he says. "You. You're, um . . ."

Gus stares at him.

"Here for the, the funeral," he says quietly.

He knows who she is.

Gus is legendary at the Picton OPP detachment. And not in

a good way. It's why Constable Journey knows all about her even though he's never met her.

I once saw her picture on a bulletin board in the staff break room at the detachment when I was nine. Across the top, some-one had written CUCKOO BIRD ALERT: APPROACH WITH CAUTION. I wasn't supposed to be in that break room, but I snuck in to get a bag of chips from the vending machine. I ripped the sign down, tore it up, and stuffed it in the garbage can.

They didn't know Gus. She wasn't crazy. She just wasn't like them. They were always saying things about procedures and proto-cols and policies back then. They liked their *P* words. Gus had her own. Purpose, persistence, possibility. She also liked *F* words. She wouldn't be told what to do or how to do it. They tried. I was there.

Back then, we were brought into the detachment a bunch of times. I always waited for her on the same bench in the same hall. At first, they didn't charge her because they felt sorry for her. But Gus being Gus, they soon got sick of her. She was charged with trespassing, theft, breaking and entering, harassment, disturbing the peace. She even got a ticket for sleeping in her car at the side of a road. They wanted her gone. They pressured Howard's parents. Told them she was messing with the investigation. The detach-ment commander, Staff Sergeant Julius Muirhead, was a friend of theirs. He told them she was *a royal pain in the ass*. He never liked her. She was an outsider from the city telling the local police com-mander how to do his job. And she was a reminder they weren't doing it. They hadn't found Howard and they had no leads.

Constable Journey's face goes red. He puts away his notepad.

The witch looks confused. She can feel things slipping away and she doesn't know why.

Everyone is staring at me. It feels like they're all whispering about us.

"I didn't do anything wrong," I shout, a little too loud. "I was just bringing the bike back for her. Someone else stole it. Borrowed it, I mean. He didn't mean to take it, I'm sure."

I say this as fast as I can so they'll all stop looking at me.

"Do you know who took the bike, Boo?" asks Gus, putting her hand on my shoulder.

"I don't," I tell her as tears fill my eyes. "I don't know anyone around here. I just returned it, that's all."

The witch *tsk, tsk, tsk*s at me. I want to run upstairs and hide under my bed but I can't.

"I think we're done here," says Gus to the constable.

Gus pulls me away, over to the grocery bags. We both kneel and start gathering the snacks that spilled out.

"She's a little liar," spits the witch.

Gus rises and lunges for the woman.

The constable jumps between them and the witch cackles.

"See. Like mother, like daughter," she shouts to the crowd.

Gus tosses a chocolate almond at the witch.

It hits her forehead and she acts like she's been shot. Her husband puffs his chest.

"Easy now, everyone," says the constable.

Gus heads back to me and we pick up the rest of our stuff. No one helps.

The constable holds out his arms and presses the family back.

"Okay, show's over, folks," the constable says, trying to get everyone to move on.

The witch recovers from her injury. She ignores the constable and walks up to the hotel manager.

"Julia, we've been coming here a very long time, and we have a lot of friends," she says.

"Mrs. McNabb, please, Mrs. McNabb, we know you're a valued . . . we appreciate your business. We-we . . ." stammers Julia.

The witch turns her back on the manager and storms toward her room with her family following. The pink girl sticks her tongue out at me.

Julia leaves a note under our door an hour later. She's sorry but our room's been double-booked and since the other people booked it first, she has to give it to them and there are no other rooms so we have to vacate the property tomorrow morning. Checkout is 10 A.M.

And even though it's not tomorrow and it's almost dusk, Gus doesn't want to spend another second in that hotel. We pack our things and leave. Gus parks around the corner on Main and starts calling motels, hotels, guesthouses, and private campgrounds and trailer parks, but the whole county is booked solid. High season.

No vacancies, they tell her, over and over.

I feel vacant. And I want to go home.

Instead, we drive to Canadian Tire.

Plan B.

4

THE DIAMONDS

WE BUY A TENT, SLEEPING BAGS, A LANTERN, AND A COOLER. THEN
we head to the Sandbanks Provincial Park, about twenty minutes
outside Picton. Gus says we're going camping. But we don't drive
to the check-in booths at the main gate to ask if there are any
campsites available. Gus knows the answer already. Instead, we
enter the park and take the long road down the finger of land that
leads to Lakeshore Beach. On one side of us is Lake Ontario, on
the other side is a stretch of sand dunes along West Lake. Howard
once told me they are the largest freshwater dunes in the world.

Before we get to the Lakeshore Beach parking area, Gus veers
onto a Parks service road that winds into the forest. A sign says NO
ENTRY but it's pretty overgrown. Gus ignores the sign and drives
until we can't go any farther. She stops and hides the car under
some cedars. We grab our supplies and trek to the dunes. It's slow
going because there's no trail and the sand is deep so we sink in as
we walk. We go up and down the dunes. At one point, we have to
duck behind a clump of cottonwoods when some late day hikers
go by. She doesn't want anyone calling the wardens on us. The
park is closing soon and then we'll have it all to ourselves.

Dusk falls. We come to a thicket of poplars next to the water's
edge where there's a small beach. Some dead logs are scattered on

the beach like benches. We dump our stuff under the poplars but we don't set up the tent. It's getting dark and we're too tired to bother. We haven't stopped moving since we left Ottawa hours ago. Gus grabs the sleeping bags and we walk down to the water. It looks just like a spot where we used to picnic and swim when I was little. We can see lights across the bay from campfires and lakeside restaurants and cottage windows. People are making s'mores and playing games and sharing stories. We're trespassing. We climb into our sleeping bags and stare up at the night sky. It's clear and there's a blanket of stars above us. This place feels magical.

I ask Gus to tell me a story. She looks out at the rippling waves a while then she tells me a story about this beach. It was the first summer we ever camped at the Sandbanks. I was only a year old so I wouldn't remember, she tells me. We made a day trip to the dunes to explore. Howard pulled me in a wagon along the shoreline. He kept making me laugh by pretending to trip and fall on his belly in the sand. He loved to make me giggle, she tells me. I look over. Her face is moonlit. She's smiling as she remembers. Gus tells me that's the day we found this beach. It's called Butterfly Beach. We had a picnic. Howard had packed everything in a small cooler bag and put it in the wagon. Wine for them, juice for me, deviled eggs, cheese, bread, olives, fresh peaches, and butter tarts. After lunch, we swam and then I fell asleep wrapped in a towel in a shady spot. Howard carved their initials inside a heart on a piece of driftwood. Then he told her he loved her for the first time. We spent the whole day there until the sun set. When it was time to go, Gus pulled the wagon and I rode on Howard's shoulders. It was a good day, she says.

Gus goes quiet. After a while, her breath deepens. She's asleep.

I slip quietly out of my sleeping bag and search for the driftwood where he carved their initials. I stumble from one log to the next. But I can't see very well so I give up. It's a warm night and

I'm sweating from all my searching. I sit and lean against a log near the shore and push my hot hands deep into the cool sand. It feels good. I wonder how deep the sand goes.

Howard knew all about these dunes. How they were made when big glaciers melted thousands of years ago. How they're always moving and changing because of the strong winds and waves off the lake. How long-lost treasures have appeared in the sand, unearthed after centuries. Like when a guide at the park found some stone netsinkers used by the St. Lawrence Iroquois to fish on this beach hundreds of years ago.

I push my cool hands deeper into the sand. Then my fingertips touch something. I wriggle the object then I grip it between my fingers and pull it from the sand. I hold it close to my eyes to get a better look. It's a small plastic baggie. Inside it are some tiny glass stones that sparkle in the moonlight. I think they're diamonds. I wonder if I've found buried treasure.

Then my heart sinks. All this is just a story I'm telling myself to feel better. Like Gus does. I suddenly feel very small and the air gets sucked from my lungs, leaving me hollow. The emptiness carries me away. I can see us from way up there in the universe. I'm sitting on Butterfly Beach and Gus is sleeping on the sand. We're not all together telling jokes or playing charades. We're all alone—just us two. A billion miles from where we really want to be. Home with Howard.

I wipe tears from my eyes as I climb back into my sleeping bag.

Even though I want to go home, I know in my heart, this is where we are supposed to be. This is where Gus brought me. And I think I know why now.

I come back down to earth and take a deep breath.

We've come back to Butterfly Beach and Prince Edward County because it's time to say goodbye.

5

THE BASEBALL CAP

SATURDAY NIGHT IT RAINS HARD. WE SET UP THE TENT AND SLEEP inside. We listen to the wind howl in the poplars. It's cloudy so there are no stars. I'm glad. The dull weather suits my sour mood. Both stick around until Sunday. The day of the funeral. There's a hot wind swirling and even though it's daytime, it looks dark. We dress in black. Mostly. Gus lets me wear my purple cords with my black blouse. We pack our suitcases and cooler in the trunk and shove the wet tent in the back seat. Gus says it doesn't matter if it gets ruined. We're going home once it's all over.

We wait in the car in the parking lot next to the Stone Chapel in Glenwood Cemetery until most of the people are inside. The Honda rocks as the wind tumbles a garbage can across the parking lot. It slams into someone's car, leaving a dent. Then it rolls across the lawn and ends up stuck between two headstones. The large maple trees around us bend and sway like giant birds trying to fly away from their roots. The obituary said 4 P.M. and that's exactly what time it is when Gus finally makes a move.

"Let's do this," she says, her jaw clenched.

She doesn't look like someone about to say goodbye.

I follow her into the chapel. Someone is singing as we come through the door. A hymn, I guess. There's organ music too. I half

expect to see Dod playing the organ, but he's not. A man in a
dark blue suit points us to a pew at the back. The chapel is packed
with people I don't know. There's a giant photo of Howard at
the front on an easel. His head looks weirdly big. He's smiling.
I don't know this photo. It looks like it was taken at a wedding
because he's wearing a suit that looks too big for him and there's
a white carnation pinned to his jacket. It doesn't look like him at
all. Not the him I remember. He never wore suits or carnations or
had a big head. There's a small table in front of the photo. On it
are candles and a red-and-blue Montreal Canadiens baseball cap
that belonged to Howard when he was a kid. His mother kept
all his childhood stuff. I don't know why it's there. Did it mean
that much to him? More than I knew? I feel like we're not even at
Howard's funeral. I hope I'm right. Should I pray on it? I've never
prayed before but we are in a chapel. It can't hurt.

Howard's parents, Kirk and Vivi, are standing at the front
next to a man in a robe. The priest, I guess. They turn to take their
seats and Vivi spots us. I wave and Gus grabs my hand, pulling
it down. Vivi looks like she's about to vomit or faint. She clings
to her husband's arm. I sit but Gus stays standing. Kirk and Vivi
look away.

They take their seats without waving or nodding or asking us
to come up front.

Gus sits. She grabs my hand and squeezes it. She never holds
my hand.

"Ouch," I whisper. She lets go.

"We shouldn't be here," she says, her legs bouncing like she's
got springs in her shoes.

Something is beginning to bubble up inside her. She's swaying back and forth now. Like the trees outside. Like she wants to
fly but she's rooted to the pew. The priest starts talking but I'm
not listening to what he's saying. Hives are springing up across my

hot neck. I clutch my dry throat. I'm having trouble swallowing. Now it's me who takes her hand. I hold it tight so she doesn't fly away. But it's no use.

"We shouldn't be here," she says again, only louder.

I take hold of her with both hands.

"Gus," I whisper. "Please."

A woman across the aisle shushes me.

Gus looks around like she's searching for an exit. Eyes wide.

"None of us should be here," she calls out.

She's no longer using an indoor voice. I don't know who she's talking to but it's not me. People turn and stare. The priest pauses. I wish in that moment I wasn't a redhead. I could pretend I'm with the woman sitting at the end of our pew. The one staring at us. But she has blond hair so I wouldn't be fooling anyone. Gus yanks her hand free from mine and rises to her feet. I shrink as low as I can in the pew. I should have seen this coming a mile away. Gus is doing Gus. She's not doing goodbye.

"This is a bloody fiasco," she shouts.

People gasp and scoff. Kirk is out of his seat. Vivi hangs on his arm like a child. Other men in the chapel rise to show they're on Kirk's side. The priest gestures for everyone to sit.

"He's not fucking dead," Gus yells.

Her voice bounces off the rafters.

Then they shudder.

The rafters, that is.

At first, I think it's God getting really mad at Gus. She always said there was no way to know if there was a God, but I'm starting to think he's real and he's miffed. The rafters groan, then the stained-glass windows start to rattle and then a sound I've never heard before begins to get louder and louder, closer and closer. It's like a freight train is rumbling down a track and it's heading straight for us. I try to think what it could be. I don't remember seeing train tracks nearby, but there have to be because the train is so loud and so close it's shaking the chapel. Then there's a loud cracking sound outside like a giant tree snapped in two. The priest looks more scared than a priest is supposed to look and everyone sees it. All eyes are on him as he sidesteps to a window and looks outside. Even from the back, I can see his eyes widen and his mouth drop open.

"Everyone get down!" he hollers, then he drops to the floor.

Someone screams. A split second later, the train hits the chapel. The last thing I see before I'm pushed off the pew is Howard's big face flying into the tumbling black sky above us where there used to be a roof. My ears pop and the air is sucked from my lungs. I hear screaming and groaning. I'm on the floor. Feet run in every direction. Wind spins purses and Kleenex boxes and Bibles in spirals. Glass rains down but it doesn't hit me because I'm under a fallen pew. The back of the bench shelters me. I don't know if Gus pushed me there or the wind blew me under or if God tucked me there for safekeeping. I curl up in the cave of the pew and cover my ears. It's so loud I think my eardrums might burst. I shut my eyes and wait for the train to leave. It feels like forever but it's probably only a few seconds and then, just like that, it's gone. The roar of the train softens until it's no more. Then everything is deadly quiet.

I open my eyes and crawl out from under the pew. Gus is right beside me. Her red hair is wild around her face like she's just touched that metal ball at the science museum. I can't help it. I laugh. She looks ridiculous. She thinks I'm delirious. Gus checks my body for blood or holes or cuts. I feel like a rag doll as she lifts my arms and pats my torso. I look up. The roof of the chapel is gone. Sunlight bursts from behind a black cloud as it rolls away and the sky clears. It's bluer than blue.

It's a miracle everyone's alive.

That's what the priest says, over and over, as he guides people out of the ruins.

The tornado came right through town with no warning. It twisted out of the stormy sky and tracked northwest across Glenwood Cemetery, down Talbot Street, then out toward the farmers' fields beyond Picton. The chapel, a dry-cleaning business, a cab company, and six houses got their roofs torn off. Because it was a warm Sunday in June and a lot of businesses were closed and people were out for Sunday drives in the county or ran to their basements when they heard the train, no one was killed. We find all this out later, but right after it happens it looks nothing like a miracle.

Gus and I wander through town. There are blank faces on all the other people wandering past us. Aimless people stumbling about in a daze. Gus is the only one who looks kind of happy.

"See? I was right," she says.

We walk around for an hour then we circle back to the cemetery. When we get there, Kirk and Vivi are standing with the priest in the parking lot. I'm surprised to see most of the guests still there too. There's a fire truck and two police cars, and more people are gathering from all directions. Maybe they heard about the chapel and have come to help. They're raking debris and picking up parts of the roof and removing branches from inside the chapel.

"I'll just be a sec," says Gus, nodding for me to wait by the car. "I've got to do something."

She crosses the parking lot and walks over to Howard's parents. The priest darts off when he sees her coming. I feel sorry for them. Their son's funeral was ruined, and Gus is probably about to give them heck for planning it in the first place.

The tornado brought down a pine tree right next to the Honda. The tree just missed crushing our car. Behind it, I notice a few gravestones have tipped over in the cemetery. Little bouquets of plastic flowers are scattered across the grass. Something else is lying there among the graves. Something blue and red. I cross the grass and pick it up. It's a baseball cap. Montreal Canadiens. The one that was sitting at the front of the chapel. It's Howard's. The tornado must have tossed it here. Maybe so I'd find it.

I hear voices behind me. A group of old men in dusty suits are talking in the parking lot. I recognize one. He guided us to our pew. He's going on about the weather like he's an actual meteorologist. He says Prince Edward County is known for its crazy summer storms. *Remember the tornadoes of 2018?* he says. Then he rattles on about La Niñas and golf-ball-size hail. How it's the cool Lake Ontario winds colliding with the hot, humid county air. He figures today's storm might just be the biggest tornado the county's seen in a decade. *Coulda been a microburst,* says another man. The meteorologist scoffs, *You don't know what you're talking about, Larry. That was easily an F3. Maybe even an F4.*

He was right. It was a tornado and a big one.

And even though there was no warning, Gus knew before anyone else did.

None of us should have been there.

The cool winds collided with the hot air and the tornado headed right for that chapel.

It put an end to that *bloody fiasco.*

Howard's parents probably think Gus brought it.

I almost think she did.

6

THE CAMPER VAN

I LOOK ACROSS THE PARKING LOT FOR GUS. SHE'S STILL TALKING to Howard's parents near the ruined chapel. Staff Sergeant Muirhead is also there. I didn't see him before, but he must have been at the funeral. I remember he's a friend of theirs. He runs a finger across his mustache as he talks. That mustache always gave me the creeps. He's looking at Howard's parents, not at Gus. Vivi's lips are pinched tight and Kirk puts his arm around her shoulders. Gus moves closer, trying to get Muirhead to make eye contact with her. She says something. I can tell from the way the veins in her neck are bulging that something bad has happened. She has her hands on her hips. My hives start tingling below the surface. I watch the four grown-ups say things I can't hear. Things I probably don't want to hear. I could run over and make them tell me, but I've turned to stone. Like the gravestones. I am heavy and frozen in place. Waiting for someone to come to me.

Then Gus looks at me. She turns away from the others and rushes over. She half stumbles as if her knees have turned to jelly. She takes me by the shoulders.

"They found the camper van," she gasps.

All the blood empties from my brain and slithers down the back of my neck.

"What? Wha-when?" I stammer.

"Two fucking weeks ago and that useless piece of shit, Muir-head, *forgot* to call me," she fumes, rolling her eyes.

"And Howard?" I ask in a voice so tiny it doesn't sound like mine.

She shakes her head.

"He wasn't inside. He wasn't anywhere. They searched the area. But they have the camper," she says. "It was found in some abandoned hangar up at Picton Airport on Macaulay Mountain, just outside town. Can you believe it?" she says. "That's why his parents went ahead with a funeral. They gave up once the camper van was found without Howard."

"But why didn't anyone tell us?" I ask.

I try to swallow away the lump in my throat but I've forgotten how.

"Vivi assumed the cops did tell us. She heard we were in town and thought we were here to get the camper van. She figured we'd never come to the funeral," she says. "Muirhead was clearly pissed she let it slip. He went on about some forensics team having to come from Kingston—how the OPP are spread thin so it took a couple of weeks but they're finally coming tomorrow. Fucking incompetent as always. The camper van is still sitting in that hangar. He said they'd release it after it was processed. Called it an active crime scene. Active my ass!"

Gus throws back her head and cackles. Now *she's* the delirious one. The old men standing nearby look shocked. I guess you're not supposed to laugh in a cemetery or after a tornado.

I look down at the baseball cap I've been clutching tight since finding it.

"But where's Howard?" I ask as tears spill from my eyes.

Gus drops to one knee. She's eye level with the cap. She glances at it then looks up at me and wipes the tears from my cheeks with both her thumbs.

"This means we can't go home yet. Okay?" she says, almost like she's asking me.

I nod and wipe my wet face with the cap.

An SUV drives past us too fast. It's Howard's parents. Vivi is looking out the passenger window. She catches my eye then looks away. I'm hurt. They left before saying hello. They used to like me when we'd visit them with Howard. Vivi used to turn down the quilt on my bed and leave a flower from her garden on my pillow. Every summer Kirk took me to Books & Company so I could pick out a new book. And every Christmas, Vivi knit me slipper socks. Now she can't say hello or wave or even crack a smile. Maybe she's forgotten how because her heart is broken too.

Muirhead is getting back into his OPP cruiser. He nods to Gus, hoping for a quick getaway, but she strides over when she spots him trying to leave. I follow. He hangs on the door, one foot inside.

"I told Kirk and Vivi I'd keep them in the loop on any findings," he says. "I can do you the same courtesy, Miss Monet."

"Gee, thanks. It *is* my van," she says.

"And it *is* their son," he says.

Right away he holds up both hands as if to stop what's about to start.

"I'll call you," he says as he gets into his car.

"I want to see it," she says.

"There's not much to see. It was cleaned out when we found it," he says. "Kids probably."

Gus stares at him and is about to open her mouth when he starts up again.

"But you can most definitely see it tomorrow. Once the team from Kingston has done their thing, the van's all yours," he says, smiling and trying not to blow his top like he used to. "Like I said, it's an active crime scene. I've had an officer posted there since we found it, even though we could use the resources elsewhere, especially today. So believe me, the scene has been secure this whole time. Be a good girl and let us do our jobs. You'll get it back soon enough. Now, if you don't mind."

He shuts his car door.

"Who found it?" she shouts at his window.

He rolls down the window. His jaw ripples like he's got a toothache.

"Hugo Remedy. He works as a security guard up there."

He drives away. I can see him reaching for his police radio and holding it to his mouth. Gus watches the cruiser weave through debris scattered on the cemetery's driveway. A tree cracks and falls somewhere in the graveyard. Someone shrieks. Sirens wail in the distance.

"Let's go." That's all Gus says, but I don't like the way she says it.

THE DRIVE THROUGH TOWN TAKES FOREVER. WE GET REROUTED twice. Once because of downed power lines and once because someone's sofa is in the middle of the road. There are people everywhere stumbling around hollow-eyed. Sleepwalkers. We reach the edge of town, pass the Bayside Hotel, then turn onto Union Street, then Church Street, then we head all the way up Macaulay Mountain, past Millennium Lookout to the airport. I don't like that the camper was found at that airport. I always thought it was the creepiest place in Picton.

We used to take this route as a shortcut to avoid going through town when summer tourists with their giant motor homes clogged Main. Church Street loops over the mountain and comes out on the other side of town at County Road 10. The road to the Sand-banks Provincial Park.

Howard told me that Picton Airport was built in 1940 to train pilots and gunners for World War II. He knew all about the history. Back then it was called Camp Picton. When the air force moved to another airfield in the sixties, a flying club started using the three runways and built some new hangars. But there was a row of long wood buildings that used to be the barracks, a drill hall, an officers' lounge, and a mess hall. They were boarded up decades ago along with most of the old hangars. The abandoned buildings looked haunted.

In the eighties, some of the buildings at one end of the field were fixed up and rented out to a yoga studio and an art gallery. But the row of broken-down buildings at the back were forgot-ten. The creepy ones were surrounded by a wire fence and left to rot.

Every time we drove past, I would look at those lonely build-ings set apart from the others, their green paint peeling off the wood siding, their shingled roofs drooping like they were about to collapse at any moment. Most of the windows were broken and had been covered with wire mesh so animals and teenagers and hoboes couldn't get in. There was a wooden tower at one end that stood watch over the lonesome camp. Maybe it used to be an air traffic control tower but it looked like a prison guard tower to me. Watching over the ghosts held captive there. The place gave me chills back then and it still does.

We turn into the entrance and drive slowly past the flying club hangars, the yoga studio, the gallery, searching for signs of an active crime scene. I don't like that's it called that. And I don't like that some kids took our stuff. At the far end of the road, we spot a NO TRESPASSING sign on the wire fence. Gus heads right for it. The gate sits open. We drive through and down a dirt road behind the old hangars. As we round the first building, we spot an OPP cruiser.

"There, up ahead," says Gus.

I recognize the policeman. It's Constable Journey from the hotel. He's standing next to some yellow police tape that's been strung across the entrance of a hangar. A man in a wrinkled uniform is talking to him. One of the hangar walls is buckled a little so the whole thing tilts to one side. Like Dod Perley. The giant front door is wide open. All I can see are dark shadows inside. We stop next to the cruiser.

Gus jumps out, leaving the car door open. The constable sees her coming. I stay put. I'm scared to take a closer look. I know Howard's not in there but it's been so long since I've seen our camper van. I don't want to cry in front of these strangers. Gus tries to go under the tape.

"Hold up, Miss Monet, you can't go in there," Constable Journey says. "The structure's not safe and the scene has to be—"

"—secured? Yeah, I know," she says, cutting him off.

"I was gonna say, processed," he says, standing in her way. "But secured works."

The other man comes up beside the constable like he's backing him up.

"You the one who found the camper?" Gus asks the man, ignoring the constable.

"Hugo Remedy in the flesh. Head of security for the airport. I was doing a walkabout of the property couple weeks back and came across it," he says, a lit cigarette bobbing in the corner of his mouth. "I nearly shit myself when I seen it. Thought someone was livin' in there."

Gus tries to move past them, but the constable blocks her way.

"I'm sorry, miss," he says.

"I won't touch anything," she says, trying to dodge around him.

The constable isn't letting her by. I'm afraid of what she might do. Gus used to take kickboxing classes. I can't bear to watch.

"The staff sergeant gave you a heads-up I might come by," she says to the constable.

"I have my orders," he says. "Besides, that roof could cave any minute."

"I took a look-see," offers Hugo. "Whatcha wanna know?"

The constable shoots Hugo a look and puts his hands on his hips, trying to look like the one in charge.

"Rest assured the OPP has thoroughly searched the surrounding area," the constable says.

"What a relief," says Gus.

"Look, I know you're not happy, but as soon as forensics dusts for prints and collects any relevant evidence, I'm sure you'll be given full access," says the constable.

"So you're telling me this guy can have a look-see and the OPP has already stomped all over the place, but I can't go in to look at my own fucking camper?" says Gus.

"She's got ya there, rookie." Hugo chuckles.

Constable Journey adjusts the caution tape. One end comes undone. The constable stoops and grabs the fallen tape. He tries to retie it to the metal frame but the other end comes undone and the whole thing falls. Gus turns her attention to Hugo.

"Tell me what you saw?" she asks.

"Nothing much, really. Just a regular old camper. Bedding, clothes, dishes. It stunk to high heaven. You'd swear someone died in there." He laughs.

"Jesus, Hugo," says the constable, shaking his head.

"You're saying our stuff is still in there?" Gus gasps.

"Yeah, no. I mean it *was* when I first found the camper but you know teenagers. These old hangars have become kind of a party place for 'em ever since my night shift guy quit a few weeks back and I can't work nights on account of the wife's gout and try finding a trained security professional. It ain't easy, let me tell ya." He takes a deep breath then continues. "But I did my duty and called it in the second I saw it. I know the staff sergeant personally. Called him direct. Lawman to lawman. His boys showed up first thing the next day. It was just crap luck those kids got in there overnight," says Hugo.

Gus turns to the constable.

"The next day," she says, glaring at him.

"We didn't realize it was *that* camper van," says the constable. "There's only two guys on duty at night. We're a small detachment."

Gus just stares at him.

"The staff sergeant has made sure there's been an officer posted out here 24/7 ever since. And a whole forensics team is coming tomorrow. They might turn up something even if the circumstances are less than . . . ideal," he says.

He looks like he's having trouble swallowing.

"Wow," says Gus. "The OPP really fucked up."

Constable Journey doesn't say anything. Gus zeroes in on Hugo again.

"This was two weeks ago?" she asks.

"Yup," he says. "I was doing my monthly rounds. It's part of my job description to check all the buildings every four weeks—like clockwork. I write it all down in my official inspection log. The owner insists on it. It's an insurance thing, liability, privilege, deductibles, legal eagle stuff," explains Hugo.

"Why didn't you see it before?" Gus asks.

Constable Journey looks just as curious as Gus to hear the answer.

"You weren't just writing it down in your official logbook and not actually doing it, were you, Hugo?" the constable says.

I think they're both starting to second-guess Hugo. I know I am.

"Swear on my ma's leaky bowel," he says, holding up three fingers in a Scout salute.

"But you did miss it," Gus points out.

"I never. It weren't there last month," says Hugo.

This is news to the constable. He stares at Hugo. Then he writes something on the notepad he pulls from his pocket. He's still got the yellow police tape wrapped around one hand.

"You're sure?" the constable asks Hugo.

"Swear on the wife's kidney stones," he says. Again, he salutes.

Gus takes a deep breath and clenches her fists. I think she's done with Hugo and done talking. I brace myself. But instead of exploding, she looks down at her feet and brings one hand to her brow. She closes her eyes and her face contorts. It looks like she's crying. But she's not.

"I think I can take it from here, Hugo," says the constable.

Hugo doesn't move.

"I'll let you know if I need you," he says.

"Technically this is my jurisdiction," says Hugo.

As the two men have a standoff, Gus glances over her shoulder at me. Her eyes dart toward the hangar then back to me. I shrink in my seat.

"If you want to give me your number, I can call you with an update," the constable offers.

Gus brings one hand to her mouth as if she might be sick. Her eyes get glassy.

"Can I get you a tissue?" he asks.

She doesn't answer. The constable tries to untangle the caution tape from his hand. Hugo tries to help him but only makes things worse. Gus shoots me another quick look. This time jerking her whole head toward the hangar. I shake my head. I can feel hives burning the back of my neck. She purses her lips tight. I nod. I have no choice.

Gus turns away from the two men. The constable searches his pockets. She walks away from the hangar, head low, face in her hands. She even bounces her shoulders like she's sobbing. Hugo gets a call on his cell and looks relieved. He hurries off with a shrug as the constable finds a used tissue in one of his pockets. He walks over and holds it out. She keeps her back to him. The constable looks a little like he might cry too.

I feel bad for him. He's young and I'm pretty sure he's new to the detachment because I don't remember seeing him around three years ago. I know most of the faces of the OPP constables from back then. He's probably a rookie like Hugo said. That's why it's his job to babysit a camper van when everyone else in the detachment is dealing with real police stuff. But even though he wasn't around, he knows who Gus is. I could tell when we first met him at the hotel. He's heard the stories about the woman who spent a year looking for her boyfriend. He knows about all the trouble Augusta Monet caused. About the shouting matches in the halls with Staff Sergeant Muirhead. About the files she copied without permission. About the police cruiser windshield she smashed with a baseball bat. His colleagues have told him all about the Cuckoo Bird.

If I were him and I'd heard these stories, I'd probably feel sorry for her too. He hasn't been around her enough to know that she doesn't cry and she uses people and she never gives up and she always has a plan B if plan A doesn't go her way.

I'm plan B today. I put on Howard's baseball cap for good luck. It's go time. I crawl across the seats and slip out the open driver's-side door. I can hear the constable talking softly to her.

"Listen, I'm sorry. I wish I could help you," he says. "I know this can't be easy."

Gus has positioned herself to make sure the constable's back is to the hangar.

It's now or never.

I dart over and race inside. My eyes take a few seconds to adjust. Then I see the camper van. The double doors on the side are wide open. I run over and look inside. It's nothing like I remember it and it smells bad. A mouse scurries across the floor next to my bed. My headlamp isn't where I left it on top of my pillow. My pillow and sleeping bag are gone. My duffel bag of clothes is gone. The three blue-and-white place mats that were laid out on our small dining table are gone.

I look back at the entrance to the hangar. No one's coming. I jump inside the camper and climb into the front seat. I sit right where Howard would have been sitting. I look straight ahead. I check under the sun visors and inside the glove box but there's nothing there. Then I remember our hiding spot inside the panel of the driver's-side door. The camper was getting old and the panel kept coming loose. You could push on the corner and it would pop out. Howard thought it was a good spot to hide our wallets when we were camping. He called it our secret compartment. I pop it open. Bingo. Inside, I find our map. It's folded open. I lift it out and right behind it is Howard's leather notebook, held closed by a thick elastic band. It's where he wrote all his notes about whatever story he was working on. He kept stray papers inside the fold of the notebook. I open it. It's stuffed with receipts, a couple of business cards and some other papers. I tuck the map inside, close the notebook, and wrap the elastic back around it. I have to get moving.

As I climb into the back of the camper, I trip and fall forward. The notebook goes flying and my hand jams into the seat belt holder. For a moment I think my arm is stuck in the gap between the holder and the seat. I try to wiggle free and as I do, my fingers graze something. I push down deeper until I find the object. I pinch it between two fingers and pull it out.

It's Howard's phone.

My face flushes with joy.

But in the next second, my heart sinks. Howard never went anywhere without his phone. He wouldn't leave it behind. He needed it for work. It's how he took photos and recorded interviews and called people and kept in touch with us.

My eyes well up. I can barely see.

I hear Gus and Constable Journey. Their voices sound closer. I wipe the tears away and pull myself up off the floor. I shove the phone in my back pocket, pick up the notebook, tuck it in the front of my pants, and hide it with my blouse. Then I climb out of the camper. I can see Gus and the constable standing by the hangar door as he tries to restring the caution tape. They're too close. I can't go out that way. I look around. There's an exit door at the back. I run over. The hinges are stiff, but I manage to pry it open just enough to squeeze through.

I spot Gus. She's pulled out her best stuff. She's now hugging the constable. He's patting her back. She waits for me to get safely back into the car before she lets him go.

"I'll personally call you to let you how things are going," he offers.

She puts her number in his phone, then walks away from the constable. Gus jumps in the car with me. He watches as she makes a dusty three-point turn. We head back down the dirt road toward the exit. We pull onto Church Street and she looks over at me.

"Did you look in the spot?" she asks.

I pull the notebook out from under my blouse and show it to her.

"That's my girl." She smiles.

She reaches over to me and taps the bill of Howard's base-ball cap.

"I knew you could do it," she says. "What else did you see?"

I stare down at Howard's notebook with the map tucked in-side as I tell her what the camper looked and smelled like. How all our stuff was gone. I tell her about the mouse.

But I don't tell her about Howard's phone.

I don't know why. I just don't.

I want it to be all mine.

At least for a little while.

7

THE NOTEBOOK

JUST DOWN THE ROAD, WE PULL OVER AT MILLENNIUM LOOKOUT. It's right above the town of Picton, but the trees have grown so tall and thick that there's no view anymore. It's almost dusk and we're the only ones parked up there. We change out of our funeral clothes. Gus sits cross-legged on the hood. I stay in the car eating stale potato chips. Her back is to me. Crickets chirp. Wind rustles the trees. The moon already hangs in the sky like a white balloon even though the sun won't set for another hour or so. Gus has her head bowed as she reads through Howard's notebook. She flips a page. Then she lifts the notebook to her face, closes her eyes, and breathes in. She's trying to smell him. To be closer to him. To remember him.

I remember everything about Howard. Like when it was pouring rain, he'd insist on going ahead to wait in line at the Mayfair Theatre for the Saturday Morning All-You-Can-Eat-Cereal Cartoon Party. The theater was just around the corner from our house. And there were only two sofas, which were the best seats in the place, so he wanted to make sure he was first in line to snag our favorite. We'd get there just before the show started and he'd be shivering wet on the sofa. And even though Gus always brought him a dry change of clothes, this one time he caught a bad cold. He said he didn't care. He was just happy we were warm and dry in our pj's. That was Howard. That *is* Howard.

The windows are rolled down and a warm breeze whispers through the Honda.

I make sure Gus isn't looking and I pull Howard's phone from my back pocket. I try the power button again. And again, nothing happens. The battery's still dead. The screen is black but, in the moonlight, I can see a fingerprint smudged on its surface. I touch the fingerprint lightly. It's larger than mine. It's Howard's. I'm close to him too. I wonder if he knows I am. I look out the car window at the moon and imagine Howard looking up at it, too, and thinking, *Will anyone ever find me?* Then I tuck the phone into my back pocket.

I MUST HAVE FALLEN ASLEEP BECAUSE THE NEXT THING I KNOW, the morning sun is blasting into the car as if someone is shining a spotlight in my face.

Gus is sitting in the driver's seat next to me. Her door is open and she has one foot hiked up, resting on the frame. She sees I'm awake and hands me a cold Pop-Tart. The map and Howard's notebook sit between us.

"That how the map was folded when you found it?" she asks.

I nod and bite off a corner of my Pop-Tart.

"He must have been going somewhere in that area then," she says.

I stare at the map. It's the same worn-out gas station map Gus has had since before I was born. It's the one she always brought on our camping trips so we could explore along the way without getting lost. Howard told her we didn't need it. He could navigate with the GPS on his phone, but she liked real maps. She trusted something she could hold in her hands, not satellites floating around in space. She was old school, he told me. He liked that about her. Howard didn't bother trying to convince her that modern technology was pretty great or that old maps can be outdated. When it was just him and me, we used his GPS.

The map is folded to a section of Prince Edward County where the blue waterways of Prince Edward Bay curve into a shape that looks like a prehistoric creature with its toothy mouth wide open. Around the bay is a grid of farmland, scattered with lakes, and darker patches of forest and marshland. There are acres and acres in the folded section. Howard could have been going anywhere. He didn't circle a destination or draw a line on the map. No clues. Just the map.

"Why do you think Howard was using your map, anyway?" I ask.

"We always used it," says Gus.

"No, we didn't. Not when you weren't there," I tell her.

She turns to look at me and I wonder if I've hurt her feelings, but she just nods.

She has owl eyes. I don't think she slept all night.

"Did you check the glove box in the camper van?" she asks.

I nod.

I put the notebook and map on my lap. I can feel Howard's phone in my back pocket. He's with me. His fingerprint is with me. It's too late to hand it over now. She'd have a fit. She'd take it from me. Then his fingerprint would be wiped away and he'd be gone.

We drive across the county and into Picton. We pull into the Tim Horton's drive-through. We need caffeine. The line wraps around the building. Halfway around, four women wearing flowy sundresses with flowers braided into their hair wander through the cars, sticking little cards under people's windshield wipers. Some people hand them money. Two of the women hold hands. Gus says they must be time travelers because they look just like hippie chicks from the 1970s. They float between the cars. As they pass by ours, one of them sticks a card in our windshield with a smile. There's dirt under her fingernails. She's wearing a bracelet just like mine, only hers is made of purple and white strings. I almost show her, but I don't. She lifts her hands to her forehead and makes a heart shape. I smile back then she moves on to the truck behind us.

The man in the pickup yells at them to *fuck off* when they get near his vehicle. I reach around the window and grab the card. It's got a picture of a sunflower painted on it in watercolors. I place it in the cupholder. As we pull up to the speaker to order, Gus chucks the card in the garbage. I wince. It's too late. I should have stopped her. I tell myself the card means nothing. It's not another thing like the pink ribbon or the baseball cap. It's not meant for me. I'm being silly.

It's okay. It's okay. It's okay.

I knock my knuckles on the car door just in case.

Howard's five-part knock.

Rat-tat-tatat-tat.

Gus asks for two large coffees, black, two breakfast sandwiches, and a box of Timbits. The cashier's voice buzzes from the speaker repeating our order. Then as we slowly snake toward the pickup window, Gus tells me what she found in Howard's notes.

All we really knew was that he had a freelance job with *Canadian Geographic* magazine. He'd been assigned to do a story about one of the world's largest bird migration paths. He'd been working on it for weeks—doing research, talking to experts, and reading everything he could on the subject. And it turned out that this migration path crossed right through Prince Edward County. He saw our annual summer camping trip as the perfect chance to do some field research and to meet one of the leading experts on bird migration who lived there.

But his notes tell us a lot more. Like who that leading expert is. He's a local naturalist named Will Stenson. For years, Stenson had been fighting with a local entrepreneur named Marica Pike over some wind park project she was planning along the shore. Stenson said the turbines would be right in the path of the migrating birds. Howard thought this was just the sort of real-life drama he needed to give his migration story *some teeth*. That's what Gus said he wrote. He asked around about the wind park and it seemed like most of the local politicians were on Pike's side. She owned a successful winery in the county; she was a soccer mom and the chair of the Prince Edward Vintners Association. Vivi and Kirk probably knew her. She helped raise money to renovate a local community center. It was all in his notes. Howard found more than one person who called her *a pillar of the community*.

On the other hand, people called Stenson *that weird bird guy*. He didn't have a lot of supporters or money for his cause. He tried to block the wind park, first with protests then through the courts. Howard quoted him as saying he was *doing it for the birds*. Howard called it a real David and Goliath story. *Birdman vs. Momzilla*, he scribbled down as a joke title.

Howard made a note about doing a deeper background check on Stenson. The story hinged on the man being a reliable source and not some crackpot. So before filling in his editor at *Canadian Geographic*, that's just what he did. According to his notes, that's when he uncovered what he called a *shit ton of red flags*.

Stenson and his wife had had a messy divorce that ended with him getting custody of his daughter, Lula. When she was fifteen, she ran away from home. This was a year before Howard met Stenson, but the rumors were still going around town and people weren't shy to spread them. Rumors about Lula's drug use and partying. About how she didn't get along with her father. One source even told Howard that Stenson was an addict and he's the one who got his daughter hooked on crystal meth. Another said she ran with a bad crowd. She had a boyfriend with a history of drug charges and that's who she ran off with. Then Howard got Stenson's criminal records. Disturbing the peace, uttering threats, and trespassing. And there was a drug possession charge. When Howard asked Stenson about all of it, he blew up. Howard wrote down the conversation, word for word, in his notebook. Stenson said it was all lies. He blamed Pike. He ranted about Lula being kidnapped and how he was being set up. Next to Stenson's name, Howard wrote a list of questions.

Is he lying or is everyone else?
Is he delusional or dangerous or both?
Is he just that weird bird guy?

Howard told Stenson he was putting a pause on the article. Stenson didn't take it well. A few days later, Stenson was arrested for attempted murder. Howard doesn't say what happened, but it looked like his David and Goliath story was toast. Or should have been, Gus said. She tells me that Howard's notes didn't stop at that point. It looked like he'd kept digging into something. A new angle? A new source? Gus couldn't tell for sure what he was up to because his notes changed. He was using some sort of shorthand and code words.

Gus spent all night trying to make sense of those last few pages, but she couldn't untangle their meaning. It looked like Howard was trying to hide what he was doing, in case someone got their hands on his notebook. But why? And who? Did it have something to do with birds or wind parks? With the attempted murder? It made no sense. Howard's notebook has left us with more questions than answers.

We're at the take-out window when Gus tells me about the last thing Howard wrote in his notebook. It was short and more like a scribble.

Meeting the Canary. Aug. 23, 11 a.m.

That was the day he disappeared.

Maybe a canary flew away with Howard.

Gus pays for our order, grabs our coffee and food, then drives on. As she's pulling out the exit of the drive-through lane, two women cross the sidewalk in front of us. One looks like she recognizes us. She elbows her friend and points. Word has spread. Word of the camper van being found. And now, right here at the local Tim's there's been a Cuckoo Bird sighting. The crazy redbird and her chick are back in town.

Birds, birds, more birds.

Gus glares at them. She's good at staring contests. They back down first and waddle on. We drive across town, eating as we go. She tells me we're heading out to Baylis Vineyards. It's about ten minutes from Picton. She knows they're closed on Mondays so, while we wait for word about the camper van, she wants to see if Howard's parents can make any sense of his notes.

But it's not until we pass the sign to Cherry Valley that she drops the bomb she's had lit this whole drive.

"I need you to stay with them for a bit," she says. "Just while I do a little digging."

"No," I say, folding my arms tight across my chest.

Her eyebrows lift. She's not expecting this from little Miss Go with the Flow. Miss Don't Push Back. Miss Do as You're Told. But I refuse to be left behind. Especially at *their* house to sit and wait and worry. *I will not do it.*

"They are not mine and I am not theirs," I tell her. "I'm yours."

When I was nine and I saw that poster of Gus at the detachment, I looked up Cuckoo Bird. I wanted to know why they called her that. I found out that Cuckoos don't make their own nests. They lay their eggs in other birds' nests. They shove out one of the other bird's eggs and leave theirs in its place, fooling the bird into thinking it's their own. That bird sits on it until it hatches. It's not because the Cuckoo is lazy. It's because she has lots of other things she needs to do and sitting on an egg isn't one of them. But I'm no egg. I'm an almost-grown-up Cuckoo Bird. I am not sitting in my shell anymore. I scowl my best scowl. Gus tries to hide her smile.

"Okay, Boo," she says.

We turn into their laneway and go up the hillside covered in neat rows of grapevines. At the top, the main house sits beside an empty parking lot and beyond is a row of guesthouses next to the main building with the tasting room and bistro. Before we get to the top, Gus stops. She reaches over and shoves the notebook and map in the glove box, then she drives on. Vivi is in the window of her kitchen, at the sink. As we crest the hill, she disappears into the house. We park and get out of the Honda. Vivi and Kirk come out onto the long veranda that runs across the front of their house. They aren't smiling or waving like they used to when we'd show up. Vivi's drying her hands on a dish towel. Kirk has his shoved deep in his pockets.

"Augusta. Bly," says Vivi like she's counting heads.

"Vivi. Kirk," says Gus.

"We slept in the car last night," I tell them because I can't think of anything else to say.

"Have you eaten?" asks Kirk. Vivi shoots him a look.

She used to bake lemon scones and we'd eat them straight out of the oven dripping in butter and topped with her homemade rhubarb jam. My mouth waters. No scones today.

"Did Howard ever talk to you about what he was working on?" Gus asks.

"The bird story. I don't understand. You know what he was doing," says Kirk.

"But did he say anything about a new angle he was chasing?" she asks.

"The answer's still the same as it was three years ago," says Vivi. "He didn't tell us much about it or anything else for that matter."

It's a weird thing to say. I always thought Howard was super-close with his parents.

"Did he mention anyone called the Canary?" Gus asks.

"As in the bird?" Kirk scrunches up his nose.

"Oh my lord, here we go again," says Vivi, twisting the dish towel. "I can't do this."

"If you could just think back—" Gus tries but Vivi cuts her off.

"You want us to relive it all one more time, is that it?" she asks.

"I want to find Howard," says Gus.

Vivi clutches Kirk like she's going to faint. He pats her arm and puts his shoulders back like he's trying to make himself look stronger than he feels.

"I understand how finding the camper has given you hope. It gave us hope until—they didn't find Howard with it. Part of me wishes they had so we would—" He swallows. "So *you* would have the closure you need to move on."

Gus clenches her fists. She's trying not to blow a fuse. But she does.

"Is that what the fucking celebration of life was all about," spits Gus.

"How dare you come to our home with your foul mouth and your insane questions about birds," says Vivi.

"It's not insane," I jump in. "Howard had a meeting with a canary that day."

Gus squeezes my shoulder. I realize she doesn't want them to know about the notebook. That's why she put it in the glove box instead of showing it to them. I clam up.

"Now you've got her playing your little games?" says Vivi.

"It was some kind of code name. He called someone the Canary," says Gus.

"You never mentioned this to the police," says Kirk.

"It only came to me when we saw the camper," explains Gus.

"You have the van. But forensics can't be done already," Kirk adds. "No one told us."

Gus hesitates. She made a mistake. It's not like her but Kirk and Vivi always throw her off kilter. She tries to right herself.

"This was last night," says Gus.

"You went to the crime scene," gasps Vivi, letting go of Kirk's arm.

"We were told to stay away," says Kirk. "Julius was very clear about that."

Gus doesn't like to be scolded.

"Oh my god. It was *you*," says Vivi, coming down the steps of her veranda.

Kirk stumbles after her. Vivi steps nose to nose with Gus.

"It wasn't teenagers at all. You were the one who took everything out of that camper," she whispers.

"We just got here. That happened two weeks ago," Gus says.

Vivi shakes her head like she doesn't believe a word Gus is saying.

"We have no idea where you've been or what you've done or what you're covering up," says Vivi.

"Now, V, you're just upset. We know it wasn't them," says Kirk.

Vivi's voice comes out weirdly calm.

"What I *do* know for sure is that my Howard would never

run away from his life, from us," she says. "Unless he had a damn good reason to."

"Stop it," I yell. Tears stream down my face.

Vivi glares at Gus. Kirk turns to his wife, wide-eyed.

"My son did not run away. He had engine trouble or ran out of gas. Someone stole his camper and ditched it in that hangar years ago," says Kirk. "That's what happened."

His legs give out. He grips the rail and sits on the veranda steps. Vivi rests a hand on his shoulder. Gus doesn't bother telling Kirk that the camper wasn't in the hangar a month ago. He looks like he can't breathe.

"They should check the gas tank," he whimpers.

"Kirk, if he ran out of gas, where did he go?" asks Gus. "He didn't just walk off a cliff."

Vivi turns to stare at Gus. She has a scary smile on her face all of a sudden.

"And there it is," she says. "The truth. We've been circling it like a bunch of bloodthirsty hyenas for three years. But we can all smell it. We're all thinking it. We all know it deep down. So let's just say it. Someone killed him. My son is dead. He's dead. Dead. Dead."

I hold up both hands, trying to stop her words. Then I cover my ears. Gus stumbles away from her. Her words are like daggers slicing at both of us. Kirk stands and tries to hug his wife, but she won't let him near her. She brings the dish towel to her mouth and screams into it. Gus pulls me away from both of them.

"What did you do to my Howard?" Vivi screeches. "What are you hiding?"

Gus trips and falls on her backside. I crumple to my knees beside her as Vivi lunges at us. Kirk grabs her by the shoulders as she gulps air and bursts into tears.

"Bad sticks to you, doesn't it, Augusta Monet? It always has and always will. We told our son. We begged him not to go through with it," she cries.

Vivi turns and buries her face in Kirk's chest. Gus is dazed. Eyes blank, mouth open. I pull her to her feet and guide her to the Honda. But Vivi's not done yet.

"He never asked you, did he?" she yells. "He'd never marry someone like you."

"Enough, V," snaps Kirk.

Gus lets me put her in the driver's seat. I pull on her seat belt then I jump in the passenger side. Vivi and Kirk stagger up the steps to their house.

Gus's phone rings. She doesn't answer it. I don't think she hears it. She's on autopilot as she backs up the car then drives down the laneway.

We head into the county. Her phone pings, letting her know there's a voice mail message. She ignores it and keeps going until we can't drive any farther when the road ends. We're at the tip of a piece of land that juts into Lake Ontario. A sign says POINT TRAVERSE. There's an old lighthouse on the edge of the point. Its windows are boarded up. We get out of the car. We walk down to the rocky shoreline and Gus checks the voice mail. There's one message. We sit on the rocks and she plays it on speaker. It's Constable Journey's voice.

Um, ma'am, Miss Monet. I'm calling to let you know the Forensics Unit folks are all done with your van. Unfortunately, they weren't able to find any new evidence pertaining to Mr. Baylis's case. Rest assured it remains an active file with our Cold Case Unit, such as it is. Anyway, call me back if you have any questions. Oh, this is Constable Able Journey. You have my number. By the way, your camper van is over at Toby's Garage on Bowery Street. Staff Sergeant Muirhead says it's all yours. But Tobias says he won't be able to get the parts he needs to get it up and running until tomorrow. You can pick it up as soon as it's ready. Costs for repairs have been covered by the OPP. So yeah. That's it, I guess. I'm sorry for all your troubles. Really. Bye now. Safe travels home.

The constable does sound sorry. I like him. Muirhead didn't even bother to call us himself. Constable Journey is the first person to say anything nice to us since we got to town.

We have nowhere to go and Gus doesn't look like she should be driving so we stay at the lighthouse the rest of the day. I think she's past exhausted. When it gets dark, we pull some boards off one of the lighthouse windows and climb inside. We set up camp at the top of the tower. It's cozy and windy and stuffy. The air smells like sardines. We get into our sleeping bags. The floorboards are painted with strokes of moonlight. I keep thinking about my old pillow from the camper. I wish it *had* been us who took all our stuff and not those stupid teenagers, but it wasn't. Vivi was wrong—about a lot of things.

I roll on my side and look at Gus. She's lying on her back staring at the cobwebbed beams above us. She needs to sleep but I don't think she can. Her mind won't let her.

"Vivi was wrong, you know," I whisper.

"I know," she says.

"No, you don't," I say. "Howard *was* going to ask you."

She turns her head to look at me.

"That summer. I was with him when he bought the ring," I tell her.

Her eyes glisten in the moonlight then she looks away and pretends to go to sleep.

IT WAS A SATURDAY. I REMEMBER BECAUSE WE WENT EARLY SO we'd get back before the line into the park got too long. Everyone from Kingston to Trenton wanted to go to the beach on a Saturday in the summer. Gus wanted to stay behind to relax in the hammock. Howard didn't argue. I didn't mind either. I got to sit up front. We drove to Picton, got groceries, then Howard said he wanted to pop by Dead People's Stuff. It was my favorite antique shop in a small barn in Bloomfield. I loved it there. The loft had loads of nooks and crannies filled with wonderful bits and bobs. Howard always bought me one treasure every time we went.

Pick whatever you want, he'd say. *Anything your heart desires.*

I always chose something tiny. He'd point to a fancy uphol-stered chair or a dining table or a lamp with gold tassels or an old trunk covered in wallpaper or a tin garden box with daisies painted on the side. But I'd always choose an old tin cup or a silver teaspoon that was bent out of shape or one of the tiny fig-urines. *Red Roses* is what the woman behind the counter called them, but I'm not sure why. They weren't red or roses. They were miniature porcelain statues of old women and rabbits and frogs and dogs and kings. I loved to stare at them and make up stories about them. There were jewelry-filled cases and baskets overflow-ing with old rings and brooches. Everything in the antique shop was worn smooth or faded or peeling, but that's usually what made the thing special. Objects became more themselves as they aged. Just like people.

That day Howard was examining a silver ring with a green stone. He was looking at it for a long time. The stone reminded me of the color of marram grass. Howard asked me if I thought my mom would like it. The lady at the counter said the ring was jade. One of a kind. Howard looked at me with this serious face.

"What do you think, Sweet Pea?" He asked it like my opinion really mattered.

I took the ring from his hand and studied it closely, just like he had done.

Then I looked up at him and that's when it hit me.

"I think she'll say yes," I said, giving it back to him.

Howard laughed and touched the end of my nose. I loved when he did that. He bought the ring and the woman put it in a tiny velvet pouch with a drawstring. Howard placed it in his pocket and told me not to tell Gus. He wanted to surprise her. He already had the spot picked out. It was a place they used to love going to when I was little. But he wanted to wait for the perfect moment. Maybe an evening with a full moon or maybe a sunset the color of rainbow sherbet. I laughed. He was happy and excited. I was too. I couldn't help it. His happy made my happy bigger. Howard was contagious like that. As we drove back to the park, he kept waving to passing cars and at people walking along the side of the road. Some of them even waved back even though they had no clue who he was. I couldn't stop giggling.

Halfway back to the campground, he pulled over and turned the car around.

"I'm an idiot! I forgot to get you something, Sweet Pea," he said.

"I don't need anything. The line into the park's probably too long already. What if we can't get back into the campground," I said. I hated being late.

"It'll be okay. Besides, we can't break the tradition. It would be bad luck." He winked and we drove back to Dead People's Stuff.

I remember his phone rang as we pulled up and he handed me a twenty. He said he had to take the call. Told me to go ahead without him. I went inside and picked out a tiny metal horse. It had tarnished hooves and there was a scratch on its saddle. It was perfect. I bought it then came back outside. I could see Howard pacing along the dirt edge of the parking lot. He kicked at the dirt. He looked upset. He saw me and made his face smile, even though his eyes couldn't.

He said something to whoever was on the phone and hung up. On the drive back to the park, Howard went quiet. His happy had gone away and so had mine with it. I wanted to ask him what was wrong and who was on the phone, but I didn't. I wish I had. Later, I couldn't find the tiny metal horse. I'd lost it.

And I never saw the jade ring again, either.

Howard disappeared the next day, probably with it still in his pocket.

The bad luck had come anyway.

AN UGLY SMELL WAKES ME. IT'S LIKE PLASTIC BURNING. I OPEN MY eyes and sit up. It's pitch-black. The moon must have moved on. A popping sound cuts through the stillness. There's a sudden roar like a plane just flew over. It's louder than the waves and rises above their dull white noise. I shove Gus's shoulder hard. She rolls over.

"Something's wrong." My voice comes out high-pitched.

She sits up fast. She smells it too. She looks around then kicks out of her sleeping bag and leaps to her feet like a ninja.

"We gotta go now!" She points to the stairwell.

I get up too and start gathering my bedding. She pulls on my elbow.

"Leave it," she shouts.

My sleeping bag falls from my arms.

I yank from her grip and grab my suitcase.

She tries to tug it from my hand, but I won't let it go. I can't.

The room is getting hazy with smoke.

"There's no time," she shouts.

I push past her toward the stairs, dragging my suitcase behind me. She grabs hold of it, lifts it onto her back with one hand, and nods for me to move. She's got it. I turn and race down the stairs ahead of her. She follows.

As we stumble down, threads of smoke crisscross the stairwell illuminated by a fiery glow that flashes through gaps in the wood beams of the old building. The smoke is being sucked inside. I can't catch my breath. Gus is coughing. We stumble through a black fog as we reach the bottom and grope for the door. We burst outside. A cloud of smoke is churning in the wind off the lake. It's moving toward us but it's not the lighthouse that's on fire. We stagger away from the smoke. My eyes sting. I turn to look back and that's when I see what's really on fire. Howard's Honda. The charred outline of the car sits in a tower of raging red flames as high as the pine trees. Gus drops my suitcase.

"Noooo!" she hollers as she runs for the car.

I can't stop her, but the heat does. It pushes her back. She shields her face. All we can do is watch as the car becomes a black ghost.

After a few minutes, Gus can't take it anymore. She turns and runs down to the lake behind the lighthouse. At first, I'm afraid she's going to jump in the water. When she doesn't, I start dragging my suitcase away from the inferno. Its wheels bump across the rocks. I make it to a spot near the rocky beach, a good enough distance from the pines if they go up in flames too. The night sky is buzzing with sparks like fireflies. Gus is bathed in an eerie orange light as she sits on a piece of wood. I let the suitcase fall on its side, then I kneel down and unzip it. I root around until I find what I'm looking for. I grab it.

Gus has her arms wrapped around her knees and she's rocking back and forth. She flinches when I come up behind her but she can't look at me.

"She was right," she says.

"Who?" I ask.

"Vivi. Bad does stick to me," she croaks.

"She was just being mean because she's sad," I tell her.

"No, she's right about me. I was there when my mother was murdered," she says, as her voice cracks. "Maybe she'd be alive if

I'd stayed in bed like I was supposed to. Maybe Howard wouldn't be gone if he hadn't met me."

I want to shout at her, but I'm afraid she'll break into a million pieces if I do. I don't want to be all alone on this rocky beach. I don't want to have to live in this lighthouse and eat pine cones to survive and stare at our ghost car forever.

"We're okay, Gus," I say softly.

"No, Boo. We're not. We may never be."

"Don't say that," I say, a little louder than I mean to.

"Cars don't just catch fire," she says.

"Maybe it was the battery," I try.

She puts her head in her hands.

"It's not just the car or Vivi. I really fucked up. I left his notebook in the glove box and now it's gone. It's all we had. I broke my own fucking rules. *Always make backups. Keep things close.* I should've taken photos of every page the second we found it."

Distant sirens howl. Flashing lights zigzag across the smoky sky.

I sit next to her on the log. She doesn't know that I took Howard's notebook from the glove box, along with the map. I put them in my suitcase so that all the things I'd been collecting along the way would be together. The ribbon, the diamonds, the map, the notebook, the baseball cap. I place the notebook in her lap. The cover shimmers in the firelight.

Gus looks down at it and gasps.

Before I can explain, she wraps her arms so tight around me I can hardly breathe. She holds me close as the sirens get louder. I hug her back and smile. When she finally lets go, a fire engine rolls toward the lighthouse. Gus tucks the notebook back in my suitcase.

We stand side by side, in our pajamas, our faces hot and our hearts racing.

Firemen are running. Flames are dancing.

She puts her arm around my shoulders.

At that moment, I feel like everything is going to be okay. We'll figure it out. We'll look for clues, we'll follow the trail that's already starting to appear. We'll get our camper van and we'll keep searching. We haven't come to say goodbye. We've come to find him. I feel so certain that we're in this together—until she speaks.

"Once we're back in Ottawa, I can go through the notebook again. You did good. Time to go home where we belong. Right, honey?" she says, squeezing me tight.

No. Not right, I think to myself. *Not right at all.*

She sounds like a mom when she calls me *honey.*

Like a sensible, protective, comforting mom and I don't like it one bit.

There's no way we're going home.

We can't.

8

THE LURE

WE'RE TAKEN BY AMBULANCE TO PRINCE EDWARD COUNTY ME-
morial Hospital. It's the middle of the night and the emergency
room is quiet. I don't feel a thing until the doctor points out the
cuts on the bottom of my feet from the rocky beach. She tells us
we're both suffering from smoke inhalation. Our cheeks look sunburnt. Gus's ankle is turning yellowish purple. The doctor says
the shock has made us numb to the pain. I think Gus has been in
shock for three years.

Sometimes she'd act like she was coming out of it—like
when she put flowers from the garden in a vase on the kitchen
table or like when she got a part-time job at Life of Pie bakery
or donated Howard's winter gloves to the Ottawa Mission. She
tried to live life, but I don't think she's ever really shaken off the
shock.

A couple of OPP constables ask Gus all kinds of questions
about how we got inside the lighthouse and how the fire started.
She lies and says the lighthouse window was already broken when
we got there. They look like they don't believe her but when she
says we're planning on leaving town tomorrow, they let it go. They
just want the Cuckoo gone. All we have is the stuff we brought
into the lighthouse. The rest of our camping gear was lost in the

fire. It's the middle of the night and we have nowhere to go and no way to get there. The constables tell us we can sleep in a cell for the night. One of them snickers. Gus doesn't want to but they insist. They drive us to the detachment, the whole way acting like we're criminals. On the seat between them is tomorrow morning's edition of the *Belleville Intelligencer*. I can see the headline on the front page.

Cold Case Van Comes Up Empty, Man Still Missing Without a Trace

I wish I could reach through the cage that separates the back seats from the front and rip the newspaper to shreds. Howard's case is not cold and he's not missing without a trace. There are traces of him everywhere. I can see his face in the reflection of the car window. I can see his silhouette under porch lights of houses we pass by. I can hear his voice in the chirps of crickets and the hum of the car wheels. I can feel him holding my hand in the back seat. Like a phantom limb, he's always there. I squeeze his hand as they let us out of the police car.

We're being led into the detachment when we run into Constable Journey coming out. He's not in his uniform. He must be going off duty. He sees Gus limping and glances at me. We must look and smell ridiculously red-faced and smoky. He stops to ask what's up. One of the constables tells him about the car fire. The other says the county's full up so it's the crowbar hotel for us. Constable Journey hesitates a second. He almost walks on, but then he looks at me again and he offers to put us up at his place.

"Your funeral."

There's more snickering as the other officers walk on, leaving us with Constable Journey.

Gus doesn't put up a fight. She's so tired she doesn't care

where they put us. Jail cell, a stranger's house. It's all the same to her. But I'm glad we're going with Constable Journey.

He makes a quick phone call, then leads us to his police car in the parking lot. He apologizes for making me ride in the back behind the cage, but there's only room for Gus up front. I don't mind. I hold Howard's hand the whole way.

The constable lives with his grandfather in a small farmhouse a couple of miles outside town. His grandfather is sitting on the front porch smoking a pipe when we pull in. The old man is wearing a bathrobe over a long nightshirt. The constable must have called him and he got out of bed to greet us. He wears his long white hair tied back in a ponytail and he has a crooked smile. He welcomes us inside. I like him right away.

The house is crammed with old things. I absolutely love it at first sight. Rusted farming tools hang on the walls like weird art. Mismatched patchwork quilts cover the sofa and armchairs. A large trunk sits in front of the sofa. Books are stacked high along the walls like leaning towers in a cityscape about to fall over. The bookshelves have no books on them but are instead lined with jars of peaches, pickled beets, chutney, and crabapple jelly. Scattered about the room are simple wooden crates stuffed with magazines. *National Wildlife Magazines*, *The Old Farmer's Almanacs*, *Canadian Outdoor Magazines*. Some lay open around the room as if they were left there in the middle of being read. I glance at the one on the sofa, open to an article called "Eat, Fly, Love, Die."

Able's grandfather is named Noble Journey. Noble and Able. I've never ever known anyone with names like that. They sound like they're from the Bible or a comic book. I like the two of them and not just because of their names. They both speak softly without any of the sharp edges of the two snickerers who drove us to the detachment. Able brings us two big wool sweaters. Mine hangs down past my knees. Noble heats up leftover rabbit stew in an iron pot on the woodstove. I can't eat mine because I like rabbits so I mostly pick at the warm bread. Noble sees I'm not eating the stew so he offers me jam and butter. The butter melts on the bread and the blueberry jam is deliciously sweet with a hint of lemon. The four of us sit at their kitchen table, talking quietly by the glowing embers of the stove. I feel at home for the first time since we came to the county—like I can just sit and eat and not have to think about anything. Able gives us his room. He takes the sofa. I fall asleep the second my head hits the pillow.

I WAKE UP LATE MORNING IN THE SAME POSITION I FELL ASLEEP in. I slip out of the bed and quietly get dressed in my cords and a T-shirt. Gus is snoring. She's still deep. I don't think she's slept this long since we left Ottawa. I tiptoe out of the room so I don't wake her.

It feels like forever since we left home, but it's only been a few days. Today's a school day. The last week before summer holidays. Rachel and Sydney must be wondering why I'm not there. Miss Haddon, my homeroom teacher, is used to it. I doubt Gus phoned the school. She's never been big on meeting the teacher or volunteering. A year ago, I learned her signature so I could sign permission slips for school field trips. It was easier that way.

Constable Journey's grandfather is reading a magazine and sipping coffee at the kitchen table. He looks up when I walk in.

"She lives," he says with a smile.

I smile back and sit across from him. He tells me Able has already gone to work but he'll come get us when our camper is ready and take us over to get it.

"Juice?" he asks.

"Coffee?" I ask.

He raises one bushy eyebrow, then rises and picks up a metal coffeepot sitting on the woodstove. His body is bent like an old man's but his brown face and big, dark eyes make him look younger than he probably is. He grabs a mug, places it in front of me, and pours steaming black coffee into it.

"Thank you," I say, placing my hands around the mug to feel the warmth.

"You hungry?" he asks.

I shake my head. He sits back down and we sip our coffee.

The skin on his neck looks like cracked earth and deep lines spider across the back of his big, rough hands—a map of where he's been and what he's done and, maybe, who he is. One corner of his mouth dips lower than the other and is darker like it's stained. I think that's where he places his pipe. It's like his whole life story is written in the wrinkles and shades of his skin.

"Was a time they would've taken you for a witch for having hair the color of fire," he says flatly. He tries hard not to smile.

"It only turned red when I sold my soul to the devil," I reply.

Noble laughs. He wasn't expecting that. It's something I heard Gus say once.

"Let's have some grub," he says, rising from his chair.

He makes scrambled eggs with beans and corn bread. I sip my coffee and pick up the magazine he was reading. It's the article I saw last night.

"Eat, Fly, Love, Die," I say out loud.

"It's about dragonflies," he tells me, as he grabs two plates from the cupboard. "Remarkable creatures. They only live about two months. Every spring they fly from Mexico or the Caribbean, all the way up here to Canada. They mate, lay their eggs, then die. The eggs turn into baby dragonflies who take up the journey where their folks left off. They head back home and it goes round and round like that—like a relay race of sorts."

He places the plates of hot food on the table, sits, and keeps talking.

"It's pretty epic if you think about it. A single dragonfly flies thousands of miles one direction and even though they die, their kid somehow knows the way back home," he says, his eyes wide.

Noble is like an old man version of Howard. Always with a good story or bit of trivia or fun fact on the tip of his tongue.

"But how do they know?" I ask Noble.

"They follow the wingbeats of their ancestors, I expect," he says, his mouth full of corn bread.

"So they can hear them?" I ask. I stop eating. His answer seems really important.

"Could be, or maybe they can see the way. This here magazine says they can see every direction all at once—three hundred sixty degrees. Imagine that," he says.

I'm imagining it.

"I wish I could see everything all at once and hear wingbeats," I say.

"I wish I could fly," he adds.

We keep eating.

An hour later, Gus is up. She hauls our suitcases onto the front porch. She's not limping anymore. Noble offers to make her breakfast even though it's almost lunchtime, but she just wants a coffee. She takes it outside and paces the porch. She's ready to leave. I'm not.

But I have no say in it. Constable Journey pulls up in his cruiser. He's already phoned Toby's Garage and made sure our camper is ready. Gus loads the suitcases into his trunk. I'm standing on the front porch next to Noble. Wisps of his long white hair are floating on the breeze. I barely know the old man, but I'm sad to be leaving him. I hold back tears. He hands me a small wooden box. A gift.

"To help you hear the wingbeats," he says.

I nod but I can't speak or I might cry.

Gus and Constable Journey are waiting.

I hug Noble and race down the steps to the cruiser.

As we're pulling away from the farmhouse, I open the wooden box.

Inside is a beautiful piece of jewelry. At first, I think it's an earring. I look closer and see that it's not that at all. It has gauzy golden wings and a spotted emerald body and a hook on one end. I saw something like this once at the Sandbanks when we walked past a man fishing off the bridge over Outlet River. He had things just like this in his tackle box.

It's a fishing lure.

And it's in the shape of a dragonfly.

9

THE MASK

THE RUSTY GARAGE SITS ON THE EDGE OF TOWN ON A GRAVEL LOT beside a field of brittle yellow grass. I think the OPP went with the cheapest mechanic in town. The constable helps us unload our stuff and introduces us to Tobias Perley, the owner. I know that last name. His fingernails are black with grease and his nose is covered in bumps. But when he smiles his teeth are bright white.

"Take good care of these two, Toby," says Constable Journey.

Gus shakes the constable's hand.

"Thank you for . . ." she says. She doesn't go on. It's hard for her because he's one of *them*. He gives her a nod, then winks at me. He jumps in his cruiser and drives off. Toby leads us to the open garage doors. He mutters about the condition of the camper van and how he had to change this and flush that and fill this and replace that. We follow him inside. There are metal shelves filled with car parts. Tools hang on a pegboard above some old tires. The garage smells of gasoline and coffee.

"No computerized whatnots to fuss with in this old clunker so it was right up my alley." Toby holds up the keys. "You're good to go."

My throat tightens. I don't know why seeing the keys takes my breath away. Even though I've already seen them with my own eyes, it's like for-real proof that the camper van was found without Howard. Howard's parents gave him the custom key chain shaped like a wine bottle that hangs from the key ring. BAYLIS VINEYARDS is written on it. He didn't take them with him. He didn't or couldn't.

Gus takes the keys.

"Did they check these for fingerprints?" Gus asks.

"Not my department." He shrugs.

Gus stares at Toby's greasy hands. She moves on.

"Did you notice anything unusual about the condition of the camper?" she asks.

"Scratched up some. Lots of mud caked in the wheel wells and undercarriage," he says. "Nothing out of the ordinary for an old beater that's been down one too many dirt roads. She's gonna have her kinks. Side doors got finicky locks. Couldn't fix 'em."

"It's always been that way," Gus says. "There's a little trick to it. If you kick the back bumper, they open right up."

"There's a nice dent on the front end," he says. "But I weren't paid to do bodywork, just to get her road ready."

"So it wasn't drivable when you got it? Hugo, the guy who found it, said it was likely moved in the last month or so," Gus says. "Is that possible?"

"'Spose, but I wouldn't put much stock in anything that ham-fisted rent-a-cop says. Hugo's been floating around this town like a turd in a swimming pool for years. Don't know how he wormed his way in with them muckety-mucks at the flying club, what with his reputation for napping on the job. Thinks he's a real cop. Even tried to be one. When they wouldn't have him, he lied about being one. Went around saying he was undercover," he says, rolling his eyes. "The guy babysits private planes for fat cats, he's never been no *O Po Po*."

Gus has tuned him out and is already reaching for the side

panel door. She slowly opens it and looks inside. A flash blinds me for a second. It came from the back corner of the garage. Someone is sitting in the shadows. I hadn't noticed them before. It's the boy who took the pink bike. Dod Perley. That's where I know the name. Tobias must be his father. Dod is sitting on a crate, hunched over a hunk of metal in his lap. Every couple of seconds sunlight glints off the metal as he moves it, spitting and polishing the object with a rag. I go over to the boy while Gus and Toby inspect the camper.

"Hi," I say softly so I don't startle him.

He doesn't look up, but he does stop polishing.

"I didn't get a chance to say hello at the church the other day. My name's Bly," I say.

"Our Dod is a man of few words," says Toby, coming up beside me.

"Is he your son?" I ask.

"He's my sister's boy. She's got three grown lads. Dod's the runt of the litter," says Toby.

A big red pickup speeds into the lot. It's going so fast that when it stops it sends up a cloud of dust that makes it disappear. When the haze settles, I stare at it. It's the biggest truck I've ever seen. The front part is huge with four doors and two rows of seats. Our Honda could have easily fit in the back cargo part. But there's something else back there. Two bloodhounds the size of small ponies rise to their feet after having crashed to the floor. We all stare as the driver's-side window rolls down.

"Speak of the devil," calls out Toby as he comes out of the shadows of the garage, one hand shielding the glaring sun.

A woman sits behind the wheel of the truck. She's got a big blond poof of hair piled on top of her head like a bird's nest. Her eyes are painted with black lines and her lips are glossy red, matching her truck. The bloodhounds are barking their heads off at Toby. The woman leans an elbow on the edge of the window and scowls.

"I swear to god, the boy rode over here on his own," he says, holding up his hands like he's being robbed.

"Dodge Randolf Perley," hollers the woman. "Get your arse into this truck right now before I tan your hide."

Dod drops the metal object he's polishing. It clatters to the concrete floor.

The woman looks over her shoulder at the dogs. "You two, shut it!"

The dogs instantly go silent.

The boy jumps up from his crate and ducks into a small office in the garage. He slams the door and peeks out a dusty window like he's playing hide-and-seek.

"Go easy, girl. The boy just wanted to hang out with his favorite uncle," says Toby.

"Don't you tell me how to raise my own flesh and blood, Toby," says the woman.

Toby kicks the dirt with the toe of his boot, like a kid.

"Wouldn't dream of telling you shit, Patience," he says.

"Dod, I can see you. Stop this foolishness. You got chores," she hollers.

The boy opens the office door a crack, his eyes fixed on his mother. Then he bursts out the door and scurries to her, passing close by me. He smells musty like wet leaves. And I'm surprised by how large he is. He's big shouldered and has huge hands. He runs around his mother's pickup and jumps in the passenger side, rocking the truck. She spots our suitcases and sleeping bags sitting in the gravel.

"What's all this then?" The woman snorts. "You skipping town, little brother?"

Gus steps out of the shadows and I follow.

"Those are ours," Gus says.

The woman's eyebrows lift as Toby picks up a bicycle lying in the dirt.

"Where you want this? In the cargo bed with them hounds?" he asks.

She ignores him so he loads it in anyway. The woman gets out of her truck and walks over to us. She isn't dressed like I thought she would be. She's wearing big rubber boots and a flannel shirt and jean shorts. She looks like a farmer only she's wearing more makeup than a farmer probably does.

"You're the two who knew that fella who went missing a few years back. From Ottawa. I heard you were in town. Had some trouble out at the lighthouse," she says, hands on hips.

"Word travels," says Gus.

"My two oldest are volunteer firefighters," she explains.

"Our car went up in flames. Engine overheated, I think," says Gus, even though I know she doesn't believe that.

"Jesus Murphy," says the woman.

"Lucky for us we got our camper back." Gus gestures toward the garage. "Now we don't have to pay to get it towed all the way back home."

My heart sinks. We are still going home.

"Lucky your car went up in flames then," says the woman.

Gus laughs. How can she laugh?

I don't feel lucky at all. I keep hoping she didn't really mean it. That we're not really leaving. Dod honks the horn and his mother jumps, hand to her heart. The dogs growl. Froth drips from their jowls. They'd be scary if their droopy faces didn't look like sad old men.

"Damn it, Dod. I nearly peed my pants," she says.

Toby shakes his head.

Patience holds out her hand to Gus.

"Name's Patience Perley. And that's my boy, Dodge—but everyone calls him Dod," she says.

Or *Dud*, like the man at the chapel told me.

"Augusta Monet. My daughter, Bly," Gus says, shaking the woman's hand.

"Sorry for your troubles, Miss Augusta," Patience says. Her eyes soften. "You're heading back to Ottawa now?"

"Sure are. This place has given us enough troubles to last a lifetime," Gus says.

Patience sighs, nods her head, and gets back in her truck.

"Don't let the fuckwads around here give you any more grief, hear me?" she calls out.

I like Patience for saying that. She's rough and loud on the outside but I think she's soft on the inside.

"Grief I'm used to. It's the fuckwads I can live without," says Gus.

They both laugh.

Patience has probably heard people talking about us and she feels sorry for us. Maybe she and Dod have had their own troubles with the fuckwads around here.

Not much good ever came from the Perleys making more Perleys.

That's what the old man at the chapel told me the day we got here.

Patience Perley knows what it's like to have a whole town be against you.

Dod looks over as his mother gets into the truck. He catches me looking at him. For a split second I think I see a smile on his lips then he looks away.

"We all got our burdens to bear, I imagine," Patience says, turning the ignition.

She slams her foot on the gas and takes off. Dust kicks up and Toby covers his face with a dirty rag. As she pulls a U-turn and they drive away, Dod sticks his head out the window like a dog. I can see his long yellow hair flipping on the wind.

We're loading the camper when I spot the piece of metal Dod dropped in the corner. I go over and pick it up. It's a hubcap that's been cut and bent and polished and reshaped. It's kind of beautiful, whatever it is. Toby spots me turning it in my hands.

"My old man owned this shop before me and his old man before him. I got motor oil in my blood. But I got no kids to pass it on to. Dod's the only one of my nephews who comes around," he says, as he comes over to me. "But he'd rather tinker with these crazy contraptions of his than learn how to change a spark plug. Probably for the best. Not like he could ever run the place. His brain ain't gonna ever catch up to his body."

"What is it?" I ask him.

"Some kind of mask, I expect. Kid makes all kinds of armor. Protection from bullies is my guess," he says.

I wish I hadn't asked. Now I feel even sorrier for Dod Perley than I did before.

"Keep it," he says. "He won't mind. He's got loads of crap like that."

I stare into the hollow eyes of the metal mask. A cold chill runs through me. Not because of the mask. It's because of the familiar rumble of the engine as Gus starts it up. A sound I've been waiting to hear ever since I lay in the hammock on our campsite three years ago waiting for Howard to come back. It crushes my heart. My eyes fill with tears.

"Tell Dod thank you from me," I say to Toby.

I clutch the mask and dip my head so he can't see my tears. I stumble to the camper, brushing them away before getting in the passenger side. I place the mask at my feet. Gus doesn't ask about it. She's used to me collecting things.

The camper smells like chlorine. I look in the back, hoping

that magically everything is there again. But it's still empty, except for our suitcases and new sleeping bags piled on the floor. I can't believe all our stuff was stolen by stupid teenagers. My pillow, my paperbacks, our place mats, our flashlights. Why would a teenager want any of that? *Our belongings.* The word makes my chest ache, especially what's at the heart of the word, which is all I'm left with. *Longings.*

I face front as Gus backs out of the garage.

I close my eyes and try to pretend I'm somewhere else.

Far from this garage and this town and this county.

Far from the fuckwads and bullies and teenagers.

But as hard as I try to be somewhere else, I'm still here and it makes my stomach turn.

I'm homesick. But not for Ottawa. Not even for our house on Ossington.

I don't want to be here or there. I grip the seat.

Five minutes down the county road I tell Gus to pull over.

"Are you sick?" she asks, looking at my clammy face.

I nod. She pulls onto the gravel shoulder and I jump out before she's even stopped the camper. I stumble into the ditch then keep going. I can't stop. I race into a cornfield and run and run. I like the feeling of the sharp husks slicing into my arms. Slashing and stinging. I can hear Gus yelling for me to stop but my legs won't let me. I want to get as far away from her as I can. I don't want to listen to her or do what she says or follow her around like an obedient puppy anymore. I hate, hate, hate, hate that she's given up.

I don't know how long I've been running but she finally catches up to me and when she does, she grabs my shoulder. I'm thrown off balance. I trip and fall. She falls too. We tumble in the dirt between the corn rows, ending up on our backs, side by side. Both of us lie there panting like we just ran a marathon.

"What the fuck, Boo?" she says, catching her breath.

"I hate you," I sob, as a river of tears bursts from my eyes.

"I know," she says calmly.

"You don't know anything," I cry. My words come out in big gulps.

"You're hungry," she says. "That's all."

She doesn't know anything about anything.

"I had corn bread and eggs," I snap. "With my friend Noble."

"You're tired, honey," she tries.

I hate when she calls me honey. I turn away from her.

"You're the one who's sick and tired of looking for him," I mumble.

"We'll come back, I promise," she says.

"You're lying. You lie all the time. You lied to the police. You lied to Howard's parents. You told Patience Perley the car overheated when you know it didn't. And now all of a sudden, you're b-being, being a"—I stammer out the words—"like you're being."

I thrash my arms and pound the dirt and scream. Gus sits up and waits for the rage to work its way through me. It takes a while but finally I go quiet and lie still. I stare up at the blue sky. Gus is leaning back on her elbows.

"What way am I being, Boo?" she asks softly.

"Not like Gus," I tell her.

She looks over then helps me to my feet. That's when I feel Howard's phone. The phone I've been hiding deep in my suitcase when I go to sleep at night. The phone that's been tucked in the back pocket of my cords every day. The phone I've kept from her ever since I found it.

"You're right. I don't think the car overheated. I think someone set it on fire. What if we'd been sleeping in it?" she says. "What if—?"

"I'm not scared," I tell her.

"It's not about being afraid," she says. "It's about keeping you safe. We've got the camper and the notebook. That's more than we expected when we came. Now we can go home and keep—"

"We're not going home," I say.

"Boo." She sighs.

I reach into my back pocket and grab Howard's phone.

I hold it out to her.

Gus blinks several times, like she's trying to get her brain to kick-start. To understand what it is I'm holding. It takes a couple of seconds.

Then I see it. She knows what it is.

Gus is back.

10

THE VIDEO

WE DRIVE INTO PICTON. THE SCRATCHES ON MY ARMS ARE TURN-
ing to pins and needles. The feeling is spreading from my head to
my toes. Gus feels it too. It's like our insides and our outsides were
jolted by electricity that still pulses through both of us. Howard's
phone did that.

Main Street is clogged with motor homes so it's annoyingly
slow going. I look out the window, my legs bouncing. The sidewalks are jam-packed with families lined up for ice cream and
teenage girls browsing long racks of bikinis and beach wraps.

We find a parking spot in a strip mall with an electronics
store called The Source. Inside, Gus buys a power cable that fits
Howard's phone, a mobile SIM card, and a mini car charger that
plugs into the camper's lighter outlet. Next, we go into Crabtree
Drugs. The pharmacist takes one look at our corn husk scratches
and recommends an antibiotic cream. She doesn't ask how we got
them but she squints at Gus when she tells her to watch for signs
of infection. She has a judgy face but when she spots my purple
cords, it softens. She tells me she had a pair just like them when
she was a young girl. I wonder to myself if my cords could actually be her old cords. Maybe when she outgrew them, she gave

them to the secondhand store and they were there all that time until I found them.

Gus buys the cream and a first aid kit and some snacks. We park behind the strip mall. She leaves the camper running, plugs Howard's phone into the charger and we wait.

11% . . . 23% . . .

We rub antibiotic cream on our scratches. I chew on gummy bears and Gus wipes down the dirty dashboard with an alcohol pad from the first aid kit.

30% . . . 45% . . . 58% . . .

I hug my knees and count the leaves on a small tree we're parked beside. Gus eats an entire family-size bag of Doritos.

75% . . . 80% . . .

She grabs the phone and turns on the power. She can't wait any longer. She taps Howard's passcode onto the screen and unlocks the phone. He's had the same one forever. We both know it. It's my birthday. I lean close as the screen lights up.

Notifications begin popping up across the photo on his home screen—the one of the three of us in our backyard. There are texts from Gus, Howard's parents, an OPP number, Howard's editor. Gus swipes the notifications off the screen one by one.

Let us know you're okay, son.
Call me.
Urgent please call this number.
Where are you?

All of them are unread texts from people trying to reach him three years ago. Gus checks his voice mail. There are messages from the same people who sent texts. All are tagged as new—never listened to until now. One stands out. The phone's robot voice tells us the message was recorded on August 23, three years ago at 1:22 P.M. The day Howard disappeared. Gus plays the message. It's a woman's voice. She sounds out of breath and scared. She's half whispering.

It's me. Did you get it? Oh my god, I hope he gave it to you before—I can't believe he's dead. Don't call me. Please. I can't do this anymore.

We can hear voices in the background as the message cuts off.

Gus plays it again. We don't know the voice. Gus checks Howard's list of recent calls but the number has been hidden by the caller. She moves on to his emails. There are lots of unread emails from his editor and a few friends, some spam, and a bunch of updates from blogs and newsletters Howard follows. Gus scrolls through the emails. She tells me that every one of them came in after he disappeared. There's nothing dated before that day. There are no folders or other emails anywhere. It's like he deleted them all. Even the trash folder is empty.

Gus opens Howard's photo app. That's when she sees it. The last picture he took. It's a selfie. She taps the small square to make the photo larger. Then we see that it's not a photo at all.

It's a video.

We look at each other then back at Howard. There's a small arrow in the middle of his frozen face—the arrow begging to be pressed. The video waiting to be played.

"Holy moly," I say, squeezing in closer to Gus.

Her hand is shaking as it hovers over the arrow.

She's not breathing at first, then she exhales and presses play.

Suddenly, Howard's face fills the screen. I gasp. Gus almost drops the phone. He's so full of life. It's like he called us for a video chat. It's like it's really him. He's looking right at us. Talking right to us. I almost shout his name but then the truth of what's happening squishes my heart so tight it feels like it could burst.

He looks exactly like he did the last time we saw him. *Exactly.* Same TRAGICALLY HIP T-shirt. Same mop of black curly hair. Same dark skin, sun-speckled and flaking a little on the tip of his sunburnt nose. Same gentle eyes. And the Band-Aid is there too. It's stuck to a small cut above his right eyebrow from where a shard of wood flew up at him as he chopped firewood with our dull camping axe the day before he disappeared.

It's Howard from three years ago. He recorded himself. The weird part is that he's in the driver's seat of the camper and it's moving. He's driving with one hand and holding the phone with the other. He would never do that. The video is bouncy and hard to watch.

Why doesn't he pull over?

I'm afraid for him. He looks distracted and he's driving too fast.

"Hey there. It's me. I don't have time to stop. I'm running late and I can't miss this meeting. It might be my only shot with this guy. But I need to tell you two something—in case things go sideways."

He laughs at himself, but it's not his laugh. It's nervous and forced.

"Cue dramatic music, dum-dum-dummm!" He smiles.

He's trying to be funny, but I can tell he's worried or scared. His mouth is quivering. His eyes dart from the road to the rear-view mirror then back to his phone—to us. Behind him, I can see dust swirling up from the road, a twisty gray monster chasing his rear bumper.

"I should have been straight with you from the get-go about

the shitstorm I've uncovered, but I didn't want to get you involved. I know you, Gus. I know you'd jump right in the thick of it with me. I'm guessing you already know something's up. You know me too well.

"The short of it is this. That migration story isn't about birds anymore. It's about something way bigger. The only trouble is that what I'm digging into could hurt some people around here if it comes out. People I care about. I was ready to walk away. Pull the bloody cork on the whole thing. But I got my hands on some pretty damning evidence and then out of nowhere I get this lead—a primary source—an insider—said he wanted to talk," he says, checking the rearview mirror again. "That's why I left this morning. To meet this guy."

"The Canary," Gus whispers.

Almost like he heard her, Howard looks back at us.

"This guy could be the linchpin that breaks the whole thing wide open—or he could be something else."

Howard's brow furrows.

Gus and I look at each other.

"What's a linchpin?" I ask her.

Gus doesn't answer. She's listening to Howard.

"I know it sounds crazy but I'm pretty sure someone's following me. I turned off the GPS on my phone and took a roundabout route to try and shake them off, but now I've got myself all turned around. This map of yours is all wrong. Sorry, it just is." He tries to smile. "Listen, I'm sure I'll be laughing later tonight about how paranoid I'm being right now. But, like I said, this is a *just-in-case* video. So here's the rest of it."

He swallows. I hate that he has such a serious face and I wish he would stop talking and driving at the same time. He's not paying attention to the road. I want him to pull over and turn around and come back to the beach. He keeps looking up ahead for something. I wish he would say what he's looking for, but he doesn't. He looks back at us and his eyes get glassy.

"I love you, Gus. And you, too, Sweet Pea. I love you both so much it hurts. If things go bad, I want you to know it's okay. I love my work and I love my life. I wouldn't change a thing. You've made me so happy. Both of you. You're my family."

Tears streak his face with tiny rivers. I can't swallow anymore. I can't look at Gus. I can barely see the video through my own tears. Howard tries to wipe his away with his driving hand but the camper swerves and he has to grab the wheel quickly. He gets back control.

"Okay, okay. Pull yourself together, man," he mutters as he stares at the road ahead.

Then he looks back at us.

"You probably think I've lost my marbles, like at Butterfly Beach." He winks.

He's making no sense as he tries to blink his tears away.

Please stop driving.

"Maybe I have. When I get back, I'm deleting this video and any and all evidence of it. You'll never even have to see it. But if you are seeing it, then you have my phone and not me. And that's on me. My fault for doing this. So, I've got to tell you this. I want you two to take care of each other. Can you do that for me? I wish I'd made it official before now. I left it way too long. I know my folks aren't always easy on you, but they love you. I love you. I guess I was waiting for the perfect—"

There's a sudden, horrible bang of metal on metal and glass breaking. Howard's eyes go wide and he pitches forward as the phone drops and the view tumbles away. He hit something. All we can see are shadows as his phone rolls to the floor. We can hear stones hammering the underside of the camper, and tires skidding in the gravel and then what sounds like a million brooms hitting the roof and sides of the camper. Branches. He's gone off the road. The view on the phone bounces violently, then it stops in place. It's jammed between the seats where I found it. We can see carpet but nothing else as the phone keeps recording.

When the brooms and stones finally quiet, we stay quiet too. We're listening. Barely breathing. We can hear distant birds twittering and the drone of cicadas. *Why can't we hear Howard? Is he injured? What did he hit? Why isn't he calling out or swearing or moving?* Something, anything.

Then we hear a soft wheezing. *Is it him?* Something rattles. It's the door handle. Is Howard trying to get out or is someone trying to get in? They stop and there's a knock. The wheezing is close but the knocking is muffled. It's on the outside. Howard's not the one knocking. The handle rattles again. It must be locked.

Suddenly, we hear glass shattering and the door opening.

That's when I want to reach over and turn off the video. It's too horrible to listen to but we can't stop. Someone is panting. There's grunting and groaning like a struggle is happening. The horn honks and there's a thud like someone fell. No one is speaking. The rustling movement continues but seems to be getting farther away like they're outside of the camper now. The muffled noises are pierced by a terrifying shriek of pain. It's Howard. I cover my ears. I can't take it. Someone is hurting him. I want to climb into the video and help him but I can't. My face is hot. The camper feels like it's tipping sideways. My vision narrows. *What are they doing to him?*

He stops shrieking and we hear shuffling and dragging sounds but they're far off now. Then there are no more sounds of the struggle. Howard has gone quiet. I strain to listen for him, for anything. All I can hear are the stupid birds. We can't see anything. Just bits of sand on the carpet of the camper. Brought there on the bottom of our sandals after a day spent swimming and playing on the beach. After another five minutes, the video cuts out. His battery must have died.

Gus lowers the phone to her lap and stares out the front window. She places her hands on the steering wheel like she's trying to transport herself back in time to see what Howard saw, to feel what he felt. My head aches, my scratches burn, and the cuts on my feet are throbbing.

"Who was that? Who took Howard?" I ask, looking at Gus.

I know she doesn't know but I ask before the question burns a hole in my chest.

Gus turns to me. She's got that look.

"That's what we're going to find out, Boo," she says.

PART TWO

11

THE EVIDENCE WALL

WE SQUEEZE DOWN THE NARROW SERVICE ROAD THEN PULL OFF into the thick woods near the beach. The place we spent our first night in the county. The place Howard mentioned in his video. The place he told Gus he loved her for the first time. That makes it our place.

Our base of operations.

Butterfly Beach Base Camp.

After watching Howard's *just-in-case* video, we spent the day gathering supplies in Picton. At Canadian Tire, we bought a kettle, coffee bodum, two mugs, two plates, two bowls, two camping chairs, a cooler, flashlights, pillows, and a Swiss Army knife. At the No Frills, we got a week's worth of string cheese, mini yogurts, canned ravioli, coffee, and cream soda. We also grabbed some roast chicken and fries from the take-out counter for dinner. Our last stop was Giant Tiger, where Gus bought a canvas shoulder bag, markers, tape, and the rest of the odds and ends on our list.

She paid cash for all our supplies. *No paper trail*, she said. She wants us off the grid so no one knows where we've been or what we're doing. The whole time we were in town, I felt like someone was watching us. Maybe it was because of what Howard said about being followed. I tried to catch them by peeking through shelves and darting into aisles and spinning around fast to look behind me but I never saw them.

It's dark when we finish setting up camp. We collapse into our new camping chairs by the firepit we dug and we eat the cold chicken and fries. After we're done eating, I dab antibiotic cream on my scratches then wrap a new bandage around the cuts on my left foot. I'm healing fast, but everything stings. Gus has her hands clasped behind her neck and she's staring at the stars. The scrapes on her arms look like words written on her skin. She has one foot propped on the cooler. A bag of ice sits on her ankle. She looks over at me and nods at the cream. I toss it over. She catches it. My foot hits the ground just as hers slips off the cooler. We both yell "*Ow!*" at the exact same moment.

We look at each other. We're both a mess. Gus rolls her eyes. She's thinking it too. And she's trying not to laugh but when a giggle bubbles out of me, she can't help herself. She laughs too. She laughs so loud she snorts. Then we both burst out. Laughter gushes from us in great waves. We laugh and laugh until it hurts. We try to stop but we can't. It keeps ebbing and flowing. I'm laughing so hard I almost fall out of my chair. Gus lets out a squeal then leaps up and runs for the woods holding herself so she doesn't pee her pants.

I can't remember the last time I laughed. Crying I'm good at. I can do that in a heartbeat. My tears are always there, just below the surface. I think we lost our laughter when we lost him. Howard was our funny bone.

Maybe for a moment tonight, he was here with us.

I WAKE FROM A DEEP SLEEP. I'M LYING ON MY SIDE, FACING THE familiar wood panels of the camper. For a second, I can't remember how old I am. But I hear Howard's voice.

It was only yesterday when he took me to the Caddy Shack to play mini golf just outside the park. Gus had stayed on the beach to read. When we got there, a big, loud group of teenagers was in front of us in line. The girls were all wearing bikini tops and short-shorts and the boys were having shoving contests and swatting at butterflies with their putters. I felt silly and young and shy around them. The teenagers all seemed so happy and confident and grown-up. After we got our putters and scorecards, we were sitting on a bench waiting for them to finish the first hole. I couldn't stop my legs from bouncing. Then Howard leaned over to me. He said he was kind of hungry and asked me if it would be okay if we skipped golf and got pizza instead. I pretended to be a little disappointed but told him that would be okay with me. The girl at the check-in shack gave Howard his money back and we spent the next hour stuffing our faces with wood-fired mushroom pizza from the Up in Smoke Pizza Co. right next door. It was way more fun than playing mini golf with teenagers watching. I'm pretty sure Howard knew it would be. He likes mini golf but he loves me.

I smile at the memory as I roll over. Suddenly the years tumble forward. I'm wrong. I'm not nine. I am almost a teenager myself.

Gus is sitting alone at the small dining table that doubles as her bed. I didn't hear her fold up her bedding and lift the table back into place, or maybe she didn't sleep at all. She's sipping coffee. When she sees me turn over, she places Howard's phone face down on the table. That's why I heard his voice. She was watching the video again. Morning sunlight pours in through the double doors beside her, which sit open to the woods.

"Java?" she asks, but doesn't wait for an answer.

She pours steaming coffee from our new thermos and hands me the mug. It's one of the two new mugs we bought in town. I wish we'd bought three. It's not right that we didn't get one for Howard. But I let the thought go.

"How long did I sleep?" I ask.

"Hours. It's almost noon. You needed it. But I'm glad you're up. I've got something to show you," she says, rocking in her seat. She's up to something.

Gus reaches over and closes the double doors beside her. There's a bunch of stuff taped to the inside. Red marker criss-crosses both doors like a cobweb connecting the bits of paper. At the bottom, she's written something. I squirm out of my sleeping bag and slip into the bench across from Gus to take a better look.

Two questions are written in marker.

Who is the Canary?
Who is the dead man from the voice mail?

I know exactly what this is.

It's an evidence wall just like the one back home.

"Number one rule: assemble all the evidence," she says.

I sip my coffee and inspect it. The papers are the ones that were tucked inside Howard's notebook—business cards, receipts, a clipping from a newspaper, a photocopy, and our map. She's taped the two business cards to the top of each door, circling them with red marker. Like two bull's-eyes. I read the cards. One says WILLIAM STENSON, NATURALIST, SOUTH BAY PRIVATE NATURE PRESERVE. The other belongs to MARICA PIKE, CEO, PIKE ENTERPRISES. A red line connects Pike's card to a newspaper article by a writer named Colton Bassett. The headline says "From Vineyards to Wind Yards" and there's a photo of a woman in her fifties with silver hair. I've seen her before. The caption on the photo says *Marica Pike.* She looks fancy and important in her high heels and pantsuit. She's not really dressed for standing on a rocky shoreline. She's pointing to a big sign that says FUTURE SITE OF PIKE WIND PARK.

The map of Prince Edward County is taped to one door—folded just like Howard had it. His receipts are taped along the bottom of the map.

There are red Xs on the map that weren't there before.

"What are the Xs?" I ask.

She's been dying for me to say something.

Gus inhales then starts talking a mile a minute. She tells me how she went through Howard's receipts and checked the recent search history in his Maps app and then marked an X on every place she could find. She even marked places she knew he'd been, like the diner where we had breakfast, like his parents' winery in Cherry Valley, and last but not least, Site 88 at Campground A on Outlet Beach at Sandbanks Provincial Park.

There's another paper taped to the doors. I lean closer. It's a photocopy of a missing person's report for a fifteen-year-old named Lula Stenson. Will Stenson's daughter. There's a picture of her on it. She was mentioned in Howard's notebook. The report says Lula was last seen at the Belleville bus station. There's a note calling her a *probable runaway*. It's dated four years ago. I do the math. She'd be nineteen now. This must have been part of Howard's background check on Will Stenson. Gus has drawn a red line from Stenson's business card to the missing person's report. She's trying to connect the dots.

"Where do you think she is now?" I ask.

"A runaway. Who knows? Might be worth trying to find out, though," she says. "That's another one of my rules. Follow every lead."

I search my brain, digging for the other rules. I find them.

"Always make backups. Always keep things close," I recite.

She smiles.

I gaze up at her wall. I know what she's trying to do, but all I can see right now is a messy paper trail with no beginning or end. No order. Gus reads my mind.

"We start with her." She points to the photo of Marica Pike on the newspaper clipping. "She was at the funeral the other day."

That's where I saw her.

"And this *X* is her winery," says Gus, pointing to an *X* on the map.

"She's the momzilla," I say, remembering what Howard called her in his notes.

"That's right. The one fighting Will Stenson over the wind park," she says.

"But what about him? The Birdman? Shouldn't we go see him too?" I ask.

"That'll be a little trickier since he's in prison, but we'll get there," she says. "For now, we stay here and we go where Howard went."

I like the sound of that. Like he's leading the way.

"We follow in Howard's footsteps," I say.

She nods.

I lean back and gaze at the evidence wall, arms folded.

"Well, Gus, it's a pretty good start," I say, trying not to smile.

She nearly spits out her coffee.

"Smart-ass," she says, wiping her mouth.

I go back over to my bed and root through my suitcase.

"It's missing something," I tell her as I search for the things I've been collecting.

The pink ribbon, the diamonds, the dragonfly lure, and the hubcap mask. I place them on the table. I tell her I found the ribbon and the diamonds the day we arrived in Picton, and the mask and the fishing lure were gifts.

"To protect us and help us hear the wingbeats," I tell her.

She touches the delicate dragonfly with her fingertips.

"It's a fishing lure. Maybe we'll catch someone with it," I say.

Gus laughs. She holds up the baggie and examines the diamonds. Then she nods toward the evidence wall. I kneel on the bench and ponder where to best place each one. First, I tape the ribbon and baggie of diamonds to the map on the spots where I found them. Then I hook the mask over one door handle and the lure over the other.

I step back. That's better. Now it's *our* evidence wall, not just hers.

Gus takes pictures of the wall with her phone. *Always have backups.*

We sit together at the table, sipping our coffees and listening to a woodpecker knocking on a nearby pine. The afternoon heat seeps in through the open windows of the camper. We take a dip in the cool waters of West Lake at the edge of Butterfly Beach, then we get dressed. We cover the firepit, hide our chairs under thick brush, then I walk out ahead of the camper to make sure the coast is clear at the end of the service road.

As we drive across the county on our very first mission, the road is splashed with sparkling summer sunlight. I feel like I can almost see Howard's footsteps as the light bounces off the highway.

But something else is there too. Something in the shadows.

I can't make it out. The glare off the road is blinding and the shadows are deep and dark.

I look away. Shut my eyes. Ghostly shapes dance across my eyelids.

We should have bought a third mug.

12

THE COASTER

PIKE WINERY IS ON THE WAY TO THE GLENORA FERRY ON THE edge of the Bay of Quinte. We stop for gas in Picton and Gus buys a map in the convenience store attached to the gas station.

It looks exactly like the one that's taped to our evidence wall in the back of the camper. I ask Gus why we don't just use that one. She says it's one of her rules. Once something is on the wall, it can't come down. It can be moved around, but never removed. I get it. It's one of the ways we're alike. We see meaning in how things are done. I think she's afraid if something comes off the wall then a hole is created that she might not ever fill. Like the hole left in our world when Howard was removed.

Before we head out, Gus puts all the same red *X*s that are on Howard's map, on our new map. Only it's not new at all. The date on both maps is the same. They're old. Who needs to buy a map when your phone has GPS?

She tucks Howard's notebook in her new canvas shoulder bag for safekeeping. She lets me hang on to his phone. I don't have one of my own and she wants me to have it *just in case*. I wish she hadn't said *just in case*.

Those words make my ears throb and I have to rub them to smooth the pain away.

With her finger, Gus traces the route for me then hands me the map. I call out the directions and fifteen minutes later we're there.

From the highway, the winery is hidden by large hickory trees but there's a big wooden sign at the entrance letting visitors know they're in the right place. The words PIKE WINERY are printed across the sign that's been carved into the shape of a fish with a cork in its mouth. Gus slows the car as we turn into the laneway. She rolls to a stop and we both look at the sign. I suddenly get why it's shaped like that. A pike is a type of fish.

"What was it Howard said in the video?" she says. "He was ready to walk away from the story. He almost pulled the plug. Only he didn't say plug, he said *cork. Pull the bloody cork.*"

"He was leaving clues for us," I say, bouncing in my seat.

"He sure was, Boo," she says, a little bouncy herself.

We drive up the long lane and park near a massive stone building marked TASTING ROOM AND BOUTIQUE. I can see a courtyard, a few other buildings, and a stone wall. The parking lot is full of cars and limousines. Some of them are decorated with paper flowers. I get a bad feeling. We get out of the camper and head for the main building. The large double doors are glittering in the sunlight. They're made of some kind of emerald-colored glass with shiny metal frames. A stone archway that looks like it belongs in a castle curves over the entrance. Grapevines hang from the archway, and a welcome sign sits in a gold stand below. Everything looks sparkling and clean, not a stray grape in sight.

I think we might be the strays. I slow down. I know we're on a mission but I'm not dressed right. *We* are not dressed right. Me in my T-shirt and cords. Gus in her secondhand jean jacket and shorts. This place is fancy. We are *not* fancy.

It's too late. The doors swing open and as they do their glass changes from emerald to deep blue. A trick of light. A couple comes out. She's in high heels. He's wearing a bow tie. Panic prickles my forearms. We should have called first. The woman glances at my cords. Her lips curl into a smirk. Another couple bursts out the doors. Gus manages to dodge them on her way in. I end up shuffled off the path. These two are also dressed up. Tuxedo, corsage, lemon-colored taffeta gown. I glance across the parking lot for signs of confetti or brides. *Are we about to crash a wedding?* The couples are pulling presents from the trunk of their car. I hear music coming from around the side of the building. I head to the corner and peek around. I can see the top of a white tent past the stone wall. A line of staff in burgundy aprons carrying trays of glasses and plates winds from a side door in the building to an entryway in the wall that leads to an enclosed garden. There are garlands and white balloons.

It's definitely a wedding.

I glance at a smaller building across the courtyard with narrow windows and a metal roof. A sign on it says THE CELLARS. A thin trail of smoke snakes up the side of the building. I'm trying to figure out what it is when a head pops out of the ground. I blink, wondering where the rest of the man is. Then I realize he's standing in a sunken stairwell beside the building. He's smoking. He looks over at me. I feel like I've been caught spying. He ducks out of sight.

"Boo! What are you doing?" Gus calls out. "Let's go."

She's holding one of the emerald doors open and nodding inside. I run over and we go in together. I brace myself. *Please don't make a scene.* But when we walk in, I'm over the moon to see a whole bunch of people dressed just like us. Shorts, T-shirts, nothing fancy. The tasting room has high ceilings strung with lights that look like falling raindrops. Another trick of light. A long bar around the room is packed with tourists busy tasting wine and laughing and talking loudly. Through a large window, I see more men in tuxedos and more women in lemon gowns. The wedding party. It's outside. Probably in the walled garden.

I breathe. My shoulders relax.

"You okay?" Gus asks. "You look pale."

I give her a big toothy grin to convince her I'm hunky-dory.

I can do this. I can.

I can stop worrying about every little thing. I can stop picturing the worst.

I can totally be less like me if I just try harder.

She's looking at me weird. My wide grin isn't working. I'm saved when a young greeter comes over. She's cradling a tablet on one arm. Her name tag says OLIVE.

"Welcome to Pike Winery. Are you here for a tasting or a tour?" she asks, not even once looking at my cords. She looks only a few years older than me.

"A tour sounds good," says Gus.

"Oh, you don't have a reservation?" she asks, gripping the tablet.

"Nope. Can we make one?"

"Um, sure. We have a bit of a wait list," she says as she moves her finger down the screen. Scrolling, scrolling, scrolling. "I could fit you in at 4:00 P.M. tomorrow, does that work?"

She smiles like she's just given us the best news ever.

"Is Marica around?" Gus asks.

The girl flinches.

"Oh. Do you—" Olive tries to ask a question but Gus cuts her off.

"I just want to say hello. I'm a fellow winemaker with Baylis Vineyards," Gus says.

"So, no appointment?" asks Olive.

Gus stares at her. Olive lets out a nervous giggle. She's no match for Gus.

"I'll see if she's available." She blinks, scurrying away.

Olive goes behind the bar and whispers into the ear of an older man. He glances at us. He whispers back and Olive disappears through a set of swinging doors. I catch a glimpse of a gleaming kitchen where people are rushing about. They're all wearing the same burgundy aprons as the staff I saw outside. For a split second when the doors are apart, I catch sight of Marica Pike talking to a man in a chef's hat. Olive approaches her then the doors close. I recognize Pike's face from the newspaper article on our evidence wall and from the funeral.

"I'm afraid she's not here at the moment."

That's what Olive tells us when she comes back. Her cheeks are flushed. There's sweat above her lip. She keeps her eyes locked on her tablet.

"A wedding and a packed house, and the boss has gone AWOL. Hmm," says Gus to me.

"Did you still want to book that—" Olive looks up at Gus and doesn't bother going on when she sees the look on her face.

"I'm sorry," says Olive, and I believe her. "Feel free to look around."

Olive looks past us.

"Welcome to Pike Winery. Are you here for a tasting or a tour?" she says to a group of women who've just arrived.

We pretend to browse the store shelves filled with Pike Winery merchandise—bottle openers shaped like fish, branded glasses and cheese boards, grape-covered napkins and jars of ice wine jelly.

"I saw her in the kitchen," I whisper to Gus.

"Yeah, me too," replies Gus.

"I think there's an entrance around the side," I tell her. "I bet it goes into the kitchen."

See, I can do this.

Gus smiles.

We head for the front doors. When we step outside, I point to the corner where I was standing before, but Gus isn't looking at me. She's staring across the parking lot at a person in a hoodie who's kneeling next to our camper van.

"Hey, you," Gus hollers.

The person quickly lifts their head and jumps to their feet. With their back to us and their hoodie up, we can't see their face. Gus breaks into a run. I run, too, pulled like a magnet after her, unable to stop my legs. The person hoists one leg over a motorbike and slams their foot down to kick-start it. Gus is almost there. The biker hits the gas and spins in a circle. The back wheel slams into Gus's leg. She tumbles sideways into the camper. Engine revving, the bike is coming straight for me. I scream and dodge out of the way as Gus dives for the driver's arm. She misses and falls into me. We both land on the hard pavement. The motorbike speeds away.

"Motherfucker," Gus yells.

The biker disappears behind the hickory trees.

Then everything got narrow. People came running and gathered around to help us, but I couldn't hear what they were saying. I remember lemon taffeta near my face and the sound of the motorbike's engine whining like a mosquito buzzing in my ear.

"NOW YOU'RE SURE YOU TWO ARE OKAY?" ASKS MARICA PIKE, AS she wrings her hands and furrows her brow.

We're sitting on a big leather sofa in a private tasting room that feels like a cave. It's windowless with dark paneling. Two sofas are arranged on either side of a low table in front of a stone fireplace and there's a long banquet table across the room. Olive hurries in with a complimentary cheese and fruit plate and bottles of sparkling water. She carefully places the bottles on Pike Winery coasters before leaving without a word. Pike sits across from us.

"We've been through worse," Gus assures her.

"It's appalling. Crime seems to be on the rise everywhere these days," Marica says, shaking her head. "We've had a few thefts in the parking lot. I don't understand it. I do hope you didn't lose anything precious."

Gus shakes her head.

Before we were led to the tasting room, Gus had checked inside the camper. Nothing looked like it had been touched and she was pretty sure we'd caught him before he got inside.

"Did you want me to call the police?" she asks.

"Fuck, no," says Gus, shaking her head. "Sorry, we have history. The cops around here are not exactly fans of mine."

Marica Pike smiles. Her dimples make her face look younger. I think she's in her fifties. Her silver hair is pinned up in a perfect swirl at the back of her head. Not a strand out of place. Her pale blue blouse is tucked neatly into a soft cream skirt. She looks like she should be in a fashion magazine.

"Well, I'm just happy no one was seriously hurt," she says.

Marica Pike slaps her knees and is about to get up but Gus isn't done with her.

"Since you're *actually* here"—Gus smiles—"we were hoping to ask you about your friend, Will Stenson."

The air suddenly goes cold like someone switched on the air-conditioning. Pike's dimples disappear and she starts to rub the inside of her palm like a child soothing herself, even though her words come out very grown-up and confident sounding.

"You said you were a winemaker? I don't believe we've met and I know all the vintners from here to the Niagara Peninsula." She chuckles, only I don't think she finds it funny.

"Maybe we're both dancing around the truth a little," Gus says, smiling and holding out her hand. "Augusta Monet and this is my daughter, Bly."

Pike lets Gus's hand hang in the cool air then slowly reaches over and shakes it. A long scar runs across her palm. She doesn't introduce herself. She doesn't have to.

"What would you like to know about Will?" she asks, smoothing her skirt and settling against the sofa back.

"We're looking into the disappearance of Howard Baylis, the journalist?" Gus says.

"Yes, three years ago. I remember," Pike answers.

"He was working on a story about bird migration. Stenson was one of his main sources," Gus says.

"Makes sense. Will always fancied himself something of an expert on the subject," she says.

"Did Howard ever reach out to you about his article?" Gus asks.

"Me? What do I know about birds? No. He never interviewed me," she says.

"That's strange because we found your business card in his notebook," Gus says.

I shift in my seat. Why is Gus telling her about the notebook when she didn't even tell Howard's parents about it? Gus puts a hand on my knee that says *I got this.*

"No doubt Will gave it to him. I was quite an obsession of his back then," Marica says.

"In what way?" asks Gus.

Pike swallows hard and begins rubbing her scar again.

"In the worst way," says Pike. "It was a difficult time for me."

"For us too," Gus mutters.

Pike doesn't seem to hear this.

"I have no idea why, but Will Stenson was convinced I was out to get him—*and* his bloody birds. It was absolutely insane. We were at odds over a minor development project. He got his say at the planning committee hearings like everyone else, but despite the fact that I agreed to numerous concessions, he was still hell-bent on sabotaging the whole thing. He vandalized our signs, harassed my surveyors. He went so far as to accuse me of kidnapping," she says, hand to chest.

"His daughter," Gus says.

"I'm a mother. It was ridiculous. He began dreaming up all sorts of conspiracy theories when it was really him conspiring to ruin my wind park. He was unhinged. The journalist knew it. Your friend. And then things came to a head and there was an awful incident at the winery."

She glances at her scar.

"Stenson attacked me with a hunting knife," she says.

"It was you. He was charged with attempted murder," says Gus.

"He got five years. The man was deeply troubled. I didn't realize how deeply at the time." Then she almost whispers, "None of us did."

Marica Pike doesn't sound as confident anymore. Like she's remembering the attack and she no longer feels right sitting here talking about it in her pretty blouse and perfect hair.

"How do you know our friend thought Stenson was coming unhinged? You said you never spoke to Howard," Gus asks.

Pike hesitates.

"I didn't say we never spoke. I said he never *interviewed* me. We talked very briefly at a Prince Edward Vintners Association gathering at his parents' winery," she says.

"And while sipping wine you chitchatted about Stenson's mental health?" Gus says, raising an eyebrow.

"I was probably oversharing and likely quite tipsy, but the man had tried to kill me so, yes, it came up," says Pike. "I don't blame Will Stenson. It was the drugs that twisted his mind. Made him beyond paranoid. I think I was just the unlucky target of his delusions. But at least the poor sod got clean in prison—one good thing to come of this, I suppose. He paid his debt, as they say, and I survived so that's that," she says, hands clasped tight.

She looks like she's clasping them so we can't see them shaking. I feel bad for her if it's true.

"*Paid his debt*? You mean he's out?" Gus asks.

Pike bites her lip. At first, I don't think she's going to answer. Then she does.

"He got early release two months ago. Folks around here were not happy. But according to the parole board, Will Stenson is no longer a danger to society," she says with a grimace.

Gus doesn't know what to say. But I know what she's thinking. For three years, she never even knew the name of Howard's source, not until we found his notebook. His editor didn't even know it. And now we find out Stenson's not in prison. He's the guy this all started with. He's the first footstep, not Pike.

"Of course, I have a restraining order against him. Although I needn't have bothered. The man's a hermit. No one ever sees him in town anymore," she says.

"He's back here in Prince Edward County?" asks Gus.

Pike nods.

"Can you tell us where he lives?" says Gus.

Pike pats down her skirt.

"Oh, I forgot to carry his address on me," says Pike.

I think she's getting sick of us. Gus smiles.

"You know Stenson's arrest didn't stop Howard," Gus says.

Pike looks at her but doesn't speak.

"And he wasn't writing about migration paths anymore," says Gus. "We found some other things in his notebook. Turns out Howard was working on something way bigger than birds."

Pike purses her lips.

"I see," she says.

Pike stands and walks to the fireplace. She places one hand

on the mantel with her back to us. She stares into the lifeless hearth.

"I would be very careful if I were you, Miss Monet," she says.

Her words feel like a threat. They send chills through me.

She turns to face us but instead of looking scary, she looks scared.

"I think your friend . . . Howard, is it? . . . he might have been led astray. Tread lightly or you may end up going down the same path as he did," she says.

Gus stands up, her fists clenched.

"It's just a caution. Will Stenson is dangerous and unpredictable, but he's also smart and manipulative. Don't go looking for him. And if you must, don't take her with you." Marica nods to me. "He likes them young."

I shiver. Someone definitely cranked the air-conditioning.

Gus folds her arms. She feels the chill too. Pike goes on.

"Even his own flesh and blood prefers living with those crazies at the commune," she says.

"Lula?" I ask, unable to keep quiet any longer.

"No one was surprised the girl ran away—but whatever possessed her to come back to these parts is beyond me," says Pike.

Olive slips into the room. She's holding her tablet to her chest. She's out of breath. I get the feeling she was supposed to come back sooner. Pike gives her an icy stare when she sees her.

"I'm sorry. It got superbusy. Um, they need you in the lavender garden for an emergency situation with the bride and stuff." She's making it up. I like that she's not a good liar.

The girl is nervous. She pastes on a smile. I wonder why Olive is so afraid of her boss. Then I notice she has the same dimples. Olive is her daughter.

"Do let me know if there's anything else I can help you with." Pike smiles.

She smooths her skirt before heading for the door.

Olive leans over the table and points to my sparkling water.

"You can keep the water—and the coaster," she says.

Pike waves at Olive, beckoning her to get moving. Olive turns and trots after Pike.

I'm superdehydrated so I down the water in gulps. Then I pick up the coaster. On the front is the fish-shaped Pike Winery logo. I flip it over. Scribbled on the back in black pen are the words *You shouldn't be here*. I show Gus. She heads for the same door. Time to go.

I pocket the coaster and we leave.

As we're driving out of the parking lot, I see a man watching us from a burgundy-colored delivery truck. I'm pretty sure it's the same guy I saw in the outdoor stairwell. He turns away so I can't see his face as we pass, but he's got the same balding head and stringy brown hair. This time I'm closer and I see a dark patch behind his ear. A birthmark maybe. Then we're gone.

I know it's just me being me, but it feels like the whole world is watching us or lying to us or warning us or afraid of us. Maybe it's because I'm supersensitive or maybe it's because there really are watchers and liars and scaredy-cats everywhere and they don't like what we're doing.

"Okay, what did we learn?" Gus asks me.

Before I can answer, she hands me Howard's notebook and tells me to make notes in it.

"Stenson's out of prison," she says.

I write it down.

"Lula is back but she doesn't live with her father," I add.

I write another note.

"A commune, I think she said," says Gus.

"Pike and Howard talked at his parents'," I add.

"Yeah, we'll have to find out when that was," she says.

I make a note. Then I look over at Gus.

"Why did you tell her about this?" I ask, holding up the notebook.

"To make her squirm. If Pike has something to hide, she'll want to know what we know," says Gus.

I squint at her. I don't get it.

"Sometimes you have to poke the bear to see what it's sitting on," she tries again.

"But what if the bear is a fish?" I ask.

She laughs.

I don't think Gus is scared anymore. Not that she ever really was. Gus is fearless. She was just afraid she was being a bad mom. She was afraid for me. I think that makes her a good mom. I'm going to try to be as brave as her from now on.

We stop at a food truck on the side of a county road and order veggie burgers and fries for dinner. Sitting in the late-afternoon sun at the picnic table, Gus tries the number on Stenson's card. It's out of service. She's not surprised. There's no address on the card so we search for it on our phones but we get nowhere. It's like Stenson doesn't want to be found. Since the county seems to be a place where everyone knows everyone, Gus asks the girl in the food truck if she knows him. She doesn't. She's only here for the summer from Toronto. Not a local. Gus figures that Stenson probably lives at one of the Xs from Howard's Maps app. She says tomorrow we'll go to every X she marked on our map until we find him.

Then she gets a better idea. She calls Constable Journey. She puts him on speaker so I can hear. The constable is surprised we're still around. Gus lies and says we're heading back to Ottawa right now, but we want to stop in to see an old friend before we leave. This friend had some trouble in the past and recently got out of prison and moved to Prince Edward County.

"It's complicated," she says. "We knew him a long time ago.

He was Howard's best friend. I know it's a lot to ask, but me and Bly just want to talk to someone who cared about Howard as much as we did."

I stare at her. I can't believe she just talked about Howard in the past tense.

She wags her chin toward the phone and mouths, *Say something.*

"Yeah, we really do" is all I can think to say. I'm mad at her.

Gus lies so easily. But I know why she's doing it so I play my part.

"It would really mean a lot to me, Constable Journey," I add.

My voice trembles, not because I'm about to cry but because I'm a terrible liar.

The constable asks for the name. He doesn't recognize it because he wasn't around when Stenson got arrested. He lived in the county when he was a kid, but he only moved back six months ago after he graduated from the Ontario Police School and got posted to Picton. I had found all this out from Noble.

We can hear the click of a keyboard. Constable Journey says he'll do a quick search on the laptop in his police cruiser. He finds William Stenson's arrest report from three years ago. He texts her Stenson's last-known home address.

"Might be an old one," he says.

"Thanks, I owe you one," says Gus.

"Safe trip home, you two," he says back.

Gus hangs up before I can say goodbye.

We check our map. The address matches one of the *X*s.

Gus eats the last bite of her veggie burger then we head to the camper. It's parked in the shade of a large oak. I remember the coaster in my pocket. I kick the back bumper and the side doors pop open. I tape the coaster to our evidence wall with the message facing out. *You shouldn't be here.*

Gus is beside me.

"She's wrong, you know. We're exactly where we should be," says Gus.

She closes the doors and just as we're about to get in, she spots the flat tire.

"That little shit," says Gus.

I come around to her side. The back tire sags around the rim. The man in the hoodie was kneeling right beside it.

Gus is getting the spare tire and jack from the wheel well when a red truck pulls in and parks by the food truck. It's Patience and Dod Perley. No dogs in the back this time. Patience hops out. She's wearing jean shorts that show half her bum. She heads for the food truck then spots us. She waves. We wave back. Then she notices the flat and comes over.

"More trouble?" she asks.

"Old tires and country roads don't mix, I guess," says Gus.

"August, was it?" she asks.

"Augusta, but you can call me Gus."

Gus never tells anyone to call her Gus unless she likes them.

"Can I help, Gus?" asks Patience. "Or, rather, can that strapping young lad in my truck give you a hand." She giggles and points a glossy red fingernail at Dod, who shrinks in his seat.

"That's okay, I can handle it," says Gus.

"I bet you can," says Patience.

"Nice nails," I tell her.

"You like? Just got them done over at Fiona's Beauty Salon," she says, wiggling her fingers. "I thought you gals had up and left town. Where you shacked up?"

Gus jacks up the camper.

"We're camping," I tell her.

Gus looks at me. I forgot we were trespassing.

"In the park?" Patience asks.

I nod.

"Good lord, you get lucky with a cancellation or something?" she asks.

"Yup" is all Gus says.

"Well, that settles it. You're probably sick to death of beans and wieners. I wouldn't forgive myself if I didn't offer you some good old Prince Edward County hospitality. You two must come join me and the boys for our Canada Day party, day after tomorrow. I won't take no for an answer," she says, hands on hips.

I look at Gus, trying to will her to say yes. She wipes sweat from her brow but says nothing.

"We're having a fish fry. JP and JW—that's my twins—they'll be out fishing first thing. Oh please come. It's just me and my three boys and we got buckets of food and I never get any female company. So much testosterone. Oh, and we're gonna roast a pig. Dod would love it. He needs a good cheering up. There'll be a bonfire and s'mores and a few fireworks."

She can barely breathe she's so excited.

I laugh.

"Can we?" I beg Gus.

She's busy wrenching the bolts off the old tire.

"We'll see. We've got a few things to take care of," she says.

"Did I mention we're having our annual horseshoe competition?" says Patience.

"It sounds so fun," I say.

"We're not here to have fun," snaps Gus.

Patience nods.

"If you change your mind, we're out on Salmon Point on the other side of the park. Last road on the left, all the way at the end. It's the big yellow house right on the water," she says.

Gus looks up at Patience. She has grease on her cheek.

"It's kind of you to invite us," says Gus.

"I wouldn't ask if I didn't mean it. Just know that you're both welcome—any time after noon—only if you like," she says with a shrug.

Her face flushes like she's embarrassed about how excited she got.

"You two lovelies take care now," she adds as she turns toward the food truck.

Gus is still changing the tire when Patience passes greasy boxes of fries through the open door of her truck to Dod. As they drive away, I wave at Dod. He doesn't wave back. I notice he has a black eye and I feel in my gut that a bully must have given it to him. Maybe that's why his mother said he needed cheering up.

"I don't see why we can't go to a Canada Day party," I say with a sulk.

"We need to stay focused," she says.

"I bet we'd be able to focus a lot better if we spent a holiday eating s'mores and having fun like normal people."

Gus looks at me.

"Who said we were normal, Boo?"

13

THE CREEPING THYME

SHE'S RIGHT. WE AREN'T NORMAL. I WAS STUPID TO THINK WE could be. By the time Gus got the tire changed, the sun was getting low and it was too late to drive across the county to Stenson's. We went back to our base camp for the night.

The spare tire didn't last long after bumping down the service road so we spent the next morning at Toby's Garage waiting for a new one. But Gus stayed focused like she said she would and now we're on our way, getting closer and closer to that *X*.

Stenson's laneway isn't really a laneway at all. It's more like two tire tracks crowded by ferns. A mound of moss between the tracks rubs the belly of our camper van. A few yards in and our front wheels get so tangled in thick fronds we can't go any farther.

"I don't think he lives here anymore," I suggest.

Gus reverses all the way back out to the highway.

We park on the shoulder.

"It's okay if you want to stay here," she says.

"No way," I tell her. "Let's go." This is me being brave.

We have no idea how far it is to his house and there's no breeze in the thick woods so it's a sticky walk down the laneway. The afternoon heat is heavy and wet. Tiny bug clouds float around our heads. The bugs keep getting stuck in the corners of my eyes and flying up my nose.

After about a half mile, the air cools as the lane dips into a valley. The bug clouds go away and I can finally take in the lush forest around me. And what's under my feet. The mossy mounds between the tire tracks are coated in tiny purply-pink flowers. I crouch and pick some. I know this plant. It's called creeping thyme. Howard planted some in our garden. He liked making tea from its leaves. The tea smelled like mint and he said that if we picked the leaves in the morning when the oils were strongest, the tea would taste better. I liked knowing our garden was full of smells and oils and tasty leaves. Howard knew all about plants and bugs and birds. It's why he was so excited about his *Canadian Geographic* assignment.

I tuck the creeping thyme in my back pocket and catch up to Gus.

I'm getting thirsty and Gus tells me to grab the water bottle from her bag. While I'm rooting around, I spot the Swiss Army knife next to Howard's notebook. I don't ask why she brought it. Maybe she's more worried about what Pike said than I thought.

Don't go looking for him. And if you must, don't take her with you.

We share what's left of the water then walk on through the thick forest of birch trees. So thick we can only see a few yards in any direction. No rooftop pokes above the trees, no mailbox sits along the lane, no smoke rises from a distant chimney. There are no sounds of human life either—no generator humming or chain saw whining or radio playing. But what we can hear is a choir all around us in the treetops—cawing and cheeping and singing and warbling. A birdman's paradise.

A mile farther, the poplar trees thin out and the lane ends at a clearing. There's an old Toyota pickup parked off to the side. It's missing a back tire and the passenger door. We stop at the entrance to the clearing. I stare across the large yard at the tin-roofed bungalow that sits there. The yard is a blanket of gold and pink and violet wildflowers—black-eyed Susans, goldenrods, and milkweeds. It's beautiful. A rain barrel sits at the corner of the house fed by a downspout. Ivy has crept up the spout, across the walls and windows and under the eaves, covering the house with green. The ivy is alive with bees. The only place the ivy hasn't taken over is the red tin roof. It's even dripping from the front porch like jellyfish tentacles.

Next to the house is a big garage. A ladder leans on the garage. It leads up to a deck that's built on top of it. All over the deck are birdhouses sitting on top of poles. The houses are different sizes, colors, and shapes. A makeshift suspension bridge hangs from the deck to a treehouse perched in the branches of a giant oak tree.

It's not just any treehouse. It's one I could happily live in for the rest of my life. It's got two stories, a wraparound walkway, and a pointy rooftop that looks like an upside-down ice cream cone. The roof is shingled with bark, and thick vines weave across the walls. It's like the whole thing is a natural part of the forest around it. There are pulleys and levers. And there's some kind of drawbridge connecting the walkway to the suspension bridge. It reminds me of a castle in a fairy tale. But what makes it so magical are the smoke bush plants surrounding the oak. Their clusters of massive pink blooms make it look like the treehouse is floating on a puffy pink cloud.

We slowly enter the clearing. I'm smiling ear to ear. Gus is on the lookout for Will Stenson, but I can't help staring in awe. If he's the one who built all this, then what they say about him can't be true. How could a dangerous person create such a beautiful place? I stop smiling when I hear the sound of metal scraping against metal.

Gus looks at me and we both turn around.

A very tall, very thin man stands about twenty feet away from us.

He's pointing a hunting rifle in our direction.

And he's blocking the way out.

We're in the open. There's nowhere to run and nothing to hide behind.

The man's wearing a faded plaid shirt, long shorts, and hiking boots. Across his face and legs are patches where the skin looks like it's been bleached by the sun or age or illness. He's like a human version of the poplars behind him—almost like he was carved from them. Like he's part of the forest. Just like his home. But I don't think he's a tree. Trees don't tremble. His hands shake, which makes the rifle shake, which makes me shake.

Gus holds her hands above her head and steps in front of me.

"Will Stenson?" she asks.

He just stares but I know it's got to be him. He kind of looks like a crazy birdman.

"We don't mean you any harm," she says.

Still nothing.

"I'm Augusta. I'm Howard Baylis's girlfriend?" she says, hoping the name rings a bell.

His eyes look down at me.

"I'm Bly," I say.

I come out from behind Gus and move toward him. She reaches out to stop me. I pull the creeping thyme plant from my back pocket and hold it out to him.

"You know you can make tea with this that tastes like mint," I tell him.

He looks at the flowering plants in my hand then back at me.

"Don't like mint," Stenson says.

Sweat trickles down his cheeks as he slowly lowers the rifle to his side.

"I got something better," he says.

He slings the rifle over his shoulder and heads past us toward his house. He leans the rifle next to the front door and goes inside. We follow but decide to wait on the porch, taking a seat on a swing at one end. The porch is freckled with droplets of light from the sun shining through the curtain of ivy surrounding it.

After a few minutes, Stenson comes back out carrying a slab of wood he's using as a tray. Balanced on it are three icy pink drinks. He places the tray on a table under the window, hands us each a glass, then takes one for himself. He sits across from us in a pine rocking chair that looks handmade. The drink smells fruity and sweet. I'm so thirsty I gulp most of it in one go. It tastes like cranberries. Gus doesn't touch hers. She sits the glass on the porch rail next to her and keeps one hand near her bag. We rock gently. I can tell she's still on alert because even though he made us an ice-cold drink and he built a magical treehouse, he also aimed a hunting rifle at us.

"Hibiscus tea," he tells me, nodding at my drink.

Stenson glances at the wildflowers in his front yard. I can see hints of gold and violet through the ivy. I wonder why he doesn't trim it back so he can see the flowers better. Maybe he likes being hidden.

"He was never found, was he?" he asks.

I know he's talking about Howard. I take another sip of my tea because my throat is suddenly very dry.

"Not yet. But the camper van he was driving turned up a couple of weeks ago," says Gus.

"Right. The camper," he says, then he pauses. "You won't find him."

I choke on the tea.

"Why would you say that?" I frown, wiping my chin.

Gus doesn't put her hand on mine or give me a look. She wants to know why too.

"She'll have buried him good and deep" is his answer.

I drop my glass. The ice cubes skim across the porch and end up under his rocking chair. I don't say sorry. I stare at him.

"She?" asks Gus, planting her feet to stop the swing from moving.

"That bitch," he says.

My brain is stuck in a horrible singsong.

Buried. Buried.

Good and deep.

Buried. Buried.

Good and deep.

"You have no idea what she's capable of," he says, more to himself than Gus.

"Pike? So tell me." Gus is talking through gritted teeth.

"Why should I?" he says.

"She sure had a lot to say about you," says Gus.

He raises an eyebrow but says nothing. He sips his tea. Swallows hard.

"About you and Lula," Gus adds.

He cringes for a second then relaxes back in his rocking chair.

"Drink your tea," he tells her.

"Fuck your tea," she says.

"My house, my rules." He laughs.

Gus knocks her drink off the porch rail.

Stenson smiles and looks away like we're not there.

"Why don't you two ladies go bother someone who gives a shit?" he says.

Gus looks at me and reaches into her bag.

"Like old man Baylis. That slimy motherfucker. It's his kid, isn't it? Go ask him and his girlfriend what's what," he says.

"Kirk? What are you talking about?" Gus looks confused.

I wish we hadn't come. *Why did we walk in?* I feel like we've made a horrible mistake. My hands are trembling. I don't want to be here.

"Figure it out. I'm done talking," he says. "Talk, talk, fucking talk. Never got me anywhere."

"Look, Will, we just want to find Howard. If you know something, I don't see why—"

He cuts her off.

"Squawk, squawk, squawk," he sings, rocking in his chair.

The ice cubes crunch under it.

Gus removes something from her shoulder bag.

"Lady, nothing I tell you changes the fact that Howard Baylis is long gone." He smiles.

I hate Will Stenson. I hate his stupid squawking face.

Gus is up and out of the swing so fast I barely see what's happening until his chair is wrenched backward and she's leaning over Stenson, his skinny poplar legs dangling, iced tea dripping from his nose, the Swiss Army knife pressed against his carotid artery.

I did a science project in grade 6 on the circulatory system. The thin line of blood along the edge of the knife reminds me of the diagram I drew showing how the blood went from the heart to the head through all these veins and arteries that looked like tree branches. The carotid arteries are the only path to the brain and right now, Gus has the knife pressed against that path.

She brings her face an inch from Stenson's.

"I was really hoping we could have a civilized conversation, but I hadn't counted on you being such a fucking asshole, so we'll do it this way instead. You're going to tell me everything you know—from the beginning. Got it?" she says, cool as a cucumber.

He nods and tries very hard not to swallow.

She doesn't take her eyes off his.

"Hey, Boo, do me a favor? Go on over to that rifle, will you?" she says to me.

I get up off the swing, walk past them, and stand beside the rifle.

"Now pick it up and bring it here," she calls out.

I pick up the rifle by one end, holding it as far away from me as I can.

I walk back over.

"Now point it at him," she says.

14

THE MARBLES

WHEN WILL STENSON WAS DONE TALKING, WE PLACED THE RIFLE on the swing and left. He didn't try to stop us. He didn't ask if we believed him. He just rocked back and forth in his chair. The tiny line of blood had dried on his neck. She hadn't cut him deep.

But I think many people had.

I wanted to believe Will Stenson. He had a story just like Pike did. Only his version was different. He wasn't the villain. She was.

He told us how Pike started spreading nasty rumors about him after he became a real thorn in her side at the planning committee hearings for her wind park. He had documented migration routes and researched how the turbines would disrupt the paths of thousands of species of birds. The few committee members who saw his point were suddenly off the committee. Then someone called in an anonymous tip to Children's Aid and a social worker came out to see Stenson and his daughter. He figured Pike was behind all of it. Nasty lies were spread about his daughter, Lula. Then drug paraphernalia and crystal meth were found on his property. He said it was all planted. He never used drugs in his life. He was being followed and so was his daughter. She begged him to stop fighting the wind park. But instead, Stenson filed a lawsuit against the project. Shortly after that Lula disappeared.

The OPP said it looked like she ran away. Lula was like a lot of kids. She was rebellious, she didn't always listen to her dad, and she missed her curfew all the time, but he knew she hadn't run away. He was convinced Pike had kidnapped her to force him to withdraw the lawsuit.

Stenson's whole story was about Pike harassing him, not the other way around.

A year later, when it looked like Pike's wind park was about to be approved, Stenson met Howard. Stenson felt a glimmer of hope. Maybe this journalist could help him save the birds from those turbines.

As Stenson put it: *The local newspapers never had a lick of interest. Goddamn Colton Bassett. Calls himself a reporter. The only reporting he ever did was to write candy-coated articles about what an upstanding citizen Marica Pike was. Figures. She single-handedly kept the lights on at the* Gazette *with her dirty advertising dollars.*

Stenson pinned all his hopes on Howard's article. He thought they were about to break the story and that the backlash and attention would put a stop to the wind park for good. But when Howard hesitated, Stenson figured Pike had gotten to him.

He went out to the winery to confront Pike. Out of nowhere, he was being arrested. It was like she knew he was coming. The cops were there in seconds. She had a bad cut on her hand. Her daughter said she'd witnessed him attack her mother. His prints were all over a hunting knife that Pike claimed she'd wrestled from him. It *was* his knife all right. He'd used it the day before to skin a rabbit. He'd been set up.

It was then that he knew he'd underestimated Pike. She'd go to any lengths to win. It worked. He was sent to prison, the migration story died, and her wind park got pushed through.

He wasn't all that surprised to learn that Lula returned soon after. Pike didn't need her anymore. He tried to see Lula after his release but she refused. She wasn't herself after what she'd been through. Stenson said he had no idea what Pike had done to her or where she'd kept her. Maybe Pike had brainwashed her and turned her against him. Lula was living in the area, at some kind of retreat, he'd heard, so he let her be. Maybe she'd come home one day. He built the treehouse for her in case she did. Pike had taken everything from him, except his home. He was done fighting her. She'd won.

Gus had removed the knife from Stenson's neck. But she had one more question. Was he just trying to get a rise out of her by saying Howard's dad had a girlfriend?

Stenson shook his head.

"It was something Howard said when he came to visit me in jail right after I was arrested. He wanted to know if there was anything he could do to help. It was kind of him. He was the only person to visit. I think he felt partly responsible. He thought he'd set me off. I didn't bother telling him Pike set me up. No point. He wouldn't have believed me. I told him to keep after Pike even though I could tell he was done with it all," said Stenson. "But he looked miserable and it wasn't just the guilt. It was something deeper. I asked if he was okay. I thought maybe Pike had threatened him. That's when he blurted out that his dad was having an affair. He regretted it the moment he said it. I felt bad for him. Then he left. A week later, I heard he'd disappeared."

IT'S DUSK WHEN WE REACH THE HIGHWAY. THE WHOLE WALK back along the two-track laneway, I can hear Howard's voice trailing along with us.

What I'm digging into could hurt some people around here if it comes out.

People I care about.

Back at base camp, Gus lights a fire while I decorate our evidence wall with the wilted creeping thyme from my back pocket.

A summer chill drifts across the dunes. We sit waist-deep in our sleeping bags by the fire. I make a crisscross slice in the end of my hot dog and slide it onto a stick. Howard taught me how to make crispy dogs. When you slice them like that and roast them on a fire, the hot dog curls into a delicious crispy octopus.

We don't talk about the affair. I don't like knowing that Howard was sad back then and that we didn't know it. He didn't tell us. Maybe he didn't know how. Maybe it hurt too much. Maybe that's why Vivi said he didn't tell them much of anything. His dad wasn't who Howard thought he was.

HOWARD USED TO CALL HIS PARENTS EVERY SUNDAY ON SKYPE. He'd say, *Time to call home*, even though he'd never lived in their new house in Cherry Valley. He had lived in Ottawa his whole life and when his parents moved to Prince Edward County after winning the lottery, he stayed behind. It was time. He was twenty-three and had a job. Kirk and Vivi had always dreamed of opening a winery and now they could. They had lots of money so they didn't need to sell the house in Ottawa. They let Howard have it. Our house. They used to joke that they did things backward—the parents left the nest instead of the kid. Vivi always felt guilty about leaving her son behind, so she set up a spare room in her new house and made it look just like Howard's childhood bedroom with all his things from when he was a kid. So he could always come home. Gus thought it was weird but I liked it. His room was my favorite place in their whole house. It was everything Howard—his old clothes and schoolbooks and model airplanes and swimming trophies. There was a globe, a telescope, and lots of Legos. I loved sleeping in that room and imagining what he was like as a kid.

I OPEN MY EYES. I MUST HAVE DOZED OFF BECAUSE, FOR A SEC-ond, I thought I was in Howard's room. But all I can see around me is the night sky. It's filled with stars but it's already turning the deep blue of dawn. The coals are glowing in our campfire. I look over at Gus. She's not in her camping chair. I wander over the dune and spot her silhouette on the beach. She's on her hands and knees. She's digging in the sand. I can see holes scattered across the beach.

"Having fun?" I call out.

She stops digging and sits back on her heels.

"You said Howard left clues for us in the video," she says.

I walk over and sink to my knees beside her.

"Yeah?" I say.

"I think I figured out another one. When he said that we're going to think he's lost all his marbles. But he mentions Butterfly Beach. *This* Butterfly Beach."

"Maybe it's just an expression," I say. "He was always saying silly stuff."

"Or maybe he lost something here . . . or hid something," she says.

I look around at all the holes she's dug. Maybe she's lost her marbles.

"Where exactly did you find those rocks?" she asks.

I don't know what she's talking about. Then I remember. She must mean the diamonds. I look left then right, trying to picture where we were sleeping that night and where I'd gone hunting.

"I don't know. I was looking for the driftwood from your story," I say.

"Where we carved our initials?" she asks. "Oh my god, that's what he meant. I called him love crazy that day. He was pointing us to this place, to that day, to the driftwood."

Before I can say anything, she looks across the beach at a large piece of driftwood. I look at it too. I think it's where I found the diamonds.

"That's the one," we both say at the same time.

Together, we scramble over to the spot. She runs her palms across the surface of the log until she finds it.

"There," she says.

I lean in. There's a heart carved in the wood and inside it are the letters *HB & AM*.

Howard Baylis and Augusta Monet.

We both start digging on either side of the log. About two feet down, my fingers touch something hard.

"I found something," I tell her.

Now, we dig together, flinging sand behind us like a pair of dogs who've caught a scent. We gradually uncover a plastic lid, then below it, a Rubbermaid tub just like the ones we stored our bungee cords and batteries and flashlights in when we camped. We pull it from the sand and open the lid. Inside are more baggies of diamonds just like the one I found here at the beach. Lots and lots of baggies. Under them Gus finds a document. She pulls it out and looks it over. Pink daylight edges over the dune.

"It looks like a list of cargo planes. See, they list what's being shipped and when and where. Ellsworth, Fort Bragg, Thule— international destinations. All in August, three years ago. These must be flight numbers," she says, pointing at the paper.

I lean closer. Printed at the top of the page is a logo that says CFD QUINTE AIRFIELD.

"That's a military airfield," I tell her, pointing to the logo.

She looks at me.

"How on earth do you know that?" she asks.

"You know those big planes that used to fly low over the beach every summer. Howard told me they were military planes. He said the air force in Trenton did their training at CFD Quinte Airfield. CFD stands for Canadian Forces Detachment," I tell her proudly.

She looks pretty impressed.

"Why would Howard be looking into military flights?" she asks.

I don't know the answer to that one.

There are some notes on the document.

Drop-offs: Aug. 13, 9:15 p.m., Aug. 20, 9:22 p.m.

Scribbled below the dates and times is *ME7*.

It's Howard's handwriting. I'd know it anywhere.

"Drop-offs," says Gus. "What was Howard up to?"

"I bet these are worth millions of dollars?" I say, holding up one of the baggies.

We hear voices.

"Shit," says Gus.

She tosses everything into the plastic tub, picks it up, and we race up the beach. We can see flashlights through the trees off in the distance. We abandon our chairs by the firepit, race across the dunes, toss the bin in the back of the camper, and jump in the front. Gus starts the engine just as the three park wardens appear in our headlights. She slams her foot down hard on the gas pedal. The same stunned look crosses each of their faces as we drive straight for them. One dives into the woods and the other two twirl out of the way just in time—their arms around each other like they're dancing. I hold my breath as we gun it past them and bump through the woods. We veer around their truck, which is parked at the end of the service road, then hit the highway.

The sky gets brighter and brighter as morning comes fast. Gus doesn't slow down until she's sure no one is following us. There's a long ribbon of red rippling across the horizon like someone fired a flare gun from a lifeboat.

I wonder if Howard sees it too.

What did he used to say?

Red sky in the morning, sailors take warning.

15

THE PHOTOGRAPH

IT FEELS LIKE THE WARNING IS MEANT FOR US. WE MIGHT HAVE found Howard's marbles but we lost our base camp. The wardens will be watching for us if we try to go back. Gus will be arrested and I don't want to think where that leaves me. But there's a trail starting to appear, and we're the only ones who can see it. We can't stop now.

I bite my nails and try to focus on the mission ahead. I don't have to ask what it is. I already guessed when we passed the sign to Cherry Valley.

But when we get there, I'm less sure. Instead of driving right up the laneway and banging on their door and making Kirk tell us all about his girlfriend, Gus parks on the road across from Baylis Vineyards. We pull off into the low ditch, hidden in the shadows of some red maples. Gus jumps in the back and hides the diamonds in the spare wheel well under the floor. She tucks the military document in Howard's notebook. Finally, she climbs back into the front seat and fills me in on the plan.

We're not banging on any doors. Howard's parents made it crystal clear how they feel about us bringing up the past, says Gus. They're not on our side and they've been hiding things. Not just the affair, but the camper van. They should have called us the second it was found. Gus doesn't trust them. She wants to take a look around their place while they're out.

And luckily, it's Canada Day and Gus knows exactly what Kirk and Vivi are doing today. What they do every July 1. Delivering cases of their special Canada Day pinot noir to local restaurants in the county. Gus and Howard were always asked to hold down the fort while they were out—in case the people staying in their guesthouses needed something.

Every year it's like clockwork.

8 A.M., they'll eat breakfast.

9 A.M., they'll head out to make the deliveries.

11 A.M., they'll be back in time for Vivi to oversee the lunch service at Baylis Bistro and for Kirk to hold his morning meeting with the tasting room staff.

That's our window. It's 8:30. While we wait, we eat cheese strings and listen to a local radio station. The DJ is holding a call-in contest. Top prize is a ride in a hot air balloon over the county. I wonder if we'd see Howard from way up. I almost ask if we can call in.

But just like that, at 8:58, Kirk and Vivi's blue SUV appears at the end of the driveway. They turn left onto the county road heading toward Picton. Once they're out of sight, we jump out and cross the highway on foot. We don't take the driveway. Instead, we climb the hill and come up behind the house so no one sees us. The sliding doors into the kitchen won't be locked. They never are. Vivi liked that about country life, that you never had to worry about someone breaking in. Guess she was wrong.

As we step inside, I ask Gus what we're looking for. She says we'll know it when we see it. That doesn't help. She heads to Kirk's office down the main floor hallway and tells me to look around the kitchen and living room. It's all one big room. Open concept. I don't know where to begin so I wing it. I lift the sofa cushions one by one. Nothing. I check under the welcome mat by the front door. Nothing. I peek into a houseplant. Only a ladybug. In the kitchen, I look inside a cookie jar on the big island. Nope. Then I check the cupboards, open the fridge, and smell the milk. I feel stupid. And hungry. I pluck a strawberry from a carton and pop it in my mouth.

I'm getting more and more nervous poking around their house without their permission. What if they come back early? It feels wrong to be here. I'm so jittery that I accidentally slam the fridge door too hard. A magnet falls off the fridge. It clatters to the kitchen tiles along with the photo it was holding. I pick them up and fumble to get them back in place on the fridge door.

The photo is of a group of women posing on the deck of a boat. The name on the side of the boat is *Princess of the Bay*. The women look about the same age. One of them looks familiar but I can't place her. They have their arms linked. Vivi is standing on the far right. She's holding on to the rail for dear life. She's wearing capri pants and a blue-striped blouse and heels. She looks like a fancy sailor but her eyes are wide. I don't think she likes boats.

There's another photo on the fridge that I've never seen before. It's of Howard at a party in his parents' garden. He's holding a wineglass but he's not looking at the camera. He's looking down. Behind him, people are gathered in small groups and there's a banner that says PRINCE EDWARD VINTNERS ASSOCIATION ANNUAL GARDEN PARTY. Everyone is smiling except for Howard. I wonder when it was taken. I lift the photo off the fridge and flip it over to see if there's a date on the back but there isn't. I look closely at the people in the background. There's a woman. She has her back to the camera but I know that swirl of silver hair. It's Marica Pike.

She told us she met Howard once.

We talked very briefly at a Prince Edward Vintners Association gathering at his parents' winery.

She told him about Stenson attacking her, so that means this photo had to have been taken around the time Howard disappeared. Stenson was already in jail. And Howard already knew about his dad's affair. He'd told Stenson about it. Maybe that's why he's not smiling. He doesn't want to be there. I look closer, trying to see into Howard's eyes but I can't. He's looking down.

Then I hear a floorboard creak. It's coming from upstairs.

I think it must be Gus until she rushes into the room. It wasn't her. But she heard it too.

She puts a finger to her lips.

Someone's in the house.

She nods to the sliding door but it's too late. They're coming down the stairs.

"Hello," she calls out in a fake-happy, out-of-breath voice like we just arrived.

She waves me over to her side and we move closer to the back door. I shove the photo of Howard in my back pocket. A man comes down the stairs and looks across the living room to the kitchen. I don't know him. He's slim, maybe thirty or forty. What's left of his hair is whisper thin. His eyes are dark caves. He's wearing a wrinkled smock with the Baylis Vineyard logo on the front. He must be an employee. Gus leans casually on the island. He looks from me to her like he's not sure what to do.

"Sorry, we didn't know anyone was here," she says, smiling. "We're staying in one of the guesthouses."

"I work here," he says, pointing to his smock.

"Kirk and Vivi went into town for a bit," she tells him, nodding to the coffee machine. "They told us to come on in and help ourselves."

"I was fixing a plumbing issue for them. Upstairs," he says.

He stays where he is near the front door. Gus grabs an apple from a bowl on the island.

"We're from out of town. Here for Canada Day," says Gus.

Why doesn't he leave? Maybe he doesn't believe us.

He smiles. Even from way across the room, I can see his small brown teeth. He gives me the creeps.

"I know who you are." He grins.

The hairs on my neck stand up.

I notice one of his hands is trembling. He tries to hide it.

Gus takes a bite of the apple.

"I don't know *you*. New here?" she asks.

I don't like the way he keeps on standing there, staring at Gus. It's like he's trying to say something without saying it. She doesn't look away. She chews her apple and stares right back. Nobody can beat Gus at a staring contest.

"I work in the back. In the kitchen," he says, looking away.

"A jack of all trades," she says. "Plumber and cook."

He smirks.

"I'll be sure to let Kirk and Vivi know you were in here," says Gus.

He turns and heads for the door. As he does, I see a birthmark by his ear. He's the creepy man I saw at Pike Winery.

"What did you say your name was?" she tries.

He doesn't answer. When the door closes behind him, Gus looks at me and shrugs. I'm trembling and my cheeks feel hot. I don't like that we were caught snooping and I don't like that Creepy Man is the one who caught us.

"Don't worry, Boo. That guy won't say a word," she says, tucking the apple core in her pocket. "He wasn't supposed to be in here either."

My throat is dry. I can't find my voice.

"I'll be right back," she says.

Gus heads upstairs. She's back down in seconds.

"We've got to get out of here," she says. Her face is white. "Move!"

She grabs my arm and we slip out the sliding doors and run down the hill. Once we're across the highway and in the camper, she slams the steering wheel with both palms.

"I knew that fucker wasn't a plumber," she says.

I want to tell her I already knew, but I need water to unlock my voice.

"The wrinkled uniform was a dead giveaway," she says. "He probably grabbed it from a laundry bin and put it on in case he was spotted. He wasn't fixing a toilet. He was trashing Howard's room. The mattress was sliced open, his model planes were smashed, clothes were tossed everywhere. What the fuck was he looking for?"

"We should call the police or tell Kirk and Vivi," I say, finally able to speak.

She shakes her head.

"Did you leave everything like you found it?" she asks.

I look at her and I know why she's asking. They'll think we did it.

"I think so." I burst into tears.

"You didn't take anything?" she asks.

"No," I gulp.

Then I remember the photo in my back pocket. I show it to her.

"I should've mentioned that rule before we went in. *Don't leave a trace*," she says.

I nod.

"Where exactly did you get this?" she asks.

"Off the fridge," I tell her.

She looks across the road.

"I have to put it back. We can't do anything about fingerprints, but it might not come to that. You didn't take anything else, did you?"

"I ate a strawberry," I say, tears streaking my cheeks.

"I'll be right back," she says and jumps out.

She's right. Who else would steal a photo of Howard? They'll know it was us.

Gus ducks low. At first, I think she tripped, then I spot the blue SUV on the highway. She's hiding. I check the time. It's only ten. They're back early. The SUV turns in and disappears up the driveway. Gus jumps back in the driver's side.

"At least we didn't get caught inside," she says.

"That man. I saw him before," I say.

"Where?" she asks.

"Pike Winery. In a delivery truck. I think he was watching us," I tell her.

She thinks on this.

"What's a guy from Pike Winery doing pretending he works here? And why was he inside the Baylis house?" she says.

Gus starts the engine. We're pulling out of the ditch when she slams on the brakes. I lurch forward in my seat then look up. The SUV is coming back down the driveway. We sink low in our seats. Kirk is alone this time. He doesn't look our way. He speeds off in the other direction. Gus pulls onto the highway and follows him.

Part of me wishes she hadn't.

16

THE SHOE

WE KEEP ABOUT A FARMER'S FIELD BETWEEN KIRK AND US. WE'RE so far back, we lose him a few times, then catch sight of the SUV on the rise of a hill or through a gap in the trees. He's heading toward Picton, but instead of going straight into the town, he takes a left toward Waring Corners. Traffic is slow moving along that stretch of road. We squeeze in behind a large motor home and keep Kirk in our sights all the way to Bloomfield.

He pulls onto a side street. We follow. He drives to the dead end and turns toward a warehouse. His SUV disappears behind the building. We pull over and park between two cars near a church about three blocks from the warehouse. We get out and walk the rest of the way on foot. We skirt the opposite side of the building from where he drove in. The warehouse looks abandoned. The windows are boarded up and it smells like garbage. We reach the back corner. Staying flat to the building, Gus peeks around. I peek around Gus. There's a woman in the passenger side of Kirk's SUV. She's left the door open on her side. She's wearing a blue shirt and white slacks. Her long wavy black hair curls down her back. She has one leg still hanging out of the SUV like she doesn't want to get all the way in. She's wearing white shoes like a nurse. We can't see her face because she's looking at

Kirk. A black Mercedes is parked next to the SUV. It's empty. It must be hers. They've come here to meet.

Suddenly, she leans over and kisses him. He jerks away. She slaps him so hard across the face that his head bounces off the window.

Gus isn't breathing. Neither am I.

Gus takes out her phone, points it at them, and starts recording a video.

I lean close to her shoulder so I can see the image on her phone. She pinches it wider, trying to zoom in. It's grainy but closer. Kirk reaches for the woman. I can't tell what he's doing at first. *Is he trying to hug her?* I look from the video to the SUV. I squint, trying to see what's happening. The woman is leaning back. I gasp when I see that Kirk has his hands around her neck. She's clawing at his arms and face. The white shoe drops from her foot as she kicks the door violently. We're not that far away. I can hear her choking. He's hurting her. He's going to kill her.

Gus's hand is shaking. Her mouth is open only she's not saying a word. She looks frozen. I grab her arm and tug. She doesn't move. I need her to do something—to help the woman. I start moving toward them but Gus grabs my shoulders and pulls me back behind the building. She holds me against the warehouse as I struggle to get free.

"What's wrong with you," I sputter.

"Stay here," she whispers. Then she lets go of me.

She looks around, searching the ground. Then she stoops, picks up a large stone, and runs for the SUV. When she's right behind it she throws the stone as hard as she can. It shatters the back window into a million tiny beads.

She races back to me.

"Run," Gus hollers.

I run.

We race along the side of the building and down the sidewalk. *Why did we park so far away?*

We run side by side toward the camper, never looking back. We jump in, lock the doors, and dive to the floor in the back. My heart is hammering against my chest like an angry fist.

Thump, thump, thumping for the woman and her poor neck.

Thump, thump, thumping for Kirk, who turned into a monster right in front of our eyes.

Gus tells me to take deep breaths. She holds my hand. I focus on the carpet fibers close to my face. They look like tiny bug legs wiggling as I pant hot breath on them. I smell chlorine. I almost throw up but I don't because someone's coming. I cover my mouth and squeeze my eyes shut.

I can hear a vehicle approaching from the direction of the warehouse. It rolls closer and closer then slows as it comes up beside us. We lie still as stones. Kirk knows the camper. He'll recognize it. The vehicle drives on. We keep lying there. Me, trying to calm my drumming heart. Gus, probably trying to figure out why she froze. A few seconds later, another vehicle passes by coming from the dead end. One of the vehicles must have been her. It had to be her. The nurse. He didn't kill her.

After a while, all we can hear is the hum of a lawn mower. Gus finally sits up. She tells me to wait where I am and then she's gone. I don't wait. I get to my feet and climb into the front seat. I watch through the window as she runs down the sidewalk then disappears around the building. I wait and watch. An old woman across the street lets her cat out the front door and glances over.

Seconds later, Gus is running back with something in her hand.

She jumps in. She has the woman's white shoe. She doesn't say anything.

"So?" I ask.

"Both vehicles were gone," says Gus, still holding the shoe.

"So she's okay if she drove away, right?" I say, trying to convince myself.

"Guess so." Gus stares at the shoe.

"You can drive without a shoe, right?" I say, continuing to reassure myself.

Gus nods. She's gone quiet. She's not helping me feel any better. I don't like it.

"Maybe it wasn't what it looked like," I suggest.

Gus doesn't agree or disagree. She just sits there, holding the stupid shoe.

"Maybe they were just play-fighting," I say.

She still gives me no comfort.

"Maybe they—" I try again, but Gus cuts me off.

"Enough," she says.

She tosses the shoe at my feet and starts the engine. She does a U-turn and heads down the street. I stare at the shoe. It has thick soles. Good arch support. It's made of rubber that looks easy to clean. It's a slip-on. No laces. A sensible shoe in a world that, right now, makes no sense at all.

We drive out of Bloomfield but I get the feeling Gus isn't headed anywhere. She looks lost. She doesn't check the map or look at road signs. Halfway back to Picton, she swings onto the shoulder of the highway near a bright yellow field of canola. She gets out without turning the engine off or shutting her door and walks over to the yellow flowers. Then she tips her head back and screams at the top of her lungs. I don't move an inch. It's a long, loud, scary scream, but when she stops, I see her shoulders relax. She takes some big breaths then she gets back in the camper.

"Pizza?" she asks, pulling onto the road. Her voice is hoarse.

I nod. I think she's okay now. Whatever was inside her had to come out. Another way she and I are alike. Hers are screams and mine are tears, but we both have to get them out. Maybe her scream has something to do with why she froze back at the warehouse.

We drive through Picton and stop at the Ultramar to get gas. It's buzzing with people excited to get where they're going. It's a holiday and everyone's waving Canadian flags or wearing red and white or orange. Cars towing tent trailers and jeeps topped with paddleboards flow in and out of the gas station. Gus points to a pizza place in a mini mall on the other side of the lot and hands me a twenty. I jump out and weave my way through the vehicles. I go into Pie Guy's Pizzeria while she fills the tank. I order a medium double-smoked bacon pizza with extra cheese, then I sit at the counter by the window and wait. The smells of melting cheese and sizzling bacon and pizza dough baking make me drool.

An OPP cruiser pulls up to the gas pump one over from Gus. I see her turn away when she spots them.

She stops pumping and fumbles with the gas cap.

One of the constables gets out. I know him. He's one of the two snickerers who drove us to the detachment when our Honda caught fire. He glances at Gus, then starts to fill up his vehicle. I can't tell if he recognizes her. Gus searches for me. Our eyes meet. She lifts her chin.

Time to go.

I ask if the pizza is ready. The young man behind the counter is playing some game on his phone tap, tap, tapping its screen. He holds up his finger. I can see the cheese bubbling through the window of the pizza oven. A drop of saliva escapes the corner of my mouth.

Gus is pulling away from the pump.

I stare at the pizza guy in desperation.

"Five more minutes," he says, then goes back to his phone.

I look out the window. I can't see our camper anymore, but

the second officer is now leaning on the roof of the cruiser talking to the first one who's pumping gas. He points. Has he spotted her? Are we about to be arrested for trespassing or breaking and entering or nearly hit-and-running over the park wardens?

I rush out of the door and search the parking lot. Gus has parked over by the washrooms at the back of the gas station. I hurry over and jump in. We circle the building and take a back exit onto Main.

"We have to go back. The pizza's almost ready," I whimper.

"Sorry, Boo, but we've got to get out of town. If those wardens caught our license plate number, Muirhead will be frothing at the mouth. He'll have his guys out looking for us. We got lucky back there, but we can't risk getting pulled over with all those baggies of god knows what," she says.

My stomach growls like there's a tiny bear inside it trying to claw its way out.

"At least we'd get fed in jail," I groan.

She doesn't care if I starve to death. She keeps driving. Farther and farther away from the bubbling, cheesy, mouthwatering pizza. She is a terrible mother and I hate her. I snap.

"I want my fucking double-smoked bacon pizza!" I holler.

She slowly looks over at me. I burst into tears.

We get caught in a holiday traffic jam, so it takes us forever to get out of town. Along the way, we pass a fish and chips stand, an outdoor market selling freshly baked pies, a grocery store, a burger joint, an ice cream vendor, and a diner before we finally reach the edge of town. We don't get followed or arrested or fed. My head aches. My stomach rumbles.

"I know somewhere we can go to get out of sight," she says.

I give her the silent treatment.

"There'll be buckets of food." She smiles.

Gus turns onto Highway 10 and we follow the signs to Salmon Point.

I don't care where we're going.

I'm too angry and hungry.

It's only when I see the big yellow house by the lake that it comes to me.

We're going to a Canada Day party.

17

THE EAGLE FEATHER

WE PULL INTO THE YARD AND THE BLOODHOUNDS COME GALLOP-
ing across the lawn. They growl and show their teeth and leap at
our windows.

Patience Perley is cranking a wheel next to a giant smoky
drum. The wheel turns a crispy pig on a stake. She's wearing a
white apron dotted with red maple leaves and a red cowboy hat.
She drops the handle of the wheel when she sees us. She waves
with both hands. A huge smile on her face.

"Bonnie! Clyde! Kennel," she hollers.

The dogs instantly obey. They hurtle across the yard to a large
kennel by the house. They squeeze through the door together and
lie down, panting and frothing at the mouth. I'm glad Bonnie
and Clyde are so well trained because they look like they could
bite my head off.

Down by the water, I can see two men arriving at a dock in a
motorboat. Dod is standing on the dock, jumping up and down.
He turns and sees us. He stops jumping, races off the dock, and
runs into a nearby wooded area.

"Dod Perley!" yells Patience. "You come back here right now.
We got company. Boys! Go get your brother!"

After they've wrestled Dod from the woods, the twins introduce themselves as JP and JW. Patience tells us their proper names are Jack Patrick Perley and Jason Wade Perley. Everyone looks happy we've come. Even Dod seems to warm up to the idea. In no time, we're put to work. Gus and I shuck the corn, the twins clean the fish, Dod folds the napkins, and Patience sets the large picnic table under the trellis next to the house. She brings out some homemade cinnamon rolls when she hears we haven't eaten all day. I devour two of them.

By midafternoon, we are gathered around the table. Bonnie and Clyde amble over, sniff our legs, then settle on the grass nearby, content to chew the strips of rawhide Patience has tossed them. Laid out on the table is a feast of corn on the cob, battered fish, roast pork, potato salad, candied carrots, coleslaw, and hot dinner rolls. *Buckets of food*, just like Patience and Gus promised. I don't eat any of the pork because all I can picture is the poor pig with his blackened eyes and that stake down his throat. But the rest of the feast is way more mouthwatering than that pizza ever could have been. I've never been happier to eat in my whole life.

Dod folded the red napkins to look just like maple leaves. I tell him I like them. He shoves an entire roll into his mouth and looks away. I notice his black eye has yellowed and faded quite a bit. I'm glad.

"Our Dodgeroo's not much of a talker," says Patience, ruffling his hair. "But he's definitely the artist in the family."

Being around the Perleys feels easy—and easy is exactly what Gus and I need right now. They tell us all about themselves as we eat. Dod is twenty and the twins are twenty-five.

"Different fathers, but brothers to the core," says Patience. "They'd move heaven and earth for each other, these boys would."

The twins look like wrestlers with thick necks, barrel chests, and small waists. And they have more in common than their looks. They both play rugby for the Belleville Bulldogs and they both work at the Lehigh Cement Plant in Picton. They're both volunteer firefighters for the county. And they eat like they're storing up for winter. Between giant helpings of pork and potato salad, the twins laugh and talk and joke and do their best to include Dod. Even when he doesn't answer, they add a *Right, Dod?* or a *Dod gets it* to whatever they're saying. I like this.

It makes me wish I had a brother or sister.

More than once, the twins compliment their mother on the food. Sometimes they say the same thing at the same time, like they can read each other's minds. Gus and I barely get a word in. But we don't mind. I think Gus is as happy as I am to be here, eating and laughing and watching this close-knit family enjoy one another's company. But Patience is a good host and she knows her boys won't stop talking so she shushes them and asks us about our life back in Ottawa. Gus tells them what grade I'm going into and what kind of house we live in. She hesitates a little so Patience changes the subject, not wanting to pry.

After dinner, the twins insist on teaching Gus the ins and outs of horseshoes. She lets them even though she knows how to play. We used to play on the beach when we were camping. Howard wasn't very good at it, but Gus was.

Patience clears the table and goes inside to do the dishes. She refuses to let me help so I go down to the dock where Dod is sitting with his toes in the cool water.

"Mind if I join you?" I ask.

He bobs his head so I sit beside him.

He kicks his feet lightly in the water. I do the same.

Then he kicks harder. Water splashes into my lap. He stops kicking and bows his head like he's done something bad. I kick my feet harder and splash him. We look at each other and both laugh.

"I like goats," he says.

"I like cows," I tell him.

"Moo-moo," he says.

"Moo-moo," I copy him.

He laughs like a kid, holding his belly.

"I like to ride my bike," he says.

"I have a bike too," I tell him. "I ride it to school."

"School-school," he says.

"Do you go to school?" I ask.

"I like the zoo," he says.

"Me too," I tell him.

"I like rain," he says.

"I like sunsets," I say, keeping the game going.

He points toward the glowing horizon. I nod.

We sit together and watch as the setting sun turns the clouds gold and orange. A flock of seagulls flies across the sky.

"Birdies," says Dod.

"You like birds?" I ask.

His face lights up. He pats the pockets of his clothes, front and back, searching for something. Then he finds it in the front pocket of his shorts.

"Birdie-birdie!" he chimes as he pulls a feather from his pocket. He's a bit of a squirrel, too, just like me. The feather is bent and missing a few bits but it's pretty. I think it's an eagle feather. He hands it to me. I shake my head.

"But it's yours," I tell him. "You found it."

He holds it close to my face until I take it.

"Thank you," I say with a nod.

He blushes and looks away.

I can hear the twins groaning loudly. I think they've figured out Gus knows how to throw a horseshoe. A screen door slams.

"Cake time," yells Patience.

Dod looks at the house then at me.

"Cake-cake," he says.

He scrambles to his feet. I put the feather in my back pocket and jump up. We race for the house. Despite the limp, Dod is fast. He easily beats me to the picnic table, where Patience has just placed a large slab of white cake. Miniature Canadian flags stick out of the cake and sparklers light it up. We all gather. I eat a huge piece of sugary cake even though I'm so full I could burst. Before he's done with his piece, Dod leaps up and runs over to a red bicycle leaning against the dog kennel.

"Bike-bike," he says, looking at me.

He wants to show me. There's an old bike lying next to the red one. The old one is twisted and rusting.

"We go ride," he says.

"Now, now. You come sit down and finish your cake, Dod. There's only the one good one. Your old one's not fit to ride no more, remember?" she says.

Patience cups a hand to her mouth like she's sharing a secret with the rest of us.

"I would've tossed that old bike long ago but he'd pitch a right fit if I did. The boy can't let go of anything."

I can relate. I'm a collector too. And I like old things.

Dod sits back down, folds his arms, and pouts.

"I know. You love to ride your bike," says Patience. "He goes all over the county on it."

"Aren't you worried about all the trucks on the highways?" Gus asks.

"He keeps mostly to the woods. He knows all the trails. Or he walks," she says.

"Walk-walk," he says.

"You know it," she says, nudging his shoulder. "He can walk all the way to Picton and back if he puts his mind to it," she says. She's proud of him.

"Bad eye," he says, frowning.

"Yes, bad eye. Dod got that shiner on one of his recent walk-abouts. He borrowed the wrong boy's bike," she tells us. "I've tried to tell him—you can't hop on any old bike just because you're tired of walking. That's why I got you that new one."

I bet that's what happened with the pink bike the day I met Dod. He got tired and borrowed it. He didn't mean to steal it.

Dod looks at his mother like a child scolded. She wraps her arm around him and kisses the top of his head. He winces.

When it gets dark, the twins set off fireworks from the dock, then we all sit around their firepit with marshmallows and choco-late and cookies. Dod insists on being the roaster for everyone. The twins try to give him advice. *Not too close. Now keep turning. Don't let it catch fire. That's it.* In the end, every marshmallow catches fire. JW keeps adding logs. The flames rise above our heads. The starless night sky fills with sparks. The yard and woods and lake vanish into blackness. It's like we're floating in a sea of sparks and the rest of the world has disappeared.

Eventually it's time for the twins to head home. They share an apartment in Picton. They tell us they're glad we came by. It made their day. I help Dod get the dogs ready for bed in their kennel. He fills their water bowls and makes sure the straw they sleep on is fluffed into a nice, big pile. He gives each bloodhound a kiss on the head and makes me do the same. I don't want to, but I do it for Dod. The dogs still scare me a little. Then Dod goes into the house without a word and doesn't come back out. I see him peek-ing from an upstairs window. I wave and he ducks out of sight.

"He doesn't do well with good-byes," explains Patience. "And there's no point in waving. He only waves to family. I taught him that to keep him out of trouble. Draw less attention to himself. In these parts, if a boy like Dod waves to the wrong person, they might take it the wrong way, if you know what I mean."

I hate that Dod is bullied.

"Thanks for everything. It's about time we headed off too," says Gus.

I wish we could stay.

Patience says we're welcome to camp in her yard for the night. We have nowhere to go and I don't feel like parking on some dark country road. Unexpectedly, my wish comes true. Gus agrees. It's late. And I think she likes the idea of staying out of sight for the night. I jump into the camper and get into my sleeping bag. It's a warm, still night. Gus tucks me in and joins Patience by the fire. When she goes, she props the side doors open a little bit to let in the breeze, but not so wide that our evidence wall is facing out.

I can hear the distant echoes of people and music from Canada Day celebrations. Laughter and singing ricochet across the bay from cottages and campsites on the other side. Patience and Gus are talking, their voices raised above the crackling fire. I can hear every word. I like knowing they're just a few feet away. I feel safe. I close my eyes and listen.

"It was my grandma Clara's house. It's been in the Perley family for a century. I was raised here and I'll take my last gasp here if I have my way," says Patience.

"It's a beautiful spot to grow up," says Gus.

"We have about a hundred acres all told across the county," she says. "My grandma left me the land and my brother, Toby, got the family business—the garage—which he successfully turned to shit but that's Tobias for ya."

"How do you manage all the land on your own without . . ." Gus pauses.

"A man?" Patience finishes her sentence for her.

"I didn't mean—" says Gus.

"It's all good. Aside from this place, most of it is worthless marshland, so there's little to no upkeep. This spring I sold off the only other parcel of any value. A stretch over near the shore of East Lake. And the boys help me out of course."

"What about the boys' fathers?" Gus asks. "They around?"

"The first one hauled his ass outta here before the twins could even walk and the second, he wasn't good for Dod. He couldn't see how special his son was. Fancies himself a big man in the county so he doesn't want people talking bad about him. Most of the time, he pretends he don't have a son. His loss," she says. "He comes sniffing around for a little sugar once in a blue moon, but we're a package deal, me and Dod. And this sweet, sweet package ain't for the takin'."

Her laugh echoes across the yard. Gus laughs too. It makes me smile.

"Did you ever get married?" asks Gus.

"Nope. Not to either one of them losers. It's why my boys got the Perley name. 'Cause they're mine and no one else's," she says.

"You're a good mum," Gus offers.

"So are you," Patience says back.

"I don't know about that," replies Gus.

"She's a great kid. *You* did that," says Patience.

I hear wood being tossed into the firepit.

"How long are you booked at the park?" asks Patience.

"We don't actually have a campsite. We've been sort of trespassing," says Gus.

"You little rebel." Patience chuckles.

"We're here looking for someone," Gus confesses.

"The one who disappeared?"

"Yeah. Howard."

"He's your man?"

"He is."

"You two married?"

"No, but we had—we *have* a pretty good life together back in

Ottawa. He works as a freelance journalist. I work at the Canadian Museum of History—at least I did. I've been on leave ever since he— Anyway, he loves his work; writing, discovering new things, talking to people," says Gus.

"What was—*is* he like?" asks Patience.

"He's the best. He's good and kind and smart. He's great with Bly. He's not her father but we've been together since she was a baby so they're super tight. She calls him Howard but he is her dad as far as I'm concerned. We're a family," Gus says. Her voice cracks.

"You miss him," says Patience.

"It's more than that. He's a part of me," says Gus. "I'm not sure if I'll ever be whole again if we don't find out what hap—" Gus stops talking.

I open my eyes and tears stream out the sides and pool in my ears.

"What do you think happened?" asks Patience.

"All I know for sure is that he started out writing a story about bird migration. Then his main source didn't check out so the story was going nowhere. Only things took a turn. Howard stumbled on something bigger. I think there's a military connection. Whatever it was, someone didn't want him looking into it. He thought he was being followed and that's when he went missing."

"Holy shit," says Patience.

"Yeah, holy shit," echoes Gus. "Some fuckwad around here knows the truth."

"Fuckwads always do," says Patience.

"I'm going to find out what happened to Howard if it's the last thing I do," says Gus.

"I'll drink to that," says Patience.

"Here's to fucking with the fuckwads," shouts Gus.

They laugh and I hear the clunk of beer cans as they toast.

But instead of making me smile, the laughing makes me sad. I miss him. I wish I could hear Howard's laugh. I hug my pillow and his phone thuds onto the floor. I've kept it tucked under there every night since we found it. I pick it up and press the home button. The screen lights up. I stare at the picture he put on his home screen.

It was taken in our backyard in Ottawa when I was six. It's me and Gus and Howard squished together in the hammock that we hung every summer between the two maples. We stopped hanging it after he was gone. Howard's arm is reached out in front of him because he's the one taking the selfie. It's a funny photo because Gus and I are both cringing in pain. We've just banged heads trying to get settled in the swaying hammock. Howard is the only one smiling with his big toothy grin. The one that lights up his whole face.

Nothing like the one in the video he made.

I place my finger over the camera app on his phone but I can't bring myself to open it and play that video—even though I want to see his face more than anything. I scroll through his texts and emails, then I tap on his phone messages and listen to one. The one with the woman's voice.

It's me. Did you get it? Oh my god, I hope he gave it to you before—I can't believe he's dead. Don't call me. Please. I can't do this anymore.

I look across the camper at the evidence wall on the back of the half-open side doors. It's dark out so I can't see it very well, but I know it's there. Written across the bottom panel of the left door. A question Gus wrote in red marker.

Who is the dead man from the voice mail?

I think I know our next mission.

18

THE MAGNET

I'M UP THE NEXT MORNING BRIGHT AND EARLY, WAY BEFORE GUS. I get dressed, make coffee, and do some digging. The Canada Day feast has perked up my entire body and the coffee I've been sipping for hours has my thoughts whizzing about like a hummingbird. Once I've done all I can do, I sit on my bed staring at the evidence wall and I wait. The morning sun slants through the windows of the camper. Gus finally stirs. She rubs her eyes. *About time. It's almost eleven.* Before she can even open her mouth to speak, a parade of words marches out of me.

"Okay, here's what I found out. The *County Gazette* stopped printing last year when they went digital, so their online archives only go back, like, twelve months. I checked. *But* their website says they have print copies of back issues from the last decade at their offices in Picton. The *Gazette*'s all local, so they write about anything that happens in the county—news, accidents, crimes, births, deaths, all of it. That's how we find out who *he* is. The dead guy in that message on Howard's phone. I even know who can help us. The reporter." I point to the newspaper clipping on our evidence wall. "Colton Bassett. He wrote the article about Pike. He probably knows all about her. We can kill two birds with one big fat stone. Not that I want to kill any birds, but you know what I mean, right?"

Gus props herself on her pillow and rubs her eyes.

"You might want to pull back on the caffeine." She smiles.

"Look. Your number one rule," I tell her, nodding to the doors beside her.

She turns her head to look at what I've added to our evidence wall. While she was sleeping right there next to it, I crawled up beside her. The nurse's shoe now sits inside the cupholder of one door and the photo of Howard and the military document are taped to the doors.

"Assemble all the evidence," I remind her.

I get up, walk over, and point to the new red *X* I've also added to the map.

"That's the military airfield. I googled it," I say.

Her eyebrows lift as she nods. I can tell she's impressed.

"This has to stay on the wall." I point to the first baggie of diamonds I found.

I see from the look on her face that she'd forgotten it was there when she hid the others.

"It's a new rule," I tell her. "Don't mess with the mojo of the evidence wall."

"Good one," she says, not like she's humoring me but like she thinks it's a good rule.

If anyone saw what we'd done to the inside of the camper doors, they'd probably think it was some weird art project—a ribbon, a dragonfly lure, a mask, a coaster, a flower, a shoe, a photo, documents, business cards, and a map covered in red *X*s. But to me, it's the beginning of a trail. And each thing matters. Whether it was given or found or dropped or stolen or it floated to us on the wind, each was meant to have a spot on our wall. I can feel it in my bones.

They are breadcrumbs.

As Gus gets dressed, I hear the squeak of the hinges on the screen door of the house. I get out of the camper van and see Dod sitting on the front porch eating a banana. I wander over and he offers me half. Gus joins us as Patience comes out of the house. She tells us we're welcome to park on her property as long as we like, but Gus says we have to go. Patience doesn't try to convince us or ask where we're going. I think she knows Gus has made up her mind. And she's right. We have a new mission waiting. Thanks to me.

Dod hovers behind his mother as Patience hands us a tin of her cinnamon rolls. She wishes us well and we say our goodbyes. Dod runs into the house without a word or a wave, but I'm not insulted. We drive back along Salmon Point Road then head for Picton.

THE *COUNTY GAZETTE* OFFICES ARE NEXT TO THE REGENT THE-atre on Main. Gus knows where they are. Three years ago, she posted notices on signposts on every street corner in Picton and bought ad space in the local paper once a week—offers of a reward with Howard's picture on them. The front desk receptionist knew her well, but Gus never met Colton Bassett or anyone else in the back offices.

It's a Saturday, almost noon, and the town is clogged with traffic again. We park in an alley a few blocks from the *Gazette* so the camper won't be spotted if they're looking for us. No one's at the front desk when we walk into the lobby, but there's a bell on the counter so Gus rings it. We hear a chair squeak, then something clatters to the floor, then footsteps patter toward us. A young woman peers around a door behind the reception desk. She pushes her glasses up the bridge of her nose and squints like an old woman.

"Sorry, we're closed. Canada Day weekend and all?" she calls out. "Yay, colonialism."

She gives us a weak little fist pump like a bored cheerleader.

"Oh, we're from out of town. We didn't know. And the door was unlocked," says Gus.

The woman slips into the lobby.

"My bad. Guess you caught me," she replies with a hoot, holding up both hands like we have a gun pointed at her.

Her long dark hair is shaved close on one side of her head and bleached white. She's wearing faded wide-leg jeans and a BLONDIE T-shirt. She can't be much older than twenty. As she comes closer, I realize *she* might be a *he*. I can't tell. She has piercings in each eyebrow, long sideburns down each cheek, and stubble on her chin. She's wearing a black bra that shows through the sheer T-shirt. Maybe she's not a *he* or a *she* but somewhere in between.

"They don't call me felonious for nothing." She laughs.

Gus looks at her with a blank stare.

"I'm just pulling your leg. I'm not a felon. No B&E going on here." Now she snorts.

"You work here?" Gus asks.

"I do at that. But full transparency, I am not actually supposed to be on said premises outside regular business hours, so this'll be *our little secret*," she whispers.

She pulls her T-shirt to her ears like she's hiding.

She's funny and strange and awkward. I don't even know her but I like her already.

"I get my best research done in the peacefulness of quiet," she adds.

Now I know why I like her. She reminds me of Howard. He can be strange and awkward too. She pulls keys from her pocket and holds them up. She wants us to leave so she can lock up behind us.

"Is Colton Bassett here?" tries Gus.

The woman bursts out laughing.

"Sorry. Um, *no*," she says. "He'll be deep in a gin coma until Monday morning. What do you want with Cole?"

"He wrote an article about Marica Pike a few years back and we were hoping to pick his brain," Gus says.

"Slim pickings." She snorts again.

The woman checks her watch, darts past us, pushes the front door open, and holds it.

"'Vineyards to Wind Yards'?" I add.

"Oh, Jesus, *that* ignominy." She grimaces. "His sole contribution was dreaming up that hideous headline. He didn't actually write the article."

"His name's on it," Gus tells her.

"Welcome to my world as Colton Bassett's intern, slash aspirin wrangler, slash designated driver, slash ghostwriter," she says with yet another snort. "Cole hasn't penned one of his own articles since they hired me four years ago when he left his way with words on a barstool around the corner. He's been searching for them in every pub across the county ever since."

She winks.

"I do the research and writing. He gives the copy a blurry-eyed once-over, makes a few scribbles with his little red pen, then puts his name on it and Bob's your uncle, or in this case, Bob's his brother and he owns the paper."

"That's not fair," I say.

She smiles and lets the door close.

"Hildy Flood at your service," she says, holding out her hand.

"Gus Monet," says Gus, taking Hildy's hand.

"I'm Bly Monet," I tell her, and she shakes mine too.

I like that. Most grown-ups don't bother shaking kids' hands. She also looks me in the eye. Howard always said you could tell a lot about a person if they looked you in the eye. You could see they were really paying attention to you and you could feel their energy. Hildy has good energy—and lots of it. Her body bobs and sways almost constantly. Maybe that's why she needs the peacefulness of quiet because she's so noisy inside.

"Don't get me wrong, it's not all *woe is me*. I get to do what I love," says Hildy.

She uses her key to lock the door.

"Come on back. You can pick my brain," she says.

Hildy leads the way into a large, bright room behind the lobby. Eight desks are arranged in two rows. There are file holders and computers and lamps on each desk. A bank of windows with crooked blinds runs along the back of the room, looking into a parking lot. Hildy drags two chairs over to her desk then sits across from us in her rolling office chair.

"7UP?" she offers.

She rolls backward to a kitchenette with a small counter, coffeemaker, sink, and fridge. We both say no thanks, so she grabs a can from the fridge for herself. The fridge is completely covered in magnets. Hildy rolls back to her desk.

"You know what? Now that I'm getting a good look at you, I remember seeing you around here a couple of years ago," she says to Gus. "We never met but I saw you out front. You had all those posters. You were looking for that journalist who disappeared, right? Howard Baylis," she says.

"Good memory," says Gus.

"Hard to forget those posters. His obituary came across my desk last week," she says.

"His parents' doing, not mine," says Gus.

"Heard they found the vehicle he was driving," she says.

"Our camper van. They did," says Gus.

"But he was never found, right?" she asks.

Gus shakes her head.

"Sorry. That's rough. You're in town for the funeral?" she asks.

"The tornado put a stop to that," says Gus.

"I guess it did," says Hildy.

"Do you remember ever seeing Howard? Did he ever come by? Maybe to ask questions or do some research?" Gus asks.

"Don't think so," says Hildy. "If he did, I wasn't the one he spoke to. I'd remember."

She pops the lid on her 7UP and takes a swig. It looks ice cold. I am so thirsty all of a sudden.

"You have questions about what's in the Pike article?" Hildy asks.

"More about what's *not* in the article," says Gus.

"That would be Cole's little red pen at work." She rolls her eyes.

Hildy tells us what she knows about Marica Pike. Gus takes notes. Some of it we already know from the article. The stuff about how Pike grew up in Cornwall and studied chemistry at Queens then got married, had a kid, and got divorced before she moved to the county. She bought land and opened a winery. It became one of the most successful wineries in Prince Edward County.

Then Hildy shares what wasn't in the article.

"There were rumors Pike's whole enterprise was backed by some casino bigwigs from the Thousand Islands, but the money trail was murky and I could never get a foothold onto it. I dug into her background a little. Her parents were small-town, working-class folks. There's no money in her family tree. But I swear it's like she's growing dollar bills on those grapevines of hers. For years she's been buying up prime land all along the peninsula with an eye to launching this massive wind park project. When it's completed, her park is going to power the entire county and beyond. That's a lot of power for one woman. She'll own more than just a few grapes. *She'll own us all*," Hildy says with an evil laugh.

"So the project has started?" Gus asks.

"It's about to. Marica Pike got the last of those pesky regulatory permits she needed this winter. Construction begins soon. Nothing can stop her now, not even Will Stenson."

"You know Stenson?" Gus asks.

"Not personally, but it's a small town. I knew all about his one-man crusade against Pike's wind park. I heard the gossip about him and his daughter. But the second I started poking around, management put the kibosh on it. I was just trying to write something real about Pike. When the Stenson angle didn't fly, I got the contact info for an old roommate of hers from university, but Cole shut that down too. Wouldn't even let me make the call. He tossed me a glossy Pike Winery brochure and the wind park investment portfolio and told me that's all the research I needed. You've read the article. It's a puff piece. I'm actually grateful they didn't put my name on it.

"Stenson left a dead bird on our doorstep when the article came out and a note that said, *Do your fucking job*. He was right, we weren't. But Pike was cozy with the Bassetts, so puffery was all she wrote." Hildy shrugs, sits back, and sips her 7UP.

She notices me eyeing her drink and nods toward the kitchenette.

"Help yourself, little sister," she tells me, and I do.

I wander over to the kitchenette, open the fridge, and grab a can. I take a closer look at the magnet collection on the fridge. They're all from local businesses and tourist spots—wineries, an ice cream parlor, a bookstore, an insurance company, Sandbanks Provincial Park, and the Prince Edward County Chamber of Commerce. I wonder if it's Hildy who collects them.

"You still have that number for Pike's roommate kicking around?" asks Gus.

"Let me find that for you," says Hildy. "It's no use to me."

Hildy starts tapping away on her laptop.

"Why the interest in Pike?" she asks.

"Just doing a little of my own digging," says Gus. "You never know where it'll lead."

Hildy nods and starts writing a number on a piece of paper.

"Do you believe what they say about Stenson?" Gus asks.

"The rumor mill sure ground his reputation to a pulp. But it doesn't make any of it true. Folks even say his kid joined a cult. What do they know? People will say anything if it gets them out of paying for the next round. I feel for the dude. The man's family left him. He lost everything. And after all that, he didn't even manage to save his beloved birds from Pike's turbines."

Gus and Hildy keep talking, but I tune them out. One of the magnets has caught my eye. It's shaped like a castle and the words *Picton Fairgrounds* are written across it. We went to the fairgrounds once when I was five. We ate cotton candy and rode the roller coaster and took a selfie in front of the castle, which was called the Crystal Palace. A clown made me an elephant out of twisted balloons, and Howard won a giant panda at the ring toss.

Mostly I remember the sky. The clouds turned coral pink as the sun went down. Howard said they looked just like my cotton candy. I didn't want the day to end. We stood in a crowd listening to a country singer strumming a guitar on the main stage. I don't remember who the musician was, but I remember Howard lifted me onto his shoulders and it felt like the clouds were close enough for me to reach up and touch them.

"I have another favor to ask," says Gus. "Is there any way we could look through your archives and check out some old back issues of the *Gazette* from three years ago?"

Hildy leaps out of her rolling chair and sends it crashing into a filing cabinet behind her.

"Hell, yeah, there's a way!" she shouts, rubbing both hands together.

It turns out Hildy is the queen of the archives. In fact, the *County Gazette*'s messy storeroom, full of old newspapers, is why she got her job in the first place. When she's not *bending the knee* to Colton Bassett, her other role is archivist. She's spent the last four years digitizing and cataloguing all the back issues that were stacked randomly on the shelves in the storeroom. She single-handedly built a search engine for the entire database. It's a big job, but she's almost done. She sounds superproud of her database. Hildy is a lot like Gus. She loves digging into the past.

Part of Hildy's job has been to track down any missing newspapers. A local hoarder has been a godsend, she tells Gus. The woman had a decade's worth of stockpiled *Gazette*s, and that's where Hildy found most of the missing issues. Once her database is finished, the *Gazette* will make the archives public.

But Hildy is *tickled pink* to have a *real-world* opportunity to take her search engine for a test drive. She enters the dates and key words Gus is looking for and after just a few keystrokes, she finds five matches and prints out the documents for us. Gus and Hildy exchange numbers, just in case Gus has more questions. Hildy tells her she's happy to help and she hopes we find what we're looking for.

As we walk back to the alley, I can feel the fairgrounds magnet pressing against my ankle. I took it off the fridge and tucked it into my sock. It reminded me of Howard and I had to have it. I told myself no one would notice. There were so many magnets. But it wasn't mine to take.

And yet, I don't run back and confess.

I don't put it right.

The old me would have in a heartbeat.

This me just keeps walking.

19

THE TWO BIRDS

HILDY WAS OUR STONE—AND MY IDEA TO GO TO THE *GAZETTE* had been a good one. She helped us kill two birds. The first one was the dead man. Three years ago, in August when everything changed for us, it also changed for five other people in the county. That week, the *Gazette* published three obituaries and two news flashes about accidental deaths.

The obituaries are all for seniors who died in long-term care homes. Natural causes. Pneumonia. Cancer. One news flash is from the day Howard went missing. August 23. It's about a young boy who drowned at West Lake. He was from Barrie, Ontario, on vacation with his parents. The other news flash is from the day before Howard disappeared. A local man broke his neck when he fell off a ladder cleaning his gutters. That has to be the man that the woman was talking about in her message on Howard's phone when she said *I can't believe he's dead*.

The local man's name was Boyd Barton. Occupation: accountant at Bayshore Casino. Survived by his wife, Annie. There's a black-and-white photo of forty-eight-year-old Boyd Barton. He has a long, twisty mustache and bushy eyebrows. I know that mustache. I tape the news flash to the evidence wall.

It's midafternoon and we're parked at Millennium Lookout

again. Gus likes it up here because it's close to town and no one seems to come around. No police, no Creepy Man, no wardens. We're sitting at the dining table in the back of the camper, eating cold ravioli straight from the can, when I remember where I saw the Mustache Man. I scan the evidence wall. I find the photo of Howard at his parents' party. There he is, standing in the background. I look at the news flash. Yep. It's him. Boyd Barton was at the party that summer.

I point to the two pictures of Boyd.

"Excellent work," she says.

She leans closer.

"Look who Boyd's staring at." She points to the woman with her back to the camera. The one with the swirly hair.

"Pike. He looks kind of like he's—" I search for the right word.

"About to lose his shit?" offers Gus.

I nod.

"Howard doesn't look thrilled to be there, either," she adds.

He *doesn't* look happy. It's a strange picture for his parents to want on their fridge but maybe they kept it because it's the last one taken of their son.

Gus picks up her phone while I finish my ravioli. She searches for a listing for Boyd and Annie Barton. She finds it and calls the number. It's disconnected.

She leans back, her eyes darting up, like she's searching her mind.

"Howard, Boyd, and Pike were all at that party," she starts. "Boyd worked as an accountant for a casino and Hildy said Pike was rumored to be in with some casino bigwigs. Same casino?"

"Maybe they knew each other," I say.

She picks up her phone again. This time she searches the Vintners Association's website and finds out that their annual event that year was August 21.

"I remember that party now. I didn't want to go because I hate making small talk, especially about wine, so we stayed behind at the campsite that day, and Howard went alone. It seemed important to him to go. I thought it was because his parents were hosting," says Gus. "The next day, Boyd had his accident. And the following day, a message is left on Howard's phone about a dead man, then Howard goes missing. I think something happened at that party."

I look at the photo. Howard's shoulders are tight and his head is bowed. I wish he could tell me what he's thinking as he stares down, his fist clenched. Then I see he's holding something. I hadn't noticed it before.

"What's that in his hand?" I say, pointing.

Gus leans in closer.

"I can't tell," she says.

We both lean in, ear to ear.

"I think it's a corkscrew," I say.

All we can see is the tip of a metal object poking from his closed fist.

"You're right," says Gus.

We sit back down. We're trying too hard to see clues. But sometimes it's just what it looks like. A corkscrew at a party where there's lots and lots of wine.

Gus moves on. She decides to try the number Hildy gave her for Pike's roommate at Queens. The other bird.

His name is Ahmed Shammas. Hildy said they shared an apartment in Kingston for five years. Gus puts her phone on speaker so I can listen in.

Ahmed picks up after five rings. He sounds half asleep. Gus says she'd like to ask him a few questions about Marica Pike. He thinks it's the police calling until Gus tells him about Howard's disappearance and how it might be connected to Pike's winery or maybe her wind park project.

"Wind park? Mare never gave one single fuck about the planet." He laughs.

He says he knows all about her being a big shot winemaker in Prince Edward County but he hasn't talked to her since Queens. Ahmed sounds tired and irritated, like he'd rather be talking about anyone else. He says he can't help.

"Why'd you think we were cops?" asks Gus.

"I was hoping she finally got what was coming to her," he says through a yawn.

"Weren't you two friends?" Gus asks.

"Two peas, once upon a time," he answers.

"Doesn't sound like you're her biggest fan. What changed?" asks Gus.

He's quiet, like he's thinking about whether or not to answer. Gus tries to encourage him.

"Listen, we're not fans of hers, either, but we lost someone we care about and we're just trying to find him. Anything you can tell us about her would be a big help," pleads Gus.

Ahmed still says nothing.

"How did you two meet?" she asks, hoping to get him talking.

He sighs.

"It was frosh week. She sat next to me on the bus to a football game. We started talking. Hit it off. She hadn't found a place to live yet and my roommate had just bailed so she moved in the next day. Lucky for both of us. At least I thought so. I know better now. Nothing is ever left to luck or chance in Marica Pike's world. Later, I figured out she already knew who I was and that my family had their name on the side of the science building. She'd probably followed me around and made sure she sat beside me on that bus.

"Mare always got what she wanted. Her dad worked at a landfill and her mom ran a day care out of their house. It's not like they could afford Queens. That didn't stop her. Step one: get herself a scholarship—a full ride. Step two: get in with the trust fund kids. I was her ticket into that world. I'll give her kudos. Mare was a smart cookie and driven as fuck. She had her whole future mapped out—literally on a vision board. She was laser focused on the road ahead. Never looked back. Like the whole time we lived together, she never once invited her parents to visit and she never called them. It was like they didn't exist. She never went home—not for Christmas or summer break—not once. She just put her head down and did the work. Studied her ass off. She wasn't like all the other douchebags on campus who couldn't see past the next kegger. She was different. I liked that about her. It rubbed off on me and I buckled down too. She helped me get through undergrad and then into grad school. Like I said, we were two peas for a few years. Then we weren't."

"What happened?" says Gus.

He laughs.

"What's so funny?" she asks.

He pauses before answering. When he does, his voice cracks a little.

"I don't even know you, but you're the first person to ask me that. My parents, my profs, the dean, my so-called friends—none of those assholes ever asked me what happened. None of them wanted to hear it. They'd already decided I was just some rich kid who threw away his golden future. The fuckup they always thought I was. The dumbass who couldn't hack grad school. And I had no proof, so what was the point in trying to tell anyone." He sighs.

Ahmed pauses, lets out a long, shaky breath like he's trying to soothe himself. Then he goes on.

"It started in the final term of grad school. Mare was burning a lot of midnight oil over at the chem lab. I barely saw her anymore. I figured she was trying to get a leg up on the other lab rats. All of us were competing for the same research positions and trying to stand out. We were rivals but we all knew the game and we played fair. Mare even came to my rescue when I failed my final thesis the first time round. She helped me with revisions and prep so I had the best shot at redefending my work.

"But this one night I go down to the lab to check on one of my experiments and that's when I see her. She's cooking. She denied it. Said it was a thing for school. The fuck it was. Nail polish remover and liquid drain cleaner? I wasn't an idiot. I told her she could get into big trouble—like life-in-prison trouble. I think she thought it was a threat. Next day, she moved out of our apartment, switched lab partners, stopped taking my calls and texts. She ghosted me. Then the day before I'm supposed to go before the committee, copies of my thesis go missing and my laptop gets wiped clean. I go down to the lab. My samples have been soaked in red food dye. The experiment I'd been working on was completely fucked and so was I. That was my last chance. Mare knew it."

"I'm really sorry that happened to you," says Gus.

"Yeah, me too. No cap and gown for Ahmed. Mare made damn sure of that," he says.

"What was she cooking?" asks Gus. I was wondering the same thing.

"Crystal meth. She was experimenting—refining the recipe. Mare didn't give a fuck about getting her master's or winning some research position—she just wanted the chem know-how and the lab access. She even told me as much in third year of undergrad. Her mom showed up out of the blue, uninvited. Mare flipped her lid. Shut the door right in her mom's face, then she started in on the wine. Mare didn't drink so she got completely blotto. She stood on the sofa, ranting and waving that wine bottle around. She'd show everyone, she said. She was going to open a big-ass lab one day. Thought she could use a winery or a brewery as a front. Said it would be the perfect cover where product could come and go and no one would suspect a thing. She already had her eye on a quiet little town with a couple of small airfields. She had it all figured out, although I doubt her plan included blurting it all out in a drunken stupor. Eventually she passed out but not before announcing at the top of her lungs that she was going to be the Crystal Queen. We never talked about it. She didn't remember anything. I thought it was bullshit. But when I caught her cooking in the lab, I remembered that rant. She knew I knew so she got my ass tossed out of grad school and I never saw her again. When I read about her winery, I knew she'd done it."

"So you think the winery's a front for a drug lab?" Gus asks.

"Like I said, Mare always had a vision for her future. I bet that wind park is just another one of her schemes. Clean energy, hah! More like a way to clean cash, I'm guessing," he says.

"You never thought about payback?" Gus asks. "Putting the cops onto her?"

Then he says something I wish he hadn't.

"I like breathing," he says.

After we hang up with Ahmed, Gus opens the windows to let in some air. We drink cream soda and wipe sweat from our foreheads. It's hot inside the camper, but I have chills.

"What's crystal meth?" I ask her.

"It's a very nasty addictive drug. Really bad stuff," she says.

"And Pike makes it and sells it?" I ask.

"Looks like she does. If Howard was on to her, he'd want to be absolutely sure he had enough evidence," Gus says. "It looks like he got his hands on some of her product."

She points to the glittery stones in the baggie on our evidence wall.

I stare at them and realize they're not diamonds at all.

"He hid them at Butterfly Beach so they wouldn't be anywhere near us," she says. "But he would have needed more. Someone to tie the drugs to her whole operation. A linchpin, like he said. Someone willing to talk. An insider. Someone who worked for Pike."

"Like an accountant?" I offer.

"Except Boyd was dead when Howard got the text that morning," says Gus. "He was meeting someone else."

"The Canary," I say.

Gus gazes up at the evidence.

"It's all here," she says.

"Where?" I ask, scanning the wall.

"It always is. We just can't see it yet," she answers.

I finish my cream soda. She's right, I can't see it.

Then her eyes narrow.

"Ahmed said something about airfields," she says to herself more than me.

Gus looks closely at the notes Howard scribbled on the CFD Quinte Airfield document, then she picks up her phone and searches for something. She smiles.

"Now that's a happy coincidence. Three years ago, those dates Howard marked down—they were both Saturdays," she announces like that's supposed to mean something to me.

I stare at her.

"Today's a Saturday," she says. Her lip curls and her eyes light up.

I know that look.

20

THE PAINTED CARD

IT'S 8:30 P.M. WHEN WE PULL OFF THE HIGHWAY INTO A FIELD and park behind a barn. The sun's almost down. We passed a farmhouse a half mile back. The blue light of a TV flickered in the living room. Everyone was in for the night. The barn is probably on their land but it's far enough away that they won't be able to see our vehicle trespassing from their front window. Gus pulls the camper behind the barn, enough to hide us, but not so far that we can't see the entrance to the large property across the road. She turns off the engine and we wait and watch Pike Winery.

Gus has a hunch that Pike was using the military airfield to transport her drugs somewhere. Just like Ahmed said. *A quiet little town with a couple of small airfields.* If that was true three years ago, maybe it still is and maybe those drop-offs still happen on Saturdays. And if Pike does have a drug lab at the winery, this is where the deliveries would come from, and the military airfield is where they'd end. Maybe Howard was staking out the winery, too, says Gus.

If he was, I like that we're doing what he did. Taking each step he took. Because eventually all those steps and all those clues and all those breadcrumbs will lead to him.

At 8:55 P.M. a burgundy truck comes down the laneway. As

it turns right, the truck passes under a streetlight and the man's face is lit up for a few seconds. Even from this far away, I can tell it's Creepy Man. He heads in the direction of Quinte Airfield. We follow.

The open farmland and the truck's headlights help keep him in our sights. We stay well back. He crisscrosses the county, along Highway 10 to Huff's Corners, where he makes a right onto Highway 62. After driving about two and a half miles, he takes a left onto Burr Road and disappears into a wooded area. Gus slows down as we approach the intersection. We can't see his lights so she turns onto Burr Road. We drive slowly until we spot his red taillights through the trees way down a narrow road. A sign by the road says MAINTENANCE ENTRANCE #7. There's a CFD Quinte Airfield logo on the sign.

Gus and I look at each other.

"ME7," I say, remembering the note Howard wrote on the military document.

"Guess we're in the right place," says Gus.

Gus turns off the headlights and drives down the dirt road. We inch along. About halfway, she turns the camper around so it's facing back the way we came, then she opens her door.

"I'll be right back," she says.

Before I can say anything, she's gone, leaving the door open and the camper running.

Suddenly I'm alone in the dark. Only I'm not alone. Birds are swooping overhead. All I can see are black shapes against a deep blue sky. They're so fast I can barely follow them. Always birds. Everywhere birds. Canaries, eagles, dead birds, cuckoo birds. Is the world trying to tell me something? One hits the roof. Then another. They're gathering. Swarming. I want to yank her door shut but I can't move. I want to scream. I want to run after Gus but I don't know where she is.

Then I see that they aren't birds. They're bats. Howard told me bats can eat thousands of bugs in a single night. I relax. *Bats are our friends*, he used to say. I slowly roll down my window.

"Thank you, friends," I call out to the bats.

They don't answer. Only the crickets and cicadas talk to me. The bats are busy eating.

I nearly scream when Gus appears. She jumps in, pulls the door shut, and slams her foot on the gas pedal. She's out of breath like she's been running.

"Fuck, fuck, fuck" is all she says as she tries to put on her seat belt.

I help her, locking it in place.

"What happened?" I ask.

"It was a drop-off all right. They were unloading crates of wine bottles. I could hear them clinking. That's how they hide the drugs. I snuck up beside the truck and right there on the front seat was a pile of baggies just like the ones Howard had. I tried to open the door but they heard me. I ran," she says, panting heavily.

I check the sideview mirror. I see headlights coming after us. We're going fast, but they're going faster and getting closer. We make it to Burr Road and Gus skids left then floors it to the highway. I grip the dashboard. The delivery truck exits the dirt lane seconds later. He's only a few yards behind us. We get lucky when we make the right onto the 62 just ahead of three cars. Creepy Man has to wait until they pass before he can follow us. Gus puts some distance between us and him. We make it to Bloomfield before we see his headlights pass the three cars, but by then we're on the far side of town. Gus turns off the main street and takes a back road into farmland. We can see fireworks in the distance coming from Picton. We head toward them down Old Belleville Road. The fireworks mean crowds and cars and places to hide.

As we crest a hill, the lights from the town glow up ahead. We're getting close.

Suddenly two headlights appear in front of us, coming straight at us.

"Hold on," says Gus.

She grips the steering wheel. I shrink in my seat.

Is it him? I can't tell. Did he find a way to get ahead of us and double back? A shortcut we didn't know about? The vehicle's high beams are on and we're blinded. He gets closer and closer. Before I know it, we're zooming past each other, inches apart. *It is him.* He rams into the back side of the camper as he passes. I hear a loud popping noise. We swerve, back and forth, skidding then spinning. It feels like we might tip over. Then we stop. A dust cloud rises in our headlights. We can't see anything. It clears. He's turning around. Gus reverses, spins the camper in the other direction, and we take off. He chases us but his headlights look crooked, like he has a flat. There's a loud flapping sound. He can't keep up and eventually, he stops. We drive on.

When we get to Picton, we're drawn to the glittering fireworks like moths to a flame. At the fairgrounds, we slow down. There are people everywhere and cars parked in the ditches and along the sidewalks. A Ferris wheel turns, and screams echo from a roller coaster. We squeeze the camper into a spot between a Winnebago and a station wagon. At the entrance, a giant portable sign on wheels is lit up with the words: HAPPY CANADA DAY WEEKEND, EH? OPEN 10 A.M. TO 11 P.M. FRIDAY TO SUNDAY.

I still have the Picton Fairgrounds magnet in my sock. The one I stole from Hildy. I pull it out and show Gus the magnet.

"See, we're supposed to be here," I tell her. "Can we go in? Please, please, please."

She doesn't ask me why I have a magnet tucked inside my sock or where I got it. She just shrugs.

"Why not?" Gus says.

I can tell she doesn't believe a magnet pulled us here. She's letting me have my way this time. She's doing it so I don't run off into any more cornfields. So I can be a kid for an hour. But she's wrong about me. I'm not a kid and I'm right about the fair. We are meant to be here.

We buy tickets and wait in line for the Ferris wheel. From the top, we can see the whole town. As we crest the highest point on the wheel, it feels like we could fly away from them all—from mean old Kirk and Creepy Man and the Crystal Queen. But we don't. We come back down to earth and wander the fairgrounds. We play Bust-A-Balloon and Gus wins a fur duck.

More birds.

We wander into the craft tent and walk past tables of quilts and wind chimes and homemade soaps. At one table, two women are selling hand-painted cards and bracelets like the one on my wrist. I recognize them from Tim Hortons. They were handing out cards just like these. Gus called them the hippie chicks. One has long braids that hang past her bum. The other is young and whisper thin with skin so pale it's almost see-through.

I knew it. We are supposed to be here. Now I can get back the card I was meant to have. The one Gus threw in the garbage. I ask Gus if we can buy one, but the woman with long braids spots my bracelet. She lifts her hands to her forehead, bending her fingers into a heart shape.

"Choose whichever one speaks to you, no charge," she says, pointing to the display of cards.

"Thank you," I tell the woman.

Gus wanders to another table. I take my time looking at each card, trying to remember what kind of flower was painted on the one I saw at Tim's. It doesn't come to me so I decide on a pretty

one painted with a cluster of blue flowers. I choose that one because the flowers are creeping thyme. Just like at Stenson's.

"Lula painted that one," says the woman with the braids.

My mouth hangs open. I look over at the pale woman.

"Are you Lula?" I ask her.

"No. Lula isn't—of this world," she says, her smile quivering.

"She's dead?" I ask, eyes wide.

"Oh, far from it. She's being reborn," says the pale woman.

The woman in braids puts a hand on the other woman's
shoulder and the pale woman seems to fold in on herself as she
looks away and starts rearranging the bracelets.

"What Tania meant to say is that Lula is alive and well," she
says.

All I can think about is Pike saying Lula lived with some *crazies at the commune*. Hildy called it a cult. I try to swallow but my
throat's gone dry. *Are the hippie chicks in a cult?*

"Let us get you a bag for that," she says, holding out her hand.
"It looks like rain."

I give her the painted card. She passes it to another young
woman at the back of the tent. I hadn't noticed her there in the
shadows. This one is sitting on an overturned milk crate next to
their supplies. She's wearing a sundress and a veil, held in place
by a string of daisies. Thin gauze hides her face, but I can see the
whites of her eyes as she places the card in a satin bag.

"Is that one of ours?" the braided woman asks, touching my
wrist.

"I don't know. I found it," I tell her, pulling my hand away.
"On the beach."

They're staring at me. *Do they think I stole it?* The braided
woman hands me the satin bag. I grab it and rush off to find Gus.
She's standing outside the craft tent.

I'm close to tears but I hold them in. I'm done with crying.

"Look. Cotton candy," she says. "You used to love that stuff. Let's get some, then we should head out. Find a safe place to hunker down for the night."

She leads me through the crowd. We line up at the cotton candy cart. I zero in on the sugary cobwebs twirling around the tub, trying to shut down my worry brain. I don't know why those hippie chicks bothered me so much. Maybe it's because they said Lula's name.

A loudspeaker announces the fairgrounds are closing in ten minutes.

Gus hands me a paper cone of pink cotton candy.

Bells, whistles, sirens, screams, music, laughter, whizzing machines flood my eardrums.

"You okay?" Gus asks.

I nod and search for a way out of the fairgrounds. I need to get away from the noise and the hippie chicks. Through a gap in the sea of people, I see Dod behind the Tilt-A-Whirl. He's not in the line out front. He's in the shadows, straddling his bike. Suddenly he falls to the ground. I think someone pushed him. Then I see a group of boys surround him and start kicking him. The crowd clots. I crane my neck. I can't see them anymore. I drop the cotton candy and run.

I bump into a man. He curses. I keep going, dodging shoulders and ducking elbows until I reach the Tilt-A-Whirl. I race around the metal railing circling the giant ride. I spot Dod crumpled against the loud generator powering the ride. He's bleeding from a cut on his forehead. Four teenage boys have formed a ring around him. One throws a bottle at Dod and it bounces off his shoulder.

"Stop it!" I yell.

They see me. I race over to Dod and stand between him and

the boys. They're young. Not much older than me. I pick up the bottle and throw it as hard as I can. It sails past them. They laugh, but then their faces darken and they scatter. Gus is there—fur duck in one hand, Swiss Army knife in the other. Those boys weren't about to mess with her.

We help Dod to his feet and Gus checks him over.

"Bullies, bad bullies, bad," chimes Dod, tears and blood streaking his dirty face.

I spot a cell phone on the ground. The screen is smashed. I pick it up. It's dead. I hand it to him anyway.

"Is this yours?" I ask.

"Trouble, I call," he says, like he's reciting instructions.

Dod searches his pockets.

"You call someone if you're in trouble?" asks Gus.

He nods. Then he spots what he's looking for on the ground. It's a small card.

He lurches for it and holds it out to us.

"Trouble, I call." He nods to the card.

Gus and I both look at it. It's a business card for the Picton OPP detachment.

"I think you're okay now," she says. "We don't need the police."

She sends me to get some paper napkins from a hot dog stand. When I come back, she presses the napkins against the cut on his forehead. The bleeding stops but he's a mess. Gus thinks he needs stitches. It doesn't look like he can ride his bike home. Gus hands him the fur duck and he hugs it close. I hate bullies.

"Let's get him to the camper," she says.

The crowds have thinned. Most of the RVs and cars have driven away. Dod leans on Gus and we walk him slowly back to where we parked. I bring the bike. The lights on the rides begin to shut down one by one. The music stops. The night air smells mossy. The sky changes quickly as dark clouds move in and flashes of far-off lightning bounce off them. The wind lifts plastic cups and candy wrappers in mini tornados. As we approach our camper, my heart skips when I see one of the side doors banging open in the wind. I look around for Creepy Man.

Gus stops in her tracks. Maybe we forgot to lock it. Or maybe someone figured out our special way of opening those doors without a key. A swift kick to the bumper and they fly open even if they're locked. But how would they know? Has someone been watching us? My skin crawls.

Gus nods to a bench at a bus stop a few feet away. I lean his bike against it then guide Dod to the bench while she goes over to inspect the camper. I sit beside Dod and watch. She grips the door handle and peers inside.

Gus goes stone-still.

Blood rushes to my brain. I stand up with shaking legs. I leave Dod where he is, napkins stuck to his forehead. I move slowly toward Gus. I don't want to see. She still hasn't moved. She's staring into the back. I get closer. The glow from a nearby lamppost lights the inside. It's not been destroyed. It looks just like we left it, but her eyes are on something I can't see.

"What is it?" I ask.

The wind kicks up and both doors fly open.

I see it now. On the dining table.

With a deafening crack of thunder, the skies open, bringing a downpour of rain so heavy and sudden it's like a dam broke. I tuck the little bag with my painted card under my shirt so it doesn't get wet. I didn't even know I was still holding it. Dod staggers over and stands next to us. He's soaking wet. We all are.

I look around for who might have done this.

The last of the fairground crowd are running for cover.

The last of the lights have turned off.

The street is almost empty.

Blood and rain streak Dod's face.

Gus looks dazed.

We stand there sopping wet staring at the photograph.

The one from our evidence wall. The one of Howard at the party.

Someone has taken our red marker and scratched out his face.

The rain splashes into the camper and onto the photo.

A river of red twists across the table.

21

THE OTHER SHOE

GUS CAN'T REACH PATIENCE PERLEY. WE DON'T HAVE HER NUM-
ber and it's not listed and Dod doesn't know it by heart. Gus
crisscrosses Band-Aids over his cut but it's deep. She doesn't want
to take him to the Picton ER. They might remember us from
the night our car caught fire, and there are always OPP milling
around. Instead, we toss his bike in the back and drive to the
only twenty-four-hour walk-in clinic in town. We saw it just the
other day. It's right beside Crabtree Drugs on Main. The nurse at
the check-in desk knows Patience and calls her. Everyone knows
everyone in small towns. After the doctor patches up Dod, we
wait with him until his mother arrives. It's just after 1 A.M. Sunday morning. The rainstorm has passed by the time she pulls up
in her big red truck. She's a mess of emotions—frantic and angry
and grateful—as she runs to Dod.

"I was up half the night, worried sick about where you'd gone
off to this time," she says, hugging him to her heaving chest.
"Why didn't you answer your phone?"

"Some boys broke it. There was a fight and Bly spotted them.
She went after those boys," Gus tells her.

"Bless your brave little heart," Patience says.

She releases him and spots the fur duck in Dod's hand.

"Quack, quack," he says.

"I won that at the fair. He can keep it," says Gus.

Patience bursts into tears.

"You two," she cries.

"We're just glad he's okay," I tell her.

She puts her arm around Dod.

"You try to be a good mum . . ." She sniffles and reaches for Gus's hand. "*You* know."

Gus takes her hand.

"We can't always be there to protect them from the world," says Gus.

"I'd do anything to keep this one safe," says Patience. "Anything."

They let go hands, then together they load Dod's bike into the truck.

"Time to get you home and in bed," says Patience.

"Zuzu," says Dod, yanking his mother's sleeve.

"Hush now, baby," she says, patting his hand.

"Zuzu," repeats Dod.

"His happy place," she says, bursting into more tears.

"Home should be a happy place and I'm sure it is because of you," says Gus.

Patience wipes her tears away and smiles.

Their red truck drives off down the glistening road. Gus and I jump into the camper. We fasten our seat belts, but she doesn't start the engine. We're both numb. It's been a long night. A high-speed chase, a showdown with bullies, but mostly, we're both rocked by what someone did to Howard's photo. Gus pulls it from her pocket. I don't even want to look at it.

"Should we put it back?" I ask.

As the words come out of my mouth, I realize that rule doesn't matter anymore. The mojo of the evidence wall has been messed with and I'm not sure we can fix it. Someone broke into our camper, saw everything on our wall, and destroyed the last photo taken of Howard. The rest of the stuff on the wall got soaked in rain. Maybe there's no mojo left. Maybe whoever did this is the same person who cleaned out the camper after Hugo found it. Maybe it wasn't teenagers at all and the mojo was gone weeks ago.

Gus doesn't answer me. She still has some of Dod's blood on her hands. She's trying to rub the red marker from Howard's face, but she rubs too hard and the coating on the photo starts to peel away. She tosses the photo on the dashboard. The missing face makes my stomach churn. I lightly tap the passenger door to calm my insides.

Howard's five-part knock.

Rat-tat-tatat-tat.

"That photo is a message," says Gus.

"What's it saying?" I ask.

"You can be disappeared too," she says.

I wish I hadn't asked.

"Whoever did that," she says, "knows what happened to Howard."

WE MUST HAVE GONE TO SLEEP BECAUSE THE NEXT THING I KNOW, I'm opening my eyes and we're both still sitting in the front seat, parked right where we were last night, only it's daylight. My neck is stiff and my mouth's dry. The sky has that pale-yellow glow it gets after a storm. Through the front windshield, I see my reflection in the glass windows of the pharmacy right in front of us. A neon OPEN sign flashes in the window. The clinic next to the pharmacy looks quiet, but there are already a dozen cars in the parking lot. It was empty last night. Gus is snoring. She has one foot resting up on the dash and her rolled-up jean jacket cradles her head.

We were in this pharmacy a few days ago when we were all scratched up from the cornfield. I remember the pharmacist liked my purple cords. She had a pair just like them when she was a kid. She had pretty black hair that looped in ringlets down her shoulders.

A flash of that bouncy black hair comes to me. But not from the pharmacy. I've seen it somewhere else.

I pick up Gus's phone from the cupholder between us. I flip through the gallery in her photo app. There are only two recent videos. One is from July 1. That's the one Gus recorded behind the warehouse in Bloomfield when we followed Kirk. I press play even though I don't want to see it again. I only watch the first part of the video—not the bad part. But right away, I can tell it's her. She has the same bouncy black hair.

And that sensible shoe she dropped. It could belong to a pharmacist.

But it's not just her hair. I've seen the pharmacist's face before. I close my eyes and scan all the places we've been and the faces we've seen over the last nine days. Then I see her on Kirk and Vivi's fridge. She's one of the women on the boat with Vivi. She knows them.

I shake Gus awake.

"W-What's wrong?" she sputters.

"It's the pharmacist," I tell her, pointing to Crabtree Drugs.

Gus rubs her eyes.

"The what?" she mumbles.

"She's the one who lost her shoe," I say.

I tell her about all the bouncy-haired connections I've made and I show her the video.

"I know we can't see her face but I know it's her," I tell her. "What if they were fighting about Howard? What if Kirk is lying about everything?"

Gus looks at me.

"Follow every lead, right?" I say.

She looks at the video.

"You're right. We can't see her face," says Gus. "But we can see her license plate."

Gus zooms in on the Mercedes parked next to Kirk's SUV. She writes down the plate number, then she asks me for Howard's phone. I give it to her, not sure what she's doing. She looks through his contacts then dials the number for a guy named Phil Browser. He's an old high school buddy of Howard's, she says. Then the name comes to me. I remember Howard telling us how Phil was always getting in trouble when they were young. In grade 11, Phil got into a fight in the boys' washroom and Howard broke it up. The principal was going to expel Phil, but Howard said he was the one who started it. Since Howard was never in trouble, he got a slap on the wrist and saved his friend from getting kicked out of school. Phil never forgot it. He finished high school and got a job at Service Ontario. He was Howard's inside source for anything motor vehicle related.

Just like she used Constable Journey to get Stenson's address, she knows Phil won't be able to turn her down. Gus is like that. She uses people if it gets her what she wants—especially if what she wants is bigger than that person's feelings or even their job. She told me her mother, Shannon, was the same way. Gus once said Shannon was like a *dog with a bone*. I guess that makes Gus part dog, and me too. Like grandmother, like mother, like daughter. Maybe it's in our blood. It must be. I was the one who sniffed out the pharmacist.

After some polite small talk, Gus asks Phil if he can look up the license plate number in the video. He hesitates at first but he does it—for Howard. The Mercedes is registered to Candice Theresa Crabtree.

We both look up at the big sign right in front of us. CRABTREE DRUGS.

"Let's go see if Candice wants her shoe back," says Gus.

THE DISPENSING COUNTER IS AT THE BACK OF THE PHARMACY. IT has three service windows. PICKUP. DROP-OFF. QUESTIONS. Behind the counter, we can see a back door marked DELIVERIES (STAFF ONLY) and sitting on the floor next to the exit, beside a recycle bin, is the other shoe. I point to it and Gus nods.

We stand in line behind a man in a foot cast. He's at the window marked QUESTIONS. He's talking quietly with a woman. It's her. She's got wavy black hair and a blue silk scarf around her neck. Her name tag says CANDICE CRABTREE, PHARMACIST.

When our turn comes, we go up to the counter. Candice doesn't look at us. She's sorting prescriptions in a small plastic tray.

"You have a question?" she asks.

I recognize her voice instantly. She's the woman who left the message on Howard's phone. She's the one who said *I can't believe he's dead.*

From the way her breath catches a little in her throat, I think Gus knows it too.

Gus places the shoe on the counter and slides it toward Candice.

Candice stops sorting and looks at Gus for the first time, then at me. Her cheeks turn bright pink and her eye twitches.

"Where did you—?" she says, keeping her voice low.

"Where you dropped it," says Gus.

"I think you're mistaken," says Candice.

"Sure looks like yours," Gus says, nodding to the other shoe on the floor.

"Please," she whispers. "I don't want it."

A man in a white smock is pouring pills onto a scale. He looks over.

"Well, then maybe Vivi would like it. I could ask her all about it," says Gus.

Candice grabs the shoe and shoves it under the counter. She glances over her shoulder.

"Everything okay?" calls out the man.

Candice smiles and waves him off. She leans closer to us.

"What do you want?" whispers Candice.

A woman gets in line behind us. Her toddler whines and tugs at her pant leg.

"We just want to talk," says Gus.

The toddler throws herself on the floor and starts wailing.

Candice looks like she's about to scream too.

"Out back. Five minutes," she says, through gritted teeth.

Gus nods and we move away from the counter. I follow Gus to the baby aisle, filled with powders, creams, diapers, and cases of formula. A girl is halfway down the aisle with her back to us. Just as we pass her, she turns and bumps into Gus, who drops her bag. It's Olive from Pike Winery. Marica's daughter. The young woman doesn't say she's sorry or anything. She puts her head down, shoulders me out of the way, and hurries off. It's like she didn't want to be caught looking at baby stuff. I wonder if she has a baby that no one knows about. Or maybe she's pregnant and her mom doesn't know and that's why she was in such a rush. I want to run after her and ask her about the message on the coaster. I want to tell her it's okay, her secret's safe with me. But she's long gone. Gus picks up her bag with a huff.

Out front, Gus double-checks that the camper is locked then we head down a side alley. Behind the pharmacy is a small, paved lot. The Mercedes is parked back there. Next to the delivery door are four plastic chairs arranged under a rickety gazebo. We sit in two of the chairs and while we wait, we listen to the voice message again.

It's me. Did you get it? Oh my god, I hope he gave it to you before—I can't believe he's dead. Don't call me. Please. I can't do this anymore.

It's definitely her. The pharmacist comes out the back door twenty minutes later. She takes a seat across from us and lights a cigarette.

"So?" she says, puffing smoke from her mouth like a blowfish.

Candice crosses her legs and pulls her elbows tight to her body. She pinches her face like she's ready for a fight. She's all brittle and closed off. A tortoise hiding inside her shell.

"We saw what happened the other day," says Gus. "Between you and Kirk Baylis."

Candice won't look at Gus. She touches the scarf around her neck. When she does, I realize she's wearing it to cover the bruises. I can't help touching my own neck as I remember how hard he grabbed her. Gus gets right to the point.

"Are you two having an affair?" asks Gus.

Candice takes another long drag off her cigarette. Her hand is trembling.

"Vivi has been my best friend since high school. We went our separate ways for a few years but I was so happy when we both ended up living in the same county," she mumbles, not answering the question.

It's like she's forgotten we're here. Gus leans in.

"Why were you fighting? Was it to do with their son's disappearance?" asks Gus.

Candice squints like she's surprised by this. I can't tell if it's because it's true or because it's not.

"I care very much about that family," says Candice. "He was my godson, I bet you didn't know that."

Candice looks at me. I want her to stop talking about Howard in the past tense.

"He never mentioned you," says Gus.

"We weren't all that close. I don't have children of my own. The godmother thing was more a kind gesture of friendship on Vivi's part. But I always asked about him," she says.

"Cut the bullshit, Candice," says Gus.

Candice's hands are shaking.

"You called Howard and left a message the day he disappeared," says Gus.

Candice tosses her cigarette into the parking lot with the flick of her finger.

"Was it Boyd Barton you were talking about?" Gus says.

Candice looks at Gus for the first time since she sat down. Her eyes widen. She's scared. A tear bubbles from the corner of one eye as the tortoise pokes her head out—just a little.

"There was no affair. Kirk loves Vivi more than anything. I confess I've been in love with him for years. But I knew he'd never love me back. He only agreed to meet me because I wouldn't stop calling and texting. I needed someone to confide in. The shame and guilt had all come back. What you saw the other day wasn't his fault. It was a desperate, broken man lashing out. I told him the truth about what I'd done. I needed him to know that it was because of me his son disappeared. I don't blame Kirk for hating me. I have to live with it, but at least now he knows," she says.

Candice uses her scarf to wipe away a tear and as she lifts it, I catch a glimpse of a purple bruise on her neck. She clears her throat. I can see her jaw clenching as she fights to hold back more tears.

"What have I done?" she whispers.

Gus rises from her chair. It tumbles backward. I'm afraid she's about to pull the knife on Candice like she did Stenson. Instead, she reaches for her and wraps her arms around the woman. Candice tries to get free but Gus hugs her close. It doesn't take long for Candice to stop struggling. She rests her cheek against Gus and the tears come. She sobs and sobs. Gus rubs her back gently. Gus knew this is what Candice needed. I guess a knife to the throat isn't always the way in. Candice finally stops crying and Gus lets her go. She rights her chair and sits back down. Candice blows her nose into her scarf and takes a deep breath with her whole body.

Then the tortoise comes all the way out of her shell and she starts to tell us the story of what happened three years ago.

I look away. I don't want to see what's in her eyes—the darkness that might be waiting to come out at the end of her story.

Instead, I stare up at the gazebo's roof. There's a clear, blue sky above the latticework. A flock of starlings is flying overhead. The birds twist and turn, moving together at the exact same time, in the exact same direction, like a giant black cloud come to life.

The birds know.

I can't stop it no matter where I look.

The darkness is coming.

I wouldn't say we were friends exactly, but Marica and I traveled in the same social circles—community fundraisers, that sort of thing. At one of these events about five years ago, we found out we had a fair bit in common—both grew up in Cornwall, both were successful business owners, both divorced.

It was around that time I got into a bit of trouble. I often went to the casino to unwind after a long week. Blackjack mostly. I had a terrible cold streak and the house finally cut me off. The debt came due and I couldn't pay it. I'd already cleaned out my savings, but I

*was about to lose everything—my pharmacy, my house.
I started getting calls at all hours. Ugly, threatening
messages. I was scared and alone.*

*Then, out of the blue, Marica asked to meet. She
said she'd taken care of it. I had no idea how she knew I
was in trouble. But this woman, whom I'd only rubbed
shoulders with at the occasional gala, had gone out on
a limb for me. She'd used her influence and made it go
away. I told her I'd pay her back but she refused. She
said it was covered. She just needed a small favor.*

*It was only supposed to be the one time, she promised.
I was grateful so I did it. She wanted me to order
some drugs through the pharmacy—cold meds, diet
pills, stimulants, opioids—the shipment was huge. I
wasn't an idiot. There are rules around these kinds
of drugs for a reason. I knew they were used to make
methamphetamines for the black market. But I turned a
blind eye because I felt I owed her. And I thought it was
just the one time.*

*But she kept coming back, month in and month
out. It took a while for me to finally clue in. She owned
me. And then I knew that my cold streak at the casino
was more than just bad luck. The debt, the threats, her
swooping in just when I needed rescuing. I'd been set up.*

*Then came the next favor. She wanted me to start
laundering money through the pharmacy. Her wind
park project was stalled and that was going to be her
golden goose. She'd planned to clean most of her dirty
money through the project's construction and beyond.
But the permits were held up in litigation and she
was making too much cash to funnel it all through
the winery. She needed a new business to absorb the*

overflow. She brought in her accountant and he showed me exactly how to cook my books.

I stalled. I knew I was one Revenue Canada audit away from my entire life crumbling to pieces. One of my colleagues was already asking questions about the after-hours deliveries. I told Marica I wanted out. That's when she sent her errand boy to my house to make sure I understood that saying no to Marica Pike was not an option. He was very persuasive. This was right before Howard disappeared.

I was living a nightmare—between midnight money drops and fabricating invoices and keeping two sets of books and trying to run my own business, I was a mess. And I was all alone. I hadn't told a soul, not even Vivi, my best friend. I was too ashamed. But I finally broke.

I called Kirk. I thought maybe he could reason with Marica. They were both on the Vintners Association board. She respected him. And the last thing she'd want was for her reputation to be sullied. I told him about the gambling debt and the threats, but before I could go on, he cut me off. He didn't want to hear another word. He wasn't about to get his family mixed up in something shady. He told me the right thing to do was to call the police and he hung up.

Kirk was wrong. The police couldn't help me. I needed him to hear the whole story, so I went to his house when I knew Vivi was out. I threw myself at Kirk and begged him to help me. Howard drove up and when he saw me in Kirk's arms—oh, the look on his face. He was devastated and so was I. Howard drove off before his father could explain. Kirk yelled at me to leave so I did.

A few days later, Howard came to the pharmacy. I could see that he was still upset. It was a busy Saturday so I took him outside. He said his father called him to explain but Howard could tell he was hiding something. Howard needed to know the truth. Were we having an affair? When I told him we weren't, he believed me. He was such a sweet, trusting young man. He took me at my word. I told him it wasn't his father who had secrets. It was me.

Howard could see I was in a terrible state. He asked me if I was okay.

I was so touched by his kindness.

Then I did something I'll regret for the rest of my days.

I told him about Marica. The whole story. At first, he was shocked to find out she had a double life, but then the wheels started turning. I think he'd had a gut feeling about her all along, but after hearing my story, he was a man on a mission. Howard said the only way he could help me was to take down Marica. He didn't want his parents involved. If Marica was in with some bad people, he didn't want Kirk and Vivi in danger. I promised I wouldn't tell a soul.

A week later, he came back to see me. He was more than excited. He'd found out why she was making so much cash. Her operation was global. Howard said he was going to blow the lid off the whole thing—expose her international routes and contacts, her money-laundering schemes, the winery, the wind park project, all of it. He said he wanted to keep me out of it. He was pretty sure he could get his hands on some physical evidence, but what he really needed was a source inside Marica's organization to go on the record.

I had an idea. I knew someone who was just as desperate as I was to get out from under Marica's thumb. Someone with their finger on the pulse of her entire operation. He was the accountant for both the casino and Pike Enterprises. Boyd Barton. I connected the two of them.

And then something went horribly wrong.

Boyd died and Howard went missing.

I was terrified they'd come for me next. But instead, Marica cut me out. There was no more contact, no more orders, no more cash. I think she was circling the wagons. She was out of my life. I wish I'd been as brave as Howard but I knew deep down I was as guilty as Marica, so I couldn't go to the police. I hated knowing what this was doing to Vivi and Kirk. It broke my heart seeing those missing person signs all over town. I felt awful for all of you. I was actually relieved when you finally left. I prayed you'd move on. I know I've tried.

And then three years go by. I think it's all over. Then suddenly the missing camper turns up and you're back in town for the funeral and all hell breaks loose again. Marica came to my house with that junkie hatchet man of hers. She said you'd been to the winery, poking around. You had Howard's notebook. But something else had changed. She'd overheard someone mention my name at the funeral, wondering why Howard's godmother wasn't there. Of course, I couldn't bring myself to show up because of what I'd done. It got Pike thinking. Was I close to Howard? Why wouldn't I come to his funeral? She put two and two together. She knew

*I was the one who introduced Boyd and Howard. She
wanted to know how much I'd told him and what
might be in that notebook. I didn't want to tell her but
her rotten-toothed little friend was, once again, very
persuasive.*

*I told them everything I knew. That Howard was
looking into her. He had evidence that her operation was
global. But when I told her that Boyd had copied some
incriminating files onto a thumb drive for Howard,
she was visibly shaken. I told her how they'd planned
to do the handoff at the annual vintners' party at his
parents'. Two strangers shaking hands in a crowd. No
one would be the wiser. But I never found out if they'd
done it. That thumb drive rattled her. Marica hates not
having control. She asked me where it was. I told her, if
Howard did get it, he probably hid it. Before the two of
them left my house, she fired her parting shot. She said
the only reason I was still alive was because I was no
one. Nothing. Like shit on her shoe. I couldn't touch her
even if I tried. No one could and no one would. She'd
make sure of that.*

Candice takes a deep breath then lights another cigarette
with a trembling hand.

My heart is vibrating. When she started talking, I couldn't
look at her, but now I can't take my eyes off the pharmacist. A
very tiny part of me feels sorry for her. She's been bruised and
hurt and threatened. But a way, way bigger part of me hates her
guts. I hate her for being a stupid gambler and for owing money
to bad people and for helping Pike get ingredients to make her
bad drugs and, most of all, I hate her for getting Howard mixed
up in her bad, bad world.

"Pike's a confident bitch, I'll give her that," says Gus.

Candice lets out a sour laugh as she blows smoke out her nostrils, and her shell hardens.

"With mob protection and the local OPP in her pocket, she's got reason to be," she says.

"What? The police?" Gus asks, leaning in.

"That's right. The fucking cops. You two keep doing what you're doing and it won't end well," she says. "I suggest you pack up your camper and your daughter and go home. Don't look back. It's been three years. Let it be. Let him rest in peace."

My chest clenches and a hiss escapes my lips. I cover my mouth.

Gus rises to her feet. She stares at Candice a moment, then she walks out from under the gazebo and across the lot. She's heard enough. I chase after her down the alley. We don't look back. We leave Candice Crabtree sitting alone under the gazebo, tucked inside her shell where she belongs.

Back in the camper, Gus sits and closes her eyes. I don't say a word. She's gathering. Like I gather objects, she gathers threads and tries to weave them together so they make sense. She's sorting through the threads of the story Candice told us. I've seen her do this before. Sometimes she does it by running her fingers across her evidence wall or by making lists or by listening to Howard's video. Sometimes she does it by staring into space or, like now, by closing her eyes and feeling her way along those threads. She looks almost—peaceful.

Let him rest in peace.

Candice is wrong.

This is no time for peace.

This is war.

And Marica Pike is the enemy.

My thoughts tumble into a messy and dizzy pool of worry and

rage. I need water. I feel sick. I decide to close my eyes too. But my brain won't stop spinning. Colors cascade across my eyeballs: purple bruises on a woman's neck, a jade ring, blue flowers on a painted card, and a horribly disfigured, red blotch on a photo— the one of Howard at his parents' party. I try to remember what his face looked like before someone scratched it away but I can't.

The photo is sitting right where we left it on the dashboard, but I don't want to look at it. I keep my eyes shut tight. I try again—try to see his face. He's not smiling. His eyes are looking down. His kind eyes. What is he looking at? His hands? No. The object he's holding.

My eyes open wide.

I lean toward the photo.

"It's not a corkscrew," I shout, as I point at it.

Gus nearly jumps out of her seat. She looks at me, then the photo.

It comes to her just as it came to me.

We both say it at the same time.

"It's the thumb drive."

22

THE PINOT NOIR

WE DON'T EVEN STOP AT TIM'S FOR COFFEE. WE DRIVE STRAIGHT down Main. It's the fastest way out of town. I keep my eyes peeled for police cruisers and delivery trucks and mobsters. I can tell Gus is on high alert too. We can't trust anyone. We pass a bus stop where a girl sits at a bench. It's Pike's daughter, Olive. Our eyes meet for a split second. I wish she hadn't seen us but it's too late now. We head out of town.

Gus takes the highway to Cherry Valley and Baylis Vineyards. We need to talk to Kirk and Vivi—even if they don't want to talk to us. They might have seen something at that party.

I bet if we show them Howard's *just-in-case* video and his notebook, we can figure this out together. Maybe they'll listen this time. Maybe they won't be angry, because we all love Howard and we all want to find him. *Maybe*s swirl under our wheels as we turn into their driveway and head up the hill to their house. But when we reach the top and see the flashing lights and the police cars and ambulances, and all the people on stretchers and the winery staff running around like chickens with their heads cut off, those *maybe*s drift up, up, and away.

Gus stops the camper and tells me to stay put. I don't see Kirk, but Vivi is standing with two OPP constables. It's them again. The snickering ones who tried to lock us up the night our Honda caught fire. Vivi stands between them like they're her personal bodyguards. They all turn and stare at us. It's only now that I notice the two constables look weirdly alike. Same buzz cuts, same uniforms, same round faces, same potbellies, same dumb expressions.

Like Tweedledum and Tweedledee.

Gus jumps out of the camper. People are scattered across the pebble stone parking lot. Some wander about dazed and hanging on to each other. Others look pale and sweaty. Some lie on the ground. A little girl cries. Then a loud knock on the window next to me lifts me off my seat. It's Kirk. I roll the window down. There's a long scratch on his cheek. I bet Candice did that.

"It's all over town," he gasps, out of breath.

I look at him blank-faced. I don't understand.

A woman near an ambulance vomits on the pebble stones.

Is it a plague?

"It's the pinot noir. Some bottles were contaminated. We're not sure how many. We've been serving it since Canada Day and everything was fine, but today when we opened some new bottles—and it's not just here. We got a call from a restaurant. We delivered cases and cases of it across the county. Who knows how many are out there. It's our special blend," he moans.

Gus comes over to Kirk. She touches his arm and he flinches.

"We need to talk," she says.

"I-I-It's not a good time," he stammers.

He's overwhelmed but Gus doesn't seem to notice. Or doesn't care. She nods for me to hand over her bag. She's going to show him Howard's phone and his notebook. I pass it to her.

She turns and Kirk is walking away.

"It's about you and Candice," she calls out to him.

He turns around and looks like he might throw up. But I don't think it's the wine. He comes back over and lowers his voice.

"It *was* you that day. I thought I saw the camper," he says.

He knows she was the one who tossed the rock at his SUV. And she knows he tried to strangle Candice.

"You bet it was me," says Gus.

"I knew it," says Vivi.

Gus spins around to find Vivi and the two constables right behind her. Vivi glares.

"Step away from the vehicle, Miss Monet," says Tweedledee.

"What the hell?" says Gus.

"Easy now," Kirk says to the two cops.

"You've come back to the scene of the crime," says Vivi, arms folded.

"You think *I* did this?" Gus says, wide-eyed.

"This all started when you came to town—our home is broken into, our personal possessions are destroyed. How could you?" Vivi spits, shaking her head. "And now you sabotage our business?"

The constables eyeball Gus. Vivi is stone-cold and weirdly calm for her. Kirk's mouth opens, but he doesn't speak. Two ambulances drive off, their sirens wailing. Suddenly, Vivi's calm gives way to howling and pointing—at me. Only it's not me. She's pointing at the front window of the camper. Everyone in the parking lot—paramedics and customers and staff—seems to stop in their tracks and stare at what she's pointing to.

There on the dash, tucked near the window, is the photo of Howard—his face scratched-out like something from a horror movie.

The constables lean closer. Kirk looks like he might cry. Gus backs away.

"Search the vehicle," commands Vivi.

The constables move in.

"The fuck you will," says Gus.

I roll up the window and lock the doors. Tweedledum knocks on the window, looking at me with lifeless eyes. He twirls one finger telling me to roll it back down. I don't. Gus squeezes in front of him.

"Leave her alone. She's just a kid," says Gus.

He grabs her elbow. She tries to jerk free but he holds tight.

"That's enough," says Kirk.

Vivi glares at her husband.

"Look what she's done to our boy," sobs Vivi. "It's sick."

Tweedledee grabs Gus by the other arm. Now they both have her. Everyone's watching.

"Get your fucking hands off me," yells Gus.

She tries to pull away. They look at each other and both let go at the same time. Gus crashes into the camper. Her elbow smacks the window and she loses her footing. She falls to the pebble stones. I unlock the door, jump out, and crouch by her side. Her bag has flipped off her shoulder and its contents have spilled out. I put my arm around her and help her up.

"What's that?" someone says.

I look where everyone else is looking. Spread across the pebble stones are the contents of Gus's bag. Chewing gum, phone, Howard's notebook, pen, wallet, Swiss Army knife—and something else that I don't recognize. A small bottle. It rolls slowly to Kirk's feet.

He picks it up and looks at the label.

"Syrup of ipecac," he reads.

"Isn't that what you give babies to make them—" says Vivi.

Right on cue, a woman—who is probably here because she heard all these good things about Baylis Vineyards' special Canada Day pinot noir—projectile vomits a dark red gush all over her husband's white shirt. Tweedledum gags.

Vivi brushes away her tears and nods to the constables.

Dee pulls out his handcuffs.

"That's not mine," says Gus, cradling her sore elbow. "I don't know how it got in there."

I do. It came to me the second Vivi said *Isn't that what you give babies?* I flashed to the moment Olive bumped into Gus in the baby aisle at the pharmacy. She must have slipped the syrup of ipecac into her bag. She was following us. Pike must have sent her. Olive tried to warn us about her mother with a message on a coaster, but she's still her daughter. And daughters do what their mothers tell them to do. Pike poisoned the wine and set up Gus. She's the one who's been trying to scare us away. The flat tire, the car fire, and now she's gone after Howard's parents and she's trying to get Gus arrested. We *did* poke the fish.

"Don't make a scene. Not in front of your kid," says Dee, holding out the handcuffs.

"We just want to have a friendly chitchat," says Dum.

"Or maybe a chit-chirp," Dee says with a smirk.

His sidekick coughs out the word *cuckoo*.

I cling to Gus's arm. Dee and Dum try to pull us apart but we stick together like glue. As Kirk tries to break up the four of us, a car speeds up the driveway and skids to a stop a few feet away. It's another OPP cruiser. Staff Sergeant Muirhead jumps out.

"What in the hell?" he says gruffly.

The constables let us go. I wrap myself tighter around Gus.

"Julius," Kirk says with relief in his voice, "thank god you're here. This is getting totally out of hand."

Vivi grabs the little bottle of syrup from Kirk and shows it to Muirhead.

"We caught her red-handed. *This* was in her bag," says Vivi.

"I've never seen it before," says Gus.

Muirhead is not listening. He's somewhere else. He should be over the moon to see Gus in trouble. *Hasn't he always hated her?*

Something's wrong.

"You two. Make yourselves useful," says Muirhead, nodding for the two constables to go help the paramedics.

Dee puts away his handcuffs, and they shuffle over to the ambulances.

"I don't understand, Julius," says Vivi. "Why isn't she being—?"

He raises a hand and this silences her.

"I need you to listen," he says, looking from Vivi to Kirk to Gus to me.

"All of you," he says.

His Adam's apple bobs like he's having trouble swallowing and that's when I know.

"There's been a development," he croaks.

Everything goes dead quiet. Even the birds. For a moment I think it's my doing. I have somehow stopped the whole world from rotating. I've clenched my fists so powerfully that no one on the planet can breathe or move or speak—including Muirhead. He can't say it.

But as fast as I found it, I lose my grip on the world and it spins out of control.

He says it.

"Two kayakers were paddling over on East Lake near Cove Beach."

I feel the earth begin to give way under my feet like a great big hole is opening up.

"They found human remains."

I am swallowed into the darkness.

AFTER WHAT FEELS LIKE A FEW SECONDS, I HEAR A HIGH-PITCHED whistle. I open my eyes. I'm looking up at a ceiling in a bright room. Gus is sitting beside me. My head feels like it weighs a thousand pounds. I can't lift it.

"You blacked out," she says softly.

I'm lying on Kirk and Vivi's sofa. Across the living room, I can see Vivi pouring steaming water into a teapot on the kitchen island. The whistling was a kettle. I can hear voices outside. Kirk isn't there. Vivi brings over a tray of blueberry muffins and tea and places it on the coffee table. She sits across from us in a wingback chair. She glances out the front window. The lights from another ambulance crisscross the wall behind her.

"So much pinot. So much red—it just kept coming and coming," she says, quietly shaking her head.

"Kind of like a zombie apocalypse?" says Gus.

Vivi stifles a laugh. She hands me a muffin. I sit up.

"How's your head, dear?" asks Vivi.

I shrug. I'm not sure why she's being nice or calling me *dear* but I like it.

"She'll be okay," says Gus. "She's one tough cookie."

I've never been called that before. I don't feel tough.

"I'm sorry for not calling you when they found the camper van. Someone should have. And I'm sorry for being so . . ." says Vivi. She doesn't finish her sentence.

"You were right about one thing," Gus says. "We did come into your house on Canada Day. I don't know what I was hoping to find but I wasn't expecting there to be a man in here. *He's* the one who trashed Howard's room. And he probably poisoned your wine. I swear, none of this was us."

"I *did* take the photo off your fridge but we didn't do that horrible thing to it," I add as I sit up.

"But why? Who's this man? What does he want?" asks Vivi.

"There are people in this town who think if they hurt you, we'll go away. Which means we're close to finding him," says Gus.

Vivi sips her tea. I try to clear the fog from my brain. *Did Muirhead say they found a body? He did.*

"You don't think it's him they found?" Vivi asks, eyes glassy.

"No. It's not Howard," says Gus.

That simple answer is all I needed.

"You're exceptionally unreasonable and far too cocky for your own good. You're reckless and irresponsible, and frankly, rude," says Vivi.

Gus says nothing. I don't think she disagrees.

"And yet you've never once given up. You're unwavering in your belief that he's still out there somewhere," says Vivi. "I don't know how you sustain it, but I do admire it."

Gus smiles. So does Vivi. It's the first time in forever since they've shared smiles.

Kirk comes through the front door.

"Sorry, love, we need you at the bistro," he says. "The staff is about to stage a mutiny."

Vivi puts down her tea, nods to us, and leaves the house.

Kirk is about to follow, but he stops. He hovers in the foyer, one hand on the door.

"You're welcome to stay if you have nowhere else," he offers.

Gus stands up before he can leave.

"We know Candice got Howard involved. He was about to expose Marica Pike's drug operation. That's why the accountant was going to give Howard the thumb drive—"

Kirk raises his hands.

"Hold up! Drug operation?" gasps Kirk. "Candy said she asked for Howard's help because she owed money to some unsavory types, but she sure in hell didn't tell me anything about Marica Pike or drugs."

"She told us. Howard was onto Pike. And at the vintners' party three years ago, she was here, and so was Howard. We just want to know if you remember anything from that party?" Gus pleads.

"Of course I do. That was the last time I saw my son. I was actually surprised he came. I thought he was angry with me. We had a misunderstanding. But he told me Candy cleared things up. He didn't stay long. He mingled a bit then left," he says.

"He didn't say or do anything unusual?" she asks.

"I don't think so," he says.

"Did you see him talking to Pike?" she asks.

"I think so, yes," he says. "I do remember one funny thing. His mother was looking for him at one point. She wanted to introduce him to a friend. I was talking to Marica at the time. I looked around, glanced at the house, and then I saw him in the upstairs window."

"What was funny?" asks Gus.

"Well, when I looked at him, he hid behind the curtain. I only remember because it reminded me of when he was a boy, playing hide-and-seek," he says. "He must have been up there looking through his old things in the spare room."

"Did Marica see him?" asks Gus.

"I don't know. Maybe," he says. "What's this about a thumb drive?"

Vivi appears in the door. She looks like she's going to cry.

"Kirk, I thought you were right behind me," she says, her voice cracking.

She puts a hand on her husband's arm like she's trying not to fall over.

"Felix just quit. I can't do this alone," she says.

He puts his hand on hers.

"Sorry, we were just saying our goodbyes," he says, his voice weak.

They cling to each other. They both look like they've aged a decade in the last hour. They shuffle out the door. Two zombies.

Saying our goodbyes?

I guess we're not as welcome as Kirk said. I don't blame him or Vivi. They've been through a lot in the last three years. And now, on top of all that stress and worry, they have an apocalypse and human remains to deal with.

THERE WAS SO MUCH MORE WE COULD HAVE SHARED WITH KIRK and Vivi—could have shown them and told them—but those *could*s are left behind on the wine-soaked gravel as we drive away. Gus tells me that Howard would want us to leave his parents out of it, so they're no longer targets. Kirk told us what he remembered. Maybe Pike remembered too. When Candice told her about the thumb drive, Gus figures that Pike probably recalled seeing Howard in the window, and she sent Creepy Man to search his room.

Maybe it's her footsteps we've been following this whole time.

23

THE WILD TURKEY

AS WE LEAVE CHERRY VALLEY, GUS'S PHONE RINGS. SHE'S DRIVING so I pick it up and check the caller ID. Hildy Flood. I show her and Gus nods. I put the phone on speaker.

"Hildy?" says Gus.

"At your service," says Hildy. "Are you still in town?"

"We are," says Gus.

"Listen, it could be nothing and the source isn't exactly one I'd stake my career on, but I overheard something and thought to myself that Augusta Monet would, at the very least, want to hear what I heard."

"Go on," says Gus.

"I was at the pub last night. The owner had called me to come scrape a gin-sodden Colton out from under a table. Hugo Remedy was there in the middle of one of his overweening, boozy rants. He works security for the flying club up on Macaulay Mountain," she says.

"We met him. He's the one who found our camper van," says Gus.

"Which is why I'm calling. Hugo was crowing about how he knew a heap more than the cops did. My reporter radar pinged.

He said if he was an OPP detective, he'd have solved the case two years ago because he knew where the camper had been that whole time."

Gus swerves onto the shoulder then quickly corrects.

"Our camper?" asks Gus, her eyes barely on the road.

"I think so," says Hildy. "That's all I caught before Colton threw up on my shoes. Full disclosure, most of our Hugo's stories have more holes in them than a honeycomb, but I thought it was worth a mention."

"Appreciate it," says Gus.

"I hope it helps. If I can do any digging for you, give me a ding-a-ling," Hildy says, then she hangs up.

Now I feel really bad for taking Hildy's magnet. She probably knows I stole it and she's still being nice to us.

Gus pulls a U-turn and heads for the Picton Airport on Macaulay Mountain.

Hugo is our next mission.

It's the weekend and the skies are clear. The flying club is buzzing as small prop planes whiz and whir along the runways and overhead. It's a perfect summer day. Only it's not. Howard is still missing and human remains have been found and the late-afternoon sun is way too bright.

Gus drives down the road behind the hangars. We stop and get out. It doesn't take long to find Hugo napping in a lawn chair between two hangars. He's leaning back against the wall, hands on his belly.

"Mr. Remedy?" Gus calls out.

He opens one eye, then rights his chair.

"Only the wife calls me that when she wants her fancy tickled," he says, rubbing his eyes with two very large fists. Tobias Perley was right. He is ham-fisted.

Hugo frees himself from his lawn chair. He stands and bends side to side, like he's getting the kinks out of his back. Then he walks over—slowly.

"What can I do ya for on this fine day, pretty ladies?" he asks, squinting into the sun.

"I don't know if you remember us. I'm Augusta. This is my daughter. You found our camper in the hangar," Gus reminds him.

He rubs his eyes again, then takes a better look at us.

"You're the bird that gave that young rookie a run for his money." He chuckles then starts coughing like his lungs are full of gravel.

"He had it coming," says Gus. "The OPP are completely incompetent. And he certainly didn't appreciate what you brought to the table. I mean, you're in charge of security for an entire airport. That's a big job. He should have given you the respect you deserve."

Gus is talking in a high voice. Not her normal one. She almost sounds sweet. She's doing it again, only instead of a hug like she gave Candice to get her talking, Gus is buttering up Hugo with sweet words and smiles.

Hugo's eyes light up when he realizes she's serious. He retucks his shirt into his baggy slacks and smooths his greasy hair. Then he fumbles in the pockets of his wrinkled uniform. He finds his cigarettes, pulls one out, and sticks it in the corner of his mouth. It fits perfectly into a divot in his lip.

"Security work takes years of specialized training," he says, his chest puffed out a little.

"I bet it does," she says, smiling.

"It's mostly a gut thing. Instincts, you know. Reading people, spotting trouble when it comes along. Not every Tom, Dick, or Larry has the gift," he says.

"I'm surprised you're not a police officer yourself," she says.

"They'd be so lucky. Cops around here don't know their asses from their arses," he says.

"That's for sure. They really messed up that crime scene," she says.

She nods to the camper van parked behind us.

He looks over at it then back at us.

"Them kids woulda never dared pull that shit on my watch," he says.

"I don't doubt it," Gus says. "They should have put you in charge from the beginning."

"That's what I told the wife," he hollers.

"You would have solved the case two years ago," she says.

"Damn straight. Second I seen it sitting in them woods I woulda cracked it," he says.

And there it is. He did see it.

Gus didn't have to pin him to the ground or hug him or hold a knife to his throat. But I can tell from the way her jaw is clenched that she's done being sweet. The smile on Hugo's face disappears as the gears click and he realizes what he just said. He digs in his pockets and finds his lighter. He flicks and flicks but it won't ignite so he gives up.

We both stare at him.

"What?" he snaps, but he knows.

"Did you put the camper in the hangar, Hugo?" she asks.

I hadn't thought of that.

"Me?" he cries. "I was the one that found it."

"So is all that stuff about seeing it two years ago just bullshit you tell people to make yourself look like a big man?" she asks, her voice back to normal.

"No! I seen it," he pleads. "I swear."

Gus takes a step closer to him. The unlit cigarette falls from his mouth.

"Talk," she says, her face an inch from his.

"I was out near Little Bluff at the conservation area. Outta nowhere I spot this wild turkey. The wife loves her some turkey," he says. "I chased the bird over a fence and into these woods. It weren't till I pulled the trigger that I looked around and seen I was on private property. But waste not want not, right? So I dragged the bird outta there by the leg. Weren't easy. Thing probably weighed a good twenty pounds and them woods was real muddy. So I'm making my way out and I catch sight of a bumper. I try to get close, but like I said, that mud was a motherfucker. The camper was tucked under some branches, but I'd seen the pictures and I got a look. It was for sure the one they'd been looking for."

"And you didn't report it," Gus says.

"Like I said, I was on private land and it weren't exactly hunting season. That's a double whammy. I woulda got a huge fuckin' fine. They put shit like that in the paper for everyone to see. I coulda lost my job *and* my small game license to boot," he whines. "You know how hard it is to get that sucker back once you lose it?"

Gus is still nose to nose with Hugo. He looks like he might be having a heart attack.

"And, the other day, when you said the camper wasn't in the hangar when you checked the month before—you could have mentioned seeing it in the woods then," she says.

"Cops woulda thought I was hiding something," he says.

"You were," she says.

"Woulda put a bull's-eye on my forehead, I tell them something like that. I ain't no thief. I'm just the unlucky duck who keeps tripping over the goddamn thing," he pleads. "Besides, when I seen that camper two years ago, it'd been missing for months. What did it matter at that point?"

Gus staggers back from Hugo almost like she's been pushed or like she can't stand being close to him another second. Then she turns and walks away—back to the camper. I don't move. I wait. I want her to come back. I want her to kick him or punch him or slap him or do something to him. Anything.

What did it matter? It's a horrible thing to say. Howard matters.

Why is Gus leaving? She opens the passenger door, grabs something, and stomps back over to Hugo. She's got the map in her hand. Gus holds it out.

"Where?" she says, through gritted teeth.

He points to a spot on the map. She leans in for a closer look. Then she stares at Hugo.

"You're a fucking coward, Hugo," she says. "And a disgrace to the uniform."

He bows his head. He can't look her in the eyes. She stares at him until he finally does.

"If I find out that you played any part in Howard not coming back to us, I'll come find you," she says, cold as ice. "And you'll wish *you* were that wild turkey."

Gus walks away but I can't. Not yet. I walk right up to him and kick him hard, right in the shin. Hugo squeals in pain. I turn and run after Gus.

We jump into the camper and drive away. In the sideview mirror, I can see him cupping his shin in his ham-fisted hands as he teeters around like a bobblehead. I hate him and I'm glad I kicked him. Only it doesn't take away the sting of what he said, or what he did two years ago. But at least we have a new lead thanks to Hildy. I try to focus on that as we take the road down the other side of Macaulay Mountain.

If the Prince Edward Land Registry Office in Picton had been open for the holiday weekend, we might have found out right away who owned the private land where Hugo said he saw the camper two years ago.

But the office was closed until Tuesday, so we never got the chance.

We didn't know at the time that everything would be different on Tuesday.

24

THE RING

WITH THE MAP ON MY LAP, I CALL OUT THE DIRECTIONS. GUS
drives as I follow the route with my finger, just like *she* used to. We
want to get there before the sun sets. I wish I'd eaten one of Vivi's
muffins. I'm starving. As if she read my mind, Gus pulls over at a
roadside stand selling home-baked pies and fresh-picked corn. She
buys a strawberry rhubarb pie, then we keep going. I direct her
along County Road 13, which runs alongside the shore of Lake
Ontario. We hardly pass any traffic. There's not much out here.

"I think it's the next left after this road," I tell her.

We come to a crossroads. As we're going through the intersection, I spot a sign hidden behind some shrubs. LITTLE BLUFF
CONSERVATION AREA. An arrow points back the way we came.

"Wait, we missed it," I tell her. "Sorry, I thought it was the
second turnoff."

Gus makes a U-turn and we backtrack then take the right
down a gravel road. We come to a small parking lot. Along one
side is a fence marked with a big sign that says PRIVATE PROPERTY.
Probably the one Hugo jumped over to chase the turkey. There's
no one else in the parking lot. It doesn't surprise us since it's almost impossible to find. We can see a few trails marked with signs
but not much else.

We park. But before we go hopping any fences, we sit at the dining table. Gus doesn't bother cutting the pie. She grabs two forks and we dig in until it's all gone. It feels good to have food in my belly but it doesn't shake loose the deep, dark dread in the pit of my stomach. It's been there ever since Muirhead told us about those kayakers. I keep picturing Howard floating in the lake. I keep hearing what Gus said to Hugo, over and over.

If I find out that you played any part in Howard not coming back to us.

Howard not coming back to us.

Howard not coming back to us.

I need to get a grip on my runaway brain. Think about something else. Like our new lead. I pull out Howard's phone and search the Maps app for our location. I check out the satellite view. Gus has been searching for information about the private property on her phone. She keeps getting linked to catalogs and directories that lead nowhere. She tries Hildy instead.

It rings once then goes to voice mail. Gus leaves Hildy a message. She asks her if she can find out who owns the tract of land near the bluffs. She gives Hildy the coordinates from our map. Longitude and latitude. Then she hangs up.

I show her the satellite image of where we are.

"That's the parking lot and the fence. See? It runs beside the county road all along that side of the forest. And there"—I point—"that looks like a gate into the forest."

We cross-check the image with our paper map but there's no road into the woods where the gate seems to be. I pinch the satellite image to zoom closer but it just gets blurry.

"Let's go take a look," says Gus.

We drive back out to the main road. I use the Maps app this time to track where we're going. The sun has set and it's getting dark fast. The sky has a creepy dark orange glow. As we drive along the road beside the wire fence, the cell service cuts out and the map stops loading. It's a dead zone. But it doesn't matter because we spot the gate. We pull onto the shoulder and get out. There's the hint of a break in the trees and it looks like there was a road here once, but it was gobbled up by the tangled forest a long time ago. The gate is padlocked. We peek over the rusty fence. It's an ugly, dark place. It doesn't fit with picture-perfect Prince Edward County and all its rolling farms and pretty vineyards and beautiful beaches. It looks forgotten. No wonder there's no cell service. No one lives around here.

Even though it's getting dark, I know Gus wants to climb the fence, but when I look at her, she's not looking into the woods. She's got her eyes on the road and a motorbike that's speeding toward us. I watch it too. It slows then stops right in the middle of the road. It's pretty far off but we can hear the engine revving.

"Do you think that's the guy who put a hole in our tire?" I ask.

Gus steps out onto the road to get a better look. I join her.

The rider lifts something from his shoulder and swings it down in front of him.

"Shit. Get in the camper. Now!" says Gus.

I stumble to the passenger-side door. Gus runs to the driver's side. We both jump in. She starts the engine.

"Get down. He's got a—" Before she gets the word out, there's a loud crack that echoes across the night, sending birds out of the forest and into the sky. He shot at us.

I duck my head. She hits the gas and we take off down the road.

The motorbike follows us all the way through Black River. It keeps following us as we pass the sunflower fields near the turnoff to the Sandbanks. Sitting low in my seat, I peek in the sideview mirror. That's when I see a second motorbike join the first.

Gus grips the steering wheel. Her eyes dart to the rearview

mirror every few seconds. We can't see their faces inside their black helmets. She doesn't turn onto a dark side road or drive too fast or try to lose them. She sticks to the main highway heading to Picton. She says they'll easily catch us if she tries to make a move.

We reach Picton and head down Main. It's quieter than I'd hoped. They stick with us, staying back and waiting. For what, I don't know. But as we reach the other side of town, I hear their engines rev. They're speeding up. One gets superclose to our bumper—so close he could touch it. Gus slams her foot on the brake and the motorbike skids out of the way. The two bikes nearly collide. They back off and that's when Gus hits the gas. I hang on. She's able to put some pavement between us and the bikes. She takes a sudden left turn and I'm flung sideways. We swerve into someone's driveway and come to a stop. An OPP police cruiser is parked in front of us. We're at Able and Noble's farmhouse.

The two men are sitting on the front porch.

They both rise from their chairs when they see us.

The two motorbikes slow then keep going down the highway.

Able comes down the steps.

"I heard you were still around," he says.

"Any chance we could park here for the night?" she asks.

He looks at his grandfather. Noble nods.

"It's fine with Pops," he says.

NOBLE MAKES US MEATLOAF SANDWICHES WITH THE LEFTOVERS from their supper. Then I take a hot bath. It's the best bath I've ever had in my whole life. When I'm changing, I find the eagle feather in the back pocket of my cords. The one Dod gave me on Canada Day. I'd forgotten all about it. I put on my pajamas and make a mental note to put it on our evidence wall before I go to sleep. Better late than never.

It's a sticky night and I find everyone out on the front porch catching a breeze. I join them, keeping an ear out for motorbikes and delivery trucks and zombies. All I can hear are crickets. A half-moon sits low in the sky. I imagine someone sitting on the curve of that moon and looking back at earth. Would they only see half a planet? Half of it light, half dark. I know they wouldn't see me. I'm in the dark half. The half without Howard.

Noble tells us the whole town is talking about what happened out at Baylis Vineyards. Able says he heard it was a busy day at the detachment but he's hoping things have quieted. He's got to go in soon. He's on the overnight shift. Noble and Able don't say anything about the kayakers or what was found on the shores of East Lake, but their eyes say it all. Gus sees it too.

"It's not him," says Gus.

Able looks at her.

"The human remains," she says. "I know it."

He doesn't ask why she's so sure. He lets it go. And he doesn't ask what we've been up to since he dropped us off at Toby's Garage. I wonder if it's because he already knows that we almost drove over some park wardens and broke into Kirk and Vivi's house and have a pile of drugs hidden in the wheel well of our camper. Probably not.

Noble gets up from his chair and goes inside the house. At first I think he's gone to bed but then I hear noises in the kitchen.

"Did you visit that friend of yours?" Able asks.

"Who?" says Gus.

"Stenson," he remembers.

"Oh yeah, we did. Thanks for that," she says.

A few minutes later, Noble comes back out. He's got a cup of hot milk for me and a glass of brandy for Gus. He says it'll help us sleep. Able goes in to change for work. I sit and sip and twirl my eagle feather between two fingers.

"That's a beauty," says Noble, eyeing the feather.

"It was a gift," I tell him.

"That eagle must have a message for you," he says.

"It does?" I ask.

"Sacred objects like that feather carry wisdom in them," he says.

"What's the eagle trying to tell me?" I ask.

"Well, let's see. An eagle can fly very high and see very far. Could be telling you to look where you're not looking," he says.

I tip the feather this way and that. The blacks shimmer in the moonlight. I can't see what it's trying to tell me but I like that it's trying.

The three of us sit quietly for a while as the crickets chitchat back and forth. Soon, Noble rises slowly from his chair.

"Are you sure you don't want to bunk inside?" asks Noble.

"We're pretty cozy in the camper, thanks," says Gus.

"Suit yourself. I think it's time to put these old bones to bed," he says.

"Good night," I say.

Noble gives me a wink and heads inside just as Able comes back out. Able straightens his gun holster and hat. It looks like he's wearing a costume and he's not really a policeman.

"Can I show you something before you go?" Gus asks.

"I'm running late and there's only two of us on tonight," he says. "Can it wait till tomorrow?"

"It won't take long," Gus insists.

There's something about the way she's looking at him that pricks my skin.

Gus once told me, there comes a time in every investigation when the darkness closes in and you can feel yourself losing your way. That's when you have to shine a light on what you have—you have to trust someone. I think she's decided to trust Able.

Able follows Gus to the camper. I trail behind them. The sky is clear and starry and that half-moon hangs there watching. Gus yanks on the side doors and lets them fall open. Our evidence wall is moonlit.

He tries to take it all in. The map marked with Xs, the article, the police report, the business cards, and the sacred objects hung like decorations. I hold my breath. He moves closer and touches things and reads things and then he points to my baggie of diamonds. Gus explains that I found them on the beach. He removes them from the wall and examines them. Gus shows him Howard's notebook. She walks him through what we've pieced together about Howard's investigation into Pike. She tells him about the missing thumb drive, the dead accountant, and the casino connection. She leaves Candice out for now. Gus plays Howard's *just-in-case* video, then she shows Able another one. It's a grainy video she shot at the military airfield. A video she forgot to show me. I lean in to watch. It's dark but I can tell it's Creepy Man. He's unloading crates from his truck with a woman in overalls.

"I know her," he says. "That's Kat. She's a fueler at CFD Quinte. Looks like a wine delivery to me."

"It's crystal meth," says Gus, nodding to the baggie in his hand.

"I thought you found this on a beach," he says.

Gus takes a deep breath. She knows it's a lot for him to take in all at once.

"I showed you this because I think I can trust you. And because we need someone on the inside," she says.

"Inside?" He squints.

"You said there are only two of you on tonight," she says.

She raises her eyebrows. I inch away from them as the air cools.

"You want me to snoop around the detachment," he says. "Why would I do that?"

"Because one of your OPP buddies is on Pike's payroll," says Gus. "Maybe more than one."

He shakes his head and starts pacing.

Now I see the real reason Gus drove to Able's house. It wasn't just to get away from the motorbikes. It was to use Able. Ever since Candice told us the local police were in with Pike, she's been wondering if they were involved in Howard's disappearance. I didn't want to think about it because it scares me.

"I got it from a reliable source," says Gus.

Able just stands there.

I know we're at a farmhouse in Prince Edward County, but it feels more like me and Gus are standing on the edge of the dark side of the planet, waiting for him to reach out and pull us into the light.

He looks down at the baggie of drugs in his hand.

"I can't help you," he says.

My heart withers.

"You think I'm crazy," says Gus.

"I mean, come on. A rusty hubcap, an old fishing lure my pops gave you. None of this proves anything. Except that you've been withholding evidence in a cold case," he says. "I don't think you're crazy. But if I'm being honest, I do think you're a little paranoid. You've been through a good deal of trauma and maybe you're seeing things that aren't there. I get it. You want to know what happened to Howard Baylis. But I'm not going to break the law because of a pink ribbon and a dead flower."

I can't look at him. He's not Able anymore. He's Constable Journey. A real policeman.

Gus closes the doors of the camper. My legs are wobbly. I sit down on the grass by the laneway.

"I'm sorry," he says. "Listen, I'll be back at nine tomorrow morning and we can talk more then. Get some rest. You look like you could both use some."

Constable Journey heads to his police cruiser. Gus leans against the camper and watches him reverse out of the laneway. The farmhouse is dark except for the front porch lights. They glow orange and night bugs swarm to their warm light. I wish I was a night bug.

"Are we paranoid?" I ask her.

I don't know what it means, but I know it's not nice.

"No, Boo, we're not," she says. "He just doesn't see it."

"I bet whatever was on that thumb drive would make him see it," I say.

She looks over at me.

"The thumb drive," she says. "Right."

She folds her arms and tips her head like she's trying to see something.

"You know, when Kirk said he saw Howard in the window, I assumed Howard was up there hiding the drive," she says. "But if he knew Pike saw him, he might have changed his mind."

"And left the party with it," I say, picking up her thoughts.

"It wasn't at Butterfly Beach, so maybe he hid it somewhere else," she says.

"Like in the camper?" I add.

I stand up and brush off the grass.

She turns to me. I know it's just the porch light, but her face is glowing. Gus jumps in the camper and I follow. We run our fingers along windowsills and inside cupboards. We peek under beds and tip out drawers to check their undersides. We lift the carpet and hunt around in the wheel well. Then Gus remembers the hidden compartment. We scramble to the front seats. *Maybe I missed it when I found the notebook.* She checks the compartment, but it's empty. I open the glove box. I don't find the thumb drive but I find something else. A small satin bag. I open the bag and pull out the little painting of the blue creeping thyme.

"I forgot all about this," I tell her, holding it up and dropping the bag between us. "They told me Lula painted it."

"Stenson's daughter?" she says, looking over. "Who told you that?"

"The hippie chicks. I should have said something at the fair, but then we saw Dod getting beat up and it rained and I forgot I even had it," I tell her.

"So that's where she lives. With the hippie chicks," she says.

Gus spots the satin bag. She picks it up. There's something printed on it. Gus holds the bag up to the dome light. It's a picture of a snake eating its own tail. Inside the circle made by the snake is the word *Gwella*. Gus flips the bag over to see if there's anything on the back and an object falls from the bag and lands in her lap.

I stare at it.

It's a silver ring with a stone the color of marram grass.

Gus picks up the jade ring.

I can't speak.

She looks over at me. I gasp. She can tell from the look on my face that I recognize it. It's the ring Howard bought her. The one he was supposed to give her three years ago. The one he carried in his pocket waiting for the perfect time to propose.

One of a kind, said the woman at the antique shop.

The memory washes over me.

What do you think, Sweet Pea?

I think she'll say yes.

Howard laughs and touches the end of my nose.

I loved when he did that.

25

THE RECORDING

WE ABANDONED OUR SEARCH FOR THE THUMB DRIVE.

We had a new mission. The hippie chicks. We needed to find out how and why they had Howard's ring. We were being led closer and closer to the truth. I could feel it. Even if Constable Journey didn't believe in us. We still did. And this breadcrumb had fallen right into Gus's lap.

Look where you're not looking.

That's what the eagle feather was telling us.

But where?

We had one clue. The word *Gwella*.

We remembered that Stenson said Lula lived at a retreat. Pike called it a commune. Maybe Gwella was a place. We searched on our phones but couldn't find anything in the county—no communes and no retreats called Gwella. All we found was a definition. The word was Welsh for *make better*. Maybe it was just something they put on their bags.

"Someone knows where they live," said Gus.

It was midnight. Too late to call or visit anyone. Too late to go roaming around the county in the dark. I think it was the warm milk but I don't even remember falling asleep.

IT'S ALL A BLUR AS DAYLIGHT FORCES MY EYELIDS OPEN. I'M IN MY bed. I look over and Gus is in the front seat talking on her phone. I bet she stayed awake the whole night to keep watch in case the motorbikes came back. I peek out the side window. The sun is still low. Constable Journey's police cruiser isn't back yet. It must be before nine.

I get dressed and climb up front just as Gus hangs up. She was talking to Hildy.

"I was right to call her. That Hildy's got her ear to the ground," she says.

I can't picture Hildy lying on the ground listening to the dirt, but I nod.

Gus says Hildy knew all about the Gwella. It's not a place. It's what the hippie chicks call themselves. They live off the grid and only come to town to sell their crafts or buy supplies. Most folks leave them be, but the ignoramuses—*Hildy's words*—don't like that a bunch of women live alone in the woods. They've been threatened and called freaks and dykes and witches. It's partly why the Gwella keep their home base a secret. And they sure don't like strangers coming by. Hildy said, we'd been warned.

"But how can we go by if she doesn't know where they live?" I ask, rubbing sleep from my eyes.

Gus smiles. It turns out that Hildy's second cousin used to date Lula and he'd gone to visit her when she came back and started living with the Gwella. They live in the woods near Half Moon Bay. No address. But Hildy said if we follow the road to the RV park, we can't miss the oil tank. Looks like a giant kettle. That's where they live.

"There's more," says Gus. "Remember the message I left her about the private land? She'd already done some digging. She got the lot number. Found out the land was subdivided and a portion was sold to Pike Enterprises."

"Pike owns the land?" I ask.

"Part of it, but she only bought it this spring. So she didn't own any of it two years ago when Hugo saw the camper. Hildy couldn't find the landowner's name, just a numbered company," says Gus. "But she offered to keep digging. She'll text if she finds anything new."

"Hildy's the best," I say.

"In the end, I'm not sure it even matters. It's possible whoever owns it didn't even know the camper was there," she says. "That land looked pretty derelict."

We check the map for Half Moon Bay. When we find it, we look at each other. We already know the way there. It's not far from Little Bluff Conservation Area and the private land.

"Weird," I say to Gus. "Maybe the Gwella own the land?"

"Only one way to find out," she says.

We fasten our seat belts. Gus turns on the engine and shifts into drive.

We don't even make it out of the laneway.

Constable Journey pulls up in his cruiser and blocks our way.

I check the time. He's back way too early.

I brace myself for the convoy of police cars that are about to swoop in behind him and surround us but they don't. His face looks drained of all color. He gets out of his car and comes over to us. Gus rolls down the window.

"I'm glad you're still here," he says.

Gus folds her arms.

"We were just leaving. You made it pretty clear whose side you're on," says Gus.

The constable shakes his head and looks from Gus to me. His eyes aren't angry, they're watery, like he's almost sorry he found us. He takes off his hat and wipes his forehead. Then I feel it. He's got news. Bad news. Gus feels it too. She grabs the steering wheel to steady herself. Before I can put my hands over my ears, he speaks.

"You were right," he says. "About everything."

He stares at the ground.

"It's Muirhead," he says.

"For fuck's sake!" she shouts. "I thought you were going to say they'd identified the remains."

He looks up from the ground and sees the dread on both our faces.

"No, god no. Sorry. The coroner's still waiting on dental records. No ID yet," he says.

"What's going on?" she asks.

As he tells us what happened, he pulls at his collar like his uniform is choking him. We don't say anything as we listen to his story.

Last night, on his way to the detachment, he kept thinking about one thing we'd shown him. The video from the military airfield. He'd dismissed it as a wine delivery. But then it struck him that commercial cargo doesn't ship from that airfield. It's strictly a military training facility. When he got to work, he decided to check the evidence room to see if our baggie matched a nasty batch of crystal meth that had been circulating in the county last summer. Some had been confiscated at a bush party so he went to find the evidence box to compare it.

Constable Smith, another rookie, was the only other person in the building. Smith was manning the front desk, or so he thought. But someone came into the evidence room. Constable Journey was behind a high shelf so he didn't see who it was at first. He was about to show himself, thinking it was Smith, when he heard voices. He recognized them. Marica Pike and Staff Sergeant Muirhead.

Civilians were definitely not allowed in the evidence room and Muirhead never showed up at night, so Constable Journey knew something was off. He stayed quiet and hidden.

Pike was angry. She said her truck was followed to the airfield. She was worried things were about to blow up. She wanted *that woman and her kid* taken care of, once and for all. It took the constable a few seconds to reach for his phone and press record.

He plays us the recording of what they said next.

"That's rich, Marica," Muirhead says. "You're hardly clean in all this."

"Yet despite the dirt under *your* greedy little fingernails, you still can't seem to do your job," she says. "His girlfriend is turning out to be a bigger pain in my ass than he was, but you haven't arrested her yet."

"On what charge?" he asks.

"Make one up. You're the top cop, aren't you?" she says. "Get your little piggies back in line."

"Nelson and Dewer have been on this from day one!" he says.

"You should have made that entire fucking van disappear the second it turned up two weeks ago," she says.

"I had it searched and wiped clean before anyone got there," he says. "But that security guard had already seen it. I had to do it by the book so there'd be no questions. Forensics didn't find a thing."

"But I bet they could tell someone messed with it," she says.

"I'm taking care of it," he says.

"Everything you're doing has only made that woman more rabid," she says.

"She's got nothing," he says. "My guys are keeping an eye on her."

"Those two piglets of yours are useless. Case in point—that fuckup at Baylis Vineyards. I did the hard part. Handed them the evidence on a poisonous platter, but you just ended up getting in the way," she says.

"It was all part of my plan," he says.

"Oh, do tell," she says.

"Those human remains presented an opportunity. So I took it. Seems they're turning out to be pretty hard to identify," he says. "At first, the coroner thought they belonged to this fisherman who went missing a year ago after his boat capsized, but he's about to change his mind. His report will say it's Howard Baylis. Drowned. Suicide most likely. Case closed. His girlfriend goes home."

"Jesus Christ. Are you an idiot? She won't believe it or she'll want proof and she doesn't scare, clearly. I've met her. She's not one to tuck her tail between her legs and go home," says Pike.

"She did two years ago. Give it time," he says.

"We don't have fucking time, Julius!" she shouts.

"I'll handle it," he mumbles.

"You know what'll happen if you don't. Career, pension, hush money, reputation—over. Life as you know it, fucking over," she hisses. "You don't want the press getting their hands on those photos of you and those very young ladies, do you? What will people think of their local hero then?"

Muirhead is quiet.

"Cuckoo bird got your tongue, Julius," she says.

He clears his throat. His voice is tight.

"Okay, okay. I'll do what needs to be done," he says.

"And what exactly do you think needs to be done, Julius?" she asks.

"You want me to spell it out?" he asks quietly.

There's a long pause.

"They won't find the bodies," he says.

"That's my good little staff sergeant," she says.

26

THE MAP

WE HIDE THE CAMPER BEHIND THE FARMHOUSE NEXT TO NOBLE'S beat-up Corolla and follow the constable inside. He stumbles through the back door of his grandfather's house like his legs have gone numb.

Noble is sitting in the kitchen. He rises when we come in. He knows something's wrong. His grandson tells him what's happened and plays the recording. I can see he loves his grandfather by the way he shares everything with him and watches his face as he does. There are no lies between these two men. The constable removes his hat and gun belt. He hangs them by the back door. He unbuttons the collar of his uniform and lays his badge on the kitchen table. That's when Constable Journey becomes Able again. I'm glad to see him.

Noble isn't sure what to do. Able can't imagine going back to work. He left early, saying he didn't feel well. And he is sick. Heartsick. He always knew Muirhead was crusty and stubborn, but he admired him. He was his mentor. And he thought his fellow rookies, Nelson and Dewer, were friends. Able can't make sense of it. He's afraid his career might be over before it's begun.

I know most of what's in that recording is bad. But one thing isn't. The human remains aren't Howard's. Muirhead said so. Gus knew they weren't all along, but I've been holding my breath since yesterday when we first heard about them. I can breathe again.

Able and Noble spend the morning talking upstairs and after lunch we all gather in the kitchen with Howard's notebook and our map. Able still looks shaky. He rocks in his chair. Gus paces. Noble leans against the kitchen sink. They trade places, moving around one another like they're doing a strange dance. I know this dance. It's what grown-ups do when things get bad. And the head of the local OPP talking about our dead bodies is bad.

"That's an old map," says Noble.

"Tell us about these?" Able says, pointing to the *X*s.

Now he's listening. Not like last night. Before Gus can speak, I jump in. I want to dance too. I prop my elbows on the table, then I point to each *X* and explain what they mean. I start at the beginning with the Picton Airport.

"Right here is where the camper was found. This is Pike Winery, where someone poked a hole in our tire and we saw Creepy Man for the first time. This is Will Stenson's place and this is Butterfly Beach, where we found the diamonds," I tell them.

"Diamonds?" asks Noble.

"Crystal meth," says Gus.

"Creepy Man?" asks Able.

"He works for Pike," says Gus. "Her delivery guy. Does other *errands* for her too."

"Like breaking into houses," I say. "Like here? This *X* is Baylis Vineyards. We caught Creepy Man inside Kirk and Vivi's house. And this is the military airfield where we followed him the other night and he chased us all the way down this road to the Picton fairgrounds. And over here is where Hugo said he saw our camper in the woods two years ago."

"Hugo Remedy?" asks Able.

I nod and keep going.

"Yep, he said he saw it right there near Little Bluff Conservation Area," I tell him. I trace my finger toward Half Moon Bay. "And over here is—"

Gus removes my hand from the map and interrupts my story.

"That's where we got the pie." She nods at me. Her way of telling me to shut up.

She doesn't want to tell them about the Gwella yet. I know why. Gus doesn't trust easily and Able let her down when she needed him most. She's not very good at giving second chances.

"You've had quite the journey," says Noble.

"We were following Howard's footsteps," I tell him.

Noble lays his hands on the map and leans in to get a closer look.

"Let's see if we can figure out where your friend was headed," he says.

"Pops knows the county like the back of his hand. He was a land surveyor before he retired," says Able. "Show him that video Howard made when he was driving."

I pull Howard's phone from my back pocket. Noble watches the video. He pauses, rewinds, then plays it again.

"It's hard to tell where he is. There's silvergrass along the highway. But there's a lot of that in the county. Wait. There. Over his shoulder," says Noble.

We all lean in to watch as he rewinds then pauses the video. He points to something.

"That's a marker," says Noble.

"It's blurry but I think that's a thirteen," says Able.

"County Road Thirteen," says Noble. "That's where he was."

We check the map. County Road 13 runs along the shore of Lake Ontario near Little Bluff. We were on that road last night when the motorbike shot at us.

Gus doesn't tell them that, either.

"Remedy told you he saw the camper there?" Able points to the woods next to the conservation area.

Gus nods.

"That's a remote stretch of road, about eighteen miles, end to end," says Noble.

"Can't be that many markers," says Able.

"In the video, your friend says he got turned around. That the map's all wrong. He's right," says Noble.

The old man points to several places on the map.

"There's the one in Cherry Valley. That one near the Glenora Ferry, and this one over at Warings Corner—none of these roads are there anymore. This map is full of roads that don't exist. I'm surprised folks still sell these relics. It wouldn't matter in most parts of the province, but in these parts, roads disappear all the time. Surveyors call them ghost roads," he says.

"How can a road disappear?" I ask.

"That's what happens in a place where wind and water and sand make the rules. Strong westerlies, high waves, and giant dunes make the land around here come alive. The farmers who settled the county back in the day made the mistake of clearing all the trees for their crops and cattle. Without the white pines and the silver maples, the dunes had nothing to cling to. They started drifting inland like a slow-moving tsunami. Sand crept across fields and buried entire roads. It took over a century of tree planting to hold back the dunes. To this day, when the winds whip up, the forces of nature can literally change the map," he says.

All four of us stare down at the old map.

"That's why we missed the turnoff to the conservation area," says Gus.

Noble runs his finger over the map and stops on a road that crosses County Road 13.

"That's one right there. That's a buried road," he says. "If a person was using an old map like this one to try to get someplace . . ."

"He'd get lost," Gus whispers.

Gus gets up from the table and walks to the sink. She keeps her back to us.

"He made the same mistake we did?" I say, my voice cracking.

We really were following in his footsteps. Gus pours herself a glass of water.

"It's best you two lie low," says Able. Gus doesn't move. "But I could go search the area and check out those woods."

"Easier said than done," says Noble. "Tricky terrain. Those woods are riddled with sinkholes and marsh. There's a network of caves that snakes from the bluffs to an underground lake below the woods. When the waves get high, the lake floods and the woods soak up all that moisture like a sponge. They're too mucky to navigate and even if you made some headway, there's a bog smack in the middle. A kind of dead zone," he says.

I shiver. Gus stares out the window above the sink.

"Pops knows everything there is to know about the land around here," says Able.

Gus turns around.

"Do you know who owns those woods?" she asks.

"Can't say I do. But I know who used to own it. Fellow by the name of Christopher McCorkell. Back in the forties. A rich New York department store owner. He bought the land on a visit to the county. The story goes that it was a real gem back then—lush forest stretching all the way to those high cliffs. A little piece of paradise with a great view of the lake. He paid a pretty penny for it. He cleared trees and set about building a grand mansion—a surprise wedding gift for his fiancée. He built a massive ornamental garden with stone walkways and terraces. He put in two pools, three tennis courts, an amusement park, and a private zoo. The whole nine yards. It was a palace fit for a queen. But before she ever stepped foot in the place, his beloved died of pneumonia. Then his little piece of heaven started to sink. No one had told him about the caves. The underground erosion got worse with each passing year. His new road flooded, his mansion's foundation began to crack, and his gardens turned to rot. Folks said the land was cursed. His heart wasn't in it anymore so he finally packed up and never came back. Years later he sold the land for peanuts," says Noble. "It's sat there ever since."

LONG AFTER EVERYONE HAS GONE TO SLEEP, I LIE AWAKE ON THE sofa thinking about the sinking mansion and the poor fiancée. I hate that Howard disappeared near a cursed forest with a sad story. I gently rub the bill of his baseball cap. I've worn it to bed every night since I found it.

Gus had barely said a word all through dinner. Able called in sick for his night shift. He was exhausted. Noble said a good night's rest would help us all see the way forward. Gus insisted we sleep in the living room. She said it was because she didn't want to put Able out of his bedroom again, but I know her too well. She's up to something. I sit up and look across the dark living room. Gus is not in the armchair. A shadow crosses the wall. It's her. She tiptoes out of the kitchen, sits, and starts pulling on her running shoes.

"Where are you going?" I ask.

She jerks her head up.

"Keep your voice down," she whispers.

"You're not going to see the Gwella all alone," I say.

"Shhhhh," she says. "Go back to sleep."

"But it's dark," I say.

"Dark is good," she replies.

A floorboard creaks above our heads. Someone is awake up-stairs. Footsteps start coming down the stairs. Gus puts a finger to her lips. Noble rounds the banister and shuffles into the kitchen. He doesn't look in the living room. He gets a glass from the cup-board and places it on the counter. The only light comes from the fridge as he opens it. Gus steps quietly across the dark living room and into the front foyer. I can see her reaching for the door. Noble pours milk into the glass. Gus slowly tries to pull open the front door without making a sound.

I don't have time to think. Her back is to me and so is Noble's. I slip off the sofa and crawl across the living room and over to the back door in the far corner of the kitchen. If he turns around, he'll see me. Noble steps back to the open fridge with the milk carton. He's humming to himself. I reach up, unlatch the screen door, and push it open. I crawl out, making sure it doesn't bang shut behind me. Then I get to my feet and race for the camper. I look over my shoulder. Gus hasn't come around the farmhouse yet. I kick the back bumper in just the right spot. The side doors fly open. I crawl in and hide underneath the dining table, pulling the doors shut. Seconds later, I hear Gus unlocking the driver's-side door. She gets in and waits. She's probably making sure No-ble goes back upstairs before she starts the engine. After a minute or two, we roll slowly out from behind the house. My heart is in my throat.

We drive for a while before I feel the wheels hit gravel and the camper come to a stop. I think she's pulled onto the shoulder. She turns off the engine. Gus climbs into the back. I hug my knees tight, trying to stay as small as I can. Her legs are right across from me, but her back is to me. She's rooting around in the drawers of the kitchenette. A beam of light flashes on and then off. She's grabbing a flashlight. She'll need it in the woods. Gus climbs back up front. The dome light comes on as she opens the

door. I have to stay close or I might lose her in the dark. I panic.
I move too fast and too soon. As I scramble to get to my feet, I
bump my head on the dining table with a loud bonk. Gus spins
around. She's clutching a gun and it's pointed right at my face.

"It's me! It's Bly!" I screech.

She drops the gun like it's burning hot and collapses like a
rag doll between the seats. But instead of getting mad at me, she
starts crying. Gus never cries. And this isn't just a tear or two.
She's weeping. I don't know what to do. I pick myself up and
search for something to make her stop. I find some paper napkins.
I hold them out to her, but she doesn't take them. She doesn't see
them through all the tears. She cries and cries in great big heaving
gulps. Whenever anyone else cries, it always makes me cry. But
not this time.

I look at the gun. *Where did she get it?* Then I know. It's Able's.
I pick it up and place it on the dining table. Then I sit and wait
until her tears have run out. Slowly, her sobs quiet and when she's
done, she looks up at me with wet stains streaking her face. I hold
out the napkins again. This time she takes them and blows her
nose.

"I could have shot you," she says, looking down at her trembling hands.

"But you didn't," I tell her. "I'm okay, see?"

I stand up so she can see there are no holes in me. I lift the
baseball cap off my head to show her there are no holes there. She
looks at my bare feet sticking out of my pajama bottoms.

"Jesus, I've become my mother and I've turned you into me,"
she says.

I don't understand at first. Then I remember the story about
her mother's death. Shannon Monet went out in her car one night
to confront a bad guy. Gus was hiding in the back seat when her
mother was killed. Gus was only eight. A kid hiding out where

she wasn't supposed to be. Seeing horrible things she wasn't meant to see.

"You didn't do this to me," I tell her.

"It's never going to stop. The past is always going to come for me. It's like a broken record that keeps skipping and skipping and playing the same song over and over, hoping I'll finally listen and I'll get it this time," she says. "I do. The past is repeating. A simple, stupid little wrong turn. My dad died because he took a wrong turn. And now Howard."

That's why she was so quiet at dinner. She was thinking about a wrong turn. I know the story of her father too. She never met him because he died before she was born. Charlie Monet was a police officer on a routine call. There was a chase, a wrong turn was taken, and he was ambushed. I see now why she's always had a hard time trusting the police even though both her parents were RCMP. Their jobs got them killed.

I know she's right.

The past is coming for us.

And it does repeat and skip and chase after us but not because it's trying to warn us. I think it's teaching us. Gus knows this, but she's not really herself right now. She did almost shoot me. Plus, she didn't eat any dinner and she hasn't slept in almost two days.

I stand. Gus stares at her feet.

"Gus, time to get up," I tell her. "We're doing this together."

I tug on her arm. She looks up at me.

"I'm not letting you disappear too," I say. "Then I'd have to find both of you all by myself."

I don't yell or cry or break out in hives or try to tap out a familiar rhythm to sooth myself. I don't do any of this. Instead, I pick the gun up and hand it to her.

Our eyes meet as she takes the gun.

27

THE KNOCK

HILDY WAS RIGHT. THE OIL TANK DOES LOOK LIKE A GIANT KET-tle. As we creep through the woods and get closer, I realize the Gwella actually live inside it. The three-story metal tank has been turned into a house. Holes have been cut out and windows added. Orange light flickers from inside. A large screen door thumps lightly in the night breeze. A wood veranda circles the lower level, lit by lanterns. Rope hammock chairs hang from the veranda's rafters. Steps lead from it to a rough patch of grass. No one is outside. We can't see anyone inside either, but we hear distant voices.

We crouch in the trees with the flashlight off. I'm wearing the slippers I had in the camper. My runners are back at Noble's house. My feet are sore from the long walk down their road, past the NO TRESPASSING sign, and past all those weird marks scratched into the trees like letters in some made-up alphabet. Now that we're here, I really wish I had my runners so I could run away fast if I need to. Worry bugs crawl up my legs.

Don't witches make strange markings in the woods?

"People used to think redheads were witches," I whisper to Gus. She keeps her eyes on the kettle house.

"People are stupid," she says. The walk did her good and she seems like herself again.

"Do you think people hate us because of our red hair?" I ask.

"People don't hate you, Boo. Me? They have trouble with me," she says.

The compound is lit up with flaming bamboo torches, just like the ones we had when we were camping. There's a row of small greenhouses near the kettle house. There's a well with a bucket, a pergola with a rough stone patio under it, and a large woodshed. Hanging on the side of the shed is a metal rack of bicycles. Pathways lead from building to building then disappear into the woods.

The voices rise and fall, almost like they're singing, only not. I don't like it. Maybe they've brainwashed Lula and she's their slave and they make her cook and clean for them. Maybe they'll do the same thing to me. I don't want to be a cult slave or get boiled in a witch's caldron. *Is that what they've done with Howard?* I shudder as my courage runs off screaming into the woods, leaving me to fend for myself.

"What's the sound?" I whisper. "Is that chanting?"

Gus gives me a *how would I know?* look.

That doesn't sound like hippie chicks to me.

The weird noises are coming from down one of the paths that leads into the very, very dark woods. We spot a thin trail of smoke snaking above the trees. A ripple of terror shoots through me. Gus starts moving. I grab her arm.

"But what if they're witches?" I croak.

She walks out into the open.

I have no choice but to follow. I'm not getting left behind. We scurry across the patch of grass in front of the house. I pray no one's looking out a window. Gus does a quick search inside the greenhouses, down the well, then around the woodshed.

Nothing. No Howard. No Lula.

Why didn't I just stay curled up on Noble's cozy sofa under his cozy blanket in his cozy farmhouse? But I know why.

We move down the path toward a glowing fire. Gus leads. I stay close. I try to focus on the gun tucked in the back of her jeans, but all I can see in my head is a chanting horde of cult people dancing around a flaming pit of snakes. I feel sick to my stomach. I see a clearing ahead. The voices are getting louder. The path narrows. I peek around Gus and see movement. People are up ahead. It's them. I tug on Gus to try to slow her down. We're getting too close. They'll see us. The flames from the fire are lighting up the path ahead. Gus stops just before she's about to step into the light. We both watch wide-eyed. It's the Gwella. Their flowy dresses move like wings, floating and rippling, silhouetted by the flames in the firepit they surround. They're holding hands as they sway and chant like one massive, winged forest creature.

A loud gong is struck. The sound came from behind us. Back at the kettle house. The Gwella suddenly stop floating. They go silent. Their silhouettes are frozen. The only movement is the flames. The only sound is the crackling from the firepit. One of the women turns to look at the path. I gasp and they all look in our direction.

"Intruders!" yells someone.

Gus stumbles backward and crashes into me. I turn to run but I can't. A woman is right behind me, aiming a crossbow at my head. The pale woman from the fair runs up beside her. She's got a spear held high. Gus drags me behind her back and pulls out the gun. She points it at the two women.

I hear footsteps behind us on the path. I turn. They're all coming. And the woman with the long braids from the fair is leading them. She's holding an axe. We're surrounded. Gus doesn't know which way to point the gun. She tries to keep me behind her while she goes back and forth between the two groups. They slowly close in.

"You're trespassing on private property," Crossbow Woman says in a booming voice.

"What have you done with him?" yells Gus.

The braided woman's face is glowing in the light of a nearby torch.

"We can't tell you what we've done, unless we know who you're talking about," she says. Her voice is icy calm.

"Howard Baylis. He disappeared not far from here. We just want him back and we'll leave you in peace," says Gus.

"You talk of peace and yet—" says the braided woman, pointing to the gun.

I'm shaking all over. And I can't keep quiet any longer.

"Where's Howard?" I cry. "And Lula?"

The braided woman looks at me. Her eyes shift to my bracelet then back to me. She takes a deep breath and slowly places her axe on the ground. She nods to the other women. They don't look like they want to but the others lower their weapons too. The braided woman walks right up to Gus, places her hand gently on the gun, and lowers it. Gus doesn't try to stop her.

"Come," says the woman. She moves past us toward the kettle house.

The other two step aside, but they're still glaring at us. We follow the braided woman. As we move down the path, I notice the faces of other women in the trees around us. Lots of them. We really are surrounded. Lit by splinters of firelight, they look like ghosts hovering in the smoky darkness of the woods. The forest floor crunches under their bare feet as they come out of the woods and trail behind us.

The braided woman leads us to the kettle house, where she sits on the top step of the veranda facing us. We stand in front of her. The other women form a semicircle behind us. It feels like we're on trial. I inch closer to Gus. When the braided woman nods, the women all sit cross-legged in the grass. I almost sit too. Gus tucks the gun in the back of her jeans.

"Lula is inside with the others, sleeping. The young ones don't attend moon ceremonies until they're ready," she says. "I don't know this Howard person."

I don't like that she says his name, but her voice is very calming. I believe her.

"They call me Ling. You've met our sentries, Steph and Tania." She nods to the two women who came at us with weapons. "We're protective of our little community. We have to be, especially of our younger sisters."

I suddenly feel like a bad person. I want her to know we don't go sneaking around in the middle of the night pointing guns at people all the time.

"I'm Bly. Do you remember me? You gave me a card at the fair. You said Lula painted it," I remind her.

"There was a ring in the bag with it," says Gus. "It belonged to Howard. We just want to know where you got it. We're not here to cause any harm."

"That may be true, but what one *means* and what *happens* can be two very different things," she says, like she's giving a sermon. "Just the other day, I caused Lula harm when I let her go to that fair. She wasn't ready. I didn't *mean* to, but it *happened* nonetheless, didn't it?"

Lula was at the fair.

Then it dawns on me. She was the girl in the shadows of the tent. The other two were talking about her like she wasn't there, but it was Lula the whole time. She had her face covered, so I didn't recognize her from the picture in the missing person's report.

"It was her," I cry. "She gave me the ring."

"Wait, what?" says Gus, turning to face me.

"She was trying to tell us something," I gasp.

"Who?" Gus says.

"Lula. She knew the ring belonged to us," I tell Gus. "That's why she put it in my bag!"

Gus takes a step toward Ling.

"We have to speak to her," says Gus.

Ling stands. There are murmurs behind us from the women sitting on the grass. She looks past us to them.

"Sisters. You may return to the fire," she says.

I turn to look. Moving as one, they rise to their feet and head back down the path. All except Steph.

"We're fine, you can go." Ling nods to Steph, who hesitates then follows the others.

Ling waves us closer as she sits back down.

"Sit a moment," Ling says.

I sit on the first step, but Gus stays standing. She's not following Ling's orders.

"You think us some sort of cult or coven of witches, no doubt," she says.

"If the pointy hat fits," says Gus.

"We prefer that, actually. Cults and witches scare people. Fear keeps us safe. It keeps them from prying. Most people anyway," she says, looking Gus up and down.

"All those women are here because they came here. They chose to be here," she says. "They come to get well, feel safe, and heal. Just as Lula did. We are a family. A safe space. A collective."

"An armed collective," adds Gus.

"Some of these women are hiding or running from very dangerous situations. The police and restraining orders often can't protect them. So we offer secrecy and, yes, we have weapons, but our strength is really in our numbers, and in our shared journey," she says.

"And you're the head witch?" asks Gus.

Ling smiles at Gus, never looking away from her gaze. I get the feeling she could match Gus in a staring contest.

"We believe that living in nature and engaging in spiritual practices, like the moon dance you witnessed, can repair the damaged parts of a soul. But on such a journey, it helps to have a leader or head witch, if you like. I prefer to think of myself as a chaperone. Most of these women feel powerless when they first come here. We encourage them to relinquish all power, all control so that when they are reborn, they can take it back fully."

There's a soft creak on the veranda. Ling turns to see who's behind her. A young girl peeks around the doorframe.

"Show yourself, little sister," says Ling.

The girl steps into the doorway but stays behind the screen door. She's wearing a white nightgown, and her long hair half covers her face. But I now see she's not a girl. She's a young woman. I recognize her from the picture.

"Lula?" I ask.

The girl doesn't answer.

"That's our Lula," says Ling.

"Is it okay with you if we talk to her?" asks Gus. She usually doesn't ask permission to do anything. She's seeing if polite works.

"You can certainly try, but she hasn't spoken since we found her—that'll be going on three years now, come this September," says Ling.

That's the month after Howard disappeared.

"Found her?" I ask.

She makes Lula sound like a stray cat.

"I remember it was a lovely autumn day. The leaves were changing color. We were foraging for elderberries along the bay. Tania found her near the shore, caked in mud. Half dead from dehydration. Terrified," she says.

"You didn't call the police, an ambulance?" Gus asks.

"We did. The police came out. Paramedics looked her over. But she became very agitated. She refused to go with them and her father was in prison, so we offered to take her in. Tania was a nurse in a previous life, so we could take care of her," she explains. "Lula chose to stay and she's been here ever since."

Lula slips out the door and stays pressed against the side of the house. I smile at her but she keeps her eyes down.

"What do you think happened to her?" I ask.

"The last time anyone in the county remembers seeing Lula was at a beach party below Little Bluff. We found her only a few miles from there. We heard someone had reported seeing her at a Belleville bus depot a few months later, but then nothing," she explains. "She'd been missing over a year by the time she came to us, so she couldn't have been on that shore the whole time. We assume she either ran away or got lost in the woods and survived somehow. She definitely experienced something traumatic. We just don't know what and we don't ask anymore."

"Do you own that land near the bluffs?" asks Gus. "Next to the conservation area?"

"We don't own any land," says Ling. "We can barely afford to lease this place."

Lula wiggles her bare toes as she rocks from side to side. She looks at my slippers. I think she likes them. I wiggle my toes and she covers her smile with both hands. Ling laughs as she watches us.

"Lula gets along with all our younger ones," Ling says. "She might not have words, but she always finds ways to communicate."

I feel sad for Lula. She looks so small and fragile. Like a young one herself.

"Why was she wearing a veil at the fair?" I ask Ling.

"She put it on. I think she was afraid of being recognized. It was her first outing and I guess she thought it would make her feel safe. But the fair was a terrible miscalculation on my part. She wasn't ready. When she left, she wouldn't stop scratching at her face and crying. She went right back to the state she was in when we found her. It's taken a couple of days, but she's slowly getting better, which is why she needs her rest."

Ling stands up again. I think this time she wants us to leave.

"Maybe one day she'll find a way to tell us her story," says Ling. "But for now, it's locked away inside her."

"Can I say goodbye to her?" I ask Ling.

She nods. I stand and very slowly climb the steps. Lula glances at my pajamas but she won't look me in the eye. She keeps rocking gently. I'm careful not to move too fast or get too close. I stop halfway up.

"Hi, Lula. I'm Bly," I tell her.

A tiny smile curves her pursed lips.

"Thank you for the ring," I say.

She meets my gaze for the first time.

"Did Howard give it to you?" I ask.

She stops rocking and looks away. Before I can say anything else, Lula turns and tiptoes back inside the house.

"Off to bed now, Lula," says Ling.

Lula hovers just behind the screen door. Ling offers Gus her hand and Gus takes it.

"I'm Augusta, by the way. Sorry about the gun and the trespassing," says Gus.

Ling squeezes Gus's hand with both of hers.

"I hope you find him," she says.

Gus nods in thanks and their hands let go. I come down the steps and follow Gus. We cross the grass in the direction of the road. We can hear the Gwella women singing at the nearby campfire. They don't sound like witches anymore.

Then we hear another sound.
It stops us both in our tracks.
It's coming from the house behind us.
We turn around. Ling looks at us.
"What is it?" she asks.
Behind her, Lula is still hovering by the door.
She's knocking lightly on the frame.
A familiar rhythm, over and over.
We know that knock.
Rat-tat-tatat-tat.

PART THREE

PART THREE

28

THE CANARY

FOLLOWING THE FADING BEAM OF THE FLASHLIGHT, WE RETRACE our steps back to the camper. We can't find words for what we're feeling, so we don't say any the whole way. I stumble along like I have rocks in my slippers—heavy-footed and wobbling.

Lula probably knows what happened to Howard, but it's buried deep inside her and she's too fragile for us to go digging for it. We might never know where she's been or what she's seen. It's not like she didn't try to tell us. Like Ling said, she finds ways to communicate. She gave us the ring, then she knocked just like Howard used to.

Rat-tat-tatat-tat.

They must have met. But what we don't know is why and how she knew to give the ring to us. We hobble down the road like Hansel and Gretel. I wonder if the knock could just be a coincidence and the ring an unlucky mistake. I can't see the breadcrumbs anymore. I wonder if they were ever there.

When we finally reach the county road, we can barely see the camper parked on the shoulder. It's clouded over. The moon is gone and it's pitch-black. Gus lights the way to the passenger door. I get in. She heads around the front of the camper. The road is deserted and lonely. Suddenly, the flashlight beam is gone and so is she. I hear a shriek. Something slams against the front bumper. A hand hits the windshield. I jump out of the camper. I can see shapes moving in the dark by the ditch. There's someone else there with Gus. They're struggling. I follow the beam of the flashlight and find it lying in the gravel. I scramble for it then shine the light on them. It's Creepy Man. He's sitting on top of Gus. He's got her arms pinned. She's clutching the gun. They're fighting for it.

"Stop, stop," he yells.

"Get off her," I scream.

He has her by the wrists.

"I don't want to hurt you," he hollers.

He slams her arm into the gravel. The gun goes flying. I run at them and kick him as hard as I can in the ribs. He howls in pain. He twists and gets hold of my leg and yanks hard. I fall on my back but I hang on to the flashlight. With one hand free, Gus punches him in the face. Blood pours from his nose.

I crawl on my belly to the ditch, searching for the gun. Using the flashlight, I find it. I grab it and roll over; flashlight in one hand, gun in the other. The gun goes off.

He screams and tumbles to the dirt. Gus crawls away from him.

"You shot me," he cries, gasping and squirming.

I drop the gun in horror and stare at my trembling hands. I can't catch my breath.

Gus staggers to my side. She picks up the gun and points it at him. He holds up a bloody hand. His pinkie is missing. I look back at my own hands, shaking violently like I have no control over them. Like they belong to someone else. I can't feel them.

"Why'd you do that?" he moans.

I open my mouth but nothing comes out.

"*You* came at me," Gus says. "I know who you are. You're Pike's errand boy."

He winces. The blood dripping down his chin starts to soak the front of his shirt.

"I just want to talk. Like I tried with that reporter—the one you been looking for. He said he'd meet me and he never showed," he says, moaning a little.

Gus sucks in air. I bite my lip and shine the flashlight at his face.

"You're the Canary," she says.

"Name's Ricky," he wheezes.

"You're lying," she says. "You set him up and lured Howard to that meeting for Pike."

"No way. He was my ticket," he whines.

"Ticket to what?" she says, still holding the gun on him.

"I was going to rat out Pike. Her going away is the only way I get my freedom," he says. "She must have caught on and one of her friends got to him first. She never said, I never asked. Played dumb. I was just happy I wasn't wearing a cement suit."

Gus looks across the road. She spots his delivery truck parked on the other side.

"How did you know where to find us?" she asks.

"I heard you were friendly with that rookie cop so I staked out his place and tailed you here," he says, sniffling.

"Did you kill Boyd Barton?" she asks.

"The accountant? He fell, I swear. I went over to talk to the guy. Maybe rough him up a little and find out what he was up to, only when he saw me, he got scared and took a header off the ladder and landed on his neck. I didn't touch the guy," he says.

Ricky looks woozy. He puts his head between his knees. I don't feel sorry for him.

"I think I'm gonna be sick." He gags.

I can't stay quiet.

"You kidnapped Lula!" I yell. "What did you do to her? She can't even talk anymore."

He cringes. He looks scared of me. He should be.

"I didn't touch Stenson's kid!" he says. "I planted drugs on her old man, but I don't mess with kids."

He lowers his head down.

"Did you find the thumb drive?" asks Gus.

He looks up. He knows we caught him at Kirk and Vivi's. He shakes his head.

"Listen, I was just doing what Pike told me to do," he whines. "But I can't do it no more."

He tries to get up but falls over, so he stays put. He cradles the hand with the missing pinkie. Gus lowers the gun. He's no threat.

"You said you wanted to talk, so talk," says Gus.

Ricky spits blood, then he starts talking really fast like he's afraid if he stops, he won't get it all out.

"Listen, I know stuff. Like where she hides her little meth lab at the winery. She's got it tucked away good. No one goes down there but her lab rats, not even me. Her guy brings up the crates. He told me it's a maze down there. Lots of tunnels and hidden rooms and shit. He weren't supposed to talk about it. She keeps things real hush-hush. The staff upstairs at the winery have no clue there's a meth lab deep in the cellars. But one time, I saw where her guy went in. I even got the entry codes," he says.

Entry codes? Tunnels? Hidden rooms?

My arms tingle with pins and needles.

"Whole operation is international. She's got a strict *no local* policy. Doesn't want some county high school kid OD'ing on her shit. Too close to home. If she knew I was skimming for my local side hustle, I'd be toast." Then he sputters, "Your reporter, h-he stole some of my stash. He tailed me, just like you did."

I knew we were following in Howard's footsteps.

"Pike's got cops on the take and a network of civilian fuelers at airfields across the US and Canada. The military don't have a clue what's happening right under their noses. The fuelers stash the product and cash in the cargo holds on training runs. I got names," he says. Then he points to his head. "It's all up here."

He looks straight into the flashlight beam. It looks like his nose exploded. His mouth is wide as he tries to get air.

"Your friend, he was my shot three years ago and I ain't had another since. He believed me. No one else was gonna take the word of a low-life junkie over the high-and-mighty Marica Pike," he says. "Except maybe you."

Gus steps close to him.

"Tell us what she did to Howard?" Gus asks.

I hold my breath.

"I swear I don't know," he says.

A car's headlights glimmer in the distance.

He pinches the bridge of his nose and tips his head back to try to stop the blood.

"You know why I told him to call me the Canary?" he croaks.

Gus doesn't answer.

"Pike has her own special recipe. She laces it with fentanyl. You think crystal meth's dangerous. Try it with a dose of fire. She knows I got a weakness for that shit, so she gets me to taste the new batches. *On the house*, she tells me. Like it's a perk of the job. But she ain't doing it to be sweet. She does it to test if the stuff's lethal. I'm her canary in a coal mine." He swallows. "So fuck her."

The headlights are getting closer.

Ricky passes out.

Gus tucks the gun in the back of her jeans. She walks behind him, loops his armpits, then drags him behind the camper. I turn the flashlight off as the car passes. They don't slow down.

The sun will be up soon. We have to get back to Able's before he wakes and finds us gone, along with his gun. Ricky has lost a lot of blood. Gus ties a dish towel around his hand. He's pretty scrawny, so it's not hard for the two of us to load him into the camper. We drive across the county—in the opposite direction of the Journey farmhouse.

We pull into Stenson's property, but this time Gus drives the camper fast down the narrow road; tree branches thump the sides and the mound of creeping thyme rubs the belly. We make it all the way to his place but we don't arrive quietly. The lights come on inside the house. Stenson comes out the front door, pointing his rifle. Gus turns off the headlights and gets out. I stay put. She holds up both hands and walks to the front of the camper.

"We have something in the back you're going to want to see," she tells him.

She nods over her shoulder.

Stenson keeps the rifle raised and follows Gus as she opens the side doors and gestures inside. Stenson looks in. Ricky is lying on the floor, passed out. He's got a crusted nose, a gory dish towel wrapped around one hand, and a blood-spattered shirt.

"Jesus. Is he dead?" asks Stenson.

"No, but he's the Canary," she says.

"Who the hell is the Canary?" he asks.

"A little birdie who works for Marica Pike," she says.

He lowers his rifle.

AFTER WE CARRY RICKY INSIDE AND BANDAGE HIS HAND, GUS lets Stenson know that we saw Lula and she's okay. The Gwella are taking good care of her. His eyes glisten when he hears this. Then Gus tells Stenson all about Pike's drug operation. He's not that surprised. He knew she was *shady as shit*, his words. Gus shows Stenson what she's got stowed in the wheel well of the camper.

The baggies of crystal meth. The evidence. She also gives him the military document and Howard's notebook. She tells him that with Ricky's help, he can be the one to bring down Pike.

"Happy to," he says. "But why me?"

"It should be you," she says. "We're on a different mission."

Ricky comes to and Stenson pumps him full of coffee and painkillers. Gus sits across from him in the front room. Paintings of birds cover the walls. I try to focus on the birds so my brain doesn't go back to the terrible, earsplitting second when I fired the gun. Great gray owls, herons, wood warblers, vultures. I didn't mean to fire it. At least I don't think I did. It happened so fast. I clasp my hands tight to stop them from shaking again. Ricky has a bag of frozen peas held to his nose. As I watch him sitting there, I still find him a little creepy but he doesn't scare me anymore. And if Howard believed him, so do I. And even though I didn't mean to do it, I feel bad that I shot off his pinkie.

"Tell us again about those hidden rooms," says Gus. "And those entry codes."

Gus picks Ricky's twitchy brain. We find out that Pike goes for a sunrise horseback ride at a nearby ranch every morning. She's never back before 7 A.M. He draws us a rough map of the property, including the door he saw. The secret way in. He figures it has to lead down to the cellars and the lab. Her security team doesn't clock in until late morning. But there are cameras. He shows us where the blind spots are.

It's 5:00 A.M. The sun rises in half an hour.

Pike Winery is about that far away.

It's now or never.

Stenson wishes us luck and we do the same.

As we bump along the dark road leading out to the highway, Gus checks her phone.

Constable Journey has left a bunch of messages.

29

THE DEED

THERE ARE LOTS OF THINGS THAT COULD HAVE MESSED UP OUR mission. Pike's daughter waking up, an alarm getting tripped, a dog barking, or even a flat tire along the way. But it wasn't any of those things.

It was the two motorbikes.

They found us again—or maybe they hadn't stopped watching us since Sunday night.

They come out of nowhere. Two bright lights crisscrossing the highway behind us. They close in fast as Gus tries to pick up speed. They have no trouble gaining on our old camper. We're still a few miles from Pike Winery and all the houses we're passing are dark. Everyone's sleeping. There's nowhere to turn off and no one to help us. The lights split apart as they pull up on either side of the camper. Gus slams her foot on the brakes hard and the bikes roar ahead, going so fast they don't stop for a few hundred yards. She shifts the camper into reverse, punches the gas, and it stalls. We can see the beams from their headlights rolling across the farmer's fields on either side of the road as they turn around. Gus turns the key but there's a grinding sound and the engine sputters. She tries again. Nothing. They're coming straight at us—two blinding yellow eyes, getting closer and closer.

"Run," hollers Gus.

She grabs her phone, shoves it in her bag, and is out the camper. I fall out my side. Gus is over to me in a flash. She grabs my arm and drags me into the ditch. We keep going into a field. It's dark. I can feel my slippers sinking into the muddy earth. I try to keep from falling. The field is wide open. There are no tall crops or barns or trees to hide behind. We stumble toward a large shape. It's a bale of hay. We dive behind it. The motorbikes have pulled up to the camper. We see the side doors open. The dome light goes on. Together, they lift one of the bikes into the back. I hear the crack as the dining table breaks to pieces. One of them jumps into the driver's seat. After a couple of false starts, the camper's engine turns over. They speed away, one on a motorbike, the other in our camper.

All we can do is watch as the taillights get smaller and smaller, then disappear over a hill. The whine of the motorbike is the last thing to fade away, then everything goes dead quiet until a rooster crows at a nearby farm. He's the first one up.

Howard once told me roosters are protectors. They crow to wake up the hens, but another reason they crow is to let the hens know that all is well in the world. The coast is clear. As my slippers sink into the mud and the morning light edges closer, I wonder if the rooster is crowing to us.

Our camper is gone. But we haven't lost everything. Gus grabbed her phone and her bag. I'm still wearing Howard's baseball cap and his phone is tucked in my back pocket along with my eagle feather, which I never did put on our evidence wall. And even though the camper is gone, we still have our mission. I check the time. It's 5:30.

"I guess we're walking the rest of the way," says Gus.

The horizon turns a deep shade of pink and the cool morning air begins to pulse with warmth. We walk out of the field then along the ditch. Gus would like to get off the main highway, but it's the quickest way to Pike's. It's quiet. No traffic yet. We've walked about a half mile when we spot a truck coming toward us. Daylight has come so they will definitely see us. The ditch is too shallow to hide in. As they drive closer, I can see it's a red truck. I brace myself for the worst, but to my relief, it's Patience Perley.

Gus flags the truck down. Patience pulls up beside us and leans out the window. Dod is next to her. Bonnie and Clyde pop up from the cargo bed and start barking their heads off. Foamy drool flies at us. She snaps her fingers and the dogs go quiet.

"Tad early for a hike," she says, smiling.

"You don't know how happy we are to see a friendly face," says Gus.

Patience looks us up and down, her gaze falling on our mud-caked shoes.

"Where you gals headed this fine morning?" she asks.

"Just a couple of miles that way." Gus points in the direction of Pike Winery.

Patience flicks a switch that unlocks the doors to the back seat of the truck.

"Don't just stand there," she says. "Hop in."

"We don't want to put you out," says Gus. "You're not headed that way."

"I'm not leaving you on the side of the highway," says Patience. "Wouldn't be right."

We get in. I lean forward and smile at Dod.

"Hi, Dod," I say.

He peers at me then quickly turns away.

I lean back as Patience makes a U-turn. Gus doesn't tell her what we're up to and Patience doesn't pry. She's happy to help.

"We moms have to look out for each other," she says.

Patience asks if we heard about the *hubbub* over in Cherry

Valley at Baylis Vineyards. We pretend we haven't, so she fills us in on all the news—how the ER was busting at the seams with barfing tourists. How there's a rumor someone spiked the wine with rat poison. How a local restaurant was seriously thinking about a class-action lawsuit against the owners of the *fancy-ass* vineyard. That's how she puts it.

"I've always said the day would come when one of those big-city types got theirs," she says. "Shoot, I plumb forgot. You know those folks, don't you?"

"We do," says Gus, but she doesn't bother reminding her how.

Patience continues breathlessly.

"Maybe it's a war of the wineries," she says. "Sour grapes if you ask me."

Patience gasps and slaps her hand to her mouth.

"Sour grapes!" She laughs. "Get it?"

Gus and I laugh too. It feels almost normal to laugh, even though nothing is normal.

"Don't like sour," mumbles Dod.

"Me either," I tell him.

Gus looks around and realizes we've gone too far.

"Oh sorry, I think we missed the turn," says Gus, leaning forward. "I should have been paying closer attention."

Patience jumps right in.

"No worries. I'll turn right around. But first, mind if I make a quick pit stop since we're headed this way?" she says. "Won't take but a sec, then we'll get you where you're going."

Gus checks the time on her phone. It's just after six. There's still time to get to the winery before Pike gets back.

"Sure thing," says Gus.

A text notification pops up on her phone. Gus opens it, reads the text, then shows it to me.

It's from Hildy.

Found an old deed to that lot on the Archives of
Ontario website. The land was owned by Clara
Perley in the 1950s. Probably still in the family since
I couldn't find any sales listed other than that parcel
sold to Pike this spring. Hope this helps.

Gus puts her phone back in her bag and stares out the window. She reaches over and holds my hand. She squeezes it. It's her way of telling me to stay calm. I hold very still, but on the inside my mind is tumbling back to Canada Day, when Patience was talking to Gus by the campfire.

It was my grandma Clara's house. We have about a hundred acres all told across the county. My grandma left me the land. This spring I sold off the only other parcel of any value.

It's Patience who owns the land by the bluffs where Hugo saw the camper.

Like an alarm going off, Noble's words about my eagle feather come back to me.

Could be telling you to look where you're not looking.

I let go of Gus's hand and pull the eagle feather from my back pocket. I stare at it, trying to will it to speak to me. Even if she owns the land, maybe Patience never goes there. It doesn't look like anyone goes in those woods. Noble said they're full of sinkholes. She wouldn't have known about the camper this whole time. She's been so nice. I want to ask Gus what she's thinking but I can't. I want to get out of this truck but I can't.

"You gals all right back there?" asks Patience, glancing into the rearview mirror. "Won't be long now."

"We're just tired," says Gus, faking a yawn.

Patience yawns, too, then Dod yawns.

"It's contagious." Patience laughs.

Dod looks over his shoulder at me and bounces in his seat.

"You go. You go," he tells me.

"He wants you to take a turn on the merry-go-round," says his mother, ruffling his hair.

I pretend to yawn. He giggles, then he spots the eagle feather in my hand.

"Birdie. My birdie," he says, clapping his hands.

"Yes, it's the one you gave me," I tell him.

He sticks out his lower lip.

"Do you want it back?" I ask.

He nods.

"Now, Dod, you know better," says Patience. "When you give someone a gift, it's theirs to keep."

"It's okay," I tell her. "He can have it back."

"Go on then," says Patience. "She said it was okay."

Dod twists around and reaches one arm over the seat. He leans closer and takes the feather gently in one of his thick, rough hands. That's when I see it. Right there on his shirt.

In the end, it's not a name on a deed or a message from an eagle that sucks the oxygen from my lungs and stops my heart. It's an object hanging from Dod Perley's front shirt pocket. It's looped through the buttonhole like a brooch. It's a dragonfly fishing lure. The one that Noble gave me. The one that was hanging on the evidence wall in our camper when it was stolen less than an hour ago.

I was right about the lure. We did catch someone with it.

A tiny whimper escapes my lips. Gus looks at me. Patience Perley is staring into the rearview mirror right at me. I try to smile but my mouth quivers. Patience looks at Dod then down at his shirt pocket. She reaches over and pulls him back around so he's facing front.

"Dod sure is a collector. Once he gets his hands on something he has a hard time letting it go," she says, trying to keep her voice light.

She speeds up. She's not making a quick pit stop. Did Gus see the fishing lure? I look over at her. She's got one hand in her bag. She did see it. She's reaching for the gun. Dod bounces in his seat.

"Almost there, baby," Patience says to Dod.

"Zuzu," he says.

"That's right," she tells him.

Out of nowhere it clicks that Dod is not making up words. He repeats words. It's what he does. He's not saying *Zuzu*. It's his way of saying *zoo*. I grip the seat to keep from being swept away by the avalanche of sights and sounds coming at me.

I see Dod and I sitting on the dock.

I like the zoo.

I hear Noble talking about the rich man who built a mansion near the bluffs.

He put in two pools, three tennis courts, an amusement park, and a private zoo.

I see Howard on the video. He's driving. He hits something.

I hear the clang of metal on metal.

Toby points to the dent in the camper's front bumper.

Dod limps over to his twisted old bike.

I hear the groundskeeper at the small white chapel.

He walks kinda funny on account of an accident a few years back.

The breadcrumbs appear in front of my eyes. The ones that were always telling me to follow Dod. The pink ribbon that trailed behind a boy on a bike. The mask that boy dropped in a garage. The magnet that brought us to the boy being bullied, and the lure that same boy took from our camper. They all led me here. Right here to this truck and to the Perleys. Gus slowly pulls the gun from her bag. I start shaking uncontrollably when I see it. My whole body this time, not just my hands. I don't want anyone else to get shot. By me or by Gus. My eyes dart from the gun to Gus.

She won't look at me. I have to stop what's about to happen. I have to get out. Right now.

"I need to pee," I say.

"We'll be there soon, doll," says Patience.

"She can go by side of the road. It's fine," Gus says. "Just pull over."

"Can't do that," says Patience.

Her words give me chills. Gus raises the gun. I reach for Gus and squeeze her leg hard. She ignores me. I sink in my seat, close my eyes, and brace for the worst.

Then Patience slows down.

"What the hell is all this?" snaps Patience, her eyes on the road ahead.

"Zoo-zoo," whines Dod.

Three police cruisers are parked across the highway, lights flashing. Four OPP officers stand on the road, blocking the way. Gus tucks the gun back into her bag. Patience slows down. We're too close for her to turn around without looking suspicious. She drives ahead, then comes to a stop. The bloodhounds go crazy. Patience rolls down her window as one of the officers comes over to the truck. He's older than the others. I don't know him but I recognize the other three. Constable Dee, Constable Dum, and Able. Only he's not Able anymore. His face is scowling and he's wearing his uniform. He's Constable Journey again.

"Sergeant Tucker. You caught me. I've been pounding back the bourbon since dawn and now I'm out for a joyride. Cuff me, Occifer!" she cackles, holding her wrists out the window.

"Mrs. Perley, you mind simmering down those dogs?" he asks.

"Bonnie! Clyde!" She snaps her fingers and the dogs stop barking.

The sergeant peers in the back seat and signals to the three behind him.

"It's them," he calls out.

The others head over. He taps on the back window.

"Please step out of the vehicle, ma'am. Slowly. Hands in the air," he says to Gus.

Gus doesn't move. I don't know what to do. I want to get out but I don't want to go with Muirhead's nasty little piglets.

"What in god's name is this all about, Emmitt?" Patience huffs.

"Mrs. Perley, Dod, stay put," he says. "You two, out."

"This is outrageous. We've done nothing wrong," says Patience, opening her door.

Sergeant Tucker pushes it shut, keeping Patience inside. She has no choice. She unlocks the doors. We get out and the four of them surround us. Constable Journey gestures to Gus's bag. She hands it to him. Dee and Dum take up positions on either side of Gus. Constable Journey looks inside her bag, then tucks it under one arm.

"She's clean," he says.

"Let's make double sure," says Dee.

"Hands on the vehicle," says Dum.

Dum grabs Gus and turns her around, pushing her hard into the truck. This upsets Bonnie and Clyde. They start barking again. Constable Journey doesn't say or do anything to stop them from hurting Gus, so I try to jump in. Dee grabs my arm and holds me tight. I bite down hard on my lip, forcing tears into my eyes, then I pretend to cry as loud as I can. The dogs are jumping and frothing. One of them snaps at Dum's head as he leans in to frisk Gus. He leaps back.

"Jesus Christ," he says. "Fuckin' mutt nearly bit my head off."

Dee lets me go and pulls his gun. He aims it at the dogs. Bonnie and Clyde go bananas.

"Bad gun, bad gun," hollers Dod from the truck.

The bloodhounds' giant paws claw over the side of the truck bed. They bare their teeth and snarl at Dee and Dum, who both step back.

"Don't you dare point that gun at my hounds," says Patience, pushing her way out of her truck, knocking into Sergeant Tucker. He steadies himself and turns his attention on the rookies.

"What the hell, Dewer? Stand down," says Sergeant Tucker.

"You heard the man, bucko," spits Patience.

Dee holsters his gun. He looks more afraid of Patience than his superior officer.

"Bad, bad, bad, bad," Dod hollers, over and over.

"Get back in the vehicle, Mrs. Perley," says Sergeant Tucker.

"Who the fuck do you think you're talking to, Emmitt?" she says, hands on hips. "I used to clean up your dirty nappies when I babysat your tiny ass."

Dum and Dee burst out laughing.

"Bad, bad, bad," Dod repeats.

Constable Journey grabs my arm. He's already handcuffed Gus.

"I got these two," he says. He starts leading us away.

Sergeant Tucker looks from Constable Journey to Patience. She's still in his face.

Dee and Dum look at each other. They don't know what to do.

"I'm talking to you, Emmitt," says Patience.

While Sergeant Tucker tries to get Patience and her dogs under control, Dee and Dum come jogging up behind us.

"We're taking them in, Journey," says Dee, grabbing Gus's elbow.

"I said I got this," says Constable Journey.

"What the fuck are you doing?" says Dum.

Constable Journey lowers his voice.

"What the boss told me to do, that's what," he says, glancing in Tucker's direction. He doesn't want him to hear.

"You're one of Muirhead's?" asks Dee. He lets go of Gus.

Journey shoves Gus and me against his police cruiser, then steps close to the constables.

"Are you two dim? Why do you think he had me take them to my place?" he whispers. "Shit. The boss didn't tell you. It's not just me, you know. There're others. Wait, maybe he's left you two out of the loop for a reason."

"He wouldn't do that," whines Dee. Dum elbows him.

"We knew," says Dum.

"Knew what?" asks Sergeant Tucker.

He comes up behind them. Dee jumps.

"Knew that our buddy here, Journey, would love to spend the rest of this fine summer day doing the paperwork on these two," says Dum.

"And a fine day it is," says Sergeant Tucker. "You good with this, Journey?"

Journey nods and the other three head for their own cars.

Constable Journey shoves Gus in the back seat. I jump in beside her, wiping away my crocodile tears. Constable Journey tosses her bag on the front seat and gets in. He finds his gun in her bag and puts it in the glove box. I look out the window.

Patience is back in her truck and the constables are laughing about something. Two motorbikes are coming down the highway in the other direction. Journey circles the other vehicles and as we pass alongside Patience and Dod, they're not looking at us. They're both looking at the motorbikes passing slowly by. Dod raises his hand and waves to them. His mother reaches out quickly and pushes his hand down. She turns her head sharply toward us and for a second, her eyes meet mine.

Patience taught her son well.

He only waves to family.

That means the two people driving those motorbikes are

family—his brothers, JW and JP. It has to be them. They slashed our tire, they shot at us and followed us, and they took our camper. That's how Dod got the dragonfly lure. From his brothers.

The Perleys have been pretending to be our friends.

Pretending to be nice.

But they're not nice at all.

30

THE MOTH

CONSTABLE JOURNEY DRIVES FAST. I GRIP THE SEAT AND WATCH his eyes in the rearview mirror. He's talking into his police radio and saying things like *persons of interest* and *BOLO* and *apprehended*. He doesn't look at me. Nothing is making sense.

A woman's voice crackles over his police radio. She confirms his message back to him and she calls off the countywide Code 9. I don't know what a Code 9 is, but I think it has something to do with us. Gus hasn't said a word since we got out of the truck, but when Constable Journey doesn't take the turn onto Main in the direction of the OPP detachment, she leans close to the cage between the seats.

"Where are we going, Able?" she asks.

Everyone has been lying to us and as much as I want to believe that he is the Able I think I know, I wonder if we'd be safer if we'd escaped from Patience on our own.

He pulls something from his breast pocket and tosses it through the small window in the cage. It's a key.

"That's for the cuffs," he says. Then he looks at me in the rearview mirror for the first time.

I unlock Gus's handcuffs and she slips them off.

"Sorry if I was a little rough back there. I had to make it look good or they wouldn't have let me take you," he says.

Gus and I look at each other. She grips my hand. He was Able all along.

"Sorry I took your gun," says Gus.

"Good thing I have a backup," he says. "Would've been hard explaining that one."

Gus rubs her wrists. I look around. I know where we're going now. To his farmhouse.

"What's with the roadblock?" asks Gus.

"Muirhead put out a BOLO on you two. He's got roadblocks across the county. Mostly around Pike Winery. I was out looking for you when I heard. I called dispatch, found out where Dewer and Nelson were posted, and told them I'd been sent to join them. Then along you came," he says. "We got lucky. If you'd come to a different roadblock, who knows what would've happened."

"What's a BOLO?" I ask him.

"It means *be on the lookout*," he says. "We don't have much time. Once Muirhead catches wind that we haven't shown up at the detachment, his boys'll be on the hunt. I figure we've got a half hour to get you out of town."

"We're not leaving town," says Gus.

Able doesn't say anything else. He pulls into his driveway and comes to a stop. Able turns off the engine, but he doesn't get out. He turns to face us.

"I haven't asked where you were or why you took my gun," he says. "But you've got to start listening to me. Muirhead is desperate, which makes him dangerous."

"He was already dangerous," says Gus.

"The guy had the whole detachment out looking for you," he says. "That makes me think Dewer and Nelson aren't the only dirty ones. You're not safe here anymore."

I can't breathe. I feel trapped behind the cage. I try the door but it's locked.

"It was the Perleys," I blurt out.

Able stares at me.

"Dod had the dragonfly and his brothers stole our camper and, and, and—" I gasp for air.

I grab the cage and pull on it as hard as I can.

"Okay, okay, easy now. Hang on. I'll let you out," he says, jumping out.

Able pulls the back door open and we scramble out. I bend and try to take deep breaths. Gus rubs my back. Able grabs her bag from the front seat.

"You all right?" he asks.

"She needs water," says Gus.

"Let's get out of sight." He nods to the house.

As we head to the house, Noble opens the front door.

"I see you found the strays," says Noble.

We all go inside.

"This one's thirsty," says Gus, nodding to me.

Noble leads us into the kitchen.

"Now what's all this about the Perley boys?" Able asks.

Noble gives me a glass of water. I drink it down as Gus turns to Able.

"Patience Perley owns that land near where Howard went missing," she tells him.

"And you think they had something to do with his disappearance?" he asks.

"They're hiding something," says Gus.

"JP and JW are good guys. I know them. We belong to the same shooting club," he says. "We get beers at Hartley's every Friday."

"They aren't good. They just pretend to be," I tell him.

"I don't understand. Why were you in her truck?" he asks.

The wail from a police siren comes down the highway. We

all wait, listening as the sound gets louder, then passes and fades. Able checks the time on his phone.

"We have to get you out of the county while we can," says Able. "You can't go home. He might have someone watching your place."

"In Ottawa?" I gulp.

"The hunting cabin?" says Noble.

"Perfect," says Able.

He turns to Gus.

"We have a cabin on the Madawaska River near Combermere. It's north of here. Two, three hours tops," he says. "You'll be safe there."

"I'll take them," says Noble.

Able nods.

"But the Perleys?" asks Gus. "They've been following us. One of them took a shot at us the other day."

"They what?" he says, eyes wide.

"They don't want us near that land," she says. "And I want to know why."

"Shit. Okay, I promise you. I'll look into the Perleys," he says. "I'll take care of Muirhead, too. If I can get that recording into the right hands, it might get someone looking into him and Pike. Then he'll have more to worry about than you two."

Gus sits at the kitchen table.

"Able, how are you going to explain how you lost us?" Gus asks.

Before he can answer, a strange thing happens. There's a loud crack from somewhere outside. A whooshing sound makes my ears feel like I've gone deaf for a split second. Able's face goes blank, then he takes a giant step backward, knocks into the table, and falls to the floor on his back. A red stain blooms on the front of his uniform near his shoulder. I don't understand what's going on until Noble hollers.

"Get down!"

Gus yanks me to the floor. Noble's already on his knees crawling to his grandson. There's another crack. The stove pings, wood splinters. *Thunk, thunk.* I look up and see a hole in the window screen. Someone's shooting at us. *Crack, crack. Thunk, thunk.*

Gus tosses Noble a dish towel and he presses it to the red stain. Able is trying to speak but no words are coming out. Noble waves Gus over. She crawls to him and he guides her hands to the bloody dish towel. He yanks off his shirt and tells her to tie it around Able's shoulder. Noble pushes the kitchen table onto its side so it shields Gus and Able. A coffee mug smashes and a sugar bowl dumps onto the floor. Some of the sugar turns pink. Noble motions for me to get behind the table with them. Able sits up. Gus wraps the wound tight as Able winces. Noble is on his feet, bending low and running into the other room. *Crack. Crack, crack.* I want it to stop. I crawl to Gus's side and curl into a tight ball. I cover my ears. Noble is back in seconds with a pair of hunting rifles. He tosses one to Able, who catches it. Able gets to his feet with Gus's help.

"Stay here," says Able, handing Gus his service revolver.

Gus hides behind the table with me.

The two men flatten themselves against the walls on either side of the back door. They nod to each other.

"They're close," says Able.

"The woodpile," says Noble.

"At least two," says Able.

"Can you shoot okay with that shoulder?" asks Noble.

"Cover me," says Able and he bursts out the back door.

Noble aims out the door and fires his rifle four times. *Crack, crack, crack, crack.*

Then he races outside.

The screen door swings shut.

It's quiet for a few terrible seconds and then the gunfire starts up again. I curl tighter. Gus pokes me and nods to the living room. She pulls me with her and we crawl from the kitchen into the living room. We hear someone holler in pain. Gus searches the room. She stumbles over to a trunk next to the sofa where Noble stores blankets. She opens it, yanks out the blankets, and points inside. I don't want to get in but I do. She covers me with a blanket and closes the lid. I can hear her laying the other blankets on top. Then, nothing. She's hiding too.

I pull the blanket over my ears, muffling the sound of gunfire. The blanket smells like mothballs. It's a sad smell like death.

The gunfire stops. I lift the blanket and listen. At first, I don't hear anything. Then there's a faint whirring sound in the distance. It gets louder. I know that sound. It's the engine of a motorbike. The whirring takes a long time to fade. When it's finally gone, I don't move. I don't know who is alive or dead or out there or in here.

I hear the squeak of the screen door. Footsteps. The door slams as it shuts. I hear voices. Gus. Then Able and Noble. I peek out from my hiding spot. Gus is walking over to me and behind her I can see Able holstering his service revolver.

"They're gone," she says. "They took off, but Able thinks he hit one of them."

I jump out of the trunk just as Able falls into his grandfather's arms and passes out.

"He's lost a lot of blood," says Noble. "Help me get him to his car."

We load Able into the back of his police cruiser and Noble hands us the keys to his Corolla. He gives us the address to their cabin.

"Neighbors will have heard the shots and called the police. Go now," he says. "I'll get him to the hospital."

Noble is trembling. Earlier in the kitchen, when he came out of the back room with a rifle in each hand, shirtless, his rough brown skin hanging from his muscles, moving swift like a hunter, he looked superhuman. He looks frail now, like a warrior after his last great battle.

I wrap my arms around him. He hugs me back.

"Thank you," says Gus, patting his arm. "He'll be okay."

Then Noble gets in and drives off. When the cruiser is out of sight, we run back into the house. Gus finds her bag where Able dropped it. She grabs one of the rifles and finds a box of bullets in a back room. She tells me to pack some food while she loads the rifle.

I feel bad taking stuff from Noble's fridge, but I know it won't be safe to stop until we reach the cabin. I find a plastic bag and start shoving food into it. Two apples, two bananas, a brick of cheese, two cans of cherry cola, and a package of butter tarts. I keep an ear out for sirens.

With our supplies gathered, we head for the back door. On the way out, Gus grabs two pairs of rubber boots sitting on a mat. I don't know why we need rubber boots at a cabin, but maybe she knows something about the Madawaska River that I don't.

Bits of metal from the bullets are strewn everywhere outside and it smells like burnt plastic. We jump into Noble's Corolla. The clock in the car says it's almost 10 A.M. We head north, away from Picton, away from Prince Edward County. I don't want to leave, but I know we have to or our bodies might never be found. We can hear sirens in the distance. It doesn't take long to reach the Skyway Bridge. We go up and over the giant bridge. It feels strange to be leaving the county. At the other side, we come to the familiar four-way stop. Gus hesitates.

A car comes to the intersection and waits for her to go through. When she doesn't, they honk.

"It's your turn," I tell her.

She doesn't go straight through. Instead, she turns right.

"You're going the wrong way," I tell her. "Noble's directions say to go that way."

I check the address I entered into the Maps app on Howard's phone. I'm right.

"You can turn that off now." She nods to the phone. "We're not going to the cabin."

We drive down Highway 2 toward Napanee, then turn right on Hamburgh Road. We follow it past Adolphustown then we take the Glenora Ferry across the Bay of Quinte. Gus has just made a great big U-turn that brings us back into Prince Edward County, on the east side.

I know where we're going now.

I should have known all along.

I roll down the window to let in the breeze. As I do, a moth flutters from my sleeve. It lands on the dash in front of me. It must have been inside the trunk with me when I was hiding.

Once when we were camping, I watched a moth fly right into our campfire. I remember Howard saying they can't stop themselves.

Moths are willing to die if it brings them closer to the light.

I close my eyes. Light dances across my lids. My hair flutters in the breeze.

I am a moth heading to the light.

And I can't stop.

31

THE BLEEDING HEART

WE PULL UP NEXT TO THE PADLOCKED GATE. THE FENCE stretches as far as I can see along the county road. We're at the woods near the bluffs. The land Patience Perley owns. The sun is high, baking hot and blinding bright on the pavement. But when I look into the woods, they are deep and dark. The sun can't find its way through the thick, tangled treetops.

Noble warned us that searching here would be hard.

They're too mucky to navigate and even if you made some headway, there's a bog smack in the middle. A kind of dead zone.

He's right. Even our phones don't work out here. Gus tucks the Corolla under the bows of a willow in the ditch, then we get out and put on the rubber boots. They're four sizes too big, but I'm glad we have them. She remembered what Noble said too. I straighten Howard's baseball cap as Gus loads the rifle. She hands me the Swiss Army knife. I tuck it in my back pocket and we head for the gate.

I'm not scared. I don't have hives and I'm not even close to tears. I just do what Gus tells me to do. I follow her over the gate. For three years, she's refused to listen to anyone. She's never turned back or looked away or given up. She's doubted herself sometimes but never ever doubted that we had to keep trying.

And she was right about me. I am becoming her. I don't need everything to be neat and tidy. I shot the pinkie off a man's hand. And even though bad people are out to get us, I will not turn back or look away, either. I can face whatever waits for us in these dark woods because I have Gus by my side and she is the bravest person I know.

We jump down onto the mud road on the other side of the gate.

It's been eleven days since we got to Prince Edward County. We've been robbed and burned, threatened, shot at, and hunted. But as we walk onto the property owned by Patience Perley—it feels like we're the ones on the hunt. And Howard's breadcrumbs have led us here, *more than once*. This time we're going in.

We're going to look where we haven't looked before.

A few yards down the overgrown road, it disappears. No more tracks, no way forward, at least not for a car or a van. I feel my first tiny pang of doubt. If our camper was hidden in these woods only a few months ago, it couldn't have been driven through this. Vines twist up the tree trunks and cobweb across the branches overhead. It's like someone took a giant blanket of ivy and draped it over the woods. That's why it's so dark. We push ahead. Gus leads. She finds a small trail between the trees. It was probably made by an animal. It's narrow but it gets us moving forward and it's something to follow. I look behind me and I can't see the road anymore.

"Maybe we should mark the path so we can find our way back," I suggest.

Gus stops and turns. She glances over my shoulder. She can't see the road, either. She pulls off her T-shirt and begins ripping it into long strips. She ties one strip to a branch right beside her. Then we walk on. I can see mosquitoes swarming the skin on her back and skittering along the band of her sports bra. I can feel them at my neck. I swat as we push deeper. Every ten steps or so, she ties another strip to a branch. Our own breadcrumbs.

As we move deeper into the woods, the earth becomes spongy and smells of rotten eggs. Maybe the rich man who sold the land to the Perleys was right. Maybe it is cursed. I push the thought from my head. Our boots make sucking sounds as we walk. Gus hands me a piece of her T-shirt then walks ahead. I tie it to a nearby tree. When I look up, I can't see Gus. She's gone. I scan the woods for her.

"Gus?" I shout.

"Over here!" I hear her muffled yelling. "Stay back. I'm down here."

I take a few steps forward, trying to follow her voice. I spot a small clearing. As I look closer I realize it's not a clearing, but an opening in the ground. I creep toward it. I peer over the edge. I see her. She's deep in a pit. Broken branches are sticking up at odd angles at the mouth. They must have been covering the hole. Like a trap.

"Are you okay?" I call down, kneeling at the edge.

"I think so," she says. She's crumpled in a heap. She slowly gets to her feet and brushes off her jeans. She steadies herself with one hand against the muddy wall of the pit and the other on the rifle. I lie flat on the ground and reach my hand down toward her. She reaches up. We're way too far apart to touch even when she holds the rifle high. The pit has got to be twenty feet deep. The walls look slick with mud. She's standing in water. Gus tries but she can't get a grip anywhere. She keeps sliding back down.

"I'm stuck," she says.

I try ripping some ivy from a tree and lowering it down to her, but it breaks when she tries to pull herself up.

"It's no good. You need to go back to the car. Look for a rope or chain, a blanket, jumper cables, anything to help get me out of here," she shouts up.

She tosses the keys up to me. I catch them.

"I'll be right back," I tell her.

I head back the way we came, searching for the torn strips of her T-shirt. The sky has clouded over and it smells like rain. I don't like the thought of her down in that pit in a downpour. I jump for joy when I spot one of our breadcrumbs. I keep going. The path winds through the trees, sometimes disappearing before showing itself again. I find another breadcrumb. I walk on. Then I stop. I can't find the next breadcrumb.

Did I go the wrong way?

I hold out the keys and press the unlock button in every direction, hoping to hear the car beep. Nothing. I turn back and retrace my steps to the last strip of cloth. *Where did I find it?* My heart feels like it's in my throat. A branch snaps behind me. I spin around. A chipmunk zips across the path. I follow her.

I move faster, stumbling over roots, my clunky, oversize boots squishing through the muck. My eyes start tearing up. *No crying. Not now.* I run, thinking I can see the narrow path ahead, but a large bush covered in berries gets in my way. I stagger around it and keep going. I'm almost there. The earth starts turning from sponge to water. My feet splash through large puddles. I stop. I can see water surrounding the trees up ahead. I'm at the bog. The dead zone.

I've gone the wrong way.

There's something else up ahead that looks like a wood platform. I keep going even as I feel the water seep into one of my boots and soak my toes. I make it to the wood planks and carefully step up onto them, out of the water. It's an old walkway of some kind. It's wobbly because some boards are missing and some are rotted, but parts of it are solid enough for me to stand on. It zigs and zags through the murky bog. I look back. Gus is waiting for me. But I'm nowhere near the road or the car and if I go back, I might get more lost. Then we'll both be alone out here. I have to be brave like Gus. I look ahead. At least this is a path. It must lead somewhere.

I step forward, slowly, carefully so I don't fall into the thick watery sludge on either side. The trees thin out. They look half dead with peeling bark and blackened water-logged roots that smell of decay and dead fish. Clouds of gnats invade my eyes and nose. Mosquitoes buzz in my ears but I don't swat. I try to stay balanced, one foot in front of the other. The uneven boardwalk slowly begins to sink into the water. I'm too unsteady to turn around. I have to keep going. At one point, I'm up to my knees in slime and my boots feel full of soupy swamp water. Then the boardwalk starts to rise again, out of the water. The walkway ends as the ground reappears, spongy but walkable. I've reached the other side of the bog. I dump the water from my boots and follow a dirt path. Thin ruts scar the path. Bicycle tire marks. Someone uses this path a lot.

I keep moving. The forest is getting thick again. Suddenly, I hear voices up ahead. I pull out the knife and ready it in one hand as I move off the path and into the low brush. A dark outline looms large through the trees. I think it's a house, but it's hard to tell. Everything is in shadow. I need to get closer. I inch forward. The voices get louder. Then I spot them a few feet in front of me. I freeze. I can see their faces.

It's Patience Perley. Dod is with her.

If they look this way, they'll see me.

I try not to move a muscle. The knife is shaking in my clenched fist.

"I know, baby. I tried, I really did." Patience is panting. "But just because you don't get your way doesn't mean you can just run off like that. I know you're sad."

She's breathing heavy like she was running. She must have been chasing him. He hangs his head. He's breathing hard too. Patience takes Dod by the arm and pulls him along behind her. He doesn't resist. They walk away from me and disappear behind the dark shape. I follow slowly. As I look up, I see that I was right. It *is* a house. Only it's more a mansion than a regular-size house. As I get closer, I can tell no one lives there anymore. Nature has moved in. Ropes of thick ivy snake in and out of holes that used to be windows and doors. One wall has collapsed into a heap of crushed stone and splintered beams. Trees have pushed up through the floorboards.

I look left and right, making sure the coast is clear, then I race to the corner of the mansion. I peek around. No Patience. No Dod. I stay pressed to the wall as I creep along the side then look around the back. I can't believe my eyes. I step out from behind the mansion and I take in the view.

Sloping down from a crumbling terrace at the back of the mansion is a huge garden. It's been carved out of the middle of the forest. It must be the size of a football field. I can still make out the old pathways and garden beds and hedgerows. There's an enormous, lopsided pergola at the center of the garden. In the distance, past a large wall of evergreens, I can see the top of a rusty Ferris wheel. There's an arched opening in the evergreens. I realize it's the entrance to a maze.

This is the palace the rich man built for his fiancée. Noble said the place was abandoned because the man thought it was cursed. But looking out at this amazing view, I don't think it's cursed at all. Even though it's not been weeded or mowed or tended to in decades, it's beautiful. Nature has spread a purple-and-gold carpet of moss and mushrooms and wildflowers across the lawn. Forget-me-nots, buttercups, black-eyed Susans, bleeding hearts, and fireweed—as far as the eye can see. Robins and sparrows swoop across the tennis court like they're playing a game. I can see two turtles at the edge of the pool—its dark green water covered with lily pads.

It is a little piece of paradise.

In the distance, a thin trail of smoke rises from the woods near the Ferris wheel. It snaps me back to reality. Patience and Dod must be out that way. It dawns on me that I'm standing out in the open. That's when I spot Patience and Dod through a gap in the hedge bordering the garden. They were walking behind it this whole time. They keep going in the other direction and disappear past the maze. Lucky for me, they never look back. I close the knife and put it in my pocket so I don't stab myself then I race full speed down the slope all the way to the bottom of the garden. I carefully make my way around the side of the maze and peek around the back.

Patience is there in a clearing. I can't see Dod. Her red truck is parked near a large garage that looks like it's been there a long time. An old maintenance shed for the garden and pool maybe. The doors to the shed are wide open. Inside, I can see stacks of firewood, garden tools, and shelves loaded with canned food and bottles of water. Across the clearing is a broken-down merry-go-round. Someone's added pieces of plywood, bits of scrap metal, and a tarp strung up with bungee cords. The whole thing looks like a giant fort. Dod's bike lies next to it. I bet it's one of his creations. The rickety shell of the Ferris wheel sits in the woods behind the merry-go-round. The rich man's amusement park.

Patience is standing next to a steel drum. That's where the smoke was coming from. She's burning something. She tosses a shoe into the drum and flames rise above its rim. Dod comes out of the shed cradling a large bowl. It looks like there's dog food in it. At first, I can't see the dogs. Then I do. They rise up from where they were hidden in the truck's cargo bed. I panic. I push backward into the hedge. The rough branches stab my skin, but

I manage to force my way through. I pop out and fall on my back inside the maze. The dogs are barking. I'm hoping it's the food they smell and not the blood trailing down my arm. But then I remember they're bloodhounds. I scramble to my feet. Any second now, those dogs are going to charge through this hedge and tear me apart. I have to run but I can't get my legs to move. Patience is yelling.

"Stop teasing those bloody dogs," hollers Patience.

The dogs are going nuts.

"Bonnie! Clyde!" she yells. Then she whistles and the dogs stop barking.

"Dod, get going. Those poor mutts think that food's for them," she shouts. "Go on now. Give the man his last meal and let's get this over and done with," she says.

The man?

My legs go weak at the knees.

I push aside some branches in the hedge and look through just in time to see Dod heading behind his merry-go-fort. There's a collection of his hubcap masks decorating his fort. He's a collector just like me. His mother said so. But her words take on a whole new meaning.

Once he gets his hands on something he has a hard time letting it go.

Dod is about to take a path leading into the woods when he turns, backtracks, and reaches for one of his masks.

"Don't bother with that," hollers Patience. "Don't matter if he sees your face now."

Dod lets go of the mask, sticks out his lower lip, and heads off down the path. One of the branches I'm holding snaps in my hand. The dogs go berserk.

"Hush now," says Patience. "He'll be right back."

A phone rings.

How does she have cell service? Maybe we're out of the dead zone.

Patience goes to her truck and grabs a chunky black phone from the front seat. It looks more like a walkie-talkie. I think it's a satellite phone. The wardens at the park have them. I can't hear what she's saying over the barking, but she doesn't look happy. After a few seconds, Patience hangs up and Dod comes trotting back without the dish. She walks to the back of the truck. She's got two dog leashes in her hand. She flicks one of the bloodhounds across the snout. It whimpers. Dod cringes. The dogs go quiet.

"Your brothers had some trouble. We have to go get them," she says.

My heart lifts. *Are they leaving?*

"No. I stay." He points to the path.

"Best you come with me, baby," she says. "I don't want you going all soft on me now."

"Not soft."

She sighs and takes his hand.

"There's no other way," she says.

He pulls away from her, folds his arms, and lowers his chin to his chest.

"We got to leave the dogs behind to make room for JW's bike. Help me so we can help your brothers," she says, holding out one of the leashes.

Dod obeys. She opens the cargo bed. I get ready to duck back into the maze and run, but the dogs stay put, even though their ears are perked. Dod grabs one dog and Patience the other. They leash them, then lead them to the merry-go-fort, where they tie them up. The dogs lie flat, with their chins to the ground. They're sulking. So is Dod.

"We'll let them have a good run in the woods as soon as we get back with your brothers," Patience says.

Mother and son jump into the red truck. I watch as it disappears down two grassy tire tracks that lead into the dark woods behind the Ferris wheel. There's another way in and out of the land.

The second they're out of sight, I push through the hedge and run for the path. The bloodhounds lift their heads. They look stunned to see me at first. Then they go crazy. They bare their teeth and growl and bark. They smell my blood and fear. I try smiling and waving, hoping they remember me. They don't. I try snapping my fingers or whistling like Patience does, but this sends them into a frenzied rage. They fight and tug and scramble at me—all claws and teeth. One dog lunges at me and gets flipped onto its back. It gags and froths as its collar digs into its throat. Maybe it's Bonnie or maybe it's Clyde, but the other one is the smart one. It's trying to escape by chewing at the knot holding its leash to the merry-go-fort. I won't get far if the dog gets free. I have to do something.

Then I get an idea.

I move fast. I don't know how long Patience and Dod will be gone. I race back to the garden and search for the wildflowers. Gus told me a story once about our old dog, Levi, and how he almost died after eating flowers from a neighbor's garden. The buds were toxic to dogs. I never forgot the name. Bleeding hearts. It sounded like a horrible way to go. But Levi survived even though he was sick for hours, Gus told me. And his heart was fine.

I cradle the buds in my shirt and race back to the clearing and into the shed, hoping I gathered enough to do the trick but not too much. I don't want them to die. I search the rows of canned food on the shelves. No dog food. Beans. Corned beef. That'll do. There's a rusty fork, a can opener, and a couple of tin mugs on top of a small fridge next to a generator. Brown water trickles from the tap into a sink full of dirty bowls and plates. I divide the corned beef between two bowls and crush the buds into the food, mixing it with the fork.

I head to the bloodhounds. They stop barking. I look around. Is the truck coming? No. It's the food. Their noses are twitching and their eyes are fixed on the bowls in my hands. They both sit and whimper. They're being good dogs. I almost can't bring myself to do it as they look at me with their droopy sad eyes. But I have to.

This is who I am now. Someone who does what she has to do.

The Perleys will be back soon. If they do come back and let the hounds loose, I'm dead.

Mission one: dose the dogs.

Mission two: find out what—or who—is down that path.

I step as close as I dare. The dogs are wiggling and drooling in anticipation. I lean down and place the bowls on the ground, just out of reach, then I kick each bowl closer with one foot and step back. The dogs dive in.

As Bonnie and Clyde devour their treats, I run for the path.

32

THE ZOO

AT FIRST, I DON'T SEE ANYTHING EXCEPT TREES AND A ROUGH dirt path. Then I spot an iron archway up ahead. It's partly hidden by overgrown brush. I walk up to it. Across the top of the archway, the metal has been twisted into the shape of a single word. ZOO.

It's Dod's zoo-zoo. I pass under the archway. The path leads down into a sheltered hollow in the forest. I enter the hollow, where a collection of large iron cages is arranged in a semicircle in a rough yard. Inside each cage is a metal shed like a shipping container with a small hatchway leading into it. The cages remind me of large dog kennels with bars running overhead and down all sides. Each cage has a padlocked gate at the front and a sign made of twisted iron hanging across it.

LEMUR. WALLABY. LYNX. YAK. CAPYBARA.

It's the rich man's private zoo.

I tug on the padlock of the first cage I come to. It won't budge. I race over to try another. The locks are solid. A porcupine sits inside the capybara cage. I leap back. I wasn't expecting to see any animals. I look over at the yak cage. A red fox is lying in the shadows inside that one. Dod has been collecting animals from the forest. Gus fell into one of his traps. I run from cage to cage. The one marked LYNX is unlocked. I check inside and the cage and shed are both empty. No lynx. No Howard. I stumble to the last cage. WALLABY. And then I see it. Lying just inside the cage. It's the bowl Dod took down the path. The food hasn't been touched.

The man's last meal.

Goose bumps cover me from my fingertips to my toes. I yank the padlock. It holds tight. I'm afraid to call out. *What if I'm wrong? What if he's not here? What if I'm too late or he's dead or he's not him anymore after all this time?*

I cling to the bars of the cage.

"Hello?" I call out, but my throat is raw and I only manage a small croak.

I hear the distant whine of a motorbike on a highway. They're coming. *It's too soon.*

I search my pockets for the Swiss Army knife. I pull it apart until I find the small screwdriver. I stick the head into the keyhole of the padlock and twist and turn.

Why didn't Gus teach me how to pick a lock? I've seen her do it. I wish she were here. She must know by now I'm not coming back for her.

I keep trying different angles but nothing is working. The sound of the motorbike is getting closer. They'll be here soon. I give up on the lock and clear my throat.

"Howard!" I holler as loud as I can.

I wait. Nothing happens. I race around the back of the wallaby cage. Maybe there's another way in, but the bars run all the way around and there are no windows or doors at the back of the shed. The only way in is the small hatchway at the front. But that's inside the cage. I run to the front again and shove the screwdriver into the padlock. One last try. The motorbike is just beyond the trees. I hear the truck too. The engines shut off. The Perleys are back.

I hear a click in the padlock. I yank on it, but the lock doesn't open.

I'm out of time. I have to get out of sight. The only place to hide is inside the shed of the lynx cage. I tug on the knife but it's jammed in the keyhole. I can't get it out. They'll know someone was here. I tug again. It's stuck. I have to hide.

As I turn away, something catches my eye. A movement inside the wallaby cage. Over by the shed. I stare at it. Everything's dead still for a few seconds, then the hatchway lifts and a shadow appears. Someone is crouched in the frame of the small opening. That someone begins to come out. It's a man. He crawls out of the shed. He shades his eyes from the white haze of the gray sky. He squints at me.

I cling to the cage as my legs give out and I dissolve to my knees. The man's shrunken face is partly hidden behind a long, dark beard and a tangle of curly black hair, but I know those eyes and I know that face.

It's not a wallaby. It's Howard. My Howard. Our Howard.

He staggers over to me and sinks to his knees in front of me. He's not wearing any shoes, and his shirt and shorts are dirty and way too big for him. They aren't his. He reaches his hand through the bars of the cage and touches the brim of the baseball cap on my head.

"Sweet Pea? Is that really you?" he asks, his voice weak.

The sound of his warm, lovely voice carries me away and I'm no longer there. I'm back to when he blew me a kiss on my first day of kindergarten and when he held my arm high when I beat him for the first time at backgammon and when he threw me above the waves and always caught me on the way down.

Great big sobs burst from me. He's alive. He's here with me. It's not a dream. He's holding my hand and talking to me. I found him. We found him. I wish Gus was here more than ever now. I can't stop crying and shaking with joy—then I hear voices. He hears them too. They're close. He nods for me to run. I squeeze his hand. I don't want to let go. He pulls away and motions for me to hide. I know he's right. I can't save him if I'm caught.

With a burst of adrenaline, I pull myself to my feet and run for the lynx cage. I stagger through the gate and scramble through the hatchway into the shed. I peek out just as Dod comes trotting down the path alone. He looks happy. I guess the bleeding hearts didn't work. I can't hear barking and I don't see Patience but I can hear her chattering in the distance. There are other voices too. The twins.

I knew it was JP and JW shooting at us when I heard their motorbikes drive off after the gunfight. Able thought he hit one of them. Sounds like he did. One of the twins hollers loudly. Patience must be trying to patch him up. Dod has just about reached Howard's cage. I can't see Howard. He must have gone back into the shed. Dod has pulled a ring of keys from his pocket. He hasn't spotted the knife hanging in the padlock yet.

Suddenly, there's a terrible scream. It's Patience.

"No, no, no, not my sweet babies," she howls.

Dod drops the keys and runs for his mother.

"Oh my god. Bonnie, Clyde, wake up," she screeches.

I hope I didn't give the dogs too much, that they're just knocked out.

But I can't think about that now.

The second Dod is out of sight, I run for the keys. Howard crawls back out of his shed. He rushes to the gate and wrenches the knife from the lock with one good yank. He nods for me to use the keys. With shaking hands, I try one. It doesn't fit. Another. That one doesn't fit either. Howard is keeping an eye on the path. He's standing close to me on the other side of the bars. He smells terrible. His steady breaths keep me calm. I try another. It fits. I turn the key and the padlock releases. Howard pushes the gate open. He steps out of the cage and pulls me into a bear hug. I hug him back. I don't care that he stinks. He lets go and takes my hand.

I'm surprised Howard can run after being locked in a cage for three years. But it is Howard. He would have never given up. He would have been waiting and getting ready for this moment all along. I see him clear as day—doing push-ups and sit-ups and jogging on the spot as he waits for his next can of corned beef or his next chance to get free.

We circle behind the Ferris wheel and push through the woods. I don't know where we're going or how we'll get out, but if we keep moving, we'll end up somewhere.

I hear angry shouts behind us. They've found the empty cage. They know Howard is free. A motorbike engine revs. It's coming closer.

We find the tire tracks and follow them. They must lead to the main road. Howard looks behind us. He tumbles into a ditch of tall grass, pulling me down next to him. We lie flat in the grass as the motorbike whizzes past and disappears down the tracks. Howard stands up and steps back onto the tracks. He looks both ways, not sure if we should go back or follow the bike. I'm just getting to my feet when the motorbike comes flying off a side trail, full speed. It catches Howard's shoulder and sends him spiraling to his back in the dirt. He lies motionless. I run over to him. Howard lifts his head. He's dazed but he's okay. JP spins on his back wheel in a full circle, guns it toward us, then comes to a skidding stop, inches from us. Dirt flies into our faces. He swings a shotgun off his shoulder and points it at us. Howard sits up. I wrap my arms around him and bury my face in his neck.

JP honks the horn on his motorbike.

"Over here," he calls out to the others.

It's not long before Patience comes walking along the tire tracks, a shotgun in her hands. I was hoping to never see her again. Patience stares at me with red eyes. She probably thought Howard got free and killed the dogs. She wasn't expecting to see me.

Without a word, they lead us at gunpoint back to the clearing near the merry-go-fort. They make us sit back-to-back on the ground. JP ties a rope around us. Howard holds my hand. It's shaking along with the rest of me. I don't want to die. I don't want to be put in a cage. And I still can't understand how the Perleys, who took such good care of us on Canada Day, have turned into such horrible people.

The fire in the steel drum is spewing black smoke. I spot Howard's TRAGICALLY HIP T-shirt on the ground next to it. They were burning his clothes. Dod is cradling one of the bloodhounds near a pool of dog vomit. Bonnie and Clyde look dead, but I see their noses quiver. JW looks like *he's* about to be dead. He's turned kind of blue and he's half smiling. His gums and lips are white. Able shot him in the leg and there's a lot of blood. His bandages have already soaked through. He's propped against the wheel of the red truck and his motorbike is in the cargo bed. JP pours water from a jug into his twin brother's mouth. Patience is pacing, her shotgun pointing to the ground. She keeps looking over at Dod and the sick dogs.

"Dod never hurt you. Not once," she says. "Why'd you have to go hurt our pups?"

She's looking at Howard like it was his doing.

"I did it," I tell her.

Howard squeezes my hand.

Patience looks at me, long and hard.

"I reckon you did," she says. "You take after your mother,

don't ya? That one doesn't scare easy, doesn't know when to quit. Like a dog with a bone." Patience chokes up.

She puts a hand to her mouth.

"Bad, bad, bad," whimpers Dod, pointing at me with teary rage.

"You're the bad one," I yell at him.

Dod shakes his head over and over.

"You pretended to like us and to be a good mom," I yell.

Howard's elbow gently nudges my back.

"I had to find out what you knew," Patience says. "What your mom knew."

Howard squirms. He's doing something behind his back. The ropes are moving back and forth, burning my arms. He still has the knife.

"Where is she?" asks Patience.

I clam up.

"Wake up, JW!" shouts JP. "He needs a fucking doctor, Ma."

JW's eyes are closed. His brother is slapping his face. Patience walks over and feels for a pulse in his neck. I glance under my arm. Howard is cutting the rope.

"He passed out," she says. "Take the truck. Go see McFadden."

"The vet?" squawks JP.

"The cops'll be all over the ER looking for the fool who got himself shot," she says. "Now pull yourself together."

"So that fuckin' cop doesn't have our backs, just his own son's." He points at Dod.

I don't understand. Is he saying Dod's dad is a cop? What did Patience say about him?

Fancies himself a big man in the county . . . pretends he don't have a son.

"Nothing we can do about that now," says Patience. "Help your brother. You, too, Dodgeroo."

Dod gently places the dog's head on the ground and ambles over. Together, Dod and JP lift their brother and lay him across the back seat of the truck. Patience leans her shotgun against the merry-go-fort as she reaches inside for a blanket.

They're distracted. Howard turns his head and whispers in my ear.

"When I say go, run and don't stop," he says. I feel the ropes loosen.

Patience walks to the truck and covers her son with the blanket. JP places his shotgun on the front seat and jumps in. Patience hands him the keys and pats the side of the truck.

"Get on now. McFadden owes me one. Don't you worry. He'll fix him up good as new," she tells JP. "Dod and I will do what we gotta do here and meet you there."

"You'll need a quick way outta here." He hands her the keys to his bike.

"Mum's gonna take care of everything, son." She kisses JP's cheek.

He nods and drives away.

Dod clings to his mother's arm as they watch the truck disappear down the lane.

"Go!" whispers Howard. He pulls the rope and it falls from us.

We scramble to our feet. I'm up. Dod and Patience turn just as I'm kicking off the rope. Dod hollers like a hyena. Patience runs for the shotgun. Howard sees it too. He lunges for the gun but his foot gets tangled in the rope. He falls flat in the dirt and the knife goes flying. Patience picks up the gun. I run to Howard as she spins around and takes aim. Dod grabs the knife and staggers to his mother's side. I block Howard with my body and hold up my hands.

"Stop," I shout. "You don't want to do this."

"You clearly don't know me," says Patience.

"Gus has gone to get the police," I tell her. "They'll be here any second. You still have time to get away."

"She wouldn't send you here alone," she says.

"You don't know *her* because she does whatever she has to do," I say.

"Enough stalling!" yells Patience.

She aims at the sky and fires. The loud crack pierces my eardrums. Dod drops the knife and covers his ears with both hands. His hear-no-evil pose.

"Get up," says Patience.

Howard and I slowly rise to our feet. She points us toward the path to the zoo. We have no choice but to take it. Howard holds my hand. I wonder if she's going to lock us up. Leave us in some cage to die. But we don't stop at the cages. Patience tells us to keep going through the zoo and behind the Ferris wheel. Maybe she's looking for a secluded spot to shoot us and bury our bodies. Muirhead would like that.

I think back to how Patience called it Howard's last meal. They were planning to kill him. Probably because they knew we were close to figuring them out. Maybe that's why they picked us up on the highway. They were going to kill all of us.

We come to a clearing. There's a small circular structure in the middle. It's made of crumbling stones. A piece of plywood sits on top of it.

"Uncover it, baby." She nods to Dod.

Dod looks scared. He shakes his head over and over.

"Do as you're told, boy," she shouts.

Dod flinches then flips the plywood off the stones. A roaring sound rises up from inside it. It's a well. But why is the water so loud? Howard puts his arm around me.

"What's that sound?" asks Howard.

"That'd be the lake," says Patience.

Noble told us about it.

There's a network of caves that snakes from the bluffs to an underground lake below the woods.

I tremble violently. Howard squeezes me tight.

"You can't," says Howard. "She's just a kid."

"I have no choice," says Patience. "My Dod's just a kid too. He doesn't know bad from good."

Dod looks at his mother with wide confused eyes.

"Bad, bad, bad," Dod says, pacing around the well.

"You never know. You might survive," Patience tells Howard.

Dod starts hitting himself in the head.

"Stop that, boy," yells Patience.

She motions us to the well with her shotgun.

"I can shoot you right here or you can take your chances down there," she says.

Together, we move slowly toward the well. Dod stops pacing and stays on the far side. He doesn't want to get too close to us. I can hear the swoosh of rushing water.

"Bad, bad, bad," he says, hitting his head again.

I feel sick. I can see the blackness inside the well as we get closer. I grip Howard's arm tighter. I don't want him to get shot trying to save me.

"Bad Dod, bad Dod," chants Dod.

"Now you hush down," snaps Patience.

Then Dod points and stares into the well.

There's an eerie half second where everyone seems frozen— Dod with his arm outstretched, Patience pointing her shotgun. We all look at Dod. He looks at his mother, then tumbles headfirst into the well. His feet disappear and he's gone.

I gasp, bracing for the sound of a splash, but instead a deafening crack echoes across the woods. Patience suddenly spins like a corkscrew and lands heavy on the ground. She drops her shotgun. Blood streams from her neck. Howard runs over, picks up the shotgun. He's not sure if he should point at Patience or the shooter. He spins toward the woods.

Then we see her.

A woman steps out of the woods at the edge of the clearing.

She's half naked, caked head to toe in mud like some wild beast. The butt of the rifle rests against her shoulder, one hand holding the gun steady, with her elbow down; the other hand on the grip, finger on the trigger. Then I see who it is. It's Gus—my incredibly brave, badass warrior mom. She keeps the rifle trained on the woman she just shot. Patience moans, lifts herself to a seated position, and touches her neck. She's dazed but the bullet that took her down only grazed her. She stares at the blood dripping from her hand. Then her glassy eyes seem to refocus. She searches the clearing.

"Where did he go?" she whimpers.

Howard is standing over her. He lowers the shotgun.

Patience looks at the well and it comes back to her.

Her face twists with pain.

"My baby. My poor little Dodgeroo. He didn't know," she cries, looking up at Howard. "He collects things. That's all. You were just one of those things—I had no idea."

She wipes away her tears.

"I was trying to be a good mum. I didn't see the harm in him having his own hideout? And he always loves animals. He told me about his zoo but I—none of us knew. Not till the twins came to mark the new property line when we sold some of the land. They found the camper and then they found you, alive." She lowers her head. "They came to me and I did what any mother would do. I protected my child. We moved that camper clear of here. We couldn't undo what Dod had done, but we couldn't set you free. My boy wouldn't last a day in a jail cell. But we aren't killers. So we left you be. Dod treated you right, didn't he? He kept you fed and warm."

Blood streams down her neck. She doesn't bother trying to stop the pulsing flow. A distant siren wails. Patience swallows hard and tries to get up but fails. Gus is still standing at the edge of the clearing with the rifle aimed at the woman. Patience glances at Gus then looks away. Her eyes are faraway like she's staring deep into the woods or the past.

"Then you came along and upended everything," she says to Gus, but she can't look at her. "When I saw you didn't scare easy and you started nosing around our land, I knew it was only a matter of time. I sent my boys to get you, but they messed that up and got your camper instead. I almost had you myself until you got lucky with those cops."

Patience looks over at Gus. The two women lock eyes.

"We were never gonna hurt you. Our plan was to bring you here," she says. "So you'd all be together. So you'd know what happened to him. You needed to know. You wanted the truth and I was going to give that to you."

Patience looks like she's about to say something else but doesn't bother when she sees Gus's face: there's no pity or forgiveness or mother-to-mother understanding—just pure disgust.

Patience lies on her back with a deep sigh.

The sirens are close now. It's over.

We aren't getting shot or tossed down a well or locked in a cage. Howard's okay. Gus is okay. I'm okay. I can't get my legs moving fast enough from where they've been frozen since Patience was shot. I race over to the wild beast. Gus drops the rifle and holds out her arms. I run to her, wrap my arms around her muddy torso, and hug her as tight as I can.

"Mama," I cry.

Our legs give out and we drop to our knees. We hold on to

each other. Howard staggers over and falls to his knees next to us. I let go of Gus.

The two of them are face-to-face.

She looks into his eyes.

Howard reaches out and gently wipes mud from her cheek.

"What took you so long?" he whispers.

Gus smiles and kisses him.

33

THE THUMB DRIVE

WHEN ABLE WOKE UP IN THE ER AND SAW HIS GRANDFATHER SITting by his bed, he knew we never made it to the cabin. Gus wouldn't go unless she was driven there. The two men rushed home and found one of their rifles missing. That's when Able knew where we'd gone. To the land we'd told him about. The land the Perleys owned. He headed there as fast as he could. He found the Corolla we'd left in the ditch, then heard the gunshot. He headed that direction until he found the back way in.

When Able came running into the woods, he couldn't believe his eyes. Patience lay bleeding on the ground and I was there with two people he didn't recognize. At least not at first. Gus and Howard both looked like wild beasts. He called for help on his police radio.

Pretty soon those dark woods filled up with light and noise. It all became one big blur as police and paramedics arrived. But not Dewer or Nelson or Muirhead.

I remember moments inside the blur.

Flashing red lights crisscrossing the treetops.

A woman in an OPP uniform handcuffing Patience to a stretcher.

An IV bag with a tube running into Howard's arm.

A bandage wrapped around Gus's hand.

She was missing four fingernails from when she clawed at the mud walls of the pit until she unearthed a tree root that she used to climb out of the hole.

And I also remember the moment Howard called his parents.

"Augusta? Is that you?" his mother said when she saw Howard's number calling.

"Mom, it's me," he said, his voice cracking. "It's Howard."

"Oh my god! Kirk, Kirk, come quick," she screeched.

There was a lot of fumbling and shouting and crying on their end.

"Son, is that really you?" she cried.

"Howard? We have you on speaker. Are you there?" said Kirk.

"I'm here. I'm okay," he said. "They found me, Gus and Bly."

Kirk and Vivi sobbed and laughed. They didn't want to hang up for the longest time. They didn't want to ever forget that moment.

JP and JW were arrested when the vet called the police on them. He'd heard about a shoot-out at the Journey farm and figured it was them. The Perleys were charged with forcible confinement, abduction, unlawful use of firearms, and attempted murder. Bonnie and Clyde had their stomachs pumped, and they got better, just like Levi had. I heard Tobias Perley took the dogs in. I was glad I hadn't killed them.

A recording of Staff Sergeant Muirhead and Marica Pike was anonymously sent to the RCMP later that day. It didn't take long for the RCMP to take over the Perley case and open up an investigation into the local OPP's involvement in Howard's disappearance. Muirhead was put on suspension and Pike was brought in for questioning. The investigators said everything we did was in self-defense. But that's not why I poisoned those dogs or why Gus shot Patience. We didn't do it for ourselves. We did it for Howard and for each other.

We stayed with Kirk and Vivi. Vivi baked dozens and dozens of lemon scones. Kirk called everyone he knew to tell them the news. Every so often Vivi would take Gus's hand in hers and tears would well up in her eyes. It was her way of thanking Gus and telling her she'd been wrong about her all along.

Howard didn't say much those first few days. Gus cut his hair and shaved his beard. He had hollow cheeks and he'd lost a lot of weight. He slept a lot. He needed time and rest and scones. None of us asked him questions. Kirk took Gus and me to Books & Company in Picton. He insisted on buying me a new book, a game, and a puzzle, then we went to a car dealership and he bought us a new car.

Day by day, Howard started to look more like the old Howard. After a week had gone by, he was ready to talk. He sat us all down and told us what happened.

He could only remember bits and pieces of the accident. That's how it started.

A boy on a bike came out of nowhere, up from the ditch and onto the road, right into the path of the camper van. Howard didn't see him until it was too late. The boy was wearing some kind of armor, which probably saved his life. Howard swerved and lost control of the camper. It careened into the ditch then slammed into the trees along the fence. Howard doesn't remember much after that. He thinks he hit his head and broke a few ribs on impact. He couldn't breathe very well. Then he passed out. He woke up in a cage, face down in the dirt. There was no one around.

Howard thought he might die that first day. The pain was bad, he was shivering, and he passed out again. When he woke up someone had laid a blanket over him and he was lying on a small cot inside a shed. And there was someone else there, in the corner. As daylight came, he saw it was a girl. She wouldn't let him get close. She was skittish. She hugged her knees and rocked a lot. And she wouldn't speak. He didn't know her name but he guessed she might be Lula. She looked about the right age and he knew Stenson believed his daughter had been kidnapped. But he knew for sure when he said her name and she gave him a tiny nod. He didn't know how she came to be there or if Pike had something to do with it, but he felt worse for her than himself. She'd likely been there months.

The boy brought them food once a day, but mostly they were alone. When the boy did come around, he always wore a metal mask and only ever muttered nonsense, if he spoke at all. He was a big kid with large, strong hands, and he walked with a bad limp. Howard figured he'd been injured when the camper hit his bike.

For days, Howard tried to reach Lula, but she seemed broken beyond repair. He passed the time by telling her all about us. He showed her the picture of us that he carried in his wallet. *That's why she recognized us at the fair.* It was in his back pocket, along with the ring. He kept them both buried in the dirt in case the boy ever decided to search him.

Howard told her that we liked camping and hiking and playing charades around the campfire. That we lived in a house in Ottawa that had a big flower garden. He called us his family. He showed her the engagement ring. She seemed to like looking at the picture and holding the ring.

It took a while, but he found small ways to communicate with her. They played X's and O's in the dirt and he taught her his favorite call-and-response knocking game. He'd knock the rhythmic call and she'd knock the reply. It was something. A small connection. Howard was glad he was there for her. He felt responsible for Lula. She reminded him of me, he said. He'd want someone to take care of me if I were ever in a bind like that. He'd want them to do whatever they could to get me out. Howard knew they had to escape.

He watched and waited and planned for days. The boy had a routine. He fed the animals first. They were skittish and hungry so they never ran. While they ate, he'd clean out their cages with a rake then lock them up again. He always fed Howard and Lula last. But he never opened their padlocked gate. Instead, he pushed the food through a small door in the bottom of the gate. Like a doggie door, Howard said. Just big enough for the bowl to slide through.

Howard talked to the boy whenever he came by. The boy never said much and Howard kept his distance. But with each passing day, he'd move a little closer and as he got friendlier and lighter, the boy would mumble or repeat a word. He even made the boy laugh once. The boy got comfortable with Howard being close. It took a couple of weeks. Howard knew he'd only get one shot. He had to be patient.

The day finally came. Howard told Lula what to do. He needed her help to pull off his plan. She shook her head a lot and Howard wasn't sure she'd be able to do her part when the time came, but he took a leap of faith. When the boy brought the food, Howard was sitting within arm's reach of the doggie door. The boy opened the door and pushed the bowls through. That's when Howard grabbed his wrist and yanked him hard, pinning him against the gate and wrenching his arm through the small door. Howard held tight. The boy squealed and squirmed like an animal caught in a trap. Howard gripped him with both hands. Lula was suddenly at his side. She *was* going to help. Lula grabbed the keys from the boy's pocket then, one by one, she tried them in the padlock until she got the right one. She unlocked the gate.

As she pushed it open, Howard lost his grip and the boy fell back. Lula squeezed through the gate and the boy lunged for her.

He caught her ankle and she fell flat on her stomach. She kicked at him as Howard crawled through the gate and bit down hard on the boy's leg. The boy screamed and let her go. Lula got up and started running. The boy and Howard scrambled to their feet. Howard turned to Lula and motioned for her to go. That's when he took his eye off Dod. A hard blow to his ribs took the wind out of him. Before he could catch his breath, the boy bodychecked him backward into the cage. Howard landed in the dirt and the boy locked the gate. Lula was gone.

The night before, Howard had given Lula the ring. He told her it was special. It would keep her safe. At first, she didn't want to take his ring, but he insisted. Howard wasn't just being nice. He knew that his plan wasn't perfect. He'd have to fight his way out. He was weak and the boy was big. It might not go his way. But he figured one of them would make it out. If it was Lula, he held out hope that, even if she couldn't tell anyone what happened to her or find her way back here, maybe by some miracle we would see the ring one day and know he was still alive and we'd find him and bring him home.

It would take almost three years, but we did. We saw all his breadcrumbs.

A FEW MONTHS LATER, WE HEARD THAT LULA HAD MADE HER way home too. The Gwella helped her find her voice and she moved back home to her dad's place—to the treehouse in the clouds that he built for her.

When Stenson had heard what happened to us out at the Perleys' land then found out the RCMP had taken over, he came forward with the evidence we'd given him. That's when things really spun out of control for Pike. The RCMP raided the winery and found her secret lab. And it was Olive who showed them the way in. She turned on her mother. And then a whole bunch of other people did too. No one was afraid of her anymore. Everyone was out to save themselves and point the finger at her. The lab rats, Candice, Kat the fueler—all of them spilled the beans.

And Ricky sang like a canary.

With his help, the RCMP had supply routes, dates, and names. Muirhead was one of those names. He was finally arrested.

But what the RCMP really needed was the money trail. And Pike's accountant, Boyd, was the only person who knew how deep and far that trail went. That's what he copied onto the thumb drive—a list of shell companies, offshore accounts, and money wire transfers—a road map of Pike's international drug network.

That thumb drive wasn't in Howard's pocket when he disappeared, and it wasn't in our camper van when JP rolled it into Cressy Marsh, where it was swallowed up forever in the dark water.

I had it.

It was tucked inside the rim of Howard's Montreal Canadiens baseball cap. The one his mother kept and placed on the altar at his funeral. The one a tornado picked up and sent my way in a cemetery. The one I wore every day since finding it even though the buckle poked the back of my head. But it wasn't the buckle. It was a thin metal thumb drive that Boyd had given Howard at the Prince Edward Vintners Association Annual Garden Party. Howard had talked to Pike at that party and he was worried she might be on to him, so he hid it but never got the chance to go back and get it.

Howard had forgotten all about it until we asked if Boyd ever gave it to him.

We turned it over to the RCMP and an international task force was launched.

The press called Pike the Crystal Queen.

Her vision for the future did come true.

Will Stenson was happy she got what she deserved and even happier the wind park project was dead. He had been wrong about Pike in one way, though. She hadn't kidnapped his daughter. As her memories slowly came back, Lula told her dad what really happened. She'd gone to a beach party down by Little Bluff. She'd been drinking and went into the woods because she felt sick. She'd passed out. Her friends thought she'd gone home to sleep it off. Dod found her the next morning. She thought he was helping her get home, but instead he led her into the woods and put her in a cage.

I bet Dod was out collecting animals for his zoo when he found Lula. He might have truly thought he was helping her or that he was meant to find her. He didn't know it was wrong to take her. His mother said as much.

He doesn't know bad from good.

Once he gets his hands on something he has a hard time letting it go.

When I think of Dod, I think of something else his mother said to us by that well.

You never know. You might survive.

Dod *did* survive. He knew those caves well and he was a strong swimmer. Patience had made sure of that since they lived by the water. He got to a ledge and waited for the waves to calm, then he climbed out of the caves and made his way down to the shore. He was found wandering the beach. I think he jumped into the well because he knew he'd done something wrong. He wasn't bad. He was just a boy in a man's body who kept what he found.

And in Howard's case, kept what was *given* to him.

When you give someone a gift, it's theirs to keep.

That's what his mother taught him—and that's how his father used him.

We found out that Staff Sergeant Julius Muirhead was Dod's biological father.

He was the *big man* ashamed to admit Dod was his son.

The most fatherly thing he ever did was to tell Dod to call if he ever got in trouble.

Trouble, I call.

That's why Dod had that OPP card at the fair.

And when Dod called his father for help after he collided with Howard, Muirhead saw his chance to get rid of Howard. Pike had been all over him to do something and now he had him. He did it for himself not Pike. He knew if she went down, he'd go with her. But Muirhead didn't want blood on his hands. That wasn't a line he would cross. But he was willing to manipulate his only son. He'd seen the zoo once and knew it was nearby and well hidden. Together, they'd moved Howard to the zoo and hid the camper in the woods.

Muirhead confessed to everything once he knew he was done for. He figured if Howard ever escaped or was found, his *half-wit son* would take the fall. His words. He told Dod that Howard was a gift and he could keep him forever. He told him to be very careful to never let Howard out. He said Howard was dangerous and if he got free, he'd hurt his mother and his brothers. He convinced Dod that he was doing a good thing for his family.

Dod believed him.

Patience was shocked and angry to hear Muirhead was behind Howard's disappearance. She thought it was all Dod's innocent misdoings, not his father's cold, calculated scheme.

When Lula's memories fully returned, the true horror of what Muirhead had done came to light. He hadn't confessed everything.

Lula had been locked up for almost a year by a masked man who never spoke to her. She was already losing her mind, but what sent her tumbling over the edge was the day Howard arrived. She peered out of the shed as they dragged him into the cage. She saw Muirhead's face. His police uniform. She knew him. He was the head of the local OPP. He'd spoken at her high school and he knew her dad. She didn't know what was happening but when he looked over and saw her, Lula thought she was about to be rescued. He looked surprised. Dod looked like a child caught with his hand in the cookie jar. At first, Muirhead didn't move and then he turned without a word, locked the gate, and left with Dod. She heard him telling Dod he was a good boy.

He just left her there. Her and Howard.

I got shivers when I heard Lula's story.

Muirhead ended up going to jail for a long time, which seemed right to me. He should be in a cage for the rest of his life. But no one thought Dod was fit to stand trial, so he was sent to a hospital. We heard Dod was released early and now he lives with his uncle and his dogs.

WHEN WE FINALLY GOT BACK HOME TO OTTAWA, WE'D BEEN away over a month. It felt like years. The grass was taller, mail was piled by the front door, and a brick of cheese in the fridge had turned green. Time hadn't stood still at the house like it had in Prince Edward County. But then it started to move fast. Summer disappeared. I started grade 8. I saw my friends again. Howard mowed the lawn and Gus started to cook more. She even tried recipes other than tuna casserole. We ate dinners on the deck and took evening walks down to Brewer Park, like a normal family. But some nights, I would sneak outside and sit on a lawn chair just to feel the wind and listen to the bugs and watch the bats and stare at the moon. It made me feel like I did back then—and there was something about that feeling that I didn't want to let go of just yet.

Gus and Howard started working on an article they were writing together. It wasn't about bird migration. His editor at *Canadian Geographic* was *giddy* about it though, her word. It was the story of a man's survival in the woods and a woman's three-year search for him that ended in a dramatic rescue. It was a love story. And *I* was a big part of it. Their working title was "Lovebirds" since it all began with the birds.

THE BURIED ROAD

I'M TRYING TO STOP COLLECTING THINGS. IT'S A HARD HABIT TO break, but the other day I saw a pair of sunglasses lying in the crosswalk. Someone had dropped them by the curb. I walked right past. I didn't pick them up or put them in my pocket. They weren't meant for me. They weren't a message or a sign or a bread-crumb. They were just sunglasses.

It's been a year since we found Howard. I wasn't sure how I'd feel coming back to the county, but now that we're here, it feels different. Or maybe I am. Back then, everything seemed to be swirling around us. The winds, the waves, the dunes, the forests, the flowers, the birds—all those birds. It was like the forces of nature were pulling us across Prince Edward County. Now when we drive by the shops and inns and happy families in motor homes, I don't feel like I'm being pulled or like everyone's watching us. I don't feel separate or lonely.

I feel at home.

We drive to the Sandbanks Provincial Park and head for the dunes. We hike to Butterfly Beach and that's where we gather. Seagulls float on the water. A sailboat drifts across the lake. The sun is about to set.

Hildy is here. So are Will and Lula. Able and Noble have

come too. Kirk and Vivi are here and they've brought the justice of the peace. And of course, there's the bride and groom. Gus is wearing a long silk dress that Vivi made for her and Howard has on a crisp white shirt and slacks. They're both barefoot. We all are. They ask me to stand with them as they say their vows. It's my job to hand Howard the jade ring.

The sky turns the color of rainbow sherbet as they are married.

Gus always says the past is all around us. But it also lives inside us and makes us who we are. It's in the color of our red hair, the lines on our fingertips, and the footsteps we leave behind us. It's in our DNA. Maybe that's why I feel different.

I know where I come from now, and I know who I am. I'm just like my mom and her mother, Shannon. Brave and unstoppable. And if there is a little bad blood inside me—that's part of me too.

Gus has told me stories of mothers and daughters who tried to run from their DNA—June and Gracie Halladay, Charlotte and May Mutchmore, Eva and Poppy Honeywell. But no matter how hard someone tries to escape who they are, the past won't let them.

It courses through our veins like a secret map of who we are and where we come from.

I think there's a buried road inside all of us.

We just have to look.

ACKNOWLEDGMENTS

THIS IS MY THIRD NOVEL. I AM AMAZED I GET TO SAY THAT. I KNOW how lucky I am to be able to follow my passion and to have my novels published. I don't take any of it for granted. And none of it is mine alone to take. I might stand at my desk by myself most days (yes, I do stand when I write), but I am not alone. I am surrounded by encouraging voices and good vibes from a bunch of very special humans.

One of my favorites is right now sitting in the next room watching a video on his phone with the volume cranked way too loud. My husband, Andy, might be a little deaf, but he is my love, my guy, my solid ground, my partner in crime. He's always there for me, eager to dive into my next novel or listen to me rant about the latest plot I'm working to untwist. And if he is the constant in my life, my daughter, Alex, is the sweetness. She is my cheerleader, my muse, my comic relief, my best friend, my reason. She is who I write for and why I try to dig deeper and do better each time. She has helped me understand what it means to be a mother, likely the reason those themes run rampant through my novels.

Another special human I'm lucky to have in my corner is my own mum, Kathleen. I appreciate her inquiries and suggestions, and our brainstorming sessions about my novels. Now in her eighties, she doesn't see herself as particularly vital, but she is to me. She is strongly opinionated, generous, well-read, smart, and always up for a good chat. And even if she doesn't think it's true, she has great ideas and insights. I am grateful she is my mum, and this novel is dedicated to her.

Those encouraging voices also include a lovely group of family and friends. They are my sisters, my support system, my steadfast advocates—Louise, Maggie, Chantal, Vivi, Jen, LA, Grace, Sarah, Jamie, Lori, and Sue. I love and appreciate you all.

I have the best agent in David Halpern and very much appreciate his associate, Janet Oshiro. David never fails to let me know he is a fan of my writing, first and foremost. He encourages me to do my thing, in whatever way makes me happy. I am honored to be part of his family of writers.

I also very much appreciate the team at HarperCollins in both the US and Canada, in particular, Sarah Stein, my editor of five years, for embracing my complicated stories, my sometimes-hard-to-love characters, and for guiding the work with good instincts and her characteristic enthusiasm. I'd like to thank David Howe for his insights that helped reshape and improve the manuscript; my wonderful publicist, Alice Tibbetts, for being my Canadian champion; and my copy editor, Laurie McGee, for her thoughtful edits and kind encouragement. And to everyone on the Harper publicity, marketing, and production teams who work tirelessly to turn my words into books, thank you for believing in me.

Connecting with readers is probably one of the best parts of being an author. I read each and every message and note sent my way, and I have loved attending all the book clubs who invited me to their lakeside homes, cottages, neighborhood gatherings, online forums, condo socials, libraries, and community centers. Special thanks to Marnie, Veronica, LuAnn and Cathy, Sheila, and Christine. It was truly the highlight of my year being able to answer your questions, listen to your insights, and share my writer's life with all of you.

Thank you to the incredibly supportive bookstagrammers, book reviewers, bloggers, podcasters, show hosts, festivals, and bookstores across North America who embraced Gus and Levi and shared them with the world. In particular, I'd like to thank

Sean Wilson from the Ottawa International Writers Festival, who is a true champion of writers and who kindly invited me to host their Scene of the Crime night and to be a guest on their podcast. The festival's affiliated bookstore, Perfect Books, has supported and promoted my novels from the get-go, as has Books on Beechwood. And I can't forget to mention Hank and Hannah at First Chapter Fun for being there for me and so many other authors.

A heartfelt thank-you to my dear friends, Kirk and Vivi, for allowing me to use your names for Howard's parents. Though the characters are quite a handful, you are not. You resemble them in name alone. I can always count on you two to be the first ones to break out the champagne to toast my successes and to read my novels. I love you for it.

I want to thank my talented friend, Jill Woodley, for aiming her discerning and artful lens in my direction to create my new author photos. Thank you to Peter Dunphy for offering his incredible talent in the creation of my book trailers. And a special nod goes out to Thomas Blake for giving me advice on how to respectfully portray the nuances of one of my characters.

Last but not least, I'd like to thank my fellow authors Hannah Mary McKinnon, Barbara Fradkin, Adrian McKinty, Sarah Priscus, Seraphina Nova Glass, Amy Tector, Michele Sinclair, Wayne Ng, Jennifer Whiteford, and Samantha Bailey for so generously offering to read this novel and/or for sharing your writerly experiences and wisdom with me.

I spent decades wanting to write a novel and when I finally decided to try, all of these wonderful encouraging voices helped me set aside my excuses and see that it was possible. As my good friend's magnetic father, Keith Spicer, always told her, "Don't give me fifty reasons why it can't be done. Give me one reason why it can."

ABOUT THE AUTHOR

KATIE TALLO grew up in Ottawa, Ontario. She has been an award-winning screenwriter and director for three decades. She began writing novels after winning an international contest in the United Kingdom for unpublished fiction. Katie is the author of *Dark August* and *Poison Lilies*. For the past twenty years, Katie and her family have embarked on annual camping trips to Prince Edward County, which is where this latest novel is set. Katie has a daughter and lives with her husband in the Wellington West neighborhood of Ottawa, Ontario.

READ MORE BY
KATIE TALLO

"Moody and riveting."
—*NEW YORK TIMES
BOOK REVIEW,
EDITOR'S CHOICE*

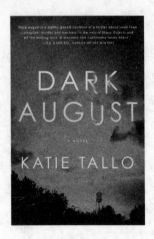

INTERNATIONAL BESTSELLER

"An imaginative thriller—
as much about family, loss,
greed, and a young woman's
attempt to find a place in the
world, as it is about solving
a long-buried mystery."

—PETER HELLER,
New York Times bestselling
author of *The Dog Stars*